P9-AFZ-573

NEBULA AWARD STORIES TEN

IN MEMORIAM

Otto O. Binder
Miriam Allen deFord
Joseph W. Ferman
John Charles Hynam (John Kippax)
P. Schuyler Miller
Hans Stefan Santesson
Charles R. Tanner
E. Mayne Hull (Mrs. A. E. Van Vogt)

Nebula Award Stories Ten

EDITED BY JAMES GUNN

HARPER & ROW, PUBLISHERS
NEW YORK
EVANSTON
SAN FRANCISCO
LONDON

Grateful acknowledgment is made for permission to reprint the following material:

"The Engine at Heartspring's Center" by Roger Zelazny. Copyright © 1974 by
Condé Nast Publications, Inc. First published in *Analog*, July 1974. Published by
permission of the author and the author's agent, Henry Morrison, Inc.

"If the Stars Are Gods" by Gordon Eklund and Gregory Benford. Copyright ©
1974 by Terry Carr. First published in *Universe 4* edited by Terry Carr and
published by Random House. Reprinted by permission of the authors.

"Twilla" by Tom Reamy. Copyright © 1974 by Mercury Press, Inc. First published
in *The Magazine of Fantasy and Science Fiction*, September 1974. Reprinted by
permission of the author and the author's agent, Virginia Kidd.

"After King Kong Fell" by Philip José Farmer. Copyright © 1973 by Roger El-
wood. First published in *Omega*, edited by Roger Elwood and published by
Walker & Co. Reprinted by permission of the author and the author's agents,
Scott Meredith Literary Agency, Inc.

"The Day Before the Revolution" by Ursula Le Guin. Copyright © 1974 by Ursula
Le Guin. First published in *Galaxy*, August 1974. Reprinted by permission of the
author and the author's agent, Virginia Kidd.

"The Rest Is Silence" by C. L. Grant. Copyright © 1974 by C. L. Grant. First
published in *The Magazine of Fantasy and Science Fiction*, September 1974.
Reprinted by permission of the author and the author's agent, Kirby McCauley.

"Born with the Dead" by Robert Silverberg. Copyright © 1974 by Robert Silverberg. First published in *The Magazine of Fantasy and Science Fiction*, April
1974. Reprinted by permission of the author and the author's agents, Scott
Meredith Literary Agency, Inc.

1. Science fiction - collections
I. Gunn, James
II. Science Fiction Writers of America

FIRST EDITION

LIBRARY OF CONGRESS CATALOG CARD NUMBER: 66-20974
ISBN: 0-06-011628-5

75 76 77 78 79 10 9 8 7 6 5 4 3 2 1

This volume of Nebula Award Stories is dedicated to

Robert A. Heinlein

who this year was presented the first Grand Master Award for a lifetime of accomplishment in science fiction

Contents

AWARD-WINNING SCIENCE FICTION 1965–1974

Introduction

This is the tenth anniversary of the founding of the Science Fiction Writers of America and of the *Nebula Award Stories*, volumes which contain the stories the writers themselves consider the best science-fiction stories of the year.

In ten years the organization has matured, and the fiction it was founded to nourish also has changed. In this book, readers will find not only those stories which won Nebula Awards, along with four of the runners-up, but an essay by Professor Robert Scholes of the English Department at Brown University describing the present position of science fiction in the broad range of contemporary literature, as well as an essay by Gordon Dickson, long-time science-fiction writer and past president of the Science Fiction Writers of America, describing ten years of Nebula Awards.

But I cannot resist adding my own analysis of the present scene, of why readers are more interested in science fiction today than at any other time in its history and of why they should be particularly interested in this volume.

Science fiction was created and read for approximately a century, give or take a decade, before 1926, but it did not exist as a genre until Hugo Gernsback* created the first science-fiction mag-

*In whose honor the World Science Fiction Conventions award "Hugos," by vote of members of each convention, for the best stories, etc. of the year.

azine, *Amazing Stories*, nearly fifty years ago. That occasion focused the attention of readers and writers on a particular medium, intensifying interest, insulating from external influences, building peculiar strengths, protecting incestuous weaknesses. Science fiction almost—but not quite—ceased to exist outside the magazines.

For some twenty years virtually no science-fiction books were published, and the two big anthologies of 1946—Groff Conklin's *The Best of Science Fiction* and Raymond J. Healy and J. Francis McComas's *Adventures in Time and Space*—not only had twenty years of neglected stories to draw upon but twenty years of suppressed desire to tap. The surge of book publishing and anthologization would continue until Tony Boucher, co-editor of the *Magazine of Fantasy and Science Fiction*, would comment in 1952 that "it's doubtful if any specialized field can lay as much proportionate stress on the anthology as science fiction does today." And he referred to the possibility of some twenty anthologies and some sixty books in all by the end of 1952.

Ten years later the numbers were four times as large. Where in 1952 four times as many mystery novels were published as science-fiction books, by 1964 the proportion had dropped to three to one. *Publishers Weekly* counted 247 science-fiction books published in 1964, up from 198 the year before.

The time seemed appropriate for the formation of an organization of science-fiction writers, something that actually had been attempted, unsuccessfully, more than a decade before and discussed intermittently since. The mystery writers were organized and the western writers had meetings, but the science-fiction writers had held back, partly because the market wasn't big enough and partly because they didn't consider themselves category writers—that is, they thought that what they wrote was, if not literature, the best method of expressing what they wished to say. And if they wanted to get together, there were always the science-fiction conventions put on by fans. Many writers had been fans; many had come directly out of the fan movement.

By 1965 conditions were changing. Not only were the numbers

of publications becoming respectable, but the monolithic position of the science-fiction magazines had begun to crumble as paperback and even hardcover publication became significant alternatives. The tidy little science-fiction world was coming apart both from internal pressures and external invasion: Writers increasingly were looking toward science fiction as full-time writing careers, something that had been possible for only a handful of writers up to that time, and they were becoming concerned about conditions; and outside writers were looking within science fiction for fresh themes, as they were beginning to search other forms of popular culture for inspiration.

Within science fiction the Milford Science Fiction Writers Conference, created by Damon Knight and James Blish and immortalized by Kurt Vonnegut, Jr., in *God Bless You, Mr. Rosewater,* celebrated its tenth anniversary in 1964. The science-fiction boom showed no signs of going bust again, and science-fiction books were being noticed outside the ghetto: *A Canticle for Leibowitz* by Walter M. Miller, Jr., was published in 1961, *Stranger in a Strange Land* by Robert Heinlein in 1962, *The Man in the High Castle* by Philip K. Dick in 1963, and *Dune* by Frank Herbert in 1965 (it won the first Nebula Award for a novel). Harlan Ellison was beginning to make noises about editing an anthology of stories too dangerous to print.

When Damon Knight sent out his announcement of the formation of the SFWA in 1965 and volunteered to be its first president and the editor of its publication fewer than one hundred writers responded, but it was enough. Since then most of the trends that had been apparent to the perceptive in 1964 have come to the maturity described by Gordon Dickson and Robert Scholes in their essays. SFWA has approximately five hundred members, all of them writers. A total of 722 science-fiction books were published in 1974, according to *Locus,* the fan news magazine; it was an increase of 10 percent over 1973, which itself had increased a whopping 47 percent over 1972. The proportion of mysteries to science fiction has dropped below two to one. Science-fiction courses were being taught in hundreds of colleges and universities across the nation and in thousands of high schools, junior high schools, and even grade schools. One part of that 1974 publishing record was twenty-nine books published by Hyperion Press, almost all of them recovered classics from the early part of the century, now returned to print primarily for libraries. Three other projects like this one came to fruition in 1975, publishing a total of well over one hundred books.

The maturity I wish to point out, however, resides in the stories contained within this book. For many years the characters in science fiction have been stereotyped as inventive, sometimes muscular young men pitting their ingenuity and their characters against the universe or rescuing the Earth from destruction or a nubile maiden from a bug-eyed-monster.

If that canard were ever true, it is no longer. The characters in this book are: an immortal man who already has lived at least one lifetime, an astronaut past middle-age, an old-maid schoolteacher, a grandfather, a seventy-two-year-old woman revolutionary suffering from the aftereffects of a stroke, a discouraged English teacher, a man approaching fifty and his already dead wife—not a steel-thewed romantic or fainting girl in the lot. That's maturity.

To my mind, however, maturity is no substitute for narrative excitement, and these stories have that as well. Consider a tender assassin, aliens who wish to speak to our sun, a lustful genie and a centuries-old nymphet, the real story of King Kong, the beginning of a revolution, an English department party that gets out of hand, and a man seeking his wife beyond the barrier of death. It isn't simply that the authors are getting older—some of them are, but some of them are still young; and science fiction always has had authors of all ages. The difference, I think, is that they no longer need depend on the natural interest of the young in the young or on action for its own sake.

A mature fiction does not discard the virtues of its youth; it reworks them into broader tapestries. We have within these covers a breadth of vision that was not available ten years ago. Not only is it exciting now; it offers magnificent prospects for the future.

What other literature can offer as much?

JAMES GUNN

Lawrence, Kansas

NEBULA AWARD STORIES TEN

ROGER ZELAZNY

The Engine at Heartspring's Center

Roger Zelazny had two Nebula-winning stories in the first Nebula Awards volume. It was a spectacular beginning for a young man who had begun writing professionally only three years before, at the age of twenty-five, while working full time for the Social Security Administration. After winning Hugos for two early novels— . . . *And Call Me Conrad* in 1966 and *Lord of Light* in 1968—he graduated to the insecurity of full-time freelance writing. His most recent books are *Damnation Alley, Nine Princes in Amber, Jack of Shadows, The Guns of Avalon, Today We Choose Faces, To Die in Italbar,* and *Sign of the Unicorn.* He was guest of honor at the 1974 World Science Fiction Convention in Washington, D.C. He returns to the tenth Nebula Award volume with a story about an immortal man-machine in a time when euthanasia is a way of life.

⌘

─────────

⌘

Let me tell you of the creature called the Bork. It was born in the heart of a dying sun. It was cast forth upon this day from the river of past/future as a piece of time pollution. It was fashioned of mud and aluminum, plastic and some evolutionary distillate of seawater. It had spun dangling from the umbilical of circumstance till, severed by its will, it had fallen a lifetime or so later, coming to rest on the shoals of a world where things go to die. It was a piece of a man in a place by the sea near a resort grown less fashionable since it had become a euthanasia colony.

Choose any of the above and you may be right.

Upon this day, he walked beside the water, poking with his forked, metallic stick at the things the last night's storm had left: some shiny bit of detritus useful to the weird sisters in their crafts shop, worth a meal there or a dollop of polishing rouge for his smoother half; purple seaweed for a salty chowder he had come to favor; a buckle, a button, a shell; a white chip from the casino.

The surf foamed and the wind was high. The heavens were a blue-gray wall, unjointed, lacking the graffiti of birds or commerce. He left a jagged track and one footprint, humming and clicking as he passed over the pale sands. It was near to the point where the fork-tailed icebirds paused for several days—a week at

4

most—in their migrations. Gone now, portions of the beach were still dotted with their rust-colored droppings. There he saw the girl again, for the third time in as many days. She had tried before to speak with him, to detain him. He had ignored her for a number of reasons. This time, however, she was not alone.

She was regaining her feet, the signs in the sand indicating flight and collapse. She had on the same red dress, torn and stained now. Her black hair—short, with heavy bangs—lay in the only small disarrays of which it was capable. Perhaps thirty feet away was a young man from the Center, advancing toward her. Behind him drifted one of the seldom seen dispatch-machines—about half the size of a man and floating that same distance above the ground, it was shaped like a tenpin, and silver, its bulbous head-end faceted and illuminated, its three ballerina skirts tinfoil-thin and gleaming, rising and falling in rhythms independent of the wind.

Hearing him, or glimpsing him peripherally, she turned away from her pursuers, said, "Help me" and then she said a name.

He paused for a long while, although the interval was undetectable to her. Then he moved to her side and stopped again.

The man and the hovering machine halted also.

"What is the matter?" he asked, his voice smooth, deep, faintly musical.

"They want to take me," she said.

"Well?"

"I do not wish to go."

"Oh. You are not ready?"

"No, I am not ready."

"Then it is but a simple matter. A misunderstanding."

He turned toward the two.

"There has been a misunderstanding," he said. "She is not ready."

"This is not your affair, Bork," the man replied. "The Center has made its determination."

"Then it will have to reexamine it. She says that she is not ready."

"Go about your business, Bork."

The man advanced. The machine followed.

The Bork raised his hands, one of flesh, the others of other things.

"No," he said.

"Get out of the way," the man said. "You are interfering."

Slowly, the Bork moved toward them. The lights in the machine began to blink. Its skirts fell. With a sizzling sound it dropped to the sand and lay unmoving. The man halted, drew back a pace.

"I will have to report this—"

"Go away," said the Bork.

The man nodded, stooped, raised the machine. He turned and carried it off with him, heading up the beach, not looking back. The Bork lowered his arms.

"There," he said to the girl. "You have more time."

He moved away then, investigating shell-shucks and driftwood. She followed him.

"They will be back," she said.

"Of course."

"What will I do then?"

"Perhaps by then you will be ready."

She shook her head. She laid her hand on his human part.

"No," she said. "I will not be ready."

"How can you tell, now?"

"I made a mistake," she said. "I should never have come here."

He halted and regarded her.

"That is unfortunate," he said. "The best thing that I can recommend is to go and speak with the therapists at the Center. They will find a way to persuade you that peace is preferable to distress."

"They were never able to persuade you," she said.

"I am different. The situation is not comparable."

"I do not wish to die."

"Then they cannot take you. The proper frame of mind is prerequisite. It is right there in the contract—Item Seven."

"They can make mistakes. Don't you think they ever make a mistake? They get cremated the same as the others."

"They are most conscientious. They have dealt fairly with me."

"Only because you are virtually immortal. The machines short out in your presence. No man could lay hands on you unless you willed it. And did they not try to dispatch you in a state of unreadiness?"

"That was the result of a misunderstanding."

"Like mine?"

"I doubt it."

He drew away from her, continuing on down the beach.

"Charles Eliot Borkman," she called.

That name again.

He halted once more, tracing lattices with his stick, poking out a design in the sand.

Then, "Why did you say that?" he asked.

"It is your name, isn't it?"

"No," he said. "That man died in deep space when a liner was jumped to the wrong coordinates, coming out too near a star gone nova."

"He was a hero. He gave half his body to the burning, preparing an escape boat for the others. And he survived."

"Perhaps a few pieces of him did. No more."

"It *was* an assassination attempt, wasn't it?"

"Who knows? Yesterday's politics are not worth the paper wasted on its promises, its threats."

"He wasn't just a politician. He was a statesman, a humanitarian. One of the very few to retire with more people loving him than hating him."

He made a chuckling noise.

"You are most gracious. But if that is the case, then the minority still had the final say. I personally think he was something of a thug. I am pleased, though, to hear that you have switched to the past tense."

"They patched you up so well that you could last forever. Because you deserved the best."

"Perhaps I already have. What do you want of me?"

"You came here to die and you changed your mind—"

"Not exactly. I've just never composed it in a fashion acceptable under the terms of Item Seven. To be at peace—"

"And neither have I. But I lack your ability to impress this fact on the Center."

"Perhaps if I went there with you and spoke to them . . ."

"No," she said. "They would only agree for so long as you were about. They call people like us life-malingerers and are much more casual about the disposition of our cases. I cannot trust them as you do without armor of my own."

"Then what would you have me do—girl?"

"Nora. Call me Nora. Protect me. That is what I want. You live near here. Let me come stay with you. Keep them away from me."

He poked at the pattern, began to scratch it out.

"You are certain that this is what you want?"

"Yes. Yes, I am."

"All right. You may come with me, then."

So Nora went to live with the Bork in his shack by the sea. During the weeks that followed, on each occasion when the representatives from the Center came about, the Bork bade them depart quickly, which they did. Finally, they stopped coming by.

Days, she would pace with him along the shores and help in the gathering of driftwood, for she liked a fire at night; and while heat and cold had long been things of indifference to him, he came in time and his fashion to enjoy the glow.

And on their walks he would poke into the dank trash heaps the sea had lofted and turn over stones to see what dwelled beneath.

"God! What do you hope to find in that?" she said, holding her breath and retreating.

"I don't know," he chuckled. "A stone? A leaf? A door? Something nice. Like that."

"Let's go watch the things in the tidepools. They're clean, at least."

"All right."

Though he ate from habit and taste rather than from necessity, her need for regular meals and her facility in preparing them led him to anticipate these occasions with something approaching a ritualistic pleasure. And it was later still, after an evening's meal, that she came to polish him for the first time. Awkward, grotesque —perhaps it could have been. But as it occurred, it was neither of these. They sat before the fire, drying, warming, watching, silent. Absently, she picked up the rag he had let fall to the floor and brushed a fleck of ash from his flame-reflecting side. Later, she did it again. Much later, and this time with full attention, she wiped all the dust from the gleaming surface before going off to her bed.

One day she asked him, "Why did you buy the one-way ticket to this place and sign the contract, if you did not wish to die?"

"But I did wish it," he said.

"And something changed your mind after that? What?"

"I found here a pleasure greater than that desire."

"Would you tell me about it?"

"Surely. I found this to be one of the few situations—perhaps the only—where I can be happy. It is in the nature of the place itself: departure, a peaceful conclusion, a joyous going. Its contemplation here pleases me, living at the end of entropy and seeing that it is good."

"But it doesn't please you enough to undertake the treatment yourself?"

"No. I find in this a reason for living, not for dying. It may seem a warped satisfaction. But then, I am warped. What of yourself?"

"I just made a mistake. That's all."

"They screen you pretty carefully, as I recall. The only reason they made a mistake in my case was that they could not anticipate anyone finding in this place an inspiration to go on living. Could your situation have been similar?"

"I don't know. Perhaps . . ."

On days when the sky was clear they would rest in the yellow warmth of the sun, playing small games and sometimes talking of the birds that passed and of the swimming, drifting, branching, floating and flowering things in their pools. She never spoke of herself, saying whether it was love, hate, despair, weariness or bitterness that had brought her to this place. Instead, she spoke of those neutral things they shared when the day was bright; and when the weather kept them indoors she watched the fire, slept or polished his armor. It was only much later that she began to sing and to hum, small snatches of tunes recently popular or tunes quite old. At these times, if she felt his eyes upon her she stopped abruptly and turned to another thing.

One night then, when the fire had burned low, as she sat buffing his plates, slowly, quite slowly, she said in a soft voice, "I believe that I am falling in love with you."

He did not speak, nor did he move. He gave no sign of having heard.

After a long while, she said, "It is most strange, finding myself feeling this way—here—under these circumstances . . ."

"Yes," he said, after a time.

After a longer while, she put down the cloth and took hold of his hand—the human one—and felt his grip tighten upon her own.

"Can you?" she said, much later.

"Yes. But I would crush you, little girl."

She ran her hands over his plates, then back and forth from flesh to metal. She pressed her lips against his only cheek that yielded.

"We'll find a way," she said, and of course they did.

In the days that followed she sang more often, sang happier things and did not break off when he regarded her. And sometimes he would awaken from the light sleep that even he required, awaken and through the smallest aperture of his lens note that she lay there or sat watching him, smiling. He sighed occasionally for the pure pleasure of feeling the rushing air within and about him, and there was a peace and a pleasure come into him of the sort he had long since relegated to the realms of madness, dream and vain desire. Occasionally, he even found himself whistling.

One day as they sat on a bank, the sun nearly vanished, the stars coming on, the deepening dark was melted about a tiny wick of falling fire and she let go of his hand and pointed.

"A ship," she said.

"Yes," he answered, retrieving her hand.

"Full of people."

"A few, I suppose."

"It is sad."

"It must be what they want, or what they want to want."

"It is still sad."

"Yes. Tonight. Tonight it is sad."

"And tomorrow?"

"Then too, I daresay."

"Where is your old delight in the graceful end, the peaceful winding-down?"

"It is not on my mind so much these days. Other things are there."

They watched the stars until the night was all black and light and filled with cold air. Then, "What is to become of us?" she said.

"Become?" he said. "If you are happy with things as they are, there is no need to change them. If you are not, then tell me what is wrong."

"Nothing," she said. "When you put it that way, nothing. It was just a small fear—a cat scratching at my heart, as they say."

"I'll scratch your heart myself," he said, raising her as if she were weightless.

Laughing, he carried her back to the shack.

It was out of a deep, drugged-seeming sleep that he dragged himself/was dragged much later, by the sound of her weeping. His time-sense felt distorted, for it seemed an abnormally long interval before her image registered, and her sobs seemed unnaturally drawn out and far apart.

"What—is—it?" he said, becoming at that moment aware of the faint, throbbing, pinprick aftereffect in his biceps.

"I did not—want you to—awaken," she said. "Please go back to sleep."

"You are from the Center, aren't you?"

She looked away.

"It does not matter," he said.

"Sleep. Please. Do not lose the—"

"—requirements of Item Seven," he finished. "You always honor a contract, don't you?"

"That is not all that it was—to me."

"You meant what you said that night?"

"I came to."

"Of course you would say that now. Item Seven—"

"You bastard!" she said, and she slapped him.

He began to chuckle, but it stopped when he saw the hypodermic on the table at her side. Two spent ampules lay with it.

"You didn't give me two shots," he said, and she looked away.

"Come on." He began to rise. "We've got to get you to the Center. Get the stuff neutralized. Get it out of you."

She shook her head.

"Too late—already. Hold me. If you want to do something for me, do that."

He wrapped all of his arms about her and they lay that way while the tides and the winds cut, blew and ebbed, grinding their edges to an ever more perfect fineness.

I think—

Let me tell you of the creature called the Bork. It was born in the heart of a dying star. It was a piece of a man and pieces of many other things. If the things went wrong, the man-piece shut them down and repaired them. If he went wrong, they shut him down and repaired him. It was so skillfully fashioned that it might have lasted forever. But if part of it should die the other pieces need not cease to function, for it could still contrive to carry on the motions the total creature had once performed. It is a thing in a place by the sea that walks beside the water, poking with its forked, metallic stick at the other things the waves have tossed. The human piece, or a piece of the human piece, is dead.

Choose any of the above.

GORDON EKLUND and
GREGORY BENFORD

If the Stars Are Gods

Gordon Eklund was born in Seattle, served four years in the Air Force, and now lives in the San Francisco Bay area. His first published story was a Nebula Award finalist in 1971. Since then he has published some four dozen stories and five novels, including *The Eclipse of Dawn, Beyond the Resurrection,* and *All Times Possible.* He is a full-time writer.

Gregory Benford is a part time writer and a full-time associate professor of physics at the University of California, Irvine, currently working in the areas of plasma turbulence and the dynamics of relativistic electron beams. He has published numerous articles on science and two science-fiction novels, *Deeper than the Darkness* and *Jupiter Project.*

They have collaborated on a Nebula Award-winning story about strange aliens and their even stranger beliefs.

§

---

§

A dog cannot be a hypocrite, but neither can he be sincere.

—LUDWIG WITTGENSTEIN

It was deceptively huge and massive, this alien starship, and somehow seemed as if it belonged almost anywhere else in the universe but here.

Reynolds stepped carefully down the narrow corridor of the ship, still replaying in his mind's eye the approach to the air lock, the act of being swallowed. The ceilings were high, the light poor, the walls made of some dull, burnished metal.

These aspects and others flitted through his mind as he walked. Reynolds was a man who appreciated the fine interlacing pleasures of careful thought, but more than that, thinking so closely of these things kept his mind occupied and drove away the smell. It was an odd thick odor, and something about it upset his careful equilibrium. It clung to him like Pacific fog. Vintage manure, Reynolds had decided the moment he passed through the air lock. Turning, he had glared at Kelly firmly encased inside her suit. He told her about the smell. "Everybody stinks," she had said, evenly, perhaps joking, perhaps not, and pushed him away in the light centrifugal gravity. Away, into a maze of tight passages that would lead him eventually to look the first certified intelligent alien beings straight in the eye. If they happened to have eyes, that is.

It amused him that this privilege should be his. More rightly, the honor should have gone to another, someone younger whose tiny paragraph in the future histories of the human race had not already been enacted. At fifty-eight, Reynolds had long since lived a full and intricate lifetime. Too full, he sometimes thought, for any one man. So then, what about this day now? What about today? It did nothing really, only succeeded in forcing the fullness of his lifetime past the point of all reasonableness into a realm of positive absurdity.

The corridor branched again. He wondered precisely where he was inside the sculpted and twisted skin of the ship. He had tried to memorize everything he saw but there was nothing, absolutely nothing but metal with thin seams, places where he had to stoop or crawl, and the same awful smell. He realized now what it was about the ship that had bothered him the first time he had seen it, through a telescope from the moon. It reminded him, both in size and shape, of a building where he had once lived not so many years ago, during the brief term of his most recent retirement, 1987 and '88, in São Paulo, Brazil: a huge ultra-modern lifting apartment complex of a distinctly radical design. There was nothing like it on Earth, the advertising posters had proclaimed; and seeing it, hating it instantly, he had agreed. Now here was something else truly like it, but not on Earth.

The building had certainly not resembled a starship, but then, neither did this thing. At one end was an intricately designed portion, a cylinder with interesting modifications. Then came a long, plain tube and at the end of that something truly absurd: a cone, opening outward away from the rest of the ship and absolutely empty. Absurd, until you realized what it was.

The starship's propulsion source was, literally, hydrogen bombs. The central tube evidently held a vast number of fusion devices. One by one the bombs were released, drifted to the mouth of the cone and were detonated. The cone was a huge shock absorber;

the kick from the bomb pushed the ship forward. A Rube Goldberg star drive—
    Directly ahead of him, the corridor neatly stopped and split, like
the twin prongs of a roasting fork. It jogged his memory: roasting
fork, yes, from the days when he still ate meat. Turning left, he
followed the proper prong. His directions had been quite clear.
    He still felt very ill at ease. Maybe it was the way he was dressed
that made everything seem so totally wrong. It didn't seem quite
right, walking through an alien maze in his shirtsleeves and plain
trousers. Pedestrian.
    But the air was breathable, as promised. Did they breathe this
particular oxygen-nitrogen balance, too? And like the smell?
    Ahead, the corridor parted, branching once more. The odor was
horribly powerful at this spot, and he ducked his head low, almost
choking, and dashed through a round opening.
    This was a big room. Like the corridor, the ceiling was a good
seven meters above the floor, but the walls were subdued pastel
shades of red, orange and yellow. The colors were mixed on all the
walls in random, patternless designs. It was very pretty, Reynolds
thought, and not at all strange. Also, standing neatly balanced near
the back wall, there were two aliens.
    When he saw the creatures, Reynolds stopped and stood tall.
Raising his eyes, he stretched to reach the level of their eyes.
While he did this, he also reacted. His first reaction was shock. This
gave way to the tickling sensation of surprise. Then pleasure and
relief. He liked the looks of these two creatures. They were certainly far kinder toward the eyes than what he had expected to
find.
    Stepping forward, Reynolds stood before both aliens, shifting his
gaze from one to the other. Which was the leader? Or were both
leaders? Or neither? He decided to wait. But neither alien made
a sound or a move. So Reynolds kept waiting.
    What had he expected to find? Men? Something like a man, that
is, with two arms and two legs and a properly positioned head,
with a nose, two eyes and a pair of floppy ears? This was what Kelly
had expected him to find—she would be disappointed now—but

Reynolds had never believed it for a moment. Kelly thought anything that spoke English had to be a man, but Reynolds was more imaginative. He knew better; he had not expected to find a man, not even a man with four arms and three legs and fourteen fingers or five ears. What he had expected to find was something truly alien. A blob, if worst came to worst, but at best something more like a shark or snake or wolf than a man. As soon as Kelly had told him that the aliens wanted to meet him—"Your man who best knows your star"—he had known this.

Now he said, "I am the man you wished to see. The one who knows the stars."

As he spoke, he carefully shared his gaze with both aliens, still searching for a leader, favoring neither over the other. One—the smaller one—twitched a nostril when Reynolds said, ". . . the stars"; the other remained motionless.

There was one Earth animal that did resemble these creatures, and this was why Reynolds felt happy and relieved. The aliens were sufficiently alien, yes. And they were surely not men. But neither did they resemble blobs or wolves or sharks or snakes. They were giraffes. Nice, kind, friendly, pleasant, smiling, silent giraffes. There were some differences, of course. The aliens' skin was a rainbow collage of pastel purples, greens, reds and yellows, similar in its random design to the colorfully painted walls. Their trunks stood higher off the ground, their necks were stouter than that of a normal giraffe. They did not have tails. Nor hooves. Instead, at the bottom of each of their four legs, they had five blunt short fingers and a single wide thick offsetting thumb.

"My name is Bradley Reynolds," he said. "I know the stars." Despite himself, their continued silence made him nervous. "Is something wrong?" he asked.

The shorter alien bowed its neck toward him. Then, in a shrill high-pitched voice that reminded him of a child, it said, "No." An excited nervous child. "That is no," it said.

"This?" Reynolds lifted his hand, having almost forgotten what was in it. Kelly had ordered him to carry the tape recorder, but now he could truthfully say, "I haven't activated it yet."

"Break it, please," the alien said.

Reynolds did not protest or argue. He let the machine fall to the floor. Then he jumped, landing on the tape recorder with both feet. The light aluminum case split wide open like the hide of a squashed apple. Once more, Reynolds jumped. Then, standing calmly, he kicked the broken bits of glass and metal toward an unoccupied corner of the room. "All right?" he asked.

Now for the first time the second alien moved. Its nostrils twitched daintily, then its legs shifted, lifting and falling. "Welcome," it said, abruptly, stopping all motion. "My name is Jonathon."

"Your name?" asked Reynolds.

"And this is Richard."

"Oh," said Reynolds, not contradicting. He understood now. Having learned the language of man, these creatures had learned his names as well.

"We wish to know your star," Jonathon said respectfully. His voice was a duplicate of the other's. Did the fact that he had not spoken until after the destruction of the tape recorder indicate that he was the leader of the two? Reynolds almost laughed, listening to the words of his own thoughts. Not *he*, he reminded himself: *it*.

"I am willing to tell you whatever you wish to know," Reynolds said.

"You are a . . . priest . . . a reverend of the sun?"

"An astronomer," Reynolds corrected.

"We would like to know everything you know. And then we would like to visit and converse with your star."

"Of course. I will gladly help you in any way I can." Kelly had cautioned him in advance that the aliens were interested in the sun, so none of this came as any surprise to him. But nobody knew what it was in particular that they wanted to know, or why, and Kelly hoped that he might be able to find out. At the moment he could think of only two possible conversational avenues to take; both were questions. He tried the first. "What is it you wish to know? Is our star greatly different from others of its type? If it is, we are unaware of this fact."

"No two stars are the same," the alien said. This was Jonathon again. Its voice began to rise in excitement. "What is it? Do you not wish to speak here? Is our craft an unsatisfactory place?"

"No, this is fine," Reynolds said, wondering if it was wise to continue concealing his puzzlement. "I will tell you what I know. Later, I can bring books."

"No!" The alien did not shout, but from the way its legs quivered and nostrils trembled, Reynolds gathered he had said something very improper indeed.

"I will tell you," he said. "In my own words."

Jonathon stood quietly rigid "Fino."

Now it was time for Reynolds to ask his second question. Ho let it fall within the long silence which had followed Jonathon's last statement. "Why do you wish to know about our star?"

"It is the reason why we have come here. On our travels, we have visited many stars. But it is yours we have sought the longest. It is so powerful. And benevolent. A rare combination, as you must know."

"Very rare," Reynolds said, thinking that this wasn't making any sense. But then, why should it? At least he had learned something of the nature of the aliens' mission, and that alone was more than anyone else had managed to learn during the months the aliens had slowly approached the moon, exploding their hydrogen bombs to decelerate.

A sudden burst of confidence surprised Reynolds. He had not felt this sure of himself in years, and just like before, there was no logical reason for his certainty. "Would you be willing to answer some questions for me? About *your* star?"

"Certainly, Bradley Reynolds."

"Can you tell me our name for your star? Its coordinates?"

"No," Jonathon said, dipping its neck. "I cannot." It blinked its right eye in a furious fashion. "Our galaxy is not this one. It is a galaxy too distant for your instruments."

"I see," said Reynolds, because he could not very well call the alien a liar, even if it was. But Jonathon's hesitancy to reveal the location of its homeworld was not unexpected; Reynolds would have acted the same in similar circumstances.

Richard spoke. "May I pay obeisance?"

Jonathon, turning to Richard, spoke in a series of shrill chirping noises. Then Richard replied in kind.

Turning back to Reynolds, Richard again asked, "May I pay obeisance?"

Reynolds could only say, "Yes." Why not?

Richard acted immediately. Its legs abruptly shot out from beneath its trunk at an angle no giraffe could have managed. Richard sat on its belly, legs spread, and its neck came down, the snout gently scraping the floor.

"Thank you," Reynolds said, bowing slightly at the waist. "But there is much we can learn from you, too." He spoke to hide his embarrassment, directing his words at Jonathon while hoping that they might serve to bring Richard back to its feet as well. When this failed to work, Reynolds launched into the speech he had been sent here to deliver. Knowing what he had to say, he ran through the words as hurriedly as possible. "We are a backward people. Compared to you, we are children in the universe. Our travels have carried us no farther than our sister planets, while you have seen stars whose light takes years to reach your home. We realize you have much to teach us, and we approach you as pupils before a grand philosopher. We are gratified at the chance to share our meager knowledge with you and wish only to be granted the privilege of listening to you in return."

"You wish to know deeply of our star?" Jonathon asked.

"Of many things," Reynolds said. "Your spacecraft, for instance. It is far beyond our meager knowledge."

Jonathon began to blink its right eye furiously. As it spoke, the speed of the blinking increased. "You wish to know that?"

"Yes, if you are willing to share your knowledge. We, too, would like to visit the stars."

Its eye moved faster than ever now. It said, "Sadly, there is nothing we can tell you of this ship. Unfortunately, we know nothing ourselves."

"Nothing?"

"The ship was a gift."

"You mean that you did not make it yourself. No. But you must have mechanics, individuals capable of repairing the craft in the event of some emergency."

"But that has never happened. I do not think the ship could fail."

"Would you explain?"

"Our race, our world, was once visited by another race of creatures. It was they who presented us with this ship. They had come to us from a distant star in order to make this gift. In return, we have used the ship only to increase the wisdom of our people."

"What can you tell me about this other race?" Reynolds asked.

"Very little, I am afraid. They came from a most ancient star near the true center of the universe."

"And were they like you? Physically?"

"No, more like you. Like people. But—please—may we be excused to converse about that which is essential. Our time is short."

Reynolds nodded, and the moment he did, Jonathon ceased to blink. Reynolds gathered that it had grown tired of lying, which wasn't surprising; Jonathon was a poor liar. Not only were the lies incredible in themselves, but every time it told a lie it blinked like a madman with an ash in his eye.

"If I tell you about our star," Jonathon said, "will you consent to tell of yours in return?" The alien tilted its head forward, long neck swaying gently from side to side. It was plain that Jonathon attached great significance to Reynolds' reply.

So Reynolds said, "Yes, gladly," though he found he could not conceive of any information about the sun which might come as a surprise to these creatures. Still, he had been sent here to discover as much about the aliens as possible without revealing anything important about mankind. This sharing of information about stars seemed a safe enough course to pursue.

"I will begin," Jonathon said, "and you must excuse my impreciseness of expression. My knowledge of your language is limited. I imagine you have a special vocabulary for the subject."

"A technical vocabulary, yes."

The alien said, "Our star is a brother to yours. Or would it be sister? During periods of the most intense communion, his wisdom —or hers?—is faultless. At times he is angry—unlike your star— but these moments are not frequent. Nor do they last for longer than a few fleeting moments. Twice he has prophesied the termi- nation of our civilization during times of great personal anger, but never has he felt it necessary to carry out his prediction. I would say that he is more kind than raging, more gentle than brutal. I believe he loves our people most truly and fully. Among the stars of the universe, his place is not great, but as our home star, we must revere him. And, of course, we do."

"Would you go on?" Reynolds asked.

Jonathon went on. Reynolds listened. The alien spoke of its personal relationship with the star, how the star had helped it during times of individual darkness. Once, the star had assisted it in choosing a proper mate; the choice proved not only perfect but divine. Throughout, Jonathon spoke of the star as a reverent Jew- ish tribesman might have spoken of the Old Testament God. For the first time, Reynolds regretted having had to dispose of the tape recorder. When he tried to tell Kelly about this conversation, she would never believe a word of it. As it spoke, the alien did not blink, not once, even briefly, for Reynolds watched carefully.

At last the alien was done. It said, "But this is only a beginning. We have so much to share, Bradley Reynolds. Once I am conver- sant with your technical vocabulary. Communication between separate entities—the great barriers of language . . ."

"I understand," said Reynolds.

"We knew you would. But now—it is your turn. Tell me about your star."

"We call it the sun," Reynolds said. Saying this, he felt more than mildly foolish—but what else? How could he tell Jonathon what it wished to know when he did not know himself? All he knew about the sun was facts. He knew how hot it was and how old it was and he knew its size and mass and magnitude. He knew about sunspots and solar winds and solar atmosphere. But that was all he knew. Was the sun a benevolent star? Was it con- stantly enraged? Did all mankind revere it with the proper quantity of love and dedication? "That is its common name. More properly, in an ancient language adopted by science, it is Sol. It lies approximately eight—"

"Oh," said Jonathon. "All of this, yes, we know. But its demeanor. Its attitudes, both normal and abnormal. You play with us, Bradley Reynolds. You joke. We understand your amusement—but, please, we are simple souls and have traveled far. We must know these other things before daring to make our personal approach to the star. Can you tell us in what fashion it has most often affected your individual life? This would help us immensely."

Although his room was totally dark, Reynolds, entering, did not bother with the light. He knew every inch of this room, knew it as well in the dark as the light. For the past four years, he had spent an average of twelve hours a day here. He knew the four walls, the desk, the bed, the bookshelves and the books, knew them more intimately than he had ever known another person. Reaching the cot without once stubbing his toe or tripping over an open book or stumbling across an unfurled map, he sat down and covered his face with his hands, feeling the wrinkles on his forehead like great wide welts. Alone, he played a game with the wrinkles, pretending that each one represented some event or facet of his life. This one here—the big one above the left eyebrow—that was Mars. And this other one—way over here almost by his right ear—that was a girl named Melissa whom he had known back in the 1970s. But he wasn't in the proper mood for the game now. He lowered his hands. He knew the wrinkles for exactly what they really were: age, purely and simply and honestly age. Each one meant nothing without the others. They represented impersonal and unavoidable erosion. On the outside, they reflected the death that was occurring on the inside.

Still, he was happy to be back here in this room. He never realized how important these familiar surroundings were to his state of mind until he was forcefully deprived of them for a length of time. Inside the alien starship, it hadn't been so bad. The time had passed quickly then; he hadn't been allowed to get homesick.

It was afterward when it had got bad. With Kelly and the others in her dank, ugly impersonal hole of an office. Those had been the unbearable hours.

But now he was home, and he would not have to leave again until they told him. He had been appointed official emissary to the aliens, though this did not fool him for a moment. He had been given the appointment only because Jonathon had refused to see anyone else. It wasn't because anyone liked him or respected him or thought him competent enough to handle the mission. He was different from them, and that made all the difference. When they were still kids, they had seen his face on the old TV networks every night of the week. Kelly wanted someone like herself to handle the aliens. Someone who knew how to take orders, someone ultimately competent, some computer facsimile of a human being. Like herself. Someone who, when given a job, performed it in the most efficient manner in the least possible time.

Kelly was the director of the moon base. She had come here two years ago, replacing Bill Newton, a contemporary of Reynolds', a friend of his. Kelly was the protégée of some U.S. Senator, some powerful idiot from the Midwest, a leader of the anti-NASA faction in the Congress. Kelly's appointment had been part of a wild attempt to subdue the Senator with favors and special attention. It had worked after a fashion. There were still Americans on the moon. Even the Russians had left two years ago.

Leaving the alien starship, he had met Kelly the instant he reached the air lock. He had managed to slip past her and pull on his suit before she could question him. He had known she wouldn't dare try to converse over the radio; too great a chance of being overheard. She would never trust him to say only the right things.

But that little game had done nothing except delay matters a few minutes. The tug had returned to the moon base and then everyone had gone straight to Kelly's office. Then the interrogation had begun. Reynolds had sat near the back of the room while the rest of them flocked around Kelly like pet sheep.

Kelly asked the first question. "What do they want?" He knew her well enough to understand exactly what she meant: What do

they want from us in return for what we want from them?
Reynolds told her: They wanted to know about the sun.

"We gathered that much," Kelly said. "But what kind of information do they want? Specifically, what are they after?"

With great difficulty, he tried to explain this too.

Kelly interrupted him quickly. "And what did you tell them?"

"Nothing," he said.

"Why?"

"Because I didn't know what to tell them."

"Didn't you ever happen to think the best thing to tell them might have been whatever it was they wished to hear?"

"I couldn't do that either," he said, "because I didn't know. You tell me: Is the sun benevolent? How does it inspire your daily life? Does it constantly rage? I don't know, and you don't know either, and it's not a thing we can risk lying about, because they may very well know themselves. To them, a star is a living entity. It's a god, but more than our gods, because they can see a star and feel its heat and never doubt that it's always there."

"Will they want you back?" she asked.

"I think so. They liked me. Or he liked me. It. I only talked to one of them."

"I thought you told us two."

So he went over the whole story for her once more, from beginning to end, hoping this time she might realize that alien beings are not human beings and should not be expected to respond in familiar ways. When he came to the part about the presence of the two aliens, he said, "Look. There are six men in this room right now besides us. But they are here only for show. The whole time, none of them will say a word or think a thought or decide a point. The other alien was in the room with Jonathon and me the whole time. But if it had not been there, nothing would have been changed. I don't know why it was there and I don't expect I ever will. But neither do I understand why you feel you have to have all these men here with you."

She utterly ignored the point. "Then that is all they are interested in? They're pilgrims and they think the sun is Mecca."

"More or less," he said, with the emphasis on "less."

"Then they won't want to talk to me—or any of us. You're the one who knows the sun. Is that correct?" She jotted a note on a pad, shaking her elbow briskly.

"That is correct."

"Reynolds," she said, looking up from her pad, "I sure as hell hope you know what you're doing."

He said, "Why?"

She did not bother to attempt to disguise her contempt. Few of them did any more and especially not Kelly. It was her opinion that Reynolds should not be here at all. Put him in a rest home back on Earth, she would say. The other astronauts—they were considerate enough to retire when life got too complicated for them. What makes this one man, Bradley Reynolds, why is he so special? All right—she would admit—ten years, twenty years ago, he was a great brave man struggling to conquer the unknown. When I was sixteen years old, I couldn't walk a dozen feet without tripping over his name or face. But what about now? What is he? I'll tell you what he is: a broken-down, wrinkled relic of an old man. So what if he's an astronomer as well as an astronaut? So what if he's the best possible man for the Lunar observatory? I still say he's more trouble than he's worth. He walks around the moon base like a dog having a dream. Nobody can communicate with him. He hasn't attended a single psychological expansion session since he's been here, and that goes back well before my time. He's a morale problem; nobody can stand the sight of him any more. And, as far as doing his job goes, he does it, yes—but that's all. His heart isn't in it. Look, he didn't even know about the aliens being in orbit until I called him in and told him they wanted to see him.

That last part was not true, of course. Reynolds, like everyone, had known about the aliens, but he did have to admit that their approach had not overly concerned him. He had not shared the hysteria which had gripped the whole of the Earth when the announcement was made that an alien starship had entered the system. The authorities had known about it for months before ever releasing the news. By the time anything was said publicly, it had been clearly determined that the aliens offered Earth no clear or present danger. But that was about all anyone had learned. Then the starship had gone into orbit around the moon, an action intended to confirm their lack of harmful intent toward Earth, and the entire problem had landed with a thud in Kelly's lap. The aliens said they wanted to meet a man who knew something about the sun, and that had turned out to be Reynolds. Then—and only then—had he had a real reason to become interested in the aliens. That day, for the first time in a half-dozen years, he had actually listened to the daily news broadcasts from Earth. He discovered —and it didn't particularly surprise him—that everyone else had long since got over their initial interest in the aliens. He gathered that war was brewing again. In Africa this time, which was a change in place if not in substance. The aliens were mentioned once, about halfway through the program, but Reynolds could tell they were no longer considered real news. A meeting between a representative of the American moon base and the aliens was being arranged, the newscaster said. It would take place aboard the aliens' ship in orbit around the moon, he added. The name Bradley Reynolds was not mentioned. I wonder if they remember me, he had thought.

"It seems to me that you could get more out of them than some babble about stars being gods," Kelly said, getting up and pacing around the room, one hand on hip. She shook her head in mock disbelief and the brown curls swirled downward, flowing like dark honey in the light gravity.

"Oh, I did," he said casually.

"What?" There was a rustling of interest in the room.

"A few facts about their planet. Some bits of detail I think fit together. It may even explain their theology."

"Explain theology with astronomy?" Kelly said sharply. "There's no mystery to sun worship. It was one of our primitive religions." A man next to her nodded.

"Not quite. Our star is relatively mild-mannered, as Jonathon would say. And our planet has a nice, comfortable orbit, nearly circular."

"Theirs doesn't?"

"No. The planet has a pronounced axial inclination, too, nothing ordinary like Earth's twenty-three degrees. Their world must be tilted at forty degrees or so to give the effects Jonathon mentioned."

"Hot summers?" one of the men he didn't know said, and Reynolds looked up in mild surprise. So the underlings were not just spear-carriers, as he had thought. Well enough.

"Right. The axial tilt causes each hemisphere to alternately slant toward and then away from their star. They have colder winters and hotter summers than we do. But there's something more, as far as I can figure it out. Jonathon says its world 'does not move in the perfect path' and that ours, on the other hand, very nearly does."

"Perfect path?" Kelly said, frowning. "An eight-fold way? The path of enlightenment?"

"More theology," said the man who had spoken.

"Not quite," Reynolds said. "Pythagoras believed the circle was a perfect form, the most beautiful of all figures. I don't see why Jonathon shouldn't."

"Astronomical bodies look like circles. Pythagoras could see the moon," Kelly said.

"And the sun," Reynolds said. "I don't know whether Jonathon's world has a moon or not. But they can see their star, and in profile it's a circle."

"So a circular orbit is a perfect orbit."

"Q.E.D. Jonathon says its planet doesn't have one, though."

"It's an ellipse."

"A very eccentric ellipse. That's my guess, anyway. Jonathon used the terms 'path-summer' and 'pole-summer,' so they do distinguish between the two effects."

"I don't get it," the man said.

"An ellipse alone gives alternate summers and winters, but in both hemispheres at the same time," Kelly said brusquely, her mouth turning slightly downward. "A 'pole-summer' must be the kind Earth has."

"Oh," the man said weakly.

"You left out the 'great-summer,' my dear," Reynolds said with a thin smile.

"What's that?" Kelly said carefully.

"When the 'pole-summer' coincides with the 'path-summer'— which it will, every so often. I wouldn't want to be around when that happens. Evidently neither do the members of Jonathon's race."

"How do they get away?" Kelly said intently.

"Migrate. One hemisphere is having a barely tolerable summer while the other is being fried alive, so they go there. The whole race."

"Nomads," Kelly said. "An entire culture born with a pack on its back," she said distantly. Reynolds raised an eyebrow. It was the first time he had ever heard her say anything that wasn't crisp, efficient and uninteresting.

"I think that's why they're grazing animals, to make it easy— even necessary—to keep on the move. A 'great-summer' wilts all the vegetation; a 'great-winter'—they must have those, too— freezes a continent solid."

"God," Kelly said quietly.

"Jonathon mentioned huge storms, winds that knocked it down, sand that buried it overnight in dunes. The drastic changes in the climate must stir up hurricanes and tornadoes."

"Which they have to migrate through," Kelly said. Reynolds noticed that the room was strangely quiet.

"Jonathon seems to have been born on one of the Treks. They don't have much shelter because of the winds and the winters that erode away the rock. It must be hard to build up any sort of technology in an environment like that. I suppose it's pretty inevitable that they turned out to believe in astrology."

"What?" Kelly said, surprised.

"Of course." Reynolds looked at her, completely deadpan. "What else should I call it? With such a premium on reading the stars correctly, so that they know the precise time of year and when the next 'great-summer' is coming—what else would they believe in? Astrology would be the obvious, unchallengeable religion—because it worked!" Reynolds smiled to himself, imagining a flock of atheist giraffes vainly fighting their way through a sandstorm.

"I see," Kelly said, clearly at a loss. The men stood around them awkwardly, not knowing quite what to say to such a barrage of unlikely ideas. Reynolds felt a surge of joy. Some lost capacity of his youth had returned: to see himself as the center of things, as the only actor onstage who moved of his own volition, spoke his own unscripted lines. *This is the way the world feels when you are winning,* he thought. This was what he had lost, what Mars had taken from him during the long trip back in utter deep silence and loneliness. He had tested himself there and found some inner core, had come to think he did not need people and the fine edge of competition with them. Work and cramped rooms had warped him.

"I think that's why they are technologically retarded, despite their age. They don't really have the feel of machines, they've never gotten used to them. When they needed a starship for their religion, they built the most awkward one imaginable that would work." Reynolds paused, feeling lightheaded. "They live inside that machine, but they don't like it. They stink it up and make it feel like a corral. They mistrusted that tape recorder of mine. They must want to know the stars very badly, to depart so much from their nature just to reach them."

Kelly's lip stiffened and her eyes narrowed. Her face, Reynolds thought, was returning to its usual expression. "This is all very well, Dr. Reynolds," she said, and it was the old Kelly, the one he knew; the Kelly who always came out on top. "But it is speculation. We need facts. Their starship is crude, but it *works.* They must have data and photographs of stars. They know things we don't. There are innumerable details we could only find by making the trip ourselves, and even using their ship, that will take centuries —Houston tells me that bomb-thrower of theirs can't go above one percent of light velocity. I want—"

"I'll try," he said. "But I'm afraid it won't be easy. Whenever I try to approach a subject it does not want to discuss, the alien begins telling me the most fantastic lies."

"Oh?" Kelly said suspiciously, and he was sorry he had mentioned that, because it had taken him another quarter-hour of explaining before she had allowed him to escape the confines of her office.

Now he was back home again—in his room. Rolling over, he lay flat on his back in the bed, eyes wide open and staring straight ahead at the emptiness of the darkness. He would have liked to go out and visit the observatory, but Kelly had said he was excused from all duties until the alien situation was resolved. He gathered she meant that as an order. She must have. One thing about Kelly: she seldom said a word unless it was meant as an order.

They came and woke him up. He had not intended to sleep. His room was still pitch-black, and far away there was a fist pounding furiously upon a door. Getting up, taking his time, he went and let the man inside. Then he turned on the light.

"Hurry and see the director," the man said breathlessly.

"What does she want now?" Reynolds asked.

"How should I know?"

Reynolds shrugged and turned to go. He knew what she wanted anyway. It had to be the aliens; Jonathon was ready to see him again. Well, that was fine, he thought, entering Kelly's office. From the turn of her expression, he saw that he had guessed correctly. And I know exactly what I'm going to tell them, he thought.

Somewhere in his sleep, Reynolds had made an important decision. He had decided he was going to tell Jonathon the truth.

Approaching the alien starship, Reynolds discovered he was no longer so strongly reminded of his old home in São Paulo. Now that he had actually been inside the ship and had met the creatures who resided there, his feelings had changed. This time he was struck by how remarkably this strange twisted chunk of metal resembled what a real starship ought to look like.

The tug banged against the side of the ship. Without having to

be told, Reynolds removed his suit and went to the air lock. Kelly
jumped out of her seat and dashed after him. She grabbed the
camera off the deck and forced it into his hands. She wanted him
to photograph the aliens. He had to admit her logic was quite
impeccable. If the aliens were as unfearsome as Reynolds claimed,
then a clear and honest photograph could only reassure the population of Earth; hysteria was still a worry to many politicians back
home. Many people still claimed that a spaceship full of green
monsters was up here orbiting the moon only a few hours' flight
from New York and Moscow. One click of the camera and this fear
would be ended.

Reynolds had told her Jonathon would never permit a photograph to be taken, but Kelly had remained adamant.

"Who cares?" he'd asked her.

"Everyone cares," she'd insisted.

"Oh, really? I listened to the news yesterday and the aliens
weren't even mentioned. Is that hysteria?"

"That's because of Africa. Wait till the war's over, then listen."

He hadn't argued with her then and he didn't intend to argue
with her now. He accepted the camera without a word, her voice
burning his ears with last-minute instructions, and plunged ahead.

The smell assaulted him immediately. As he entered the spaceship, the odor seemed to rise up from nowhere and surround him.
He made himself push forward. Last time, the odor had been a
problem only for a short time. He was sure he could overcome it
again this time.

It was cold in the ship. He wore only light pants and a light shirt
without underwear, because last time it had been rather warm.
Had Jonathon, noticing his discomfort, lowered the ship's temperature accordingly?

He turned the first corner and glanced briefly at the distant
ceiling. He called out, "Hello!" but there was only a slight echo.
He spoke again and the echo was the same, flat and hard.

Another turn. He was moving much faster than before. The
tight passages no longer caused him to pause and think. He simply
plunged ahead, trusting his own knowledge. At Kelly's urging he

was wearing a radio attached to his belt. He noticed that it was beeping furiously at him. Apparently Kelly had neglected some important last-minute direction. He didn't mind. He already had enough orders to ignore; one less would make little difference.

Here was the place. Pausing in the doorway, he removed the radio, turning it off. Then he placed the camera on the floor beside it and stepped into the room.

Despite the chill in the air, the room was not otherwise different from before. There were two aliens standing against the farthest wall. Reynolds went straight toward them, holding his hands over his head in greeting. One was taller than the other. Reynolds spoke to it. "Are you Jonathon?"

"Yes," Jonathon said, in its child's piping voice. "And this is Richard."

"May I pay obeisance?" Richard asked eagerly.

Reynolds nodded. "If you wish."

Jonathon waited until Richard had regained its feet, then said, "We wish to discuss your star now."

"All right," Reynolds said. "But there's something I have to tell you first." Saying this, for the first time since he had made his decision, he wasn't sure. Was the truth really the best solution in this situation? Kelly wanted him to lie: tell them whatever they wanted to hear, making certain he didn't tell them quite everything. Kelly was afraid the aliens might go sailing off to the sun once they had learned what they had come here to learn. She wanted a chance to get engineers and scientists inside their ship before the aliens left. And wasn't this a real possibility? What if Kelly was right and the aliens went away? Then what would he say?

"You want to tell us that your sun is not a conscious being," Jonathon said. "Am I correct?"

The problem was instantly solved. Reynolds felt no more compulsion to lie. He said, "Yes."

"I am afraid that you are wrong," said Jonathon.

"We live here, don't we? Wouldn't we know? You asked for me because I know our sun, and I do. But there are other men on our

homeworld who know far more than I do. But no one has ever
discovered the last shred of evidence to support your theory."

"A theory is a guess," Jonathon said. "We do not guess; we
know."

"Then," Reynolds said, "explain it to me. Because I don't know."
He watched the alien's eyes carefully, waiting for the first indication of a blinking fit.

But Jonathon's gaze remained steady and certain. "Would you
like to hear of our journey?" it asked.

"Yes."

"We left our homeworld a great many of your years ago. I
cannot tell you exactly when, for reasons I'm certain you can
understand, but I will reveal that it was more than a century ago.
In that time we have visited nine stars. The ones we would visit
were chosen for us beforehand. Our priests—our leaders—determined the stars that were within our reach and also able to help
in our quest. You see, we have journeyed here in order to ask
certain questions."

"Questions of the stars?"

"Yes, of course. The questions we have are questions only a star
may answer."

"And what are they?" Reynolds asked.

"We have discovered the existence of other universes parallel
with our own. Certain creatures—devils and demons—have come
from these universes in order to attack and capture our stars. We
feel we must—"

"Oh, yes," Reynolds said. "I understand. We've run across several of these creatures recently." And he blinked, matching the
twitching of Jonathon's eye. "They are awfully fearsome, aren't
they?" When Jonathon stopped, he stopped too. He said, "You
don't have to tell me everything. But can you tell me this: these
other stars you have visited, have they been able to answer any of
your questions?"

"Oh, yes. We have learned much from them. These stars were
very great—very different from our own."

"But they weren't able to answer all your questions?"

"If they had, we would not be here now."

"And you believe our star may be able to help you?"

"All may help, but the one we seek is the one that can save us."

"When do you plan to go to the sun?"

"At once," Jonathon said. "As soon as you leave. I am afraid there is little else you can tell us."

"I'd like to ask you to stay," Reynolds said. And he forced himself to go ahead. He knew he could not convince Jonathon without revealing everything, yet, by doing so, he might also be putting an end to all his hopes. Still, he told the alien about Kelly and, more generally, he told it what the attitude of man was toward their visit. He told it what man wished to know from them, and why.

Jonathon seemed amazed. It moved about the floor as Reynolds spoke, its feet clanking dully. Then it stopped and stood, its feet only a few inches apart, a position that impressed Reynolds as one of incredulous amazement. "Your people wish to travel farther into space? You want to visit the stars? But why, Reynolds? Your people do not believe. Why?"

Reynolds smiled. Each time Jonathon said something to him, he felt he knew these people—and how they thought and reacted— a little better than he had before. There was another question he would very much have liked to ask Jonathon. How long have your people possessed the means of visiting the stars? A very long time, he imagined. Perhaps a longer time than the whole lifespan of the human race. And why hadn't they gone before now? Reynolds thought he knew: because, until now, they had had no reason for going.

Now Reynolds tried to answer Jonathon's question. If anyone could, it should be him. "We wish to go to the stars because we are a dissatisfied people. Because we do not live a very long time as individuals, we feel we must place an important part of our lives into the human race as a whole. In a sense, we surrender a portion of our individual person in return for a sense of greater immortality. What is an accomplishment for man as a race is also an accomplishment for each individual man. And what are these accomplishments? Basically this: anything a man does that no other man

has done before—whether it is good or evil or neither one or both
—is considered by us to be a great accomplishment."

And—to add emphasis to the point—he blinked once.

Then, holding his eyes steady, he said, "I want you to teach me
to talk to the stars. I want you to stay here around the moon long
enough to do that."

Instantly Jonathon said, "No."

There was an added force to the way it said it, an emphasis its
voice had not previously possessed. Then Reynolds realized what
that was: at the same moment Jonathon had spoken, Richard too
had said, "No."

"Then you may be doomed to fail," Reynolds said. "Didn't I tell
you? I know our star better than any man available to you. Teach
me to talk to the stars and I may be able to help you with this one.
Or would you prefer to continue wandering the galaxy forever,
failing to find what you seek wherever you go?"

"You are a sensible man, Reynolds. You may be correct. We will
ask our home star and see."

"Do that. And if it says yes and I promise to do what you wish,
then I must ask you to promise me something in return. I want you
to allow a team of our scientists and technicians to enter and
inspect your ship. You will answer their questions to the best of
your ability. And that means truthfully."

"We always tell the truth," Jonathon said, blinking savagely.

The moon had made one full circuit of the Earth since Reynolds'
initial meeting with the aliens, and he was quite satisfied with the
progress he had made up to now, especially during the past ten
days after Kelly had stopped accompanying him in his daily shut-
tles to and from the orbiting starship. As a matter of fact, in all that
time, he had not had a single face-to-face meeting with her and
they had talked on the phone only once. And she wasn't here now
either, which was strange, since it was noon and she always ate
here with the others.

Reynolds had a table to himself in the cafeteria. The food was
poor, but it always was, and he was used to that by now. What did
bother him, now that he was thinking about it, was Kelly's ab-

sence. Most days he skipped lunch himself. He tried to remember the last time he had come here. It was more than a week ago, he remembered—more than ten days ago. He didn't like the sound of that answer.

Leaning over, he attracted the attention of a girl at an adjoining table. He knew her vaguely. Her father had been an important wheel in NASA when Reynolds was still a star astronaut. He couldn't remember the man's name. His daughter had a tiny cute face and a billowing body about two sizes too big for the head. Also, she had a brain that was much too limited for much of anything. She worked in the administrative section, which meant she slept with most of the men on the base at one time or another.

"Have you seen Kelly?" he asked her.

"Must be in her office."

"No, I mean when was the last time you saw her here?"

"In here? Oh—" The girl thought for a moment. "Doesn't she eat with the other chiefs?"

Kelly never ate with the other chiefs. She always ate in the cafeteria—for morale purposes—and the fact that the girl did not remember having seen her meant that it had been several days at least since Kelly had last put in an appearance. Leaving his lunch where it lay, Reynolds got up, nodded politely at the girl, who stared at him as if he were a freak, and hurried away.

It wasn't a long walk, but he ran. He had no intention of going to see Kelly. He knew that would prove useless. Instead, he was going to see John Sims. At fifty-two, Sims was the second oldest man in the base. Like Reynolds, he was a former astronaut. In 1987, when Reynolds, then a famous man, was living in São Paulo, Sims had commanded the first (and only) truly successful Mars expedition. During those few months, the world had heard his name, but people forgot quickly, and Sims was one of the things they forgot. He had never done more than what he was expected to do; the threat of death had never come near Sims's expedition. Reynolds, on the other hand, had failed. On Mars with him, three men had died. Yet it was he—Reynolds, the failure—who had been the hero, not Sims.

And maybe I'm a hero again, he thought as he knocked evenly

on the door to Sims's office. Maybe down there the world is once
more reading about me daily. He hadn't listened to a news broadcast since the night before his first trip to the ship. Had the story
been released to the public yet? He couldn't see any reason why
it should be suppressed, but that seldom was important. He would
ask Sims. Sims would know.

The door opened and Reynolds went inside. Sims was a huge
man who wore his black hair in a crewcut. The style had been out
of fashion for thirty or forty years; Reynolds doubted there was
another crewcut man in the universe. But he could not imagine
Sims any other way.

"What's wrong?" Sims asked, guessing accurately the first time.
He led Reynolds to a chair and sat him down. The office was big
but empty. A local phone sat upon the desk along with a couple
of daily status reports. Sims was assistant administrative chief,
whatever that meant. Reynolds had never understood the functions of the position, if any. But there was one thing that was clear:
Sims knew more about the inner workings of the moon base than
any other man. And that included the director as well.

"I want to know about Vonda," Reynolds said. With Sims, everything stood on a first-name basis. Vonda was Vonda Kelly. The
name tasted strangely upon Reynolds' lips. "Why isn't she eating
at the cafeteria?"

Sims answered unhesitantly. "Because she's afraid to leave her
desk."

"It has something to do with the aliens?"

"It does, but I shouldn't tell you what. She doesn't want you to
know."

"Tell me. Please." His desperation cleared the smile from Sims's
lips. And he had almost added: for old times' sake. He was glad he
had controlled himself.

"The main reason is the war," Sims said. "If it starts, she wants
to know at once."

"Will it?"

Sims shook his head. "I'm smart but I'm not God. As usual, I
imagine everything will work out as long as no one makes a stupid

mistake. The worst will be a small local war lasting maybe a month. But how long can you depend upon politicians to act intelligently? It goes against the grain with them."

"But what about the aliens?"

"Well, as I said, that's part of it too." Sims stuck his pipe in his mouth. Reynolds had never seen it lit, never seen him smoking it, but the pipe was invariably there between his teeth. "A group of men are coming here from Washington, arriving tomorrow. They vant to talk with your pets. It seems nobody—least of all Vonda —is very happy with your progress."

"I am."

Sims shrugged, as if to say: that is of no significance.

"The aliens will never agree to see them," Reynolds said.

"How are they going to stop them? Withdraw the welcome mat? Turn out the lights? That won't work."

"But that will ruin everything. All my work up until now."

"What work?" Sims got up and walked around his desk until he stood hovering above Reynolds. "As far as anybody can see, you haven't accomplished a damn thing since you went up there. People want results, Bradley, not a lot of noise. All you've given anyone is the noise. This isn't a private game of yours. This is one of the most significant events in the history of the human race. If anyone ought to know that, it's you. Christ." And he wandered back to his chair again, jiggling his pipe.

"What is it they want from me?" Reynolds said. "Look—I got them what they asked for. The aliens have agreed to let a team of scientists study their ship."

"We want more than that now. Among other things, we want an alien to come down and visit Washington. Think of the propaganda value of that, and right now is a time when we damn well need something like that. Here we are, the only country with sense enough to stay on the moon. And being here has finally paid off in a way the politicians can understand. They've given you a month in which to play around—after all, you're a hero and the publicity is good—but how much longer do you expect them to wait? No, they want action and I'm afraid they want it now."

Reynolds was ready to go. He had found out as much as he was apt to find here. And he already knew what he was going to have to do. He would go and find Kelly and tell her she had to keep the men from Earth away from the aliens. If she wouldn't agree, then he would go up and tell the aliens and they would leave for the sun. But what if Kelly wouldn't let him go? He had to consider that. He knew; he would tell her this: If you don't let me see them, if you try to keep me away, they'll know something is wrong and they'll leave without a backward glance. Maybe he could tell her the aliens were telepaths; he doubted she would know any better.

He had the plan all worked out so that it could not fail.

He had his hand on the doorknob when Sims called him back. "There's another thing I better tell you, Bradley."

"All right. What's that?"

"Vonda. She's on your side. She told them to stay away, but it wasn't enough. She's been relieved of duty. A replacement is coming with the others."

"Oh," said Reynolds.

Properly suited, Reynolds sat in the cockpit of the shuttle tug, watching the pilot beside him going through the ritual of a final inspection prior to take-off. The dead desolate surface of the moon stretched briefly away from where the tug sat, the horizon so near that it almost looked touchable. Reynolds liked the moon. If he had not, he would never have elected to return here to stay. It was the Earth he hated. Better than the moon was space itself, the dark endless void beyond the reach of man's ugly grasping hands. That was where Reynolds was going now. Up. Out. Into the void. He was impatient to leave.

The pilot's voice came to him softly through the suit radio, a low murmur, not loud enough for him to understand what the man was saying. The pilot was talking to himself as he worked, using the rumble of his own voice as a way of patterning his mind so that it would not lose concentration. The pilot was a young man in his middle twenties, probably on loan from the Air Force, a lieutenant or, at most, a junior Air Force captain. He was barely old enough to remember when space had really been a frontier. Mankind had decided to go out, and Reynolds had been one of the men chosen to take the giant steps, but now it was late—the giant steps of twenty years ago were mere tentative contusions in the dust of the centuries—and man was coming back. From where he sat, looking out, Reynolds could see exactly 50 percent of the present American space program: the protruding bubble of the moon base. The other half was the orbiting space lab that circled the Earth itself, a battered relic of the expansive seventies. Well beyond the nearby horizon—maybe a hundred miles away—there had once been another bubble, but it was gone now. The brave men who had lived and worked and struggled and died and survived there —they were all gone too. Where? The Russians still maintained an orbiting space station, so some of their former moon colonists were undoubtedly there, but where were the rest? In Siberia? Working there? Hadn't the Russians decided that Siberia—the old barless prison state of the czars and early Communists—was a more practical frontier than the moon?

And weren't they maybe right? Reynolds did not like to think so, for he had poured his life into this—into the moon and the void beyond. But at times, like now, peering through the artificial window of his suit, seeing the bare bubble of the base clinging to the edge of this dead world like a wart on an old woman's face, starkly vulnerable, he found it hard to see the point of it. He was an old enough man to recall the first time he had ever been moved by the spirit of conquest. As a schoolboy, he remembered the first time men conquered Mount Everest—it was around 1956 or '57 —and he had religiously followed the newspaper reports. Afterward, a movie had been made, and watching that film, seeing the shadows of pale mountaineers clinging to the edge of that white god, he had decided that was what he wanted to be. And he had never been taught otherwise; only by the time he was old enough to act, all the mountains had long since been conquered. And he had ended up as an astronomer, able if nothing else to gaze outward at the distant shining peaks of the void, and from there he had been pointed toward space. So he had gone to Mars and become famous, but fame had turned him inward, so that now, without the brilliance of his past, he would have been nobody but another of those anonymous old men who dot the cities of the world, inhabiting identically bleak book-lined rooms, eating daily in bad restaurants, their minds always a billion miles away from the dead shells of their bodies.

"We can go now, Dr. Reynolds," the pilot was saying.

Reynolds grunted in reply, his mind several miles distant from his waiting body. He was thinking that there was something, after all. How could he think in terms of pointlessness and futility when he alone had actually seen them with his own eyes? Creatures, intelligent beings, born far away, light-years from the insignificant world of man? Didn't that in itself prove something? Yes. He was sure that it did. But what?

The tug lifted with a murmur from the surface of the moon. Crouched deeply within his seat, Reynolds thought that it wouldn't be long now.

And they found us, he thought, we did not find them. And when had they gone into space? Late. Very late. At a moment in their history comparable to man a hundred thousand years from now. They had avoided space until a pressing reason had come for venturing out, and then they had gone. He remembered that he had been unable to explain to Jonathon why man wanted to visit the stars when he did not believe in the divinity of the suns. Was there a reason? And, if so, did it make sense?

The journey was not long.

It didn't smell. The air ran clean and sharp and sweet through the corridors, and if there was any odor to it, the odor was one of purity and freshness, almost pine needles or mint. The air was good for his spirits. As soon as Reynolds came aboard the starship, his depression and melancholy were forgotten. Perhaps he was only letting the apparent grimness of the situation get the better of him. It had been too long a time since he'd last had to fight. Jonathon would know what to do. The alien was more than three hundred years old, a product of a civilization and culture that had reached its maturity at a time when man was not yet man, when he was barely a skinny undersized ape, a carrion eater upon the hot plains of Africa.

When Reynolds reached the meeting room, he saw that Jonathon and Richard were not alone this time. The third alien—Reynolds sensed it was someone important—was introduced as Vergnan. No adopted Earth name for it.

"This is ours who best knows the stars," Jonathon said. "It has spoken with yours and hopes it may be able to assist you."

Reynolds had almost forgotten that part. The sudden pressures of the past few hours had driven everything else from his mind. His training. His unsuccessful attempts to speak to the stars. He had failed. Jonathon had been unable to teach him, but he thought that was probably because he simply did not believe.

"Now we shall leave you," Jonathon said.

"But—" said Reynolds.

"We are not permitted to stay."

"But there's something I must tell you."

It was too late. Jonathon and Richard headed for the corridor, walking with surprising gracefulness. Their long necks bobbed, their skinny legs shook, but they still managed to move as swiftly and sleekly as any cat, almost rippling as they went.

Reynolds turned toward Vergnan. Should he tell this one about the visitors from Earth? He did not think so. Vergnan was old, his skin much paler than the others', almost totally hairless. His eyes were wrinkled and one ear was torn.

Vergnan's eyes were closed.

Remembering his lessons, Reynolds too closed his eyes.

And kept them closed. In the dark, time passed more quickly than it seemed, but he was positive that five minutes went by.

Then the alien began to speak. No—he did not speak; he simply sang, his voice trilling with the high searching notes of a well-tuned violin, dashing up and down the scale, a pleasant sound, soothing, cool. Reynolds tried desperately to concentrate upon the song, ignoring the existence of all other sensations, recognizing nothing and no one but Vergnan. Reynolds ignored the taste and smell of the air and the distant throbbing of the ship's machinery. The alien sang deeper and clearer, his voice rising higher and higher, directed now at the stars. Jonathon, too, had sung, but never like this. When Jonathon sang, its voice had dashed away in a frightened search, shifting and darting wildly about, seeking vainly a place to land. Vergnan sang without doubt. It—*he*— was certain. Reynolds sensed the overwhelming maleness of this being, his patriarchal strength and dignity. His voice and song never struggled or wavered. He knew always exactly where he was going.

Had he felt something? Reynolds did not know. If so, then what? No, no, he thought, and concentrated more fully upon the voice, too intently to allow for the logic of thought. Within, he felt strong, alive, renewed, resurrected. *I am a new man. Reynolds is dead. He is another.* These thoughts came to him like the whispering words of another. *Go, Reynolds. Fly. Leave. Fly.*

Then he realized that he was singing too. He could not imitate Vergnan, for his voice was too alien, but he tried and heard his own voice coming frighteningly near, almost fading into and being lost within the constant tones of the other. The two voices suddenly became one—mingling indiscriminately—merging—and that one voice rose higher, floating, then higher again, rising, farther, going farther out—farther and deeper.

Then he felt it. Reynolds. And he knew it for what it was.

The Sun.

More ancient than the whole of the Earth itself. A greater, vaster being, more powerful and knowing. Divinity as a ball of heat and energy.

Reynolds spoke to the stars.

And, knowing this, balking at the concept, he drew back instinctively in fear, his voice faltering, dwindling, collapsing. Reynolds scurried back, seeking the Earth, but, grasping, pulling, Vergnan drew him on. Beyond the shallow exterior light of the sun, he witnessed the totality of that which lay hidden within. The core. The impenetrable darkness within. Fear gripped him once more. He begged to be allowed to flee. Tears streaking his face with the heat of fire, he pleaded. Vergnan benignly drew him on. *Come forward—come—see—know.* Forces coiled to a point.

And he saw.

Could he describe it as evil? Thought was an absurdity. Not thinking, instead sensing and feeling, he experienced the wholeness of this entity—a star—the sun—and saw that it was not evil. He sensed the sheer totality of its opening nothingness. Sensation was absent. Colder than cold, more terrifying than hate, more sordid than fear, blacker than evil. The vast inner whole nothingness of everything that was anything, of all.

I have seen enough. No!

Yes, cried Vergnan, agreeing.

To stay a moment longer would mean never returning again. Vergnan knew this too, and he released Reynolds, allowed him to go.

And still he sang. The song was different from before. Struggling within himself, Reynolds sang too, trying to match his voice to that of the alien. It was easier this time. The two voices merged, mingled, became one.

And then Reynolds awoke.

He was lying on the floor in the starship, the rainbow walls swirling brightly around him.

Vergnan stepped over him. He saw the alien's protruding belly as he passed. He did not look down or back, but continued onward, out the door, gone, as quick and cold as the inner soul of the sun itself. For a brief moment, he hated Vergnan more deeply than he had ever hated anything in his life. Then he sat up, gripping himself, forcing a return to sanity. I am all right now, he insisted. I am back. I am alive. The walls ceased spinning. At his back the floor shed its clinging coat of roughness. The shadows in the corners of his eyes dispersed.

Jonathon entered the room alone. "Now you have seen," it said, crossing the room and assuming its usual place beside the wall.

"Yes," said Reynolds, not attempting to stand.

"And now you know why we search. For centuries our star was kind to us, loving, but now it too—like yours—is changed."

"You are looking for a new home?"

"True."

"And?"

"And we find nothing. All are alike. We have seen nine, visiting all. They are nothing."

"Then you leave here too?"

"We must, but first we will approach your star. Not until we have drawn so close that we have seen everything, not until then can we dare admit our failure. This time we thought we had succeeded. When we met you, this is what we thought, for you are unlike your star. We felt that the star could not produce you—or your race—without the presence of benevolence. But it is gone now. We meet only the blackness. We struggle to penetrate to a deeper core. And fail."

"I am not typical of my race," Reynolds said.

"We shall see."

He remained with Jonathon until he felt strong enough to stand. The floor hummed. Feeling it with moist palms, he planted a kiss upon the creased cold metal. A wind swept through the room, carrying a hint of returned life. Jonathon faded, rippled, returned to a sharp outline of crisp reality. Reynolds was suddenly hungry and the oily taste of meat swirled up through his nostrils. The cords in his neck stood out with the strain until, gradually, the tension passed from him.

He left and went to the tug. During the great fall to the silver moon he said not a word, thought not a thought. The trip was long.

Reynolds lay on his back in the dark room, staring upward at the faint shadow of a ceiling, refusing to see.

Hypnosis? Or a more powerful alien equivalent of the same? Wasn't that, as an explanation, more likely than admitting that he had indeed communicated with the sun, discovering a force greater than evil, blacker than black? Or—here was another theory: wasn't it possible that these aliens, because of the conditions on their own world, so thoroughly accepted the consciousness of the stars that they could make him believe as well? Similar things had happened on Earth. Religious miracles, the curing of diseases through faith, men who claimed to have spoken with God. What about flying saucers and little green men and all the other incidents of mass hysteria? Wasn't that the answer here? Hysteria? Hypnosis? Perhaps even a drug of some sort: a drug released into the air. Reynolds had plenty of possible solutions—he could choose one or all—but he decided that he did not really care.

He had gone into this thing knowing exactly what he was doing and now that it had happened he did not regret the experience. He had found a way of fulfilling his required mission while at the same time experiencing something personal that no other man would ever know. Whether he had actually seen the sun was immaterial; the experience, as such, was still his own. Nobody could ever take that away from him.

It was some time after this when he realized that a fist was pounding on the door. He decided he might as well ignore that, because sometimes when you ignored things, they went away. But the knocking did not go away—it only got louder. Finally Reynolds got up. He opened the door.

Kelly glared at his nakedness and said, "Did I wake you?"

"No."

"May I come in?"

"No."

"I've got something to tell you." She forced her way past him, sliding into the room. Then Reynolds saw that she wasn't alone. A big, red-faced beefy man followed, forcing his way into the room too.

Reynolds shut the door, cutting off the corridor light, but the big man went over and turned on the overhead light. "All right," he said, as though it were an order.

"Who the hell are you?" Reynolds said.

"Forget him," Kelly said. "I'll talk."

"Talk," said Reynolds.

"The committee is here. The men from Washington. They arrived an hour ago and I've kept them busy since. You may not believe this, but I'm on your side."

"Sims told me."

"He told me he told you."

"I knew he would. Mind telling me why? He didn't know."

"Because I'm not an idiot," Kelly said. "I've known enough petty bureaucrats in my life. Those things up there are alien beings. You can't send these fools up there to go stomping all over their toes."

Reynolds gathered this would not be over soon. He put on his pants.

"This is George O'Hara," Kelly said. "He's the new director."

"I want to offer my resignation," Reynolds said casually, fixing the snaps of his shirt.

"You have to accompany us to the starship," O'Hara said.

"I want you to," Kelly said. "You owe this to someone. If not me, then the aliens. If you had told me the truth, this might never have happened. If anyone is to blame for this mess, it's you, Reynolds. Why won't you tell me what's been going on up there the last month? It has to be something."

"It is," Reynolds said. "Don't laugh, but I was trying to talk to the sun. I told you that's why the aliens came here. They're taking a cruise of the galaxy, pausing here and there to chat with the stars."

"Don't be frivolous. And, yes, you told me all that."

"I have to be frivolous. Otherwise, it sounds too ridiculous. I made an agreement with them. I wanted to learn to talk to the sun. I told them, since I lived here, I could find out what they wanted to know better than they could. I could tell they were doubtful, but they let me go ahead. In return for my favor, when I was done, whether I succeeded or failed, they would give us what we wanted. A team of men could go and freely examine their ship. They would describe their voyage to us—where they had been, what they had found. They promised cooperation in return for my chat with the sun."

"So, then nothing happened?"

"I didn't say that. I talked with the sun today. And saw it. And now I'm not going to do anything except sit on my hands. You can take it from here."

"What are you talking about?"

He knew he could not answer that. "I failed," he said. "I didn't find out anything they didn't know."

"Well, will you go with us or not? That's all I want to know right now." She was losing her patience, but there was also more than a minor note of pleading in her voice. He knew he ought to feel satisfied hearing that, but he didn't.

"Oh, hell," Reynolds said. "Yes—all right—I will go. But don't ask me why. Just give me an hour to get ready."

"Good man," O'Hara said, beaming happily.

Ignoring him, Reynolds opened his closets and began tossing clothes and other belongings into various boxes and crates.

"What do you think you'll need all that for?" Kelly asked him.

"I don't think I'm coming back," Reynolds said.

"They won't hurt you," she said.

"No. I won't be coming back because I won't be wanting to come back."

"You can't do that," O'Hara said.

"Sure I can," said Reynolds.

It took the base's entire fleet of seven shuttle tugs to ferry the delegation from Washington up to the starship. At that, a good quarter of the group had to be left behind for lack of room. Reynolds had requested and received permission to call the starship prior to departure, so the aliens were aware of what was coming up to meet them. They had not protested, but Reynolds knew they wouldn't, at least not over the radio. Like almost all mechanical or electronic gadgets, a radio was a fearsome object to them.

Kelly and Reynolds arrived with the first group and entered the air lock. At intervals of a minute or two, the others arrived. When the entire party was clustered in the lock, the last tug holding to the hull in preparation for the return trip, Reynolds signaled that it was time to move out.

"Wait a minute," one of the men called. "We're not all here. Acton and Dodd went back to the tug to get suits."

"Then they'll have to stay there," Reynolds said. "The air is pure here—nobody needs a suit."

"But," said another man, pinching his nose. "This smell. It's awful."

Reynolds smiled. He had barely noticed the odor. Compared to the stench of the first few days, this was nothing today. "The aliens won't talk if you're wearing suits. They have a taboo against artificial communication. The smell gets better as you go farther inside. Until then, hold your nose, breathe through your mouth."

"It's making me almost sick," confided a man at Reynolds' elbow. "You're sure what you say is true, Doctor?"

"Cross my heart," Reynolds said. The two men who had left to fetch the suits returned. Reynolds wasted another minute lecturing them.

"Stop enjoying yourself so much," Kelly whispered when they were at last under way.

Before they reached the first of the tight passages where crawling was necessary, three men had dropped away, dashing back toward the tug. Working from a hasty map given him by the aliens, he was leading the party toward a section of the ship where he had never been before. The walk was less difficult than usual. In most places a man could walk comfortably and the ceilings were high enough to accommodate the aliens themselves. Reynolds ignored the occasional shouted exclamation from the men behind. He steered a silent course toward his destination.

The room, when they reached it, was huge, big as a basketball gymnasium, the ceiling lost in the deep shadows above. Turning, Reynolds counted the aliens present: fifteen . . . twenty . . . thirty . . . forty . . . forty-five . . . forty-six. That had to be about all. He wondered if this was the full crew.

Then he counted his own people: twenty-two. Better than he had expected—only six lost en route, victims of the smell.

He spoke directly to the alien who stood in front of the others. "Greetings," he said. The alien wasn't Vergnan, but it could have been Jonathon.

From behind, he heard, "They're just like giraffes."

"And they even seem intelligent," said another.

"Exceedingly so. Their eyes."

"And friendly too."

"Hello, Reynolds," the alien said. "Are these the ones?"

"Jonathon?" asked Reynolds.

"Yes."

"These are the ones."

"They are your leaders—they wish to question my people."

"They do."

"May I serve as our spokesman in order to save time?"

"Of course," Reynolds said. He turned and faced his party, looking from face to face, hoping to spot a single glimmer of intelligence, no matter how minute. But he found nothing. "Gentlemen?" he said. "You heard?"

"His name is Jonathon?" said one.

"It is a convenient expression. Do you have a real question?"

"Yes," the man said. He continued speaking to Reynolds. "Where is your homeworld located?"

Jonathon ignored the man's rudeness and promptly named a star.

"Where is that?" the man asked, speaking directly to the alien now.

Reynolds told him it lay some thirty light-years from Earth. As a star, it was very much like the sun, though somewhat larger.

"Exactly how many miles in a light-year?" a man wanted to know.

Reynolds tried to explain. The man claimed he understood, though Reynolds remained skeptical.

It was time for another question.

"Why have you come to our world?"

"Our mission is purely one of exploration and discovery," Jonathon said.

"Have you discovered any other intelligent races besides our own?"

"Yes. Several."

This answer elicited a murmur of surprise from the men. Reynolds wondered who they were, how they had been chosen for this mission. Not what they were, but who. What made them tick. He

knew what they were: politicians, NASA bureaucrats, a sprinkling
of real scientists. But who?

"Are any of these people aggressive?" asked a man, almost certainly a politician. "Do they pose a threat to you—or—or to us?"

"No," Jonathon said. "None."

Reynolds was barely hearing the questions and answers now.
His attention was focused upon Jonathon's eyes. He had stopped
blinking now. The last two questions—the ones dealing with intelligent life forms—he had told the truth. Reynolds thought he was
beginning to understand. He had underestimated these creatures.
Plainly, they had encountered other races during their travels
before coming to Earth. They were experienced. Jonathon was
lying—yes—but unlike before, he was lying well, only when the
truth would not suffice.

"How long do you intend to remain in orbit about our moon?"

"Until the moment you and your friends leave our craft. Then
we shall depart."

This set up an immediate clamor among the men. Waving his
arms furiously, Reynolds attempted to silence them. The man who
had been unfamiliar with the term "light-year" shouted out an
invitation for Jonathon to visit Earth.

This did what Reynolds himself could not do. The others fell
silent in order to hear Jonathon's reply.

"It is impossible," Jonathon said. "Our established schedule re-
quires us to depart immediately."

"Is it this man's fault?" demanded a voice. "He should have
asked you himself long before now."

"No," Jonathon said. "I could not have come—or any of my
people—because we were uncertain of your peaceful intentions.
Not until we came to know Reynolds well did we fully comprehend the benevolence of your race." The alien blinked rapidly
now.

He stopped during the technical questions. The politicians and
bureaucrats stepped back to speak among themselves and the
scientists came forward. Reynolds was amazed at the intelligence
of their questions. To this extent at least, the expedition had not
been wholly a farce.

Then the questions were over and all the men came forward to listen to Jonathon's last words.

"We will soon return to our homeworld and when we do we shall tell the leaders of our race of the greatness and glory of the human race. In passing here, we have come to know your star and through it you people who live beneath its soothing rays. I consider your visit here a personal honor to me as an individual. I am sure my brothers share my pride and only regret an inability to utter their gratitude."

Then Jonathon ceased blinking and looked hard at Reynolds. "Will you be going too?"

"No," Reynolds said. "I'd like to talk to you alone if I can."

"Certainly," Jonathon said.

Several of the men in the party protested to Kelly or O'Hara, but there was nothing they could do. One by one they left the chamber to wait in the corridor. Kelly was the last to leave. "Don't be a fool," she cautioned.

"I won't," he said.

When the men had gone, Jonathon took Reynolds away from the central room. It was only a brief walk to the old room where they had always met before. As if practicing a routine, Jonathon promptly marched to the farthest wall and stood there waiting. Reynolds smiled. "Thank you," he said.

"You are welcome."

"For lying to them. I was afraid they would offend you with their stupidity. I thought you would show your contempt by lying badly, offending them in return. I underestimated you. You handled them very well."

"But you have something you wish to ask of me?"

"Yes," Reynolds said. "I want you to take me away with you."

As always, Jonathon remained expressionless. Still, for a long time, it said nothing. Then, "Why do you wish this? We shall never return here."

"I don't care. I told you before: I am not typical of my race. I can never be happy here."

"But are you typical of my race? Would you not be unhappy with us?"

"I don't know. But I'd like to try."

"It is impossible," Jonathon said.

"But—but—why?"

"Because we have neither the time nor the abilities to care for you. Our mission is a most desperate one. Already, during our absence, our homeworld may have gone mad. We must hurry. Our time is growing brief. And you will not be of any help to us. I am sorry, but you know that is true."

"I can talk to the stars."

"No," Jonathon said. "You cannot."

"But I did."

"Vergnan did. Without him, you could not."

"Your answer is final? There's no one else I can ask? The captain?"

"I am the captain."

Reynolds nodded. He had carried his suitcases and crates all this way and now he would have to haul them home again. Home? No, not home. Only the moon. "Could you find out if they left a tug for me?" he asked.

"Yes. One moment."

Jonathon rippled lightly away, disappearing into the corridor. Reynolds turned and looked at the walls. Again, as he stared, the rainbow patterns appeared to shift and dance and swirl of their own volition. Watching this, he felt sad, but his sadness was not that of grief. It was the sadness of emptiness and aloneness. This emptiness had so long been a part of him that he sometimes forgot it was there. He knew it now. He knew, whether consciously aware of it or not, that he had spent the past ten years of his life searching vainly for a way of filling this void. Perhaps even more than that: perhaps his whole life had been nothing more than a search for that one moment of real completion. Only twice had he ever really come close. The first time had been on Mars. When he had lived and watched while the others had died. Then he had not been alone or empty. And the other time had been right here in this very room—with Vergnan. Only twice in his life had he been allowed to approach the edge of true meaning. Twice in fifty-eight long and endless years. Would it ever happen again? When? How?

Jonathon returned, pausing in the doorway. "A pilot is there," it said.

Reynolds went toward the door, ready to leave. "Are you still planning to visit our sun?" he asked.

"Oh, yes. We shall continue trying, searching. We know nothing else. You do not believe—even after what Vergnan showed you—do you, Reynolds?"

"No, I do not believe."

"I understand," Jonathon said. "And I sympathize. All of us—even I—sometimes we have doubts."

Reynolds continued forward into the corridor. Behind, he heard a heavy clipping noise and turned to see Jonathon coming after him. He waited for the alien to join him and then they walked together. In the narrow corridor, there was barely room for both.

Reynolds did not try to talk. As far as he could see, there was nothing left to be said that might possibly be said in so short a time as that which remained. Better to say nothing, he thought, than to say too little.

The air lock was open. Past it, Reynolds glimpsed the squat bulk of the shuttle tug clinging to the creased skin of the starship.

There was nothing left to say. Turning to Jonathon, he said, "Goodbye," and as he said it, for the first time he wondered about what he was going back to. More than likely, he would find himself a hero once again. A celebrity. But that was all right: fame was fleeting; it was bearable. Two hundred forty thousand miles was still a great distance. He would be all right.

As if reading his thoughts, Jonathon asked, "Will you be remaining here or will you return to your homeworld?"

The question surprised Reynolds; it was the first time the alien had ever evidenced a personal interest in him. "I'll stay here. I'm happier."

"And there will be a new director?"

"Yes. How did you know that? But I think I'm going to be famous again. I can get Kelly retained."

"You could have the job yourself," Jonathon said.

"But I don't want it. How do you know all this? About Kelly and so on?"

"I listen to the stars," Jonathon said in its high warbling voice.

"They are alive, aren't they?" Reynolds said suddenly.

"Of course. We are permitted to see them for what they are. You do not. But you are young."

"They are balls of ionized gas. Thermonuclear reactions."

The alien moved, shifting its neck as though a joint lay in the middle of it. Reynolds did not understand the gesture. Nor would he ever. Time had run out at last.

Jonathon said, "When they come to you, they assume a disguise you can see. That is how they spend their time in this universe. Think of them as doorways."

"Through which I cannot pass."

"Yes."

Reynolds smiled, nodded and passed into the lock. It contracted behind him, engulfing the image of his friend. A few moments of drifting silence, then the other end of the lock furled open.

The pilot was a stranger. Ignoring the man, Reynolds dressed, strapped himself down and thought about Jonathon. What was it that it had said? I listen to the stars. Yes, and the stars had told it that Kelly had been fired?

He did not like that part. But the part he liked even less was this: when it said it, Jonathon had not blinked.

(1) It had been telling the truth. (2) It could lie without flicking a lash.

Choose one.

Reynolds did, and the tug fell toward the moon.

TOM REAMY

Twilla

Tom Reamy began writing science fiction only a few years ago after a career in Dallas as a technical writer for the aerospace industry. Laid off there, he went to Los Angeles and tried his talents on film, screen-writing and acting as property manager on *Flesh Gordon*. Although many science-fiction writers came out of fandom and many still keep up their fan activities, Tom may be the first to have a story nominated for a Nebula Award and to publish a fanzine *(Nickelodeon)*, that has been nominated for a Hugo. He has not yet had a novel published, but if he can find time from his graphic design studio and his labors as editor and designer of the publications for the 1976 World Science Fiction Convention to be held in Kansas City, readers may find more such stories as this deceptively commonplace story where incredible events lie in wait for a simple Kansas town.

Twilla Gilbreath blew into Miss Mahan's life like a pink butterfly wing that same day in early December that the blue norther dropped the temperature forty degrees in two hours. Mr. Choate, the principal, ushered Twilla and her parents into Miss Mahan's ninth-grade homeroom shortly after the tardy bell rang. She had just checked the roll: all seventeen ninth-graders were present except for Sammy Stocker, who was in the Liberal hospital having his appendix removed. She was telling the class how nice it would be if they sent a get-well card when the door opened.

"Goooood morning, Miss Mahan." Mr. Choate smiled cheerfully. He always smiled cheerfully first thing in the morning, but soured as the day wore on. You could practically tell time by Mr. Choate's mouth. "We have a new ninth-grader for you this morning, Miss Mahan. This is Mr. and Mrs. Gilbreath and their daughter, Twilla."

Several things happened at once. Miss Mahan shook hands with the parents; she threw a severe glance at the class when she heard a snigger—but it was only Alice May Turner, who would probably giggle if she were being devoured by a bear; and she had to forcibly keep her eyebrows from rising when she got a good look at Twilla. Good Lord, she thought, and felt her smile falter.

Miss Mahan had never in her life, even when it was fashionable

for a child to look like that, seen anyone so perfectly . . . pink and
. . . doll-like. She wasn't sure why she got such an impression of
pinkness, because the child was dressed in yellow and had golden
hair (*that's* the color they mean when they say golden hair, she
thought with wonder) done in, of all things, drop curls, with a big
yellow bow in back. Twilla looked up at her with a sweet radiant
sunny smile and clear periwinkle-blue eyes.

Miss Mahan detested her on sight.

She thought she saw, when Alice May giggled, the smile freeze
and the lovely eyes dart toward the class, but she wasn't sure. It
all happened in an instant, and then Mr. Choate continued his
Cheerful Charlie routine.

"Mr Gilbreath has bought the old Peacock place."

"Really?" she said, tearing her eyes from Twilla. "I didn't know
it was for sale."

Mr. Gilbreath chuckled. "Not the entire farm, of course. I'm no
farmer. Only the house and grounds. Such a charming old place.
The owner lives in Wichita and had no use for them."

"I would think the house is pretty run-down," Miss Mahan said,
glancing at Twilla, still radiating at the world. "No one's lived in
it since Wash and Grace Elizabeth died ten years ago."

"It is a little," Mrs. Gilbreath said pleasantly.

"But structurally sound," interjected Mr. Gilbreath pleasantly.

"We'll enjoy fixing it up," Mrs. Gilbreath continued pleasantly.

"Miss Mahan teaches English to the four upper grades," said Mr.
Choate, bringing them back to the subject, "as well as speech and
drama. Miss Mahan has been with the Hawley school system for
thirty-one years."

The Gilbreaths smiled pleasantly. "My . . . ah . . . Twilla seems
very young to be in the ninth grade." That get-up makes her look
about eleven, Miss Mahan thought.

The Gilbreaths beamed at their daughter. "Twilla is only thirteen," Mrs. Gilbreath crooned, pride swelling her like yeast. "She's
such an intelligent child. She was able to skip the second grade."

"I see. From where have you moved?"

"Boston," replied Mr. Gilbreath.

"Boston. I hope . . . ah . . . Twilla doesn't find it difficult to adjust to a small-town school. I'm sure Hawley, Kansas, is quite unlike Boston."

Mr. Gilbreath touched Twilla lovingly on the shoulder. "I'm sure she'll have no trouble."

"Well." Mr. Choate rubbed his palms together. "Twilla is in good hands. Shall I show you around the rest of the school?"

"Of course," smiled Mrs. Gilbreath.

They departed with fond murmurings and good-bys, leaving Twilla like a buttercup stranded in a cabbage patch. Miss Mahan mentally shook her head. She hadn't seen a family like that since Dick and Jane and Spot and Puff were sent the way of *McGuffey's Reader*. Mr. and Mrs. Gilbreath were in their middle thirties, good-looking without being glamorous, their clothes nice though as oddly wrong as Twilla's. They seemed cut with some outdated Ideal Family template. Surely, there must be an older brother, a dog, and a cat somewhere.

"Well . . . ah, Twilla," Miss Mahan said, trying to reinforce the normal routine, "if you will take a seat—that one there, behind Alice May Turner. Alice May, will you wave a flag or something so Twilla will know which one?" Alice May giggled. "Thank you, dear." Twilla moved gracefully toward the empty desk. Miss Mahan felt as if she should say something to the child. "I hope you will . . . ah . . . enjoy going to school in Hawley, dear."

Twilla sat primly and glowed at her. "I'm sure I shall, Miss Mahan," she said, speaking for the first time. Her voice was like the tinkle of fairy bells—just as Miss Mahan was afraid it would be.

"Good," she said and went back to the subject of a get-well card for Sammy Stocker. She had done this so often—there had been a great many sick children in thirty-one years—it had become almost a ritual needing only a small portion of her attention. The rest she devoted to the covert observation of Twilla Gilbreath.

Twilla sat at her desk, displaying excellent posture, with her hands folded neatly before her, seemingly paying attention to the Great Greeting Card Debate, but actually giving the rest of the class careful scrutiny. Miss Mahan marveled at the surreptitious calculation in the girl's face. She realizes she's something of a green monkey, Miss Mahan thought, and I'll bet my pension she doesn't let the situation stand.

And the class surveyed Twilla, in their superior position of established territorial rights, with open curiosity—and with the posture of so many sacks of corn meal. Some of them looked at her, Miss Mahan was afraid, with rude amusement—especially the girls, and especially Wanda O'Dell, who had bloomed suddenly last summer like a plump rose. Oh, yes, Wanda was going to be a problem. Just like her five older sisters. Thank goodness, she sighed, Wanda was the last of them.

Children, Miss Mahan sighed again, but fondly.

Children?

They were children when she started teaching and certainly were when *she* was fifteen, but, now, she wasn't sure. Fifteen is such an awkward, indefinite age. Take Ronnie Dwyer: he looks like a prepubescent thirteen at most. And Carter Redwine, actually a couple of months younger than Ronnie, could pass for seventeen easily and was anything but prepubescent. Poor Carter, a child in a man's body. To make matters worse, he was the best looking boy in town; and to make matters even worse yet, he was well aware of it.

And, she noticed, so was Twilla. Forget it, Little Pink Princess. Carter already has more than he can handle, Miss Mahan chuckled to herself. Can't you see those dark circles under his eyes? They didn't get there from studying. And then she blushed inwardly.

Oh, the poor children. They think they have so many secrets. If they only knew. Between the tattletales and the teachers' gossip she doubted if the whole student body had three secrets between them.

Miss Mahan admonished herself for having such untidy thoughts. She didn't use to think about things like that, but then, fifteen-year-olds didn't lead such overtly sexual lives back then. She remembered reading somewhere that only 35 percent of the children in America were still virgins at fifteen. But those sounded like Big City statistics, not applicable to Hawley.

Then she sighed. It was all beyond her. The bell rang just as the get-well card situation was settled. The children rose reluctantly to go to their first class: algebra with Mr. Whittaker. She noticed that Twilla had cozied up to Alice May, though she still kept her eye on Carter Redwine. Carter was not unaware and with deliberate lordly indifference sauntered from the room with his hand on Wanda O'Dell's shoulder. Miss Mahan thought the glint she observed in Twilla's eyes might lead to an interesting turn of events.

Children.

She cleared her mind of random speculation and geared it to *Macbeth* as the senior class filed in with everything on their minds but Shakespeare. Raynelle Franklin, Mr. Choate's secretary, lurked nervously among them, looking like a chicken who suddenly finds herself with a pack of coyotes. She edged her middle-aged body to Miss Mahan's desk, accepted the absentee report, and scuttled out. Miss Mahan looked forward to Raynelle's performance every morning.

During lunch period, Miss Mahan walked to the dime store for a get-well card which the ninth-grade class would sign that afternoon when they returned for English. She glanced at the sky and unconsciously pulled her gray tweed coat tighter about her. The sky had turned a cobalt blue in the north. It wouldn't be long now. Though the temperature must be down to thirty-five already, it seemed colder. She guessed her blood was getting thin; she knew her flesh was. Old age, she thought, old age. Thin blood, thin flesh, and brittle bones. She sometimes felt as if she were turning into a bird.

She almost bumped into Twilla's parents emerging from the dry-goods store, their arms loaded with packages. Their pleasant smiles turned on. Click, click. They chatted trivialities for a moment, adding new dimensions to Twilla's already flawless character. Miss Mahan had certainly seen her share of blindly doting parents, but this was unbelievable. She had seen the cold calculation with which Twilla had studied the class, and that was hardly the attribute of an angel. Something didn't jibe somewhere. She speculated on the contents of the packages, but thought she knew. Then she couldn't resist; she asked if Twilla were an only child. She was. Well, there went that.

She looked at the clock on the tower of the courthouse and, subtracting fourteen minutes, decided she'd better hurry if she wanted to eat lunch and have a rest before her one-o'clock class.

The teachers' lounge was a reasonably comfortable room where students were forbidden to enter on pain of death—though it seemed to be a continuing game on their part to try. Miss Mahan hung her coat on a hanger and shivered. "Has anyone heard a weather forecast?" she asked the room in general.

Mrs. Latham (home economics) looked up from her needlepoint and shook her head vaguely. Poor old dear, thought Miss Mahan. Due to retire this year, I think. Seems like she's been here since Creation. She taught me when I was in school. Leo Whittaker (math) was reading a copy of *Playboy*. Probably took it from one of the children. "Supposed to be below twenty by five," he said, then grinned and held up the magazine. "Ronnie Dwyer."

Miss Mahan raised her eyebrows. Loretta McBride (history/civics) tsked, shook her head, and went back to her book. Miss Mahan retrieved her carton of orange juice from the small refrigerator and drank it with her fried egg sandwich. She put part of the sandwich back in the Baggie. She hardly had any appetite at all anymore. Guess what they say is true: the older you get . . .

She began to crochet on her interminable afghan. The little squares were swiftly becoming a pain in the neck, and she regretted ever starting it. She looked at Mrs. Latham and her needlepoint. She sighed, I guess it's expected of us old ladies. Anyway, it gave her something to hide behind when she didn't feel like joining the conversation. But today she felt like talking, though it didn't seem as if anyone else did.

She finished a square and snipped the yarn. "What do you think of the Shirley Temple doll who joined our merry group this morning?"

Mrs. Latham looked up and smiled. "Charming child."

"Yes," said Loretta, putting away the book, "absolutely charming. And smart as a whip. Really knows her American History. Joined in the discussion as if she'd been in the class all semester." Miss McBride was one of the few outsiders teaching in Hawley who gave every indication of remaining. Usually they came and went as soon as greener pastures opened up. Most were like Miss Mahan, Mrs. Latham, and Leo Whittaker, living their entire lives there.

It was practically incestuous, she thought. Mrs. Latham had taught her, she had taught Leo, and he was undoubtedly teaching part of the next group. Miss Mahan had to admit that Leo had been something of a surprise. He was only twenty-five and had given no indication in high school that he was destined for anything better than a hanging. She wondered how long it would be before Leo connected his students' inability to keep secrets from the teachers with his own disreputable youth.

Now here he was. Two years in the army, four years in college, his second year of teaching, married to Lana Redwine (Carter's cousin and one of the nicest girls in town) with a baby due in a couple of months. You never can tell. You just never can tell.

"Well, Leo," Miss Mahan asked, bemused, "what did you think of Twilla Gilbreath?"

"Oh, I don't know. She seems very intelligent—at least in algebra. Quiet and well-behaved—unlike a few others. Dresses kinda funny. Seems to have set her sights on my cousin-in-law." He grinned. "Fat chance!" Miss Mahan wouldn't say Leo was handsome—not in the way Carter Redwine was—but that grin was the reason half the girls in school had a crush on him.

"Oh? You noticed that too? I imagine she may have a few surprises up her sleeve. I don't think our Twilla is the fairy-tale princess she's made out to be." She began another square.

"You must be mistaken, Miss Mahan," Loretta said, wide-eyed. "The child is an absolute darling. And the very idea: a baby like that running after Carter Redwine. I never heard of such a thing!"

"Really?" Miss Mahan smiled to herself and completed a shell stitch. "We shall see what we shall see."

The norther hit during the ninth-grade English class, bringing a merciful, if only temporary, halt to the sufferings of Silas Marner. The glass in the windows rattled and pinged. The wind played on the downspouts like a mad flautist. Sand ticked against the windows, and the guard lights came on in the school yard. Outside had become a murky indigo, as if the world were under water. Miss Mahan switched on the lights, making the windows seem even darker. Garbage cans rolled down the street, but you could hardly hear them above the howl of the wind. And the downtown Christmas decorations were whipping loose, as they always did at least once every year.

The sand was only temporary; a cloud of it blown along before the storm, but the wind could last all night or all week. Miss Mahan remembered when she was a girl during the great drought of the thirties, when the sand wasn't temporary, when it came like a mile-high solid tidal wave of blown-away farmland, when you couldn't tell noon from midnight, when houses were half buried after the wind finally died down. She shuddered.

"All right, children. Settle down. You've all seen northers before."

Leo and Loretta were right about one thing: Twilla was intelligent. She was also perceptive, imaginative . . . and adaptable. She had already dropped the Little Mary Sunshine routine, though Miss Mahan couldn't imagine why she had used it in the first place. It must have been a pose—as if the child had somehow confused the present and 1905.

The temperature had dropped to eighteen by the time school was out. The wind hit Miss Mahan like icy needles. Her gray tweed coat did about as much good as tissue paper. She grabbed at her scarf as it threatened to leave her head and almost lost her briefcase. She walked as fast as her aging legs would go and made it to her six-year-old Plymouth. The car started like a top, billowing a cloud of steam from the exhaust pipe to be whipped away by the wind.

She sat for a moment, getting her breath back, letting the car warm up. She saw Twilla, huddled against the wind, dash to a new black Chrysler and get in with her parents. The car backed out and moved away. Miss Mahan wasn't the least surprised that little Miss Gilbreath wasn't riding the school bus. The old Peacock place was a mile off the highway at Miller's Corners, a once-upon-a-time town eight miles east of Hawley.

Well, I guess I'm not much better, she thought. I only live four blocks away—but I'll be darned if I'll walk it today. She always did walk except when the weather was bad, and, oddly enough, the older she got, the worse the weather seemed to get.

She pulled into the old carriage house that served equally well with automobiles and walked hurriedly across the yard into the big, rather ancient house that had belonged to her grandfather. She knew it was silly to live all alone in such a great pile—she had shut off the upstairs and hadn't been up in months—but it was equally silly not to live there. It was paid for and her grandfather had set up a trust fund to pay the taxes. It was a very nice house, really; cool in the summer, but (she turned up the fire) a drafty old barn in the winter.

She turned on the television to see if there were any weather bulletins. While it warmed up, she closed off all the downstairs rooms except the kitchen, her bedroom, and the parlor, putting rolled-up towels along the bottoms of the doors to keep the cold air out. She returned to the parlor to see the television screen covered with snow and horizontal streaks of lightning.

She knew it. The aerial had blown down again. She turned off the set and put on a kettle for tea.

The wind had laid somewhat by the time Miss Mahan reached school the next morning, but still blew in fitful gusts. The air was the color of ice and so cold she expected to hear it crackle as she moved through it. The windows in her room were steamed over, and she was busily wiping them when Twilla arrived. Although Miss Mahan had expected something like this, she stared nevertheless.

Twilla's hair was still the color of spun elfin gold, but the drop curls were missing. Instead, it fell in soft folds to below her shoulders in a style much too adult for a thirteen-year-old. But, then, this morning Twilla looked as much like thirteen as Mrs. Latham.

All the physical things were there: the hair, just the right amount of make-up, a short stylish skirt, a pale-green jersey that displayed her small but adequate breasts, a lovely antique pendant on a gold chain nestling between them.

But it wasn't only the physical things—any thirteen-year-old would have appeared more mature with a similar overhaul—it was something in the face, in her bearing: an attitude of casual sophistication, a confidence usually attainable only by those secure in their power. Twilla smiled. Shirley Temple and Mary Pickford were gone; this was the smile of a conqueror.

Miss Mahan realized her face was hanging out, but before she was forced to say anything, several students, after a prelude of clanging locker doors, barged in. Twilla turned to look at them, and the moment was electric. Their inane chatter stopped as if someone had thrown a switch. They gaped. Twilla gave them time for the full effect, then strolled to them and began chatting as if nothing were new.

Miss Mahan sat at her desk feeling a little weak in the knees. She waited for Carter Redwine to arrive as, obviously, was Twilla. When he did, it was almost anticlimactic. His recently acquired worldliness and sexual sophistication melted away in one callow gawk. But he recovered quickly and his feelers popped up, testing the situation. Twilla moved to her desk, giving him a satisfied smile. Wanda O'Dell looked as if she'd eaten a bug.

Miss Mahan had to admit to the obvious. Twilla was a stunning beauty. But the whole thing was . . . curious . . . to say the least.

The conversation in the teachers' lounge was devoted almost exclusively to the transformation of Twilla Gilbreath. Mrs. Latham had noted it vaguely. Loretta McBride ceded reluctantly to Miss Mahan's observations of the previous day. Leo Whittaker expressed a masculine appreciation of the new Twilla, earning a fishy look from Loretta. "I never saw Carter act so goofy," he said, grinning.

But neither they nor any of the others noted the obvious strangeness of it all. At least, Miss Mahan thought, it seems obvious to me.

That day Miss Mahan set out on a campaign of Twilla watching. She even went upstairs to her grandfather's study and purloined one of the blank journals from the bottom drawer of his desk. She curled up in the big chair, after building a fire in the parlor fireplace—the first one this year—and opened the journal to the first page ruled with pale-blue lines. She wrote *Twilla,* after rejecting *The Twilla Gilbreath Affair, The Peculiar Case of Twilla Gilbreath,* and others in a similar vein.

She felt silly and conspiratorial and almost put the journal away, but, instead, wrote farther down the page: *Is my life so empty that I must fill it by spying on a student?*

She thought about what she had written and decided it was either unfair to Twilla or unfair to herself, but let it remain. She turned to the second page and wrote *Tuesday, the 5th* at the top. She filled that page and the next with her impressions of Twilla's first day. She headed the fourth page *Wednesday, the 6th* and noted the events of the day just ending.

On rereading, she thought perhaps she might have overemphasized the oddities, the incongruities, and the anachronisms; but, after all, that was what it was about, wasn't it?

It began snowing during the night. Miss Mahan drove to school through a fantasy landscape. The wind was still blowing, and the steely flakes came down almost horizontally. She loved snow, always had, but she preferred the Christmas-card variety when the big fluffy flakes floated down through still, crisp air like so many pillow fights.

She knew there had been developments as soon as Carter Redwine entered the room. His handsome face was glum and sullen and looked as if he hadn't slept. He sat at his desk with his head hunched between his shoulders and didn't look up until Twilla came in. Miss Mahan darted her eyes from one to the other. Carter looked away again, his neck and ears glowing red. Twilla ignored him; more than that—she consigned him to total nonexistence.

Miss Mahan was dumfounded. What on earth . . . ? Had Carter made advances and been rebuffed? That wouldn't explain it. Surely he had been turned down before. Hadn't he? Of course, she knew he had. Leo, who viewed his cousin-in-law's adventures with bemused affection, had been laughing about it in the teachers' lounge one day. "He'll settle down," Leo had said, "he just has a new toy." Which made her blush after she'd thought about it awhile.

Surely, he hadn't tried to take Twilla . . . by force? She couldn't believe that. Despite everything, Carter was a very decent boy. He had just developed too early, was too handsome, and knew too many willing girls. What then? Was it the first pangs of love? That look on his face wasn't lovesickness. It was red, roaring mortification. Then she knew what must have happened. Carter had not been rebuffed, maybe even encouraged. But, whatever she had expected, he had been inadequate.

Twilla had made another error. She had failed to realize that Carter, despite the way he looked, was only fifteen. Then the ugly enormity of it struck her. My God, she thought, Twilla is only thirteen. What had she wanted from Carter that he was too inexperienced or naïve to give her?

Friday, the 8th

Billy Jermyn came in this morning with a black eye. It's all over school that Carter gave it to him in gym yesterday when Billy teased him about Twilla. What did she do to humiliate him so? I've never known Carter to fight. I guess that's one secret that'll never penetrate the teachers' lounge.

Twilla is taking over the class. I've seen it coming since Wednesday. It's subtle but pretty obvious when you know what to look for. The others defer to her in lots of little ways. Twilla is being very gracious about it. Butter wouldn't melt in her mouth. (Wonder where that little saying came from? —doesn't make sense when you analyze it.)

I also wonder who Twilla's got her amorous sights on, now that Carter failed to make the grade. She hasn't shown an interest in anyone in particular that I've noticed. And there's been no gossip in the lounge. The flap created by Carter has probably shown her the wisdom of keeping her romances to herself. She's adaptable.

Sonny Bowen offered to put my TV aerial back up for me. I knew one of them would. Bless their conniving little hearts.

TGIF!

Miss Mahan closed the journal and sat watching a log in the fireplace that was about to fall. The whole Twilla affair was curious, but no more curious than her own attitude. She should have been scandalized (you didn't see too many thirteen-year-old combinations of Madame Bovary and the Dragon Lady—even these days), but she only felt fascination. Somehow it didn't seem quite real; more as if she were watching a movie. She smiled slightly. Wonder if it would be rated R or X, she thought. R, I guess. Haven't seen anyone with their clothes off yet.

The log fell, making her jump. She laughed in embarrassment, banked the fire, and went to bed.

The snow was still falling Monday morning, though the fierceness of the storm had passed. There was little wind, and the temperature had risen somewhat. That's more like it, Miss Mahan said to herself, watching the big soft flakes float down in random zigzags.

The bell rang, and she turned away from the windows to watch the ninth-grade homeroom clatter out. The Gilbreaths must have been out of town over the weekend, she observed. Twilla didn't get that outfit in Hawley. But she was still wearing that lovely, rather barbaric pendant around her neck. She sighed. Two days away from Twilla had made her wonder if she weren't getting senile; if she weren't making a mystery out of a molehill; if she weren't imagining the whole thing. Twilla was certainly a picture of normalcy this morning.

Raynelle Franklin came for the absentee report looking more like a frightened chicken than ever. She followed an evasive course to Miss Mahan's desk and took the report as if she were afraid of being struck. There were only two names on the report: Sammy Stocker and Yvonne Wilkins.

Raynelle glanced at the names and paled. "Haven't you *heard?*" she whispered.

"Heard what?"

Raynelle looked warily at the senior class shuffling in and backed away, motioning for Miss Mahan to follow. Miss Mahan groaned and followed her into the hall. Students were milling about everywhere, chattering and banging locker doors. Raynelle grimaced in distress.

"Raynelle, will you stand still and tell me!" Miss Mahan commanded in exasperation.

"Someone will hear," she pleaded.

"Hear *what?*"

Raynelle fluttered her hands and blew air through her teeth. She looked quickly around and then huddled against Miss Mahan. "Yvonne Wilkins," she hissed.

"Well?"

"She's . . . she's . . . *dead!*"

Miss Mahan thought Raynelle was about to faint. She grabbed her arm. "How?" she asked in her no-nonsense voice.

"I don't know," Raynelle gasped. "No one will tell me."

Miss Mahan thought for a moment. "Go on with what you were doing." She released Raynelle and marched into Mr. Choate's office.

Mr. Choate looked up with a start. He was already wearing his three-o'clock face. "I see you've heard." He was resigned.

"Yes. What is going on? Raynelle was having a conniption fit." Miss Mahan looked at him over her glasses the same way she would a recalcitrant student.

"Miss Mahan," he sighed, "Sheriff Walker thought it best if the whole thing were kept quiet."

"Quiet? Why?"

"He didn't want a panic."

"Panic? What did she die of, bubonic plague?"

"No." He looked at her as if he wished she would vanish. "I guess I might as well tell you. It'll be all over town by ten o'clock anyway. Yvonne was murdered." He said the last word as if he'd never heard it before.

Miss Mahan felt her knees giving way and quickly sat down. "This is unbelievable," she said weakly. Mr. Choate nodded. "Why does Robin Walker want to keep it quiet? What happened?"

"Miss Mahan, I've told you all I can tell you."

"Surely Robin knows secrecy will only make it worse? Making

a mystery out of it is guaranteed to create a panic."

Mr. Choate shrugged. "I have my instructions. You're late for your class."

Miss Mahan went back to her room in a daze, her imagination ringing up possibilities like a cash register. She couldn't keep her mind on *Macbeth* and the class was restless. They obviously didn't know yet, but their radar had picked up something they couldn't explain.

When the class was over, she went into the hall and saw the news moving through like a shock wave. She accomplished absolutely nothing the rest of the morning. The children were fidgety and kept whispering among themselves. She was as disturbed as they and made only halfhearted attempts to restore order.

At lunch time she bundled up and trounced through the snow to the courthouse. It was too hot inside, and the heat only accentuated the courthouse smell. She didn't know what it was, but they all smelled the same. Maybe it was the state-issue disinfectant. The Hawley courthouse hadn't changed since she could remember. The same wooden benches lined the hall; the same ceiling fans encircled the round lights. No, she corrected herself, there was a change: the brass spittoons had been removed some twelve years ago. It seemed subtly wrong without the spittoons.

She was removing her coat when Rose Newcastle emerged in a huff from the sheriff's office, her heels popping on the marble floor, sending echoes ringing down the hall. Rose was the last of the three Willet girls, the daughters of old Judge Willet. People still called them the Willet girls, although Rose was considerably older than Miss Mahan. She was a widow now, her husband having finally died of insignificance.

"Hello, Rose," she said, feeling trapped. Rose puffed to a halt like a plump locomotive.

"Oh, Miss Mahan, isn't it *awful!*" she wailed. "And Robin Walker absolutely refuses to do anything! We could all be murdered in our beds!"

"I'm sure he's doing everything he can, Rose. What did he tell you?"

"*Nothing!* Absolutely nothing! If my father were still alive, I'd have that man's job. I told him he'd better watch his step come next election. I told him, as a civic leader in this town, I had a right to know what's going on. I told him I had a good mind to organize a citizens' committee to investigate the whole affair."

"Give him a chance. Robin is a very conscientious man."

"He's a child."

"Come on, Rose. He's at least thirty. I taught him for four years, and I have complete confidence in him. You'll have to excuse me. I'm here to see him myself."

"He won't tell you anything," Rose said, sounding slightly mollified.

"Perhaps," Miss Mahan said. Rose echoed off down the hall. "He might have if you haven't put his tail over the dashboard," she muttered and pushed open the door.

Loreen Whittaker, Leo's aunt by marriage, looked up and smiled. "Hello, Miss Mahan. What can I do for you?"

"Hello, Loreen. I'd like to see Robin, if I may."

Loreen chuckled. "He gave me strict orders to let no one in but the governor—right after Mrs. Newcastle left."

Miss Mahan grimaced. "I met her in the hall. Would you ask him? It's important."

Loreen arose from her desk and went into the sheriff's private office. Miss Mahan felt that she and Robin were good friends. She had not only taught him, but his sister, Mary Ellen; and his little brother, Curtis, was a senior this year. She liked all of them and thought they liked her. Robin's son was in the second grade and was a little doll. She was looking forward to teaching him, too.

Loreen came out of his office, grinning. "He said you could come in but I was to frisk you first." Her smile wavered. "Try to cheer him up, Miss Mahan. It's the first . . . murder we've had since he's been in office, and it's getting to him."

Miss Mahan nodded and went in. The sheriff sat hunched over his desk. His hair was mussed where he had been running his hand through it. There was a harried look on his face, but he dredged up a thin smile for her.

"You aren't gonna give me trouble, too, are you?" he asked warily.

"I ran into Rose in the hall," she smiled back at him.

He motioned her to a chair. "What's the penalty for punching a civic leader in the nose?"

"You should know that better than I."

He grunted. "Yeah." He leaned back in the chair and stretched his long legs. "I can't discuss Yvonne Wilkins, if that's what you're here for."

"That's why I'm here. Don't you think this secrecy is worse than the facts? People will be imagining all sorts of horrible things."

"I doubt if anything they could imagine would be worse than the actual facts, Miss Mahan. You'll have to trust me. I have to do it this way." He ran his fingers through his hair again. "I'm afraid I may be in over my head on this. There's just me and five deputies for the whole county. And we haven't anything to work on. Nothing."

"Where did they find her?"

"Okay," he sighed. "I'll tell you this much. Yvonne went out yesterday afternoon in her father's car to visit Linda Murray. When she didn't come home last night, Mr. Wilkins called the Murrays and they said Yvonne left about six-thirty. He was afraid she'd had an accident in the snow; so he called me. We found her about three this morning out on the dirt road nearly to the old Weatherly place. She was in the car . . . dead. It's been snowing for five days. There wasn't a track of any kind and no fingerprints that didn't belong. And that's all you're gonna worm out of me."

Miss Mahan had an idea. "Had she been molested?"

Robin looked at her as if he'd been betrayed. "Yes," he said simply.

"But," she protested, "why the big mystery? I know it's horrible, but it's not likely to cause a . . . a panic."

He got up and paced around the office. "Miss Mahan, I can't tell you any more."

"Is there more? Is there more than rape and murder?" She felt something like panic rising in her.

Robin squatted in front of her, taking her hands in his. "If there's anyone in town I'd tell, it would be you. You know that. I've loved you ever since I was fourteen years old. If you keep after me, I'll tell you. So have a little pity on a friend and stop pushing."

She felt her eyes burning and motioned for him to get up. "Robin, you're not playing fair." She stood up and he held her coat for her. "You always were able to get around me. Okay, you win."

"Thank you, Miss Mahan," he said, genuinely relieved, and kissed her on the forehead. She stopped in the hall and dabbed at her eyes.

But I haven't given up yet, she thought as she huddled in her coat on the way to Paul Sullivan's office. The bell tinkled on the door, and the nurse materialized from somewhere.

"Miss Mahan. What are you doing out in this weather?"

"I'd like to see the doctor, Elaine." She hung her coat on the rack.

"He's with the little Archer girl now. She slipped on the snow and twisted her ankle."

"I'll wait." She sat and picked up a magazine without looking at it. Elaine Holliday had been one of her students. Who in town hadn't? she wondered. Elaine wanted to talk about the murder, as did Louise Archer when she emerged with her limping daughter, but Miss Mahan wasn't in the mood for gossip and speculation. She marched into Dr. Sullivan's sanctum.

"Hello, Paul," she said before he could open his mouth. "I've just been to see Robin. He told me Yvonne had been raped, but he wouldn't tell me what the big mystery is. I know you're what passes for the County Medical Examiner; so you know as much as he does. I've known you for fifty years and even thought at one time you might propose to me, but you didn't. So don't give me any kind of runaround. Tell me what happened to Yvonne." She plopped into a chair and glared at him.

He shook his head in dismay. "I thought I might propose to you at one time too, but right now is a good example of why I didn't. You were so independent and bullheaded, you scared me to death."

"Don't change the subject."

"You won't like it."

"I don't expect to."

"There's no way I can 'put it delicately,' as they say."

"You don't know high-school kids. I doubt if you *know* anything indelicate that I haven't heard from them."

"Even if I tell you everything I know about it, it'll still be a mystery. It is to me."

"Quit stalling."

"Okay, you asked for it. And if you repeat this to anyone, I'll wring your scrawny old neck."

"I won't."

"All right. Yvonne was . . . how can I say it? . . . she was sexually mutilated. She was split open. Not cut—torn, ripped. As if someone had forced a two-by-four into her—probably something larger than that."

"Had they?" Miss Mahan felt her throat beginning to burn from the bile rising in it.

"No. At least there was no evidence of it. No splinters, no soil, no foreign matter of any kind."

"My Lord," she moaned. "How she must have suffered."

"Yes," he said softly, "but only for a few seconds. She must have lost consciousness almost immediately. And she was dead long before they finished with her."

"They? What makes you think there was more than one?"

"Are you sure you want to hear the rest of it?"

"Yes," she said, but she didn't.

"I said we found no foreign matter, but we found semen."

"Wasn't that to be expected?"

· "Yes, I suppose. But not in such an amount."

"What do you mean?"

"We found nearly a hundred and fifty cc's. There was probably even more. A lot of it had drained out onto the car seat." His voice was dull.

She shook her head, confused. "A hundred and fifty cc's?"

"About a cupful."

She felt nauseous. "How much . . . how much . . . ?"

"The average male produces about two or three cc's. Maybe four."

"Does that mean she was . . . what? . . . fifty times?"

"And fifty different men."

"That's impossible."

"Yes. I know. One of the deputies took it to Wichita to be analyzed. To see if it's human."

"Human?"

"Yes. We thought someone might . . ."

She held up hei hand. "You don't need to go . . . go any further." They sat for a while, not saying anything.

After a bit he said, "You can see why Robin wanted to keep it quiet?"

"Yes." She shivered, wishing she had her coat even though the office was warm. "Is there any more?"

He shook his head and slumped morosely deep in the chair. "No. Only that Robin is pretty sure she was . . . killed somewhere else and then taken out on the old road because there was almost no blood in or around the car. How they ever drove so far out on that road in the snow is another mystery, although a minor one. The deputy was about to give up and turn around, and he had on snow chains."

Miss Mahan was late for her one-o'clock class. The children hadn't become unruly as they usually did, but were subdued and talking in hushed voices. A discussion of *Silas Marner* proved futile; so she told them to sit quietly and read. She didn't feel any more like classwork than they did. She noticed that Twilla's eyes were bright with suppressed excitement. Well, she thought, I guess you can't expect her to react like the others. She hardly knew Yvonne.

It had stopped snowing by the time Mr. Choate circulated a memo that school would be closed Wednesday for the funeral. Apparently Robin had managed to keep a lid on knowledge of the rape. There was speculation on the subject, but she could tell it was only speculation.

When she got home, she saw the Twilla journal lying beside the big chair in front of the cold fireplace. Strange, Twilla had hardly crossed her mind all day. She guessed it only proved how silly and stupid her Twilla watching really was. She put the journal away in the library table drawer and decided that was enough of that nonsense.

Tuesday, the 12th
This morning I saw Twilla jab Alice May Turner in the thigh with a large darning needle.

Miss Mahan stopped in the middle of a sentence and stared in disbelief. She walked slowly to Twilla's desk, feeling every eye in the class following her. "What's going on here?" she asked in a deathly quiet voice. Twilla looked up at her with such total incomprehension that she wondered if she had imagined the whole thing. But she looked at Alice May and saw her mouth tight and trembling and the tears being held in her eyes only by surface tension.

"What do you mean, Miss Mahan?" Twilla asked in a bewildered voice.

"Why did you stick Alice May with a needle?"

"Miss Mahan! I didn't!"

"I saw you."

"But I didn't!" Twilla's eyes were becoming damp, as if she were about to cry in injured innocence.

"Don't bother to cry," Miss Mahan said calmly. "I'm not impressed." Twilla's mouth tightened for the briefest instant. Miss Mahan turned to Alice May. "Did she jab you with a needle?"

Alice May blinked and a tear rolled down each cheek. "No, ma'am," she answered in a strained voice.

"Then why are you crying?" Miss Mahan demanded.

"I'm not crying," Alice May insisted, wiping her face.

"I think both of you had better come with me to Mr. Choate."

Mr. Choate wouldn't or, I guess, couldn't do anything. They both lied their heads off, insisting that nothing happened. Twilla even had the gall

to accuse me of spying on her and persecuting her. I think Mr. Choate
believed me. He could hardly help it when Alice May began rubbing her
thigh in the midst of her denials.

Miss Mahan sent Twilla back to the room and kept Alice May in
the hall. Alice May began to snuffle and wouldn't look at her.
"Alice May, dear," she said patiently. "I saw what Twilla did. Why
are you fibbing to me?"

"I'm not!" she wailed softly.

"Alice May, I don't want any more of this nonsense!" Why on
earth did Twilla do it? she wondered. Alice May was such a silly
harmless girl. Why would anyone want to hurt her?

"Miss Mahan, I can't tell you," she sobbed.

"Here." Miss Mahan gave her a handkerchief. Alice May took it
and rubbed at her red eyes. "Why can't you tell me? What's going
on between you and Twilla?"

"Nothing," she sniffed.

"Alice May, I promise to drop the whole subject if you'll just tell
me the truth."

Alice May finally looked at her. "Will you?"

"Yes," she groaned in exasperation.

"Well, my . . . my giggling gets on her nerves."

"What?"

"She told me if I didn't stop, I'd be sorry."

"Why didn't you pick up something and brain her with it?"

Alice May's eyes widened in disbelief. "Miss Mahan, I couldn't
do that!"

"She didn't mind hurting you, did she?"

"I'm . . . I'm afraid of her. Everybody is."

"Why? What has she done?"

"I don't know. Nothing. I'm just afraid. You promise not to let
her know I told you?"

"I promise. Now, go to the restroom and wash your face."

Twilla kept watching me the rest of the period. I imagine she suspects
Alice May spilled the beans. The other children were very quiet and
expectant as if they thought Twilla and I would go at each other tooth and

claw. I wonder whom they would root for if we did.

I'll have to admit to a great deal of perverse pleasure in tarnishing Twilla's reputation in the teachers' lounge. I was a little surprised to find a few of the others had become somewhat disenchanted with her also. They didn't have such a concrete example of viciousness as I had, but she was making them uncomfortable.

I also discovered who Twilla's romantic (if you can call it that) interest is since Carter flunked out.

Leo Whittaker!

I was never so shocked and disappointed in my life. An affair between a teacher and a student is bad enough but—Leo! No wonder she was being quiet about it. I thought he acted a bit peculiar when we discussed Twilla. So I said bold as brass: "I wonder whom she's sleeping with?" He turned red and left the room, looking guilty as sin.

I don't know what to do about it. I've got to do something. But what? What? What? I can't do anything to hurt Leo, because it'll also hurt poor Lana.

How could Leo be so stupid?

Dark clouds hung oppressively low the morning of the funeral. They scudded across the sky so rapidly that Miss Mahan got dizzy looking at them. She stood with the large group huddled against the cold outside the First Christian Church of Hawley, waiting for the formation of the procession to the County Line Cemetery. The services had drawn a capacity crowd, mostly from curiosity, she was afraid. The entire ninth grade was there, with the exception of Sammy Stocker, of course, and Twilla. Only two teachers were missing: Mrs. Bryson (first grade), who had the flu, and Leo Whittaker. Leo's absence was peculiar because Lana was there, looking pale and beautifully pregnant. She was with Carter Redwine and his parents. Carter seems to be recovering nicely from his little misadventure, she thought.

She spotted Paul Sullivan and crunched through the snow to his side. He saw her coming and frowned. "Hello, Paul. Did you get the report from Wichita?"

"Do you think this is the place to discuss it?"

"Why not? No one will overhear. Did you?"

He sighed. "Yes."

"Well?"

"It was human—although there were certain peculiarities."

"What peculiarities?"

He cocked his eyes at her. "If I told you, would it mean anything?"

She shrugged. "What else?"

"Well, it all came from the same person—as far as they could tell. At least, there was nothing to indicate that it didn't. Also, all the sperm was the same age."

"What does that mean?"

"The thought occurred to us that someone might be trying to create a grisly hoax. That someone might have . . . well . . . saved it up until they had that much."

"I get the picture," she grimaced. She thought a moment. "Can't they . . . ah . . . freeze it? Haven't I read something about that?"

"You can't do it in your Frigidaire. If the person who did it had the knowledge and the laboratory equipment to do that . . . well . . . it's as improbable as the other theories."

"Robin hasn't learned anything yet?"

"I don't know. Some of us aren't as nosy as others."

She smiled at him as she spotted Lana Whittaker moving toward the Redwine car. She began edging away. "Will you keep me posted?"

"No."

"Thank you, Paul." She caught up with Lana. "Hello, dear."

Lana started and turned, then smiled thinly. "Hello, Miss Mahan."

She exchanged greetings with Mr. and Mrs. Redwine and Carter as they entered their car. "Should you be out in this weather, Lana?"

Lana shrugged. She looked a little haggard and her eyes were puffy. "I'll be all right."

Miss Mahan took her arm. "Come on. My car is right here. Get in out of the cold and talk to me. We'll have plenty of time before they get this mess untangled." Lana went unprotesting and sat in the car staring straight ahead. Miss Mahan started the car and switched on the heater although it was still fairly warm. She turned and looked at Lana.

"When you were in school," she said quietly, "you came to me with all your problems. It made me feel a little like I had a daughter of my own."

Lana turned and looked at her with love and pain in her eyes. "I'm not a little girl any more, Miss Mahan. I'm a married lady with a baby on the way. I should be able to solve my own problems."

"Where's Leo?"

Lana leaned back against the seat and put her fingers on the sides of her nose. "I don't know," she said simply, as if her tears had been used up. "He went out last night and I haven't seen him since. I told my aunt and uncle he went to Liberal to buy some things for the baby."

"Did you call Robin? Maybe he had an accident."

"No. There was no accident. I thought so the first time."

"When was that?"

"Last Friday night. He didn't come in until after midnight. The same thing Saturday. He didn't show up until dawn Monday and Tuesday. This time he didn't come back at all."

"What did he say?"

"Nothing. He wouldn't say anything. Miss Mahan, I know he still loves me; I can tell. He seems genuinely sorry and ashamed of what he's doing, but he keeps . . . keeps doing it. I've tried to think who she might be, but I can't imagine anyone. He's so tired and worn out when he comes home, it would be funny if it . . . if it were happening to someone else."

"Do you still love him?"

Lana smiled. "Oh, yes," she said softly. "More than anything. I love him so much it—" she blushed— "it gives me goosebumps. I was crazy about Leo even when we were in high school, but he was so wild he scared me to death. I thought . . . I thought he had changed."

"I think he has." Miss Mahan took Lana's hand as she saw Robin get in his car and pull out with the pallbearers and the hearse directly behind him. "They're starting. You'd better go back to your car. I'm glad you told me. I'll do all I can to help."

Lana opened the car door. "I appreciate it, Miss Mahan, but I really don't see what you can do."

"We shall see what we shall see."

Miss Mahan managed to hang back until she was last in the funeral procession. The highway had been cleared of snow, and she hoped it wouldn't start again before they all got back to town. She turned off the highway at Miller's Corners, down the dirt road to the old Peacock place. There was nothing left of Miller's Corners now except a few scattered farmhouses. The café had been moved into Hawley eight years ago, and the Gulf station had been closed when George Cutsinger died last fall. The Gulf people had even taken down the signs.

If the Gilbreaths were fixing up the old Peacock farm, they must have started on the inside. It was still as gray and weary-looking as it was ten years ago, if not more so. The black Chrysler was in the old carriage house, and smoke drifted this way and that from one of the chimneys.

She parked and sat looking at the house a moment before getting out. The snow was clean and undisturbed on the front walk. She guessed they must use the back door; it was closer to the carriage house.

No one answered her knock, but she knew they were home. She waited and knocked again. Still no response. She took a deep breath and pushed open the door. "Mrs. Gilbreath?" she called. She listened carefully but there was not a sound. She could hear the melting snow dripping from the eaves and the little ticking sounds an old house makes. She went in and closed the door behind her. "Mrs. Gilbreath?" she called again, hearing nothing but a faint echo. The house was warm but even more dilapidated than the last time she was in it.

She stepped into the parlor and saw them both sitting there. "Oh!" she gasped, startled, and then laughed in embarrassment. "I didn't mean to barge in, but no one answered my knock." Mr.

and Mrs. Gilbreath sat in high-back easy chairs facing away from her. She could only see the tops of their heads. They didn't move.

"Mrs. Gilbreath?" she said, beginning to feel queasy. She walked slowly around them, her eyes fixed so intently on the chairs that she momentarily experienced an optical illusion that the chairs were turning slowly to face her. She blinked and took an involuntary step backward. They sat in the chairs dressed to go out, their eyes focused on nothing. Neither of them moved, not even the slight movements of breathing, nor did their eyes blink. She stared at them in astonishment, fearing they were dead.

Miss Mahan approached them cautiously and touched Mrs. Gilbreath on the arm. The flesh was warm and soft. She quickly drew her hand back with a gasp. Then she reached again and shook the woman's shoulder. "Mrs. Gilbreath," she whispered.

"She won't answer you." Miss Mahan gave a little shriek and looked up with a jerk. Twilla was strolling down the stairs, tying the sash on a rather barbaric-looking floor-length fur robe. The antique pendant she always wore was around her neck. She stopped at the foot of the stairs and leaned against the newel post. She smiled. "They're only simulacra, you know."

"What?" Miss Mahan was bewildered. She hadn't expected Twilla to be here. She thought she would be with Leo.

Twilla indicated her parents. "Watch." Miss Mahan jerked her head back toward the people in the chairs. Suddenly, their heads twisted on their necks until the blank faces looked at each other. Then they grimaced and stuck out their tongues. The faces became expressionless again, and the heads swiveled back to stare at nothing.

Twilla's laugh trilled through the house. Miss Mahan jerked her eyes back to the beautiful child, feeling like a puppet herself. "They're rather clever, don't you think?" she cooed as she walked toward Miss Mahan, the fur robe making a soft sound against the floor. "I'm glad you came, Miss Mahan. It saves me the trouble of going to you."

"What?" Miss Mahan felt out of control. Her heart was beating like a hammer, and she clutched the back of Mrs. Gilbreath's chair to keep from falling.

Twilla smiled at her panic. "I haven't been unaware of your interest in me, you know. I had decided it was time to get you out of the way before you became a problem."

"Get me out of the way?"

"Of course."

"What are you?" She felt her voice rising to a screech but she couldn't stop it. "What are these things pretending to be your parents?"

Twilla laughed. "A thirteen-year-old is quite limited in this society. I had to have parents to do the things I couldn't do myself." She shrugged. "There are other ways, but this is the least bothersome."

"I won't let you get me out of the way," Miss Mahan hissed, dismissing the things she didn't understand and concentrating on that single threat, trying to pull her reeling senses together.

"Don't be difficult, Miss Mahan. There's nothing you can do to stop me." Twilla's face had become petulant, and then she smiled slyly. "Come with me. I want to show you something." Miss Mahan didn't budge. Twilla took a few steps and then turned back. "Come along, now. Don't you want all your questions answered?"

She started up the stairs. Miss Mahan followed her. Her legs felt mechanical. Halfway up she turned and looked back at the two figures sitting in the chairs like department-store dummies. Twilla called to her and she continued to the top.

A hallway ran the length of the house upstairs with bedroom doors on either side. Twilla opened one of them and motioned Miss Mahan in. The house wasn't as old as her own, but it still had the fourteen-foot ceilings. But the ceilings, as well as the walls, had been removed. This side of the hall was one big area, opening into the attic, the roof at least twenty feet overhead, with what appeared to be some sort of trap door recently built into it. The area was empty except for a large gray mass hunched in one corner like a partially collapsed tent.

"He's asleep," Twilla said and whistled. The mass stirred. The tent unfolded slowly, rustling like canvas sliding on canvas. Bony ribs spread gracefully, stretching the canvaslike flesh into vast bat wings which lifted out and up to bump against the roof. The wings trembled slightly as they stretched lazily and then settled, folding neatly behind the thing sitting on the floor.

It was a man, or almost a man. He would have been about sixteen feet tall had he been standing. His body was massively muscled and covered with purplish gray scales that shimmered metallically even in the dim light. His chest, shoulders, and back bulged with great wing-controlling muscles. He stretched his arms and yawned, then rubbed at his eyes with horny fists. His head was hairless and scaled; his ears rose to points reaching above the crown of his skull. The face was angelically beautiful, but the large liquid eyes were dull, and the mouth was slack like an idiot's. He scratched his hip with two-inch talons, making the sound of a rasp on metal. He was completely naked and emphatically male. His massive sex lay along his heavy thigh like a great purple-headed snake.

"This is Dazreel," Twilla said pleasantly. The creature perked up at the sound of his name and looked toward them. "He's a djinn," Twilla continued. He turned his empty gaze away and began idly fondling himself. Twilla sighed. "I'm afraid Dazreel's pleasures are rather limited."

Miss Mahan ran.

She clattered down the stairs, clutching frantically at the banister to keep her balance. She lost her left shoe and stumbled on the bottom step, hitting her knees painfully on the floor. She reeled to her feet, unaware of her shins shining through her torn stockings. Twilla's crystal laughter pealing down the stairs hardly penetrated the shimmering white layer of panic blanketing her mind.

She bruised her hands on the front door, clawing at it, trying to open it the wrong way. She careened across the porch, into the snow, not feeling the cold on her stockinged left foot. But her lopsided gait caused her to fall, sprawling on her face, burying her arms to the elbows in the snow. She crawled a few feet before gaining enough momentum to regain her feet. Her whole front was frosted with white, but she didn't notice.

She locked the car doors, praying it would start. But she released the clutch too quickly, and it bucked and stalled. She ground the starter and turned her head to see Twilla standing on the porch, her arms hugging a pillar, her cheek caressing it, her smile mocking. The motor caught. Miss Mahan turned the car in a tight circle. The rear wheels lost traction and the car fishtailed.

Take it easy, she screamed at herself. You've made it. You've gotten away. Don't end up in the bar ditch.

She was halfway to Miller's Corners when the loose snow began whipping in a cloud around her. She half heard the dull boom of air being compressed by vast wings. A shadow fell over her, and Dazreel landed astraddle the hood of her car. The metal collapsed with a hollow *whump* as the djinn leaned down to peer curiously at her through the windshield. She began screaming, tearing her throat with short hysterical mindless shrieks that seemed to come from a great distance.

Her screams ended suddenly with a grunt as the front wheels struck the ditch, bringing the car to an abrupt halt. Dazreel lost his balance and flopped over backward with a glitter of purplish gray and a tangle of canvas-flesh into the snow drifts. Miss Mahan watched in paralyzed shock as he got to his feet, grinning an idiot grin, shaking the snow from his wings, and walked around the car. His wings kept opening and closing slightly to give him balance. Her head turned in quick jerks like a wooden doll, following his movements. He leaned over the car from behind, and the glass of both side windows crumbled with a gravelly sound as his huge fingers poked through to grasp the tops of the doors.

The dim light became even dimmer as his wings spread in a mantle over the car. The snow swirled into the air, and she could see the tips of each wing as it made a downward stroke. The car shifted and groaned and rose from the ground.

She fainted.

A smiling angel face floated out of a golden mist. Soft pink lips moved solicitously, but no sound emerged. Miss Mahan felt a glass of water at her mouth and she drank greedily, soothing her raw throat. Sound returned.

"Are you feeling better, Miss Mahan? We don't want you to have a heart attack just yet, do we?" Twilla's eyes glittered with excitement.

Miss Mahan sucked oxygen, fighting the fog in her brain. Then, raw red fingers of anger tore away the silvery panic. She looked at the beautiful monstrous child kneeling before her, the extravagant robe parted enough at the top to reveal a small perfect bare breast. The nipple looked as if it had been rouged. "I'm feeling quite myself again, thank you."

Twilla rose and moved to a facing chair. They were in the parlor. Miss Mahan looked around, but the djinn was absent. Only the parent dolls were there in the same positions.

"Dazreel is back upstairs," Twilla assured her, watching her speculatively. "You have nothing to fear." She smiled slightly. "He will have only virgins."

Miss Mahan felt the blood draining from her face, and she weaved in the chair, feeling the panic creeping back. Twilla threw her head back, and her crystal laugh was harsh and strident, like a chandelier tumbling down marble stairs.

"Miss Mahan, you never cease to amaze me," she gasped. "Imagine! And at your age, too."

The anger returned in full control. "It's none of your business," she stated unequivocally.

"I'm ever so glad you decided to pay me a visit, Miss Mahan. It's —what do you say?—killing two birds with one stone?"

"What do you mean?"

"Dazreel has, as I said, limited but strong appetites. If they aren't satisfied, he becomes quite unmanageable. And don't think he will reject you because you're a scrawny old crow. He has no taste at all and only one criterion: virginity." Twilla was almost fidgety with anticipation.

"What possible difference could it make to that monster?" I must be losing my mind, Miss Mahan thought. I'm sitting here having a calm conversation with this wretched child who is going to kill me!

Twilla was thoughtful. "I really don't know. I never thought about it. That's just the way it's always been. It could be a personal idiosyncrasy, or perhaps it's religious." She shrugged. "Something like *kosher*, do you think? Anyway, you can't fool him."

"I don't understand any of this," Miss Mahan said in confusion. "Did you say he was a . . . a djinn?"

"Surely you've heard of them. King Solomon banished the entire race, if you remember." She smiled, pleased. "But I saved Dazreel."

"How old are you?" Miss Mahan breathed.

Twilla chuckled. "You wouldn't believe me if I told you. Don't let the body mislead you. It's relatively new. Dazreel has great power if you can control him. But he's crafty and very literal. One wrong move and . . ." She ran her forefinger across her throat.

"But . . ." Miss Mahan was completely confused. "If this is all true, why are you going to school in Hawley, Kansas, for heaven's sake?"

Twilla sighed. "Boredom is the curse of the immortal, Miss Mahan. I thought it might offer some diversion."

"If you're so bored with life, why don't you die?"

"Don't be absurd!"

"How could you be so inhuman? What you did to Yvonne . . . does life mean nothing to you?"

Twilla shifted in irritation. "Don't be tiresome. How could your brief, insignificant lives concern me?"

There was a restless sound from above. Twilla glanced at the stairs. "Dazreel is becoming impatient." She turned back to Miss Mahan with a smirk. "Are you ready to meet your lover, Miss Mahan?"

Miss Mahan sat frozen, the blood roaring in her ears. "You might as well go," Twilla continued. "It's inevitable. Think of your dignity, Miss Mahan. Do you really want to go kicking and screaming? Or perhaps you'd like another run in the snow?"

Miss Mahan stood up suddenly. "I won't give you the satisfaction," she said calmly. She walked to the stairs, bobbing up and down with one shoe off. Twilla rose and ran after her, circling her in glee.

Twilla leaned against the newel post, blocking the stairs. She

smiled wistfully. "I rather envy you, Miss Mahan. I've often wished
. . . Dazreel knows the ancient Oriental arts, and sex *was* an art."
She grimaced. "Now it's like two goats in heat!" Her smile re-
turned. "I've often wished I had the capacity."

Miss Mahan ignored her and marched slowly up the stairs with
lopsided dignity. Twilla clapped her hands and backed up ahead
of her, taunting her, encouraging her, plucking at her gray tweed
coat. Twilla danced around her, swirling the fur robe with graceful
turns. Miss Mahan looked straight ahead, one hand on the banister
for balance.

Then, at the third step from the top, she stumbled. She fell
against the railing and then to her knees. She shifted and sat on
the step, rubbing her shins.

"Don't lose heart now, Miss Mahan," Twilla sang. "We're almost
there." Twilla tugged at her coat sleeve. Miss Mahan clutched
Twilla's wrist as if she needed help in getting up. Then she heaved
with all her might. Twilla's laughter became a gasp and then a
shriek as she plummeted down the stairs with a series of very
satisfying thumps and crashes. Miss Mahan hurried after her, but
the fall had done the job.

Twilla lay on her back a few feet from the bottom step, her body
twisted at the wrong angle. She was absolutely motionless except
for her face. It contorted in fury, and her eyes were metallic with
hate. Her rose-petal lips writhed and spewed the most vile ob-
scenities Miss Mahan had ever imagined, some of them in languages she'd never heard.

"Dazreel!" Twilla keened. "Dazreel! Dazreel!" over and over. A
howl reverberated through the house. It shook. Plaster crashed
and wood splintered. Dazreel appeared at the top of the stairs,
barely able to squeeze through the opening.

Twilla continued her call. Miss Mahan took a trembling step
backward. Dazreel started down the steps. Miraculously they
didn't collapse. Only the banister splintered and swayed outward.

Miss Mahan commanded herself to think. What did she know
about djinns? Very little, practically nothing. Wasn't there supposed to be a controlling device of some sort? A lamp? A bottle?

A magic ring? A talisman? Something. She looked at Twilla and then at the djinn. She almost fainted. Dazreel approached the bottom of the stairs with an enormous erection.

She looked frantically at Twilla. She's not wearing rings. Then something caught her eye.

The pendant! Was it the pendant? It had slipped up and over her shoulder and beneath her neck. Miss Mahan scrambled for it. She pushed Twilla's head aside. The child screamed in horrible agony. She grasped the pendant and pulled. The chain cut into the soft flesh of Twilla's neck and then snapped, leaving a red line that oozed blood.

She looked at Dazreel. He had stopped and was looking at her tentatively. It was the pendant! "Give it back," Twilla groaned. "Give it back. Please. Please, give it back. It won't do you any good. You don't know how to use it." Dazreel took another step. He stretched his hand toward her. His eyes implored.

Miss Mahan threw the pendant at him. Twilla screamed, and the hair on the back of Miss Mahan's neck bristled. It was not a scream of pain or rage, but of the damned. Dazreel's huge hand darted out and caught the pendant. He held his fist to his face and opened his fingers, gazing at what he held. He looked at Miss Mahan and smiled an angelic smile. Then he rippled, like heat waves on the desert, and . . . vanished.

Miss Mahan sat on the bottom step, weak with relief, gulping air. She looked at Twilla, as motionless as the parent dolls in the chairs. Only her face moved, twisting in sobs of self-pity. Miss Mahan almost felt sorry for her . . . but not quite.

She stood up and walked through the kitchen and out the back door. She thought she knew where it would be. Everyone kept it there. She went to the shed behind the carriage house, floundering through the snow drift. She scooped away the snow to get the door open. She stepped in and looked around. There was almost no light. The scudding clouds seemed even lower and darker, and the single window in the shed was completely grimed over.

She spotted it behind some shovels, misted over with cobwebs. She pushed the shovels aside, grasped the handle and lifted the gasoline can. It was heavy. She shook it. There was a satisfying slosh. She smiled grimly and started back to the house.

Then she stopped and gaped when she saw Leo Whittaker's car parked out of sight behind the house. She hurried on, letting the heavy can bounce against the ground with every other step. She opened the kitchen door and shrieked.

Mrs. Gilbreath stood in the doorway, smiling pleasantly at her and holding a butcher knife. Without reasoning, without even thinking, Miss Mahan took the handle of the heavy gasoline can in both hands and swung it as hard as she could.

The sharp rim around the bottom caught Mrs. Gilbreath across the face, destroying one eye, shearing away her nose, and opening one cheek. Her expression didn't change. Blood flowed over her pleasant smile as she staggered drunkenly backward.

Miss Mahan lost her balance completely. The momentum of the gasoline can swung her around and she sat in the snow, flat on her skinny bottom. The can slipped from her fingers and bounced across the ground with a descending scale of clangs. She lurched to her feet and looked in the kitchen door. Mrs. Gilbreath had slammed back against the wall and was sitting on the floor, still smiling her gory smile, her right arm twitching like a metronome.

Miss Mahan scrambled after the gasoline can and hid it in the pantry. She ducked up the kitchen stairs when she heard footsteps.

Mr. Gilbreath walked through the kitchen, ignoring Mrs. Gilbreath, and went out the back door. Miss Mahan hurried up the stairs. Oh Lord, she thought, I'll be so sore, I can't move for a week.

She entered the upstairs hall from the opposite end. She stepped carefully over the debris from the wall shattered by the djinn. She looked in the bedrooms on the other side. The first one was empty, with a layer of dust, but the second . . . She stared. It looked like a set from a Maria Montez movie. A fire burned in the fireplace, and Leo Whittaker lay stark naked on the fur-covered bed.

"Leo Whittaker!" she bellowed. "Get up from there and put your clothes on this instant!" But he didn't move. He was alive; his chest moved gently as he breathed. She went to him, trying to keep from looking at his nakedness. Then she thought, what the dickens? There's no point in being a prude at this stage. Her eyes widened in admiration. Then she ceded him a few additional points for being able to satisfy Twilla. Why couldn't she have found a beautiful man like that when she was twenty-three, she wondered. She sighed. It wouldn't have made any difference, she guessed.

She put her hand on his shoulder and shook him. He moaned softly and shifted on the bed. "Leo! Wake up! What's the matter with you?" She shook him again. He acted drugged or something. She saw a long golden hair on his stomach and plucked it off, throwing it on the floor. She took a deep breath and slapped him in the face. He grunted. His head lifted slightly and then fell back. "Leo!" she shouted and slapped him again. His body jerked, and his eyes clicked open but didn't focus.

"Leo!" Slap!

"Owww," he said and looked at her. "Miss Mahan?"

"Leo, are you awake?"

"Miss Mahan? What are you doing here? Is Lana all right?" He sat up in the bed and saw the room. He grunted in bewilderment.

"Leo. Get up and get dressed. Hurry!" she commanded. She heard the starter of a car grinding. Leo looked at himself, turned red, and tried to move in every direction at once. Miss Mahan grinned and went to the window. She could hear Leo thumping and bumping as he tried to put his clothes on. The car motor caught, and steam billowed from the carriage house. "Hurry, Leo!" The black Chrysler began slowly backing out, Mr. Gilbreath at the wheel. Then the motor stalled and died.

He's trying to get away, she thought. No, he's only a puppet. He's planning to take Twilla away! She turned back to Leo. He was dressed, sitting on the edge of the bed, putting on his shoes. He looked at her shame-faced, like a little boy.

"Leo," she said in her sternest, most no-nonsense unruly-child voice. The car motor started again. "Don't ask any questions. Go down the kitchen stairs and to your car. Hurry as fast as you can. Don't let Mr. Gilbreath see you. Bring your car around to the front and to the end of the lane. Block the lane so Mr. Gilbreath can't get out. Keep yourself locked in your car because he's dangerous. Do you understand?"

"No," he said, shaking his head.

"Never mind. Will you do what I said?"

He nodded.

"All right, then. Hurry!" They left the bedroom. Leo gave it one last bewildered glance. They ran down the kitchen stairs as fast as they could, Leo keeping her steady. She propelled him out the back door before he could see Mrs. Gilbreath still smiling and twitching. The black Chrysler was just pulling around to the front of the house.

She ran to the pantry, retrieved the gasoline can, and staggered into the entry hall. She could see Mr. Gilbreath getting out of the car. She locked the door and hobbled into the parlor. Twilla had been moved to the divan and covered with a quilt. He shouldn't have moved her, Miss Mahan thought; with an injury like that it could have killed her.

Twilla saw her enter and began screeching curses at her. Miss Mahan shook her head. She put the gasoline can down by the divan and tried to unscrew the cap on the spout. It wouldn't budge. It was rusted solid. Miss Mahan growled in frustration. The front door began to rattle and clatter.

Twilla's curses stopped suddenly, and Miss Mahan looked at her. Twilla was staring at her in round-eyed horror. Miss Mahan went to the fireplace and got the poker. Twilla's eyes followed her. She drew the poker back and swung it as hard as she could at the gasoline can. It made a very satisfactory hole. She swung the poker several more times and tossed it away. She picked up the can as Twilla began to scream and plead. She rested it on the back of the divan and stripped away the blanket. She tipped it over, and pale-pink streams of gasoline fell on Twilla.

Glass shattered in the front door. Miss Mahan left the can resting on the back of the divan, still gurgling out its contents, and went to the fireplace again. She picked up the box of matches as Mr. Gilbreath walked in. His expression didn't change as he hurried toward her. She took a handful of wooden matches. She struck them all on the side of the box and tossed them on Twilla.

Twilla's screams and the flames ballooned upward together. Mr. Gilbreath shifted directions and waded into the flames, reaching for Twilla. Miss Mahan ran out of the house as fast as she could.

She was past the black Chrysler, its motor still running, when the gasoline can exploded. Leo had parked his car where she told him. Now he jumped out and ran to her. They looked at the old Peacock house.

It was old and dry as dust. The flames engulfed it completely. The snow was melting in a widening circle around it. They had to back all the way to Leo's car because of the heat.

They heard a siren and turned to see Sheriff Walker's car hurrying down the lane, followed by some of the funeral procession on its way back to Hawley. The ones who hadn't turned down the road were stopped on the highway, looking.

"Leo, dear," she said. "Do you know what you're doing here?"

He rubbed his hand across his face, his eyes still a little bleary. "Yes. I think so. It all seems like a dream. Twilla . . . Miss Mahan," he said in pain. "I don't know why I did it."

"I do," she said soothingly and put her arm around him. "And it wasn't your fault. You have to believe that. Don't tell Lana or anyone. Forget it ever happened. Do you understand?"

He nodded as Robin Walker got out of his car and ran toward them. He looks very handsome in his uniform, she thought. My, my, I've suddenly become very conscious of good-looking men. Too bad it's thirty years too late.

"Miss Mahan? Leo? What's going on here?" Robin asked in bewilderment. "Is anyone still in there?" He looked at her feet. "Miss Mahan, why are you running around in the snow with only one shoe on?"

She followed his gaze. "I'll declare," she said in astonishment. "I didn't know I'd lost it. Leo. Robin, let's get in your car. I have a lot to tell you both."

Miss Mahan sat before the fireplace in her comfortable old house, tearing the pages from her Twilla journal and feeding them one at a time to the fire. Paul Sullivan had doctored her cuts and bruises, and she felt wonderful—stiff and sore, to be sure—but wonderful. Tomorrow the news would be all over town that, with brilliant detective work, Robin Walker, aided by Leo Whittaker, had discovered that Twilla Gilbreath's father was Yvonne's killer. In an attempt to arrest him the house had burned and all three had perished.

She had told Robin and Leo everything that happened—well, almost everything. She had left out her own near encounter with Dazreel and a few other related items. She had also given the impression—sort of—that the house had burned by accident. Poor sweet Robin hadn't believed a word of it. But after hearing Leo's account, taking a look at her demolished car, and seeing the footprints in the snow, he finally, grudgingly, agreed to go along with it. And it did explain all the mysteries of Yvonne's death.

She knew the *public* story was full of holes and loose ends, but she also knew the people in Hawley. They wanted to hear that an outsider had done it, and they wanted to hear that he had been discovered. Their own imaginations would fill in the gaps.

Lana Whittaker didn't really believe that Leo was working with Robin all those nights he was away, but they loved each other enough. They'd be all right.

She fed the last pages to the fire and looked around her parlor. She decided to put up a tree this year. She hadn't bothered with one in years. And a party. She'd have a party. There hadn't been more than three people in the house at one time in ages.

She hobbled creakily up the stairs, humming "Deck the Hall with Boughs of Holly," considerably off key, heading for the attic to search for the box of Christmas-tree ornaments.

GORDON R. DICKSON

Ten Years of
Nebula Awards

Gordon Dickson is one of the few writers of science fiction to have earned a degree in creative writing; after two additional years of graduate work, he became a freelance writer in 1950 and has written, uninterruptedly, ever since. In that quarter of a century he has published more than two hundred short stories and won a Hugo (for "Soldier, Ask Not") and a Nebula (for "Call Him Lord"). He has also published some thirty novels, of which the best known are those that belong to his *Dorsai* cycle, eventually to be composed of three historical novels, three contemporary novels, and an expanding number of futuristic novels. He served for two years as president of the Science Fiction Writers of America.

We have now had ten years' worth of science-fiction novels and shorter works which have been voted winners of the Nebula Award; and whatever else may be said about these stories, they cannot be denied the label of "representative." The winners as a group are the result of a decade of selections by those who themselves write in the field and who have endeavored annually to choose the best work that was being done.

This being the case, it is a temptation to examine these stories for evidence that the genre—as it has commonly come to be referred to in recent years—is developing and for further indications of the direction in which that development is headed. Unfortunately, ten years of winners, while representing considerable fictional wordage, cover too brief a time to show evidence of any really enduring trend. In addition, the word "genre" does not really tell the whole story about that part of the current literary map generally regarded as being held under the name of science fiction; and moreover, readers, critics, and in fact authors themselves tend to an instinctive parochiality in the matter of time. It is not only easy but tempting to believe that the historical currents with which anyone is concerned make a significant and sudden turn for the better or worse in that person's own professional lifetime.

Inhabitants of previous periods have entertained this same thought, and time has proved then mistaken. To guard against such error in the present instance, it might help to imagine a bookshelf holding in book form all the Nebula-winning stories to date. Picture this bookshelf as containing ten volumes that are novels, three volumes that together contain ten novellas, two volumes containing ten novelets, and one volume containing nine short stories,* all arranged on the shelf in no particular order.

On surveying and reading the stories in these volumes, the primary characteristic that surfaces is that, irrespective of their date of publication, they are all strong stories that do not fall easily into any specific groupings, temporal or otherwise. Story by story, they stand apart from each other—even when there is more than one winner by a particular writer—and the general impression they give is that they are works of fiction written by distinct and highly individualistic authors.

The effect, in fact, is not so much that of a "genre" as of a separate and developing current of literature, with a diversity of style and theme as large as that of the so-called literary mainstream itself.

To many critics whose knowledge and understanding of science fiction is cursory, such a statement about the diversity of the work by its authors may sound bold indeed. However, two factors make it at least possible that the statement has a basis in truth. One is that as the past ten years of Nebula winners show, and as knowledgeable readers in this field have long been aware, there has never existed a single "master" type of science fiction. Rather what has been considered science fiction at any particular time has been given its character by as many strong authors as were then appearing in print with it and who, by what they wrote, defined the field rather than adapted themselves to it.

The other factor is that beyond such independence of the authors concerned, a true and viable development in the field of literature has two requirements. One is that its examples must

*In 1970 there was no award for short story.

establish themselves in what, effectively, is the marketplace. They must create a supporting readership willing to pay to read them, not merely because this readership has been told science fiction is something everybody is reading or should read but for the sheerly personal pleasure of finding a piece of fiction that interests and entertains individually. Without such a real-life readership any literary development takes place, in effect, under laboratory conditions only; and no true estimate of its chances for survival in succeeding decades can be made.

The other requirement for a literary development is that the attitude of those creating the works involved be primarily occupied with the effectiveness of what they do and only secondarily with current praise and approval of it. It is a truism in art that the self-conscious artist is unlikely to be productive of great work. Certainly there has been considerable evidence that this is true both of literary art over the centuries and of science fiction in this past decade. The outstanding examples here being those of professional writers outside the field of science fiction who have tried to do a science-fictional work and, failing, discovered that it is a type of literature that goes a great deal deeper than the display of a few surface characteristics and techniques.

The difference, in fact, between true science fiction and even expert imitations is a profound one, as those members of the Science Fiction Writers of America who have voted these Nebula Awards are professionally aware. The writers represented on our hypothetical shelf are those who have experimented successfully, and they have been successful precisely because they experimented for the sake of their writing and not because they hoped to gain for themselves the name of experimentalist.

These two factors of individuality and responsibility have been visible in science fiction from the 1940s to the present. They are particularly visible in the winners of the award during the past ten years. Therefore, it seems entirely possible that even if the award winners of this decade do not cover a sufficient span of time to give us a certain picture of the direction in which science fiction is developing, they do present evidence from which, for the first time, we may try to paint a picture of what the field is, in present character and in its possible eventual relationship to the historical current of literature in general.

In the area of identity, three specific characteristics of science fiction show themselves almost at once to the inquiring eye. The first is that science fiction, as the Nebula winners themselves show —from "He Who Shapes" by Roger Zelazny in 1965 to "Born with the Dead" by Robert Silverberg in 1974—is a literature of ideas and thematic argument. Secondly, that it is a literature characterized by experimentation with style—as in "Repent, Harlequin!" by Harlan Ellison, 1965, *BABEL-17* by Samuel Delany and "The Last Castle" by Jack Vance, 1966, "The Planners" by Kate Wilhelm in 1968, and a large number of others, moving forward down the years to 1975. Third, it is a literature remarkable for the existence of a community attitude among its practitioners, one that has avoided fostering a pattern of sterile imitation within the group while successfully encouraging ideational conflict among its members—with resultant benefit to the readers.

Unfortunately these characteristics have not been free of occasional misunderstandings. The word "ideas" has encountered some semantic ghettoization. There is an argument to the effect that science fiction was formerly a literature of ideas but has since developed into a literature of human values. While these two terms do indicate a difference of a kind, they are still siblings of the same philosophical family. The general term "ideas" can be stretched to encompass them both. Ideas about things, which were characteristic during the period of technological science fiction in the 1940s, have in fact generally given way to ideas about human relationships and potentials in the current literature. But these two patterns of science fiction are still brother and sister, as the definite kinship, even in the past ten years, shows in the cases of such stories as "The Secret Place" by Richard McKenna, a 1966 winner, and "The Day Before the Revolution" by Ursula K. Le Guin, this year's winner in the short-story division.

The second point, that of experimentation, has occasionally been obscured by the fact that we have just recently gone through a period of experimentation in science fiction. In the past few years a great many attempts have been made to stretch the effective limits of presently known writing techniques. Most of these, of course, were statistically doomed to be unsuccessful; and unfortunately some of the unsuccessful ones, as older readers, critics, and writers have occasionally recognized, duplicate earlier literary experiments in the mainstream. It is an easy assumption that literary experiment is a periodic phenomenon, productive mainly of failures.

But the assumption is wrong. Literary techniques and attitudes are and have always been in a process of evolution, no matter how fast or how slowly, and the means by which evolution is accomplished is the actual enlargement of techniques and literary limits resulting from successful experiments. It is beside the point that the successes are in the small minority. An art is judged by its best examples, not by its worst.

The third point, that of community, sometimes has been considered only an idiosyncrasy of the field rather than an actual source of strength. A close look shows that at no time before in history has a group of writers this numerous been able to communicate so intimately to form in fact the community to which I refer. Such a community was a physical impossibility before our present time. As Ben Bova, science-fiction author and editor of *Analog* magazine, has remarked, the long-distance telephone and the jet plane are what make it workable.

Traditionally, the conditions of existence for the professional writer—and I do not hold the publishing industry blameless for a good many of these—have tended to keep him at a distance from his fellow professionals. In almost all fields of writing before 1950, at a social occasion attended by two or more established writers, the writers metaphorically, if not actually, eyed each other from opposite ends of the room with all the mistrust of natural enemies.

Since the 1950s, however, and specifically in the science-fiction area, this situation has changed. Science-fiction writers nowadays are together on a number of occasions, professional, academic, and social; and accordingly they are able to compare notes over the whole range of their work and lives. This new—it is a temptation to call it futuristic—community interaction is one of the factors that have kept the field constantly renewed and alive.

A number of the stylized misconceptions of science fiction fail in the face of the science fiction written in the last decade. Dramatically so in the case of Nebula winners such as Robert Silverberg, Ursula Le Guin, and Gene Wolfe, but clearly in the case of any who have received the award since its inception. For many years outside communities have taken a single aspect of science fiction and run off with it, proclaiming the part to be the whole. Hollywood early seized on the concept of the monster and called that "science fiction" (or, more likely, "sci-fi") in some thousands of movie advertisements. Critics who could not be bothered to read more than the flap copy of the books they reviewed extracted the idea of future science and technology and made of this a buzzing, light-blinking piece of Rube Goldberg hardware, which they pilloried in thousands of columns of newspaper type.

Meanwhile, the actual writers in the actual field, as these award-winning stories show, were writing the full-fleshed, three-dimensional works of literate art that historically have always been found near the heart of memorable literature. Not all the science-fiction writers were doing this at all times, to be sure. Not even a majority of those writing science fiction at any one time were doing it. But neither have a majority of those in any other area of writing ever done so at any one time. To repeat what was said earlier, we judge an art by its best examples, not by its worst.

Happily, in recent years with the serious attention of the much larger audience that has grown up into the future our earlier writers hypothesized, and with the attention of serious academics, the era of the monster and the hardware is finally coming to an end. If anything further were needed to end it, the hypothetical ten-year shelf of Nebula winners does the task. Since the commencement of the award in 1965, this shelf reveals no monsters and no hardware. Instead, what is found on it are stories of human beings under new and different life pressures, life pressures that may not yet have come to be but which can lie within the bounds of some possible future or alternate present for any one of us.

It is not prophecy but freedom to entertain all concepts that is being celebrated here. The proof of its worth is in the endurance of the best things being written in this literary area. Their endurance and their translation into other media—into movies, into radio and television, even into serious comics, often some years after the original publication—are some evidence of their worth and the artistry of their authors. It is interesting to note that there are none—without exception—among these writers who have won Nebulas to the present date who have not gone on to gather an ever-growing audience and who are not now seeing their earlier works collected or reprinted for a continually enlarging readership. I know of no other award, literary or otherwise, of which that statement can be made.

Finally, and this is the important point, the conditions that produced such consistently good and unusual writing are still at work. The instinct to experiment, the sense of responsibility, the fascination with the human spirit and its possibilities, the community attitude, all are currently being put to work by new people even as they are being kept at work by the old. As the awards for this year were being handed out, the next generation of science-fiction writers, with all the individuality, power, and vitality that is traditional in this literature, were in the field and being heard from. Their names are already familiar. Haldeman, Dozois, Bryant, Lanier, Eisenstein, Grant—the list goes on. And behind them in the further dawn a wave of even newer faces are taking on identity—Catherine Callaghan, Arsen Darnay, Roland Green, and others. How soon will we see you walking toward the head table at award time in the years to come?

ROBERT SCHOLES

As the Wall Crumbles

Robert Scholes is a professor of English at Brown University. Born in Brooklyn, New York, in 1929, he received his B.A. from Yale in 1950, his Ph.D. from Cornell in 1959. He has written many books and essays on literary theory and on modern fiction. His most recent works are *Structuralism in Literature* (Yale, paperbound, 1975) and a study of science fiction entitled *Structural Fabulation* (Notre Dame, 1975).

For some time in literary circles—or circles with literary preten-sions—it has been possible to acquire virtue automatically by ut-tering hostile noises at the mention of science fiction, with the vehemence of the noises in direct proportion to the noise-maker's ignorance of the subject. I regret to report, however, that this particular path to meritorious eminence is becoming beset with pitfalls for the unwary. There are people around who have read the stuff and are just militant enough about it to challenge such casual remarks. Something is going on here, of which this change in behavior is a symptom. The wall between sf and mainstream, between fans and critics, is coming down. It is not coming down all at once, like the walls of Jericho in that old sf tale about the sun standing still. Oh, no. It is being dismantled brick by brick, and the whole job may never be completed. But holes are appearing here and there, and communications are being sent back and forth. From my point of view, as an "academic critic" (a man who likes to talk about books and accepts money from universities for doing so) the great benefit of all this is that the literary riches inside the wall are becoming more accessible. And a lot of what's in there is too good and too important to be left to the "fans." The rest of the world needs it too.

When people ask me, more or less politely, "What's so hot about science fiction, huh?"—and they do ask, more and more, all the time—I answer, more or less politely, "Literary quality and ideas that we need to hear." That's the short version of my reply. The long version might fill a book—and as a matter of fact it has. Another version, of intermediate length, will occupy these few pages in the tenth volume of *Nebula Award Stories.* Most readers of this volume, of course, don't need to be told that sf is interesting. Their interest is no doubt the thing that has brought them to the volume in the first place. But even for the initiate I may be able to put this interest into a broader perspective, as an aspect of the whole literary situation at the present time, which is itself an aspect of the entire system of literature.

If we think of all fiction as a kind of separate territory within the domain of literature as a whole, we can see that this territory is subdivided into smaller sections, sort of like pieces of real estate. The divisions are fictional (like real-estate divisions) and subject to revision, though some of the major boundaries, like that between realism and fantasy, seem based on natural features of the terrain —something like a hill or a river, there, not just a surveyor's dividing line. This territory has some curious features. First of all, the boundaries are continually shifting, and no two surveys ever coincide exactly, though there may be some agreement from one to another. Also, the value of different tracts is subject to change from time to time. What we have learned to call science fiction was a neglected corner of the territory of fantasy until the past century, a kind of swamp or bog that defied productive use. But after Wells and Stapledon and a few others blazed some trails through it, people went to work: draining, clearing, building, mining. It will never look like Kansas (as Dorothy observed to Toto), but too many folks have struck oil on this land now for the establishment to continue ignoring it. Land values are going up, and the critics, publishers, and academic investors are trying to buy in while they can. In fact, sf is doing a land-office business.

There you have it, in the form of a fable, but let me also put it in more explicit and academic terms. Science fiction is attracting the attention of the literary establishment because it has qualities that are needed, which other forms of fiction cannot provide. Some of these qualities are purely literary. They have to do with the ability of sf writers to tell stories. Pleasure in fiction is rooted in our response to narrative movement—to story itself. This is a fundamental kind of pleasure, almost physical, and closely connected to physical sensations like those of motion and sex. Above all, our sexual experiences exhibit a narrative structure: a beginning, middle, and end—a tension, climax, and resolution. Much modern fiction in the "mainstream," especially that most admired in academic circles, has encumbered this pure fictional movement with such a weight of analysis and subtle refinement of consciousness that as fiction it has become overburdened. We may read it with interest and enlightenment, but we do not get from it the pure fictional pleasure that lies at the heart of our need for narration.

One result of this situation is that many people may resort, more or less guiltily, to "lesser" forms of fiction—outside the mainstream of serious literature—for a narrative "fix," a shot of joyful storytelling. A world in which values are clear (with heroes and heroines, villains and villainesses), and action is fast and furious, has extraordinary appeal for people enmeshed in lives of muddled complexity. But such fiction may be so empty of meaning, so far removed from the concerns of experience, that we feel more and more guilty about indulging in it. Thus, what most people need in fiction is something that satisfies their legitimate desire for the pleasures of storytelling, without making them feel ashamed of having some childish and anti-social impulse. We need recreational texts, good stories that leave us refreshed without any feeling of guilt. We need stories that are genuinely adult in their concerns and ideas while satisfying our elemental need for wonder and delight.

Science fiction at its best answers this need better than any other form of contemporary fiction. And it does more. The ancient epics satisfied this same need by telling stories about the distant past: an age of heroes and monsters. And the great novels of the last century satisfied this need by telling dramatic stories of ordinary people in present time or the very recent past. And both of these great literary forms, the epic and the novel, also served to make the values of their culture explicit and available for their audiences. These fictions were a moral force as well as an entertainment. But, as it happens, the major moral problems of our age are centered in the future. The great questions are how we shall leave the earth for future generations, how we shall shape our environment, our genetic heritage, and our intellectual imperatives, so that our descendants may live decent lives. Of all our present actions, especially those involving large political decisions about population control and food distribution, or the spread of scientific knowledge and technological skill, we must ask not whether our ancestors would approve, nor even whether it is right for us now, but how it will affect *them*—the unborn, unconceived, uncreated. Thus, to act morally we need to know *them*, which means to imagine *them* under various aspects, as they might be if this should happen or that. We need, as Olaf Stapledon tried to tell us, to act in the light of our best knowledge, to imagine the world as being better than ourselves might see it. To do this is to raise the consciousness of the whole human race.

For the past half-century or more, the single group of people who have done the most to achieve this beautiful and perhaps impossible goal have been the writers of science fiction. Only they, of all men and women of letters, have made a real and consistent effort to give us living images of the future consequences of present actions. Only they, by conceiving parallel and alternate universes, have helped to sharpen our perception of our own world as a thing not necessary and inevitable but brought into being by the actions of innumerable men and women. "Things might be otherwise!" That is one of the great messages of science fiction. And another one is, "If you keep on doing *this*, they will get worse." These messages are optimistic in the best sense. They restore our faith in human power to act in the world and remind us that we have some control over our collective destiny. But they also remind us that some choices come only once; some doors, once opened, may never be closed; some processes, once begun, may never be reversed.

As the epic claimed the past and the novel the present, science fiction claims the future as its literary domain. It offers us imaginative feedback on the future consequences of present actions. It does other things as well, of course, not all of them important or admirable. It offers us idealized versions of fascist states. It gives us the same old adventures, over and over again, with only the costumes and scenery altered. And in various ways it fails frequently to live up to its high potential. But so does every other form of fiction that has ever existed. The "mainstream," too, has been choked with sewage from time to time, and in ancient days there must have been plenty of bad epics being sung that have not survived the winnowing of the ages. But sf should not use this as an excuse. At present, this form of fiction is so alive, so accessible, that its writers and readers may form an uncritical club devoted to mutual admiration. Hence the real value that Hugo and Nebula awards have held over the past decade or so. They suggest that there *are* standards, even within the protective walls of the sf community. And these standards are not low. In the area of full-length fiction, for instance, the past twenty-five years of Hugo Award winners compares very favorably to the list of Pulitzer Prize winners over the same quarter of a century. But it is beginning to get more difficult to tell which books should be considered for which award, as the dividing wall comes down and the territory is reorganized.

The new "discovery" of sf by the academic and critical community is going to have some effect on the whole situation of science fiction. I hope that ultimately some good will come of this, in the form of better rewards and recognition for sf writers. At some point in time academic critics like myself may be able to persuade the major reviewing media, like the *New York Times Book Review*, to treat the strongest works of sf as they would treat any other valuable works of fiction, instead of relegating all sf to a "Department" as if it were mere entertainment. It pains me that major efforts of the recent past, like John Brunner's *The Sheep Look Up* and Ursula K. Le Guin's *The Dispossessed*, were not reviewed seriously on the front page of the *Book Review*. So the battle is far from won, though victory is sure to come, ultimately.

On the other side of the question, we may well ask whether the academic and critical "discovery" of sf may have any bad side effects. It is likely to produce a rash of unnecessary anthologies for classroom use, but this is not a serious problem. It may also—perhaps inevitably—lead writers into a greater solemnity, so that their writing begins to resemble more closely those mainstream fictions that it has been defined against. As the mainstream borrows concepts and literary strategies from sf, science fiction itself is in some danger of accepting the cumbersome properties of realistic narration discarded by mainstream fiction. When fiction gets too analytical, too introspective, too big and heavy, it goes the way of the dinosaur.

But the literary situation will not stand still. And for those who have loved sf as a sub-literary kind of fiction, there is no real alternative now. The ghetto walls are coming down whether the ordinary fan wants them to or not and whether the literary critics want them to or not. The strength and vitality of science fiction, which is bursting with new ideas, vividly imagined by a host of talented young writers, is in such marked contrast to the exhausted situation of the novel of psycho-social analysis that the machinery of the marketplace alone would be sufficient to bring sf to the center of our literary consciousness. The contrast between the two situations is so great that an enormous potential for exchange of energy has been established. Already there has been serious leakage from sf into mainstream fiction. Writers like Golding, Burgess, Lessing, Burroughs, Barth, and above all Pynchon have borrowed techniques, strategies, and ideas from science fiction. And there has been some exchange in the other direction, too. Brunner, Dick, Disch, Delany, and Le Guin, for example, have all written passages that, except for their settings in future or alternate locations, could be taken for parts of realistic or naturalistic novels. At some point, probably in the very near future, it will no longer be possible to maintain the distinction between "mainstream" and "sf"—because sf will have taken over the center and become the mainstream.

And what will this do to those pleasant aspects of ghetto exis-

tence which have made the world of sf such a remarkable place
to inhabit, where fans and writers mingle at conferences, where
fans become writers themselves, without losing their ability to
admire the work of their fellows, where costumes and high jinks
share the spotlights with serious reports on the future of the bio-
sphere—what will become of all this if sf and mainstream merge?
Honestly, I don't know. But I'm worried. The fact that the world
of sf has had enough tolerance for freaks in Star Trek T-shirts to
rub elbows with philosophers of the future has been important as
well as charming—not just because tolerance is a great virtue
presently in short supply but because the vitality of sf as a literary
form has been based in part on this vital interaction between fans
and writers, philosophers and freaks. No writers in the world have
had the kind of immediate and vigorous feedback from audiences
that sf writers enjoy. And this must continue if sf itself is to retain
its vitality. Still, as the wall around the sf ghetto is dismantled, and
the major talents in the field receive more recognition from the
larger world of letters, the spirit of comradery which was based in
part on isolation and a sense of common indignities shared is
bound to diminish. Perhaps, in the future, sf itself will become a
tired form of fiction, self-conscious and cumbersome, ready to be
pushed aside by some vigorous upstart who has gained strength
while protected by another wall around another ghetto. This is the
way the system of literature works, and if we who love science
fiction can't accept the processes of change, then we love it in vain
and haven't learned one of the great lessons it teaches. The "popular" forms of literature always grow in strength until they are
ready to challenge the mainstream forms and displace them from
the center of attention and acclaim. Right now, sf is moving in on
the mainstream and is ready to take over from the traditional
novel. Let us who love science fiction for once turn our eyes away
from the future and concentrate on the present. So what if some
day sf itself will be old and tired. Now it is young and strong and
about to win big. For those who have suffered the indignities of
the ghetto, there are some scores to be paid. This is going to be
fun.

PHILIP JOSÉ FARMER

After King Kong Fell

Philip José Farmer is a grandfather who writes about grandfathers in a way few grandfathers write. He has been a reader of science fiction since 1928 and a writer of science fiction since the early Fifties, when he won an award as the most promising new writer of 1952. He won a Hugo for his 1967 novella "Riders of the Purple Wage" and another in 1972 for his novel *To Your Scattered Bodies Go,* which is the first novel in his popular *Riverworld* series. He was guest of honor at the 1968 World Science Fiction Convention in Oakland. After working as a technical writer in Los Angeles, he has returned to prolific full-time writing in which he is fascinated as much by the heroes of his youth as by the characters he creates. In recent times he has written popular biographies of such fictional characters as Tarzan and Doc Savage and is at work on a biography of Allan Quatermain. He recently completed a screen treatment for the motion picture *Doc Savage: Archenemy of Evil.* In the following story he continues his mythmaking.

The first half of the movie was grim and gray and somewhat tedious. Mr. Howller did not mind. That was, after all, realism. Those times had been grim and gray. Moreover, behind the tediousness was the promise of something vast and horrifying. The creeping pace and the measured ritualistic movements of the actors gave intimations of the workings of the gods. Unhurriedly, but with utmost confidence, the gods were directing events toward the climax.

Mr. Howller had felt that at the age of fifteen, and he felt it now while watching the show on TV at the age of fifty-five. Of course, when he first saw it in 1933, he had known what was coming. Hadn't he lived through some of the events only two years before that?

The old freighter, the *Wanderer*, was nosing blindly through the fog toward the surflike roar of the natives' drums. And then: the commercial. Mr. Howller rose and stepped into the hall and called down the steps loudly enough for Jill to hear him on the front porch. He thought, commercials could be a blessing. They give us time to get into the bathroom or the kitchen, or time to light up a cigarette and decide about continuing to watch this show or go on to that show.

And why couldn't real life have its commercials?

Wouldn't it be something to be grateful for if reality stopped in mid-course while the Big Salesman made His pitch? The car about to smash into you, the bullet on its way to your brain, the first cancer cell about to break loose, the boss reaching for the phone to call you in so he can fire you, the spermatozoon about to be launched toward the ovum, the final insult about to be hurled at the once, and perhaps still, beloved, the final drink of alcohol which would rupture the abused blood vessel, the decision which would lead to the light that would surely fail?

If only you could step out while the commercial interrupted these, think about it, talk about it, and then, returning to the set, switch it to another channel.

But that one is having technical difficulties, and the one after that is a talk show whose guest is the archangel Gabriel himself and after some urging by the host he agrees to blow his trumpet, and . . .

Jill entered, sat down, and began to munch the cookies and drink the lemonade he had prepared for her. Jill was six and a half years old and beautiful, but then what granddaughter wasn't beautiful? Jill was also unhappy because she had just quarreled with her best friend, Amy, who had stalked off with threats never to see Jill again. Mr. Howller reminded her that this had happened before and that Amy always came back the next day, if not sooner. To take her mind off of Amy, Mr. Howller gave her a brief outline of what had happened in the movie. Jill listened without enthusiasm, but she became excited enough once the movie had resumed. And when Kong was feeling over the edge of the abyss for John Driscoll, played by Bruce Cabot, she got into her grandfather's lap. She gave a little scream and put her hands over her eyes when Kong carried Ann Redman into the jungle (Ann played by Fay Wray).

But by the time Kong lay dead on Fifth Avenue, she was rooting for him, as millions had before her. Mr. Howller squeezed her and kissed her and said, "When your mother was about your age, I took her to see this. And when it was over, she was crying, too."

Jill sniffled and let him dry the tears with his handkerchief.

When the Roadrunner cartoon came on, she got off his lap and went back to her cookie-munching. After a while she said, "Grandpa, the coyote falls off the cliff so far you can't even see him. When he hits, the whole earth shakes. But he always comes back, good as new. Why can he fall so far and not get hurt? Why couldn't King Kong fall and be just like new?"

Her grandparents and her mother had explained many times the distinction between a "live" and a "taped" show. It did not seem to make any difference how many times they explained. Somehow, in the years of watching TV, she had gotten the fixed idea that people in "live" shows actually suffered pain, sorrow, and death. The only shows she could endure seeing were those that her elders labeled as "taped." This worried Mr. Howller more than he admitted to his wife and daughter. Jill was a very bright child, but what if too many TV shows at too early an age had done her some irreparable harm? What if, a few years from now, she could easily see, and even define, the distinction between reality and unreality on the screen but deep down in her there was a child that still could not distinguish?

"You know that the Roadrunner is a series of pictures that move. People draw pictures, and people can do anything with pictures. So the Roadrunner is drawn again and again, and he's back in the next show with his wounds all healed and he's ready to make a jackass of himself again."

"A jackass? But he's a coyote."

"Now . . ."

Mr. Howller stopped. Jill was grinning.

"O.K., now you're pulling my leg."

"But is King Kong alive or is he taped?"

"Taped. Like the Disney I took you to see last week. *Bedknobs and Broomsticks.*"

"Then *King Kong* didn't happen?"

"Oh, yes, it really happened. But this is a movie they made about King Kong after what really happened was all over. So it's not exactly like it really was, and actors took the parts of Ann Redman and Carl Denham and all the others. Except King Kong himself. He was a toy model."

Jill was silent for a minute and then she said, "You mean, there really *was* a King Kong? How do you know, Grandpa?"

"Because I was there in New York when Kong went on his rampage. I was in the theater when he broke loose, and I was in the crowd that gathered around Kong's body after he fell off the Empire State Building. I was thirteen then, just seven years older than you are now. I was with my parents, and they were visiting my Aunt Thea. She was beautiful, and she had golden hair just like Fay Wray's—I mean, Ann Redman's. She'd married a very rich man, and they had a big apartment high up in the clouds. In the Empire State Building itoclf."

"High up in the clouds! That must've been fun, Grundpa!"

It would have been, he thought, if there had not been so much tension in that apartment. Unclo Nate and Aunt Thea should have been happy because they were so rich and lived in such a swell place. But they weren't. No one said anything to young Tim Howller, but he felt the suppressed anger, heard the bite of tone, and saw the tightening lips. His aunt and uncle were having trouble of some sort, and his parents were upset by it. But they all tried to pretend everything was as sweet as honey when he was around.

Young Howller had been eager to accept the pretense. He didn't like to think that anybody could be mad at his tall, blond, and beautiful aunt. He was passionately in love with her; he ached for her in the daytime; at nights he had fantasies about her of which he was ashamed when he awoke. But not for long. She was a thousand times more desirable than Fay Wray or Claudette Colbert or Elissa Landi.

But that night, when they were all going to see the premiere of *The Eighth Wonder of the World*, King Kong himself, young Howller had managed to ignore whatever it was that was bugging his elders. And even they seemed to be having a good time. Uncle Nate, over his parents' weak protests, had purchased orchestra seats for them. These were twenty dollars apiece, big money in Depression days, enough to feed a family for a month. Everybody got all dressed up, and Aunt Thea looked too beautiful to be real. Young Howller was so excited that he thought his heart was going to climb up and out through his throat. For days the newspapers had been full of stories about King Kong—speculations, rather, since Carl Denham wasn't telling them much. And he, Tim Howller, would be one of the lucky few to see the monster first.

Boy, wait until he got back to the kids in seventh grade at Busiris, Illinois! Would their eyes ever pop when he told them all about it!

But his happiness was too good to last. Aunt Thea suddenly said she had a headache and couldn't possibly go. Then she and Uncle Nate went into their bedroom, and even in the front room, three rooms and a hallway distant, young Tim could hear their voices. After a while Uncle Nate, slamming doors behind him, came out. He was red-faced and scowling, but he wasn't going to call the party off. All four of them, very uncomfortable and silent, rode in a taxi to the theater on Times Square. But when they got inside, even Uncle Nate forgot the quarrel or at least he seemed to. There was the big stage with its towering silvery curtains and through the curtains came a vibration of excitement and of delicious danger. And even through the curtains the hot hairy ape-stink filled the theater.

"Did King Kong get loose just like in the movie?" Jill said.

Mr. Howller started. "What? Oh, yes, he sure did. Just like in the movie."

"Were you scared, Grandpa? Did you run away like everybody else?"

He hesitated. Jill's image of her grandfather had been cast in a heroic mold. To her he was a giant of Herculean strength and perfect courage, her defender and champion. So far he had managed to live up to the image, mainly because the demands she made were not too much for him. In time she would see the cracks and the sawdust oozing out. But she was too young to disillusion now.

"No, I didn't run," he said. "I waited until the theater was cleared of the crowd."

This was true. The big man who'd been sitting in the seat before him had leaped up yelling as Kong began tearing the bars out of his cage, had whirled and jumped over the back of his seat, and his knee had hit young Howller on the jaw. And so young Howller had been stretched out senseless on the floor under the seats while the mob screamed and tore at each other and trampled the fallen.

Later he was glad that he had been knocked out. It gave him a good excuse for not keeping cool, for not acting heroically in the situation. He knew that if he had not been unconscious, he would have been as frenzied as the others, and he would have abandoned his parents, thinking only in his terror of his own salvation. Of course, his parents had deserted him, though they claimed that they had been swept away from him by the mob. This *could* be true; maybe his folks *had* actually tried to get to him. But he had not really thought they had, and for years he had looked down on them because of their flight. When he got older, he realized that he would have done the same thing, and he knew that his contempt for them was really a disguised contempt for himself.

He had awakened with a sore jaw and a headache. The police and the ambulance men were there and starting to take care of the hurt and to haul away the dead. He staggered past them out into the lobby and, not seeing his parents there, went outside. The sidewalks and the streets were plugged with thousands of men, women, and children, on foot and in cars, fleeing northward.

He had not known where Kong was. He should have been able to figure it out, since the frantic mob was leaving the midtown part of Manhattan. But he could think of only two things. Where were his parents? And was Aunt Thea safe? And then he had a third thing to consider. He discovered that he had wet his pants. When he had seen the great ape burst loose, he had wet his pants.

Under the circumstances, he should have paid no attention to this. Certainly no one else did. But he was a very sensitive and shy boy of thirteen, and, for some reason, the need for getting dry underwear and trousers seemed even more important than finding his parents. In retrospect he would tell himself that he would have gone south anyway. But he knew deep down that if his pants had not been wet he might not have dared return to the Empire State Building.

It was impossible to buck the flow of the thousands moving like

lava up Broadway. He went east on 43rd Street until he came to
Fifth Avenue, where he started southward. There was a crowd to
fight against here, too, but it was much smaller than that on Broadway. He was able to thread his way through it, though he often had
to go out into the street and dodge the cars. These, fortunately,
were not able to move faster than about three miles an hour.

"Many people got impatient because the cars wouldn't go
faster," he told Jill, "and they just abandoned them and struck out
on foot."

"Wasn't it noisy, Grandpa?"

"Noisy? I've never heard such noise. I think that everyone in
Manhattan, except those hiding under their beds, was yelling or
talking. And every driver in Manhattan was blowing his car's horn.
And then there were the sirens of the fire trucks and police cars
and ambulances. Yes, it was noisy."

Several times he tried to stop a fugitive so he could find out what
was going on. But even when he did succeed in halting someone
for a few seconds, he couldn't make himself heard. By then, as he
found out later, the radio had broadcast the news. Kong had
chased John Driscoll and Ann Redman out of the theater and
across the street to their hotel. They had gone up to Driscoll's
room, where they thought they were safe. But Kong had climbed
up, using windows as ladder steps, reached into the room, knocked
Driscoll out, grabbed Ann, and had then leaped away with her. He
had headed, as Carl Denham figured he would, toward the tallest
structure on the island. On King Kong's own island, he lived on
the highest point, Skull Mountain, where he was truly monarch of
all he surveyed. Here he would climb to the top of the Empire
State Building, Manhattan's Skull Mountain.

Tim Howller had not known this, but he was able to infer
that Kong had traveled down Fifth Avenue from 38th Street
on. He passed a dozen cars with their tops flattened down by
the ape's fist or turned over on their sides or tops. He saw
three sheet-covered bodies on the sidewalks, and he overheard
a policeman telling a reporter that Kong had climbed up several buildings on his way south and reached into windows and

pulled people out and thrown them down onto the pavement.

"But you said King Kong was carrying Ann Redman in the crook of his arm, Grandpa," Jill said. "He only had one arm to climb with, Grandpa, so . . . so wouldn't he fall off the building when he reached in to grab those poor people?"

"A very shrewd observation, my little chickadee," Mr. Howller said, using the W. C. Fields voice that usually sent her into giggles. "But his arms were long enough for him to drape Ann Redman over the arm he used to hang on with while he reached in with the other. And to forestall your next question, even if you had not thought of it, he could turn over an automobile with only one hand."

"But . . . but why'd he take time out to do that if he wanted to get to the top of the Empire State Building?"

"I don't know why *people* often do the things they do," Mr. Howller said. "So how would I know why an *ape* does the things he does?"

When he was a block away from the Empire State, a plane crashed onto the middle of the avenue two blocks behind him and burned furiously. Tim Howller watched it for a few minutes, then he looked upward and saw the red and green lights of the five planes and the silvery bodies slipping in and out of the search-lights.

"Five airplanes, Grandpa? But the movie . . ."

"Yes, I know. The movie showed about fourteen or fifteen. But the book says that there were six to begin with, and the book is much more accurate. The movie also shows King Kong's last stand taking place in the daylight. But it didn't; it was still nighttime."

The Army Air Force plane must have been going at least 250 mph as it dived down toward the giant ape standing on the top of the observation tower. Kong had put Ann Redman by his feet so he could hang on to the tower with one hand and grab out with the other at the planes. One had come too close, and he had seized the left biplane structure and ripped it off. Given the energy of the plane, his hand should have been torn off, too, or at least he should have been pulled loose from his hold on the tower and gone down with the plane. But he hadn't let loose, and that told something of the enormous strength of that towering body. It also told something of the relative fragility of the biplane.

Young Howller had watched the efforts of the firemen to extinguish the fire and then he had turned back toward the Empire State Building. By then it was all over. All over for King Kong, anyway. It was, in after years, one of Mr. Howller's greatest regrets that he had not seen the monstrous dark body falling through the beams of the searchlights—blackness, then the flash of blackness through the whiteness of the highest beam, blackness, the flash through the next beam, blackness, the flash through the third beam, blackness, the flash through the lowest beam. Dot, dash, dot, dash, Mr. Howller was to think afterward. A code transmitted unconsciously by the great ape and received unconsciously by those who witnessed the fall. Or by those who would hear of it and think about it. Or was he going too far in conceiving this? Wasn't he always looking for codes? And, when he found them, unable to decipher them?

Since he had been thirteen, he had been trying to equate the great falls in man's myths and legends and to find some sort of intelligence in them. The fall of the tower of Babel, of Lucifer, of Vulcan, of Icarus, and, finally, of King Kong. But he wasn't equal to the task; he didn't have the genius to perceive what the falls meant, he couldn't screen out the—to use an electronic term—the "noise." All he could come up with were folk adages. What goes up must come down. The bigger they are, the harder they fall.

"What'd you say, Grandpa?"

"I was thinking out loud, if you can call that thinking," Mr. Howller said.

Young Howller had been one of the first on the scene, and so he got a place in the front of the crowd. He had not completely forgotten his parents or Aunt Thea, but the danger was over, and he could not make himself leave to search for them. And he had even forgotten about his soaked pants. The body was only about thirty feet from him. It lay on its back on the sidewalk, just as in the movie. But the dead Kong did not look as big or as dignified as in the movie. He was spread out more like an apeskin rug than a body, and blood and bowels and their contents had splashed out around him.

After a while Carl Denham, the man responsible for capturing Kong and bringing him to New York, appeared. As in the movie, Denham spoke his classical lines by the body: "It was Beauty. As always, Beauty killed the Beast."

This was the most appropriately dramatic place for the lines to be spoken, of course, and the proper place to end the movie.

But the book had Denham speaking these lines as he leaned over the parapet of the observation tower to look down at Kong on the sidewalk. His only audience was a police sergeant.

Both the book and the movie were true. Or half true. Denham did speak those lines way up on the 102nd floor of the tower. But, showman that he was, he also spoke them when he got down to the sidewalk, where the newsmen could hear them.

Young Howller didn't hear Denham's remarks. He was too far away. Besides, at that moment he felt a tap on his shoulder and heard a man say, "Hey, kid, there's somebody trying to get your attention!"

Young Howller went into his mother's arms and wept for at least a minute. His father reached past his mother and touched him briefly on the forehead, as if blessing him, and then gave his shoulder a squeeze. When he was able to talk, Tim Howller asked his mother what had happened to them. They, as near as they could remember, had been pushed out by the crowd, though they had fought to get to him, and had run up Broadway after they found themselves in the street because King Kong had appeared. They had managed to get back to the theater, had not been able to locate Tim, and had walked back to the Empire State Building.

"What happened to Uncle Nate?" Tim said.

Uncle Nate, his mother said, had caught up with them on Fifth Avenue and just now was trying to get past the police cordon into the building so he could check on Aunt Thea.

"She must be all right!" young Howller said. "The ape climbed up her side of the building, but she could easily get away from him, her apartment's so big!"

"Well, yes," his father had said. "But if she went to bed with her

headache, she would've been right next to the window. But don't
worry. If she'd been hurt, we'd know it. And maybe she wasn't
even home."

Young Tim had asked him what he meant by that, but his father
had only shrugged.

The three of them stood in the front line of the crowd, waiting
for Uncle Nate to bring news of Aunt Thea, even though they
weren't really worried about her, and waiting to see what happened to Kong. Mayor Jimmy Walker showed up and conferred
with the officials. Then the governor himself, Franklin Delano
Roosevelt, arrived with much noise of siren and motorcycle. A
minute later a big black limousine with flashing red lights and a
siren pulled up. Standing on the runningboard was a giant with
bronze hair and strange-looking gold-flecked eyes. He jumped off
the runningboard and strode up to the mayor, governor, and police commissioner and talked briefly with them. Tim Howller
asked the man next to him what the giant's name was, but the man
replied that he didn't know because he was from out of town also.
The giant finished talking and strode up to the crowd, which
opened for him as if it were the Red Sea and he were Moses, and
he had no trouble at all getting through the police cordon. Tim
then asked the man on the right of his parents if he knew the
yellow-eyed giant's name. This man, tall and thin, was with a
beautiful woman dressed up in an evening gown and a mink coat.
He turned his head when Tim called to him and presented a
hawklike face and eyes that burned so brightly that Tim wondered
if he took dope. Those eyes also told him that here was a man who
asked questions, not one who gave answers. Tim didn't repeat his
question, and a moment later the man said, in a whispering voice
that still carried a long distance, "Come on, Margo. I've work to
do." And the two melted into the crowd.

Mr. Howller told Jill about the two men, and she said, "What
about them, Grandpa?"

"I don't really know," he said. "Often I've wondered . . . Well,
never mind. Whoever they were, they're irrelevant to what happened to King Kong. But I'll say one thing about New York—you

sure see a lot of strange characters there."

Young Howller had expected that the mess would quickly be cleaned up. And it was true that the sanitation department had sent a big truck with a big crane and a number of men with hoses, scoop shovels, and brooms. But a dozen people at least stopped the cleanup almost before it began. Carl Denham wanted no one to touch the body except the taxidermists he had called in. If he couldn't exhibit a live Kong, he would exhibit a dead one. A colonel from Roosevelt Field claimed the body and, when asked why the Air Force wanted it, could not give an explanation. Rather, he refused to give one, and it was not until an hour later that a phone call from the White House forced him to reveal the real reason. A general wanted the skin for a trophy because Kong was the only ape ever shot down in aerial combat.

A lawyer for the owners of the Empire State Building appeared with a claim for possession of the body. His clients wanted reimbursement for the damage done to the building.

A representative of the transit system wanted Kong's body so it could be sold to help pay for the damage the ape had done to the Sixth Avenue Elevated.

The owner of the theater from which Kong had escaped arrived with his lawyer and announced he intended to sue Denham for an amount which would cover the sums he would have to pay to those who were inevitably going to sue him.

The police ordered the body seized as evidence in the trial for involuntary manslaughter and criminal negligence in which Denham and the theater owner would be defendants in due process.

The manslaughter charges were later dropped, but Denham did serve a year before being paroled. On being released, he was killed by a religious fanatic, a native brought back by the second expedition to Kong's island. He was, in fact, the witch doctor. He had murdered Denham because Denham had abducted and slain his god, Kong.

His Majesty's New York consul showed up with papers which proved that Kong's island was in British waters. Therefore, Denham had no right to anything removed from the island without permission of His Majesty's government.

Denham was in a lot of trouble. But the worst blow of all was to come next day. He would be handed notification that he was being sued by Ann Redman. She wanted compensation to the tune of ten million dollars for various physical indignities and injuries suffered during her two abductions by the ape, plus the mental anguish these had caused her. Unfortunately for her, Denham went to prison without a penny in his pocket, and she dropped the suit. Thus, the public never found out exactly what the "physical indignities and injuries" were, but this did not keep it from making many speculations. Ann Redman also sued John Driscoll, though for a different reason. She claimed breach of promise. Driscoll, interviewed by newsmen, made his famous remark that she should have been suing Kong, not him. This convinced most of the public that what it had suspected had indeed happened. Just how it could have been done was difficult to explain, but the public had never lacked wiseacres who would not only attempt the difficult but would not draw back even at the impossible.

Actually, Mr. Howller thought, the deed was not beyond possibility. Take an adult male gorilla who stood six feet high and weighed 350 pounds. According to Swiss zoo director Ernst Lang, he would have a full erection only two inches long. How did Professor Lang know this? Did he enter the cage during a mating and measure the phallus? Not very likely. Even the timid and amiable gorilla would scarcely submit to this type of handling in that kind of situation. Never mind. Professor Lang said it was so, and so it must be. Perhaps he used a telescope with gradations across the lens like those on a submarine's periscope. In any event, until someone entered the cage and slapped down a ruler during the action, Professor Lang's word would have to be taken as the last word.

By mathematical extrapolation, using the square-cube law, a gorilla twenty feet tall would have an erect penis about twenty-one inches long. What the diameter would be was another guess and perhaps a vital one, for Ann Redman anyway. Whatever anyone else thought about the possibility, Kong must have decided

that he would never know unless he tried. Just how well he succeeded, only he and his victim knew, since the attempt would
have taken place before Driscoll and Denham got to the observation tower and before the searchlight beams centered on their
target.

But Ann Redman must have told her lover, John Driscoll, the
truth, and he turned out not to be such a strong man after all.

"What're you thinking about, Grandpa?"

Mr. Howller looked at the screen. The Roadrunner had been
succeeded by the Pink Panther, who was enduring as much pain
and violence as the poor old coyote.

"Nothing," he said. "I'm just watching the Pink Panther with
you."

"But you didn't say what happened to King Kong," she said.

"Oh," he said, "we stood around until dawn, and then the big
shots finally came to some sort of agreement. The body just
couldn't be left there much longer, if for no other reason than that
it was blocking traffic. Blocking traffic meant that business would
be held up. And lots of people would lose lots of money. And so
Kong's body was taken away by the Police Department, though it
used the Sanitation Department's crane, and it was kept in an
icehouse until its ownership could be thrashed out."

"Poor Kong."

"No," he said, "not poor Kong. He was dead and out of it."

"He went to heaven?"

"As much as anybody," Mr. Howller said.

"But he killed a lot of people, and he carried off that nice girl.
Wasn't he bad?"

"No, he wasn't bad. He was an animal, and he didn't know the
difference between good and evil. Anyway, even if he'd been
human, he would've been doing what any human would have
done."

"What do you mean, Grandpa?"

"Well, if you were captured by people only a foot tall and carried off to a far place and put in a cage, wouldn't you try to escape?
And if these people tried to put you back in, or got so scared that

they tried to kill you right now, wouldn't you step on them?"

"Sure, I'd step on them, Grandpa."

"You'd be justified, too. And King Kong was justified. He was only acting according to the dictates of his instincts."

"What?"

"He was an animal, and so he can't be blamed, no matter what he did. He wasn't evil. It was what happened around Kong that was evil."

"What do you mean?" Jill said.

"He brought out the bad and the good in the people."

But mostly bad, he thought, and he encouraged Jill to forget about Kong and concentrate on the Pink Panther. And as he looked at the screen, he saw it through tears. Even after forty-two years, he thought, tears. This was what the fall of Kong had meant to him.

The crane had hooked the corpse and lifted it up. And there were two flattened-out bodies under Kong; he must have dropped them onto the sidewalk on his way up and then fallen on them from the tower. But how explain the nakedness of the corpses of the man and the woman?

The hair of the woman was long and, in a small area not covered by blood, yellow. And part of her face was recognizable.

Young Tim had not known until then that Uncle Nate had returned from looking for Aunt Thea. Uncle Nate gave a long wailing cry that sounded as if he, too, were falling from the top of the Empire State Building.

A second later young Tim Howller was wailing. But where Uncle Nate's was the cry of betrayal, and perhaps of revenge satisfied, Tim's was both of betrayal and of grief for the death of one he had passionately loved with a thirteen-year-old's love, for one whom the thirteen-year-old in him still loved.

"Grandpa, are there any more King Kongs?"

"No," Mr. Howller said. To say yes would force him to try to explain something that she could not understand. When she got older, she would know that every dawn saw the death of the old Kong and the birth of the new.

URSULA LE GUIN

The Day Before the Revolution

"The Day Before the Revolution" won the Nebula Award for the best science-fiction short story of 1974. Ursula's *The Dispossessed* won the Nebula Award and the Hugo Award for the best novel of 1974. The Le Guin award-winning spree began with her 1969 novel *The Left Hand of Darkness,* which won both the Nebula and Hugo awards and to my mind did more to exploit the potential of the science-fiction novel than anything published to that time; and it continued with her Hugo novella of 1971, "The Word for World Is Forest," her Hugo short story of 1973, "The Ones Who Walk Away from Omelas," and the 1973 National Book Award in children's literature for her novel *The Farthest Shore.* Ursula comes naturally to writing and to science: her mother was an author, her father an anthropologist; her husband is a Portland State College professor of French history, and she herself, besides her family of three children, possesses an advanced degree in French and Italian Renaissance literature. The story that follows is cut from the same fictional tapestry as *The Dispossessed.*

The speaker's voice was loud as empty beer-trucks in a stone street, and the people at the meeting were jammed up close, cobblestones, that great voice booming over them. Taviri was somewhere on the other side of the hall. She had to get to him. She wormed and pushed her way among the dark-clothed, close-packed people. She did not hear the words, nor see the faces: only the booming, and the bodies pressed one behind the other. She could not see Taviri, she was too short. A broad black-vested belly and chest loomed up blocking her way. She must get through to Taviri. Sweating, she jabbed fiercely with her fist. It was like hitting stones, he did not move at all, but the huge lungs let out right over her head a prodigious noise, a bellow. She cowered. Then she understood that the bellow had not been at her. Others were shouting. The speaker had said something, something fine about taxes or shadows. Thrilled, she joined the shouting—"Yes! Yes!"— and shoving on, came out easily into the open expanse of the Regimental Drill Field in Parheo. Overhead the evening sky lay deep and colorless, and all around her nodded the tall weeds with dry, white, close-floreted heads. She had never known what they were called. The flowers nodded above her head, swaying in the wind that always blew across the fields in the dusk. She ran among them, and they whipped lithe aside and stood up again swaying, silent. Taviri stood among the tall weeds in his good suit, the dark grey one that made him look like a professor or a play-actor, harshly elegant. He did not look happy, but he was laughing, and saying something to her. The sound of his voice made her cry, and she reached out to catch hold of his hand, but she did not stop, quite. She could not stop. "Oh, Taviri," she said, "it's just on there!" The queer sweet smell of the white weeds was heavy as she went on. There were thorns, tangles underfoot, there were slopes, pits. She feared to fall . . . she stopped.

Sun, bright morning-glare, straight in the eyes, relentless. She had forgotten to pull the blind last night. She turned her back on the sun, but the right side wasn't comfortable. No use. Day. She sighed twice, sat up, got her legs over the edge of the bed, and sat hunched in her nightdress looking down at her feet.

The toes, compressed by a lifetime of cheap shoes, were almost square where they touched each other, and bulged out above in corns; the nails were discolored and shapeless. Between the knob-like ankle bones ran fine, dry wrinkles. The brief little plain at the base of the toes had kept its delicacy, but the skin was the color of mud, and knotted veins crossed the instep. Disgusting. Sad, depressing. Mean. Pitiful. She tried on all the words, and they all fit, like hideous little hats. Hideous: yes, that one too. To look at oneself and find it hideous, what a job! But then, when she hadn't been hideous, had she sat around and stared at herself like this? Not much! A proper body's not an object, not an implement, not a belonging to be admired, it's just you, yourself. Only when it's no longer you, but yours, a thing owned, do you worry about it— Is it in good shape? Will it do? Will it last?

"Who cares?" said Laia fiercely, and stood up.

It made her giddy to stand up suddenly. She had to put out her hand to the bedtable, for she dreaded falling. At that she thought of reaching out to Taviri, in the dream.

What had he said? She could not remember. She was not sure if she had even touched his hand. She frowned, trying to force memory. It had been so long since she had dreamed about Taviri;

and now not even to remember what he had said!

It was gone, it was gone. She stood there hunched in her night-dress, frowning, one hand on the bedtable. How long was it since she had thought of him—let alone dreamed of him—even thought of him, as "Taviri"? How long since she had said his name?

Asieo said. When Asieo and I were in prison in the North. Before I met Asieo. Asieo's theory of reciprocity. Oh yes, she talked about him, talked about him too much no doubt, maundered, dragged him in. But as "Asieo," the last name, the public man. The private man was gone, utterly gone. There were so few left who had even known him. They had all used to be in jail. One laughed about it on those days, all the friends in all the jails. But they weren't even there, these days. They were in the prison cemeteries. Or in the common graves.

"Oh, oh my dear," Laia said out loud, and she sank down onto the bed again because she could not stand up under the remembrance of those first weeks in the Fort, in the cell, those first weeks of the nine years in the Fort in Drio, in the cell, those first weeks after they told her that Asieo had been killed in the fighting in Capitol Square and had been buried with the Fourteen Hundred in the lime-ditches behind Oring Gate. In the cell. Her hands fell into the old position on her lap, the left clenched and locked inside the grip of the right, the right thumb working back and forth a little pressing and rubbing on the knuckle of the left first finger. Hours, days, nights. She had thought of them all, each one, each one of the fourteen hundred, how they lay, how the quicklime worked on the flesh, how the bones touched in the burning dark. Who touched him? How did the slender bones of the hand lie now? Hours, years.

"Taviri, I have never forgotten you!" she whispered, and the stupidity of it brought her back to morning-light and the rumpled bed. Of course she hadn't forgotten him. These things go without saying between husband and wife. There were her ugly old feet flat on the floor again, just as before. She had got nowhere at all, she had gone in a circle. She stood up with a grunt of effort and disapproval, and went to the closet for her dressing gown.

The young people went about the halls of the House in becoming immodesty, but she was too old for that. She didn't want to spoil some young man's breakfast with the sight of her. Besides, they had grown up in the principle of freedom of dress and sex and all the rest, and she hadn't. All she had done was invent it. It's not the same.

Like speaking of Asieo as "my husband." They winced. The word she should use as a good Odonian, of course, was "partner." But why the hell did she have to be a good Odonian?

She shuffled down the hall to the bathrooms. Mairo was there, washing her hair in a lavatory. Laia looked at the long, sleek, wet hank with admiration. She got out of the Houso so seldom now that she didn't know when she had last seen a respectably shaven scalp, but still the sight of a full head of hair gave her pleasure, vigorous pleasure. How many times had she been jeered at, *Longhair, Longhair,* had her hair pulled by policemen or young toughs, had her hair shaved off down to the scalp by a grinning soldier at each new prison? And then had grown it all over again, through the fuzz, to the frizz, to the curls, to the mane . . . In the old days. For God's love, couldn't she think of anything today but the old days?

Dressed, her bed made, she went down to commons. It was a good breakfast, but she had never got her appetite back since the damned stroke. She drank two cups of herb tea, but couldn't finish the piece of fruit she had taken. How she had craved fruit as a child, badly enough to steal it; and in the Fort—oh for God's love stop it! She smiled and replied to the greetings and friendly inquiries of the other breakfasters and big Aevi who was serving the counter this morning. It was he who had tempted her with the peach, "Look at this, I've been saving it for you," and how could she refuse? Anyway she had always loved fruit, and never got enough; once when she was six or seven she had stolen a piece off a vendor's cart in River Street. But it was hard to eat when everyone was talking so excitedly. There was news from Thu, real news. She was inclined to discount it at first, being wary of enthusiasms, but after she had read the article in the paper, and read between the lines of it, she thought, with a strange kind of certainty, deep

but cold, Why, this is it; it has come. And in Thu, not here. Thu
will break before this country does; the Revolution will first pre-
vail there. As if that mattered! There will be no more nations. And
yet it did matter somehow, it made her a little cold and sad—
envious, in fact. Of all the infinite stupidities. She did not join the
talk much, and soon got up to go back to her room, feeling sorry
for herself. She could not share their excitement. She was out of
it, really out of it. It's not easy, she said to herself in justification,
laboriously climbing the stairs, to accept being out of it when
you've been in it, in the center of it, for fifty years. Oh for God's
love. Whining!

She got the stairs and the self-pity behind her, entering her
room. It was a good room, and it was good to be by herself. It was
a great relief. Even if it wasn't strictly fair. Some of the kids in the
attics were living five to a room no bigger than this. There were
always more people wanting to live in an Odonian House than
could be properly accommodated. She had this big room all to
herself only because she was an old woman who had had a stroke.
And maybe because she was Odo. If she hadn't been Odo, but
merely the old woman with a stroke, would she have had it? Very
likely. After all who the hell wanted to room with a drooling old
woman? But it was hard to be sure. Favoritism, elitism, leader-
worship, they crept back and cropped out everywhere. But she
had never hoped to see them eradicated in her lifetime, in one
generation; only Time works the great changes. Meanwhile this
was a nice, large, sunny room, proper for a drooling old woman
who had started a world revolution.

Her secretary would be coming in an hour to help her dispatch
the day's work. She shuffled over to the desk, a beautiful, big piece,
a present from the Nio Cabinetmakers' Syndicate because somebody had heard her remark once that the only piece of furniture
she had ever really longed for was a desk with drawers and enough
room on top . . . damn, the top was practically covered with papers
with notes clipped to them, mostly in Noi's small clear handwriting: Urgent.—Northern Provinces.—Consult w/R.T.?

Her own handwriting had never been the same since Asieo's

death. It was odd, when you thought about it. After all, within five
years after his death she had written the whole *Analogy*. And
there were those letters, which the tall guard with the watery grey
eyes, what was his name, never mind, had smuggled out of the
Fort for her for two years. *The Prison Letters* they called them
now, there were a dozen different editions of them. All that stuff,
the letters which people kept telling her were so full of "spiritual
strength"—which probably meant she had been lying herself blue
in the face when she wrote them, trying to keep her spirits up—
and the *Analogy* which was certainly the solidest intellectual
work she had ever done, all of that had been written in the Fort
in Drio, in the cell, after Asieo's death. One had to do something,
and in the Fort they let one have paper and pens. . . . But it had
all been written in the hasty, scribbling hand which she had never
felt was hers, not her own like the round, black scrollings of the
manuscript of *Society Without Government*, forty-five years old.
Taviri had taken not only her body's and her heart's desire to the
quicklime with him, but even her good clear handwriting.

But he had left her the revolution.
How brave of you to go on, to work, to write, in prison, after such
a defeat for the Movement, after your partner's death, people had
used to say. Damn fools. What else had there been to do? Bravery,
courage—what was courage? She had never figured it out. Not
fearing, some said. Fearing yet going on, others said. But what
could one do but go on? Had one any real choice, ever?
To die was merely to go on in another direction.
If you wanted to come home you had to keep going on, that was
what she meant when she wrote, "True journey is return," but it
had never been more than an intuition, and she was farther than
ever now from being able to rationalise it. She bent down, too
suddenly, so that she grunted a little at the creak in her bones, and
began to root in a bottom drawer of the desk. Her hand came to
an age-softened folder and drew it out, recognizing it by touch
before sight confirmed: the manuscript of *Syndical Organization
in Revolutionary Transition*. He had printed the title on the

folder and written his name under it, Taviri Odo Asieo, IX 741.
There was an elegant handwriting, every letter well-formed, bold,
and fluent. But he had preferred to use a voiceprinter. The manuscript was all in voiceprint, and high quality too, hesitancies ad-
justed and idiosyncrasies of speech normalized. You couldn't see
there how he had said "o" deep in his throat as they did on the
North Coast. There was nothing of him there but his mind. She
had nothing of him at all except his name written on the folder.
She hadn't kept his letters, it was sentimental to keep letters.
Besides, she never kept anything. She couldn't think of anything
that she had ever owned for more than a few years, except this
ramshackle old body, of course, and she was stuck with that. . . .

Dualizing again. "She" and "it." Age and illness made one dual-
ist, made one escapist; the mind insisted, *It's not me, it's not me.*
But it was. Maybe the mystics could detach mind from body, she
had always rather wistfully envied them the chance, without hope
of emulating them. Escape had never been her game. She had
sought for freedom here, now, body and soul.

First self-pity, then self-praise, and here she still sat, for God's
love, holding Asieo's name in her hand, why? Didn't she know his
name without looking it up? What was wrong with her? She raised
the folder to her lips and kissed the handwritten name firmly and
squarely, replaced the folder in the back of the bottom drawer,
shut the drawer, and straightened up in the chair. Her right hand
tingled. She scratched it, and then shook it in the air, spitefully. It
had never quite got over the stroke. Neither had her right leg, or
right eye, or the right corner of her mouth. They were sluggish,
inept, they tingled. They made her feel like a robot with a short
circuit.

And time was getting on, Noi would be coming, what had she
been doing ever since breakfast?

She got up so hastily that she lurched, and grabbed at the
chairback to make sure she did not fall. She went down the hall
to the bathroom and looked in the big mirror there. Her grey
knot was loose and droopy, she hadn't done it up well before
breakfast. She struggled with it awhile. It was hard to keep her

arms up in the air. Amai, running in to piss, stopped and said, "Let me do it!" and knotted it up tight and neat in no time, with her round, strong, pretty fingers, smiling and silent. Amai was twenty, less than a third of Laia's age. Her parents had both been members of the Movement, one killed in the insurrection of '60, the other still recruiting in the South Provinces. Amai had grown up in Odonian Houses, born to the Revolution, a true daughter of anarchy. And so quiet and free and beautiful a child, enough to make you cry when you thought: this is what we worked for, this is what we meant, this is it, here she is, alive, the kindly, lovely future.

Laia Osaieo Odo's right eye wept several little tears as she stood between the lavatories and the latrines having her hair done up by the daughter she had not borne; but her left eye, the strong one, did not weep, nor did it know what the right eye did.

She thanked Amai and hurried back to her room. She had noticed, in the mirror, a stain on her collar. Peach juice, probably. Damned old dribbler. She didn't want Noi to come in and find her with drool on her collar.

As the clean shirt went on over her head, she thought, What's so special about Noi?

She fastened the collar-frogs with her left hand, slowly.

Noi was thirty or so, a slight, muscular fellow with a soft voice and alert dark eyes. That's what was special about Noi. It was that simple. Good old sex. She had never been drawn to a fair man or a fat one, or the tall fellows with big biceps, never, not even when she was fourteen and fell in love with every passing fart. Dark, spare, and fiery, that was the recipe. Taviri, of course. This boy wasn't a patch on Taviri for brains, nor even for looks, but there it was: She didn't want him to see her with dribble on her collar and her hair coming undone.

Her thin, grey hair.

Noi came in, just pausing in the open doorway—my God, she hadn't even shut the door while changing her shirt!—She looked at him and saw herself. The old woman.

You could brush your hair and change your shirt, or you could wear last week's shirt and last night's braids, or you could put on cloth of gold and dust your shaven scalp with diamond powder. None of it would make the slightest difference. The old woman would look a little less, or a little more, grotesque.

One keeps oneself neat out of mere decency, mere sanity, awareness of other people.

And finally even that goes, and one dribbles unashamed.

"Good morning," the young man said in his gentle voice.

"Hello, Noi."

No, by God, it was *not* out of mere decency. Decency be damned. Because the man she had loved, and to whom her age would not have mattered—because he was dead, must she pretend she had no sex? Must she suppress the truth, like a damned puritan authoritarian? Even six months ago, before the stroke, she had made men look at her and like to look at her; and now, though she could give no pleasure, by God she could please herself.

When she was six years old, and Papa's friend Gadeo used to come by to talk politics with Papa after dinner, she would put on the gold-colored necklace that Mama had found on a trash-heap and brought home for her. It was so short that it always got hidden under her collar where nobody could see it. She liked it that way. She knew she had it on. She sat on the doorstep and listened to them talk, and knew that she looked nice for Gadeo. He was dark, with white teeth that flashed. Sometimes he called her "pretty Laia." "There's my pretty Laia!" Sixty-six years ago.

"What? My head's dull. I had a terrible night." It was true. She had slept even less than usual.

"I was asking if you'd seen the papers this morning."

She nodded.

"Pleased about Soinehe?"

Soinehe was the province in Thu which had declared its secession from the Thuvian State last night.

He was pleased about it. His white teeth flashed in his dark, alert face. Pretty Laia.

"Yes. And apprehensive."

"I know. But it's the real thing, this time. It's the beginning of the end of the Government in Thu. They haven't even tried to order troops into Soinehe, you know. It would merely provoke the soldiers into rebellion sooner, and they know it."

She agreed with him. She herself had felt that certainty. But she could not share his delight. After a lifetime of living on hope because there is nothing but hope, one loses the taste for victory. A real sense of triumph must be preceded by real despair. She had unlearned despair a long time ago. There were no more triumphs. One went on.

"Shall we do those letters today?"

"All right. Which letters?"

"To the people in the North," he said without impatience.

"In the North?"

"Parheo, Oaidun."

She had been born in Parheo, the dirty city on the dirty river. She had not come here to the capital till she was twenty-two and ready to bring the Revolution. Though in those days, before she and the others had thought it through, it had been a very green and puerile revolution. Strikes for better wages, representation for women. Votes and wages—Power and Money, for the love of God! Well, one does learn a little, after all, in fifty years.

But then one must forget it all.

"Start with Oaidun," she said, sitting down in the armchair. Noi was at the desk ready to work. He read out excerpts from the letters she was to answer. She tried to pay attention, and succeeded well enough that she dictated one whole letter and started on another. "Remember that at this stage your brotherhood is vulnerable to the threat of . . . no, to the danger . . . to . . ." She groped till Noi suggested, "The danger of leader-worship?"

"All right. And that nothing is so soon corrupted by power-seeking as altruism. No. And that nothing corrupts altruism—no. Oh for God's love you know what I'm trying to say, Noi, you write it. They know it too, it's just the same old stuff, why can't they read my books!"

"Touch," Noi said gently, smiling, citing one of the central Odonian themes.

"All right, but I'm tired of being touched. If you'll write the letter I'll sign it, but I can't be bothered with it this morning." He was looking at her with a little question or concern. She said, irritable, "There is something else I have to do!"

When Noi had gone she sat down at the desk and moved the papers about, pretending to be doing something, because she had been startled, frightened, by the words she had said. She had nothing else to do. She never had had anything else to do. This was her work: her lifework. The speaking tours and the meetings and the streets were out of reach for her now, but she could still write, and that was her work. And anyhow if she had had anything else to do, Noi would have known it; he kept her schedule, and tactfully reminded her of things, like the visit from the foreign students this afternoon.

Oh, damn. She liked the young, and there was always something to learn from a foreigner, but she was tired of new faces, and tired of being on view. She learned from them, but they didn't learn from her; they had learnt all she had to teach long ago, from her books, from the Movement. They just came to look, as if she were the Great Tower in Rodarred, or the Canyon of the Tulaevea. A phenomenon, a monument. They were awed, adoring. She snarled at them: Think your own thoughts!—That's not anarchism, that's mere obscurantism.—You don't think liberty and discipline are incompatible, do you?—They accepted their tonguelashing meekly as children, gratefully, as if she were some kind of All-Mother, the idol of the Big Sheltering Womb. She! She who had mined the shipyards at Seissero, and had cursed Premier Inoilte to his face in front of a crowd of seven thousand, telling him he would have cut off his own balls and had them bronzed and sold as souvenirs, if he thought there was any profit in it—she who had screeched, and sworn, and kicked policemen, and spat at priests, and pissed in public on the big brass plaque in Capitol Square that said HERE WAS FOUNDED THE SOVEREIGN NATION STATE OF A-IO ETC. ETC. pssssssss to all that! And now she was everybody's grandmama, the dear old lady, the sweet old monument, come worship at the womb. The fire's out, boys, it's safe to come up close.

"No, I won't," Laia said out loud. "I will not." She was not self-conscious about talking to herself, because she always had talked to herself. "Laia's invisible audience," Taviri had used to say, as she went through the room muttering. "You needn't come, I won't be here," she told the invisible audience now. She had just decided what it was she had to do. She had to go out. To go into the streets.

It was inconsiderate to disappoint the foreign students. It was erratic, typically senile. It was un-Odonian. Pssssss to all that. What was the good working for freedom all your life and ending up without any freedom at all? She would go out for a walk.

"What is an anarchist? One who, choosing, accepts the responsibility of choice."

On the way downstairs she decided, scowling, to stay and see the foreign students. But then she would go out.

They were very young students, very earnest: doe-eyed, shaggy, charming creatures from the Western Hemisphere, Benbili and the Kingdom of Mand, the girls in white trousers, the boys in long kilts, warlike and archaic. They spoke of their hopes. "We in Mand are so very far from the Revolution that maybe we are near it," said one of the girls, wistful and smiling: "The Circle of Life!" and she showed the extremes meeting, in the circle of her slender, dark-skinned fingers. Amai and Aevi served them white wine and brown bread, the hospitality of the House. But the visitors, unpresumptuous, all rose to take their leave after barely half an hour. "No, no, no," Laia said, "stay here, talk with Aevi and Amai. It's just that I get stiff sitting down, you see, I have to change about. It has been so good to meet you, will you come back to see me, my little brothers and sisters, soon?" For her heart went out to them, and theirs to her, and she exchanged kisses all round, laughing, delighted by the dark young cheeks, the affectionate eyes, the scented hair, before she shuffled off. She was really a little tired, but to go up and take a nap would be a defeat. She had wanted to go out. She would go out. She had not been alone outdoors since —when? since winter! before the stroke. No wonder she was get-

ting morbid. It had been a regular jail sentence. Outside, the
streets, that's where she lived.

She went quietly out the side door of the House, past the vegeta-
ble patch, to the street. The narrow strip of sour city dirt had been
beautifully gardened and was producing a fine crop of beans and
ceea, but Laia's eye for farming was unenlightened. Of course it
had been clear that anarchist communities, even in the time of
transition, must work towards optimal self-support, but how that
was to be managed in the way of actual dirt and plants wasn't her
business. There were farmers and agronomists for that. Her job
was the streets, the noisy, stinking streets of stone, where she had
grown up and lived all her life, except for the fifteen years in
prison.

She looked up fondly at the façade of the House. That it had
been built as a bank gave peculiar satisfaction to its present occu-
pants. They kept their sacks of meal in the bombproof money-
vault, and aged their cider in kegs in safe-deposit boxes. Over the
fussy columns that faced the street, carved letters still read, "NA-
TIONAL INVESTORS AND GRAIN FACTORS BANKING ASSOCIATION."
The Movement was not strong on names. They had no flag. Slo-
gans came and went as the need did. There was always the Circle
of Life to scratch on walls and pavements where Authority would
have to see it. But when it came to names they were indifferent,
accepting and ignoring whatever they got called, afraid of being
pinned down and penned in, unafraid of being absurd. So this best
known and second oldest of all the cooperative Houses had no
name except The Bank.

It faced on a wide and quiet street, but only a block away began
the Temeba, an open market, once famous as a center for black-
market psychogenics and teratogenics, now reduced to vegetables, secondhand clothes, and miserable sideshows. Its crapulous
vitality was gone, leaving only half-paralysed alcoholics, addicts,
cripples, hucksters, and fifth-rate whores, pawnshops, gambling
dens, fortunetellers, body sculptors, and cheap hotels. Laia turned
to the Temeba as water seeks its level.

She had never feared or despised the city. It was her country.

There would not be slums like this, if the Revolution prevailed. But there would be misery. There would always be misery, waste, cruelty. She had never pretended to be changing the human condition, to be Mama taking tragedy away from the children so they won't hurt themselves. Anything but. So long as people were free to choose, if they chose to drink flybane and live in sewers, it was their business. Just so long as it wasn't the business of Business, the source of profit and the means of power for other people. She had felt all that before she knew anything; before she wrote the first pamphlet, before she left Parheo, before she knew what "capital" meant, before she'd been farther than River Street where she played rolltaggie kneeling on scabby knees on the pavement with the other six-year-olds. She had known it: that she, and the other kids, and her parents, and their parents, and the drunks and whores and all of River Street, was at the bottom of something— was the foundation, the reality, the source.

But will you drag civilisation down into the mud? cried the shocked decent people, later on, and she had tried for years to explain to them that if all you had was mud, then if you were God you made it into human beings, and if you were human you tried to make it into houses where human beings could live. But nobody who thought he was better than mud would understand. Now, water seeking its level, mud to mud, Laia shuffled through the foul, noisy street, and all the ugly weakness of her old age was at home. The sleepy whores, their lacquered hair-arrangements dilapidated and askew, the one-eyed woman wearily yelling her vegetables to sell, the halfwit beggar slapping flies, these were her countrywomen. They looked like her, they were all sad, disgusting, mean, pitiful, hideous. They were her sisters, her own people.

She did not feel very well. It had been a long time since she had walked so far, four or five blocks, by herself, in the noise and push and stinking summer heat of the streets. She had wanted to get to Koly Park, the triangle of scruffy grass at the end of the Temeba, and sit there for a while with the other old men and women who always sat there, to see what it was like to sit there and be old; but it was too far. If she didn't turn back now, she might get a dizzy spell, and she had a dread of falling down, falling down and having to lie there and look up at the people come to stare at the old woman in a fit. She turned and started home, frowning with effort and self-disgust. She could feel her face very red, and a swimming feeling came and went in her ears. It got a bit much, she was really afraid she might keel over. She saw a doorstep in the shade and made for it, let herself down cautiously, sat, sighed.

Nearby was a fruit-seller, sitting silent behind his dusty, withered stock. People went by. Nobody bought from him. Nobody looked at her. Odo, who was Odo? Famous revolutionary, author of *Community, The Analogy,* etc. etc. She, who was she? An old woman with grey hair and a red face sitting on a dirty doorstep in a slum, muttering to herself.

True? Was that she? Certainly it was what anybody passing her saw. But was it she, herself, any more than the famous revolutionary, etc., was? No. It was not. But who was she, then?

The one who loved Taviri.

Yes. True enough. But not enough. That was gone; he had been dead so long.

"Who am I?" Laia muttered to her invisible audience, and they knew the answer and told it to her with one voice. She was the little girl with scabby knees, sitting on the doorstep staring down through the dirty golden haze of River Street in the heat of late summer, the six-year-old, the sixteen-year-old, the fierce, cross, dream-ridden girl, untouched, untouchable. She was herself. Indeed she had been the tireless worker and thinker, but a bloodclot in a vein had taken that woman away from her. Indeed she had been the lover, the swimmer in the midst of life, but Taviri, dying, had taken that woman away with him. There was nothing left, really, but the foundations. She had come home; she had never left home. "True voyage is return." Dust and mud and a doorstep in the slums. And beyond, at the far end of the street, the field full of tall dry weeds blowing in the wind as night came.

"Laia! What are you doing here? Are you all right?"

One of the people from the House, of course, a nice woman, a bit fanatical and always talking. Laia could not remember her name though she had known her for years. She let herself be taken home, the woman talking all the way. In the big cool common-room (once occupied by tellers counting money behind polished counters supervised by armed guards) Laia sat down in a chair. She was unable just as yet to face climbing the stairs, though she would have liked to be alone. The woman kept on talking, and other excited people came in. It appeared that a demonstration was being planned. Events in Thu were moving so fast that the mood here had caught fire, and something must be done. Day after tomorrow, no, tomorrow, there was to be a march, a big one, from Old Town to Capitol Square—the old route. "Another Ninth Month Uprising," said a young man, fiery and laughing, glancing at Laia. He had not even been born at the time of the Ninth Month Uprising, it was all history to him. Now he wanted to make some history of his own. The room had filled up. A general meeting would be held here, tomorrow, at eight in the morning. "You must talk, Laia."

"Tomorrow? Oh, I won't be here tomorrow," she said brusquely. Whoever had asked her smiled, another one laughed, though Amai glanced round at her with a puzzled look. They went on talking and shouting. The Revolution. What on earth had made her say that? What a thing to say on the eve of the Revolution, even if it was true.

She waited her time, managed to get up and, for all her clumsiness, to slip away unnoticed among the people busy with their planning and excitement. She got to the hall, to the stairs, and began to climb them one by one. "The general strike," a voice, two voices, ten voices were saying in the room below, behind her. "The general strike," Laia muttered, resting for a moment on the landing. Above, ahead, in her room, what awaited her? The private stroke. That was mildly funny. She started up the second flight of stairs, one by one, one leg at a time, like a small child. She was dizzy, but she was no longer afraid to fall. On ahead, on there, the dry white flowers nodded and whispered in the open fields of evening. Seventy-two years and she had never had time to learn what they were called.

C. L. GRANT

The Rest Is Silence

C. L. Grant is executive secretary of the Science Fiction Writers of America. Like all SFWA's officers, he also is a working science-fiction writer. He lives in New Jersey, has a bachelor's degree in history, a wife, two years of service in Vietnam, a teaching position in high school (until recently), and has sold twenty-three science-fiction stories in addition to the following novelette, a story that suggests (like Tom Reamy's "Twilla") that more goes on in high school than any of us remember.

Beware of dreamers: *that would be my epitaph if I could have a grave to go to when I die. But all there is now is a rambling, shrinking house, and a fog that wisps away my words as I speak. I have committed suicide (unaware) and have been murdered for it (all too aware); but if I have to shift the unbearable blame for this madness elsewhere, it has to go to Julius Caesar, late of Rome and the Elizabethan stage. After all, if he hadn't gotten himself so famously killed, Shakespeare would have never written a play about it nor would I have had to teach it. Yet he did, and I did, so here we are. And now I know all too well just where that is.*

After the fact, events have a diabolical way of falling into place that makes a curse of hindsight and hell for the present. Case in point: a Wednesday in October and a perfectly ordinary English Department meeting. Chandler Jolliet, the commandingly tall chairman, was quietly and efficiently razoring our confidence in our collective abilities. Apparently a virgin member of our troupe had decided not to concentrate on *Julius Caesar*'s examination of power, but rather on the in-depth characterization of the conspirators, Brutus in particular. God forbid that we should deviate from the chartered lanes of the courses of study, but this youngster, fresh from college with stars in his eyes, had taken it upon himself to do just that, and we were all suffering for it. Jolliet's

147

sycophants and friends were murmuring and nodding; and the rest of us, who had endured this brand of tirade before, were daydreaming, planning our Christmas vacations and plotting assassinations of our own. And when the hour-and-a-half tantrum was over, we nodded our heads in sage obeisance and shuffled out, as slaves must have done before the overseer's whip. In the hall, however, the culprit, Marty Schubert, cornered me and Valerie Stern to press his case.

"I don't understand," he said. "What's so holy about *Caesar* that I can't talk about something new for a change? I'm not saying Jollie's way is better or worse, but for God's sake, what the hell does he have against me? What did I do that he hates me?"

"Not a thing," Val said, guiding him gently by the arm away from Jolliet's open office door. "It's just his way of breaking you in." She looked back at me and smiled. "Eddie's been through it. So have I. You just have to grin and bear it."

"Why?" he demanded as anguish and anger gathered in his features like thunderclouds.

"Because we need the jobs, Marty," I said, not liking the sound of my voice, so recently like his, so recently crushed. "There are too many teachers and not enough jobs. Val, me, and a few others, we've been around much too long to go hunting for other positions. Who'd hire us when they could have newcomers at half the salary? The only thing we can do is play the game, Sam. Play the game and hope he has a heart attack, or a lingering case of diarrhea."

Marty stared, not quite sure if I were serious. Finally he decided I wasn't and laughed. But his cheeks were still flushed and his eyes glinting, as if he'd been repeatedly slapped. We signed out in silence, and in the parking lot Val and I watched him slump to his car and drive slowly away. Val, her eyes hidden by uncut bangs as black as my mood, shook her head. "He's a smart kid, Eddie. It's a shame to see the old bastard do him in like that."

I could only shrug, and she accepted that as a sign of the times under which we lived. We parted, silently, and I drove home much faster than I'd intended, for there was nothing for me there.

The apartment was still the hospital-white, bare-floored cell I'd resigned myself to when I finally realized there was no place else for me to go. I wasn't clever enough to quit and enter business, nor was I ambitious enough to climb out of the classroom into administration. Sometimes I entertained the spirit of Mr. Chips and envisioned thousands of ex-students tearfully waving goodbye at my retirement. A farce for all that: I could barely remember the names of kids I'd taught the year before, much less those I'd challenged in my virgin year.

It rained that night, if I recall correctly. My unlisted telephone continuod collecting dust. The end of a perfect day. And the world kept spinning.

The following morning, however, with the sun barely risen, the telephone scared the hell out of me by working.

"Eddie?"

"Marty, that you?" I was still asleep. I must have been, or his actor's deep voice would have identified him immediately.

"Eddie, listen, I can't go back. Not after what he's done to me."

That woke me up. "Whoa, son, hang on a minute. Don't let that creep get to you like that."

"I'm sorry, Eddie, but I can't do it. I understand your position, really, and I'm not kidding, but I've been thinking it over. In fact, I haven't slept all night. I just can't go back and face him. Would you do me a favor and stop over on your way in? You can take my books and stuff in with you. My resignation too."

Since I was still rather foggy, all I did was mumble an agreement, take a shower and fix myself some instant breakfast. I made a quick call to the school, telling the secretary I might be a little late, car trouble, and hung up before she could get too nosy. On the way to Marty's rented duplex, I kept the window rolled down to wake me up. I was worried. Marty was one of the brightest, most dedicated teachers I had known, and somehow I had to keep him with us. If for no other reason than he actually liked the kids he worked with, and they, in turn, held him in enormous respect.

He opened his front door immediately when I knocked. He was dressed for work, but unshaven, and his breath as he welcomed me told me what he'd been thinking with. He was sober, though, and solemnly waved me to a chair.

"Marty, listen—"

"I know, I know, Ed. I'm cutting my career out from under me, right? Nobody's going to hire a teacher who quit before Christmas for reasons like mine, right? You want me to last out the year, find another school and then tell him to shove it. Right?"

All I could do was nod, and he laughed at my confusion and the wind spilling from my best noble speech. To my surprise, he nodded too.

"Well, you are right. I've been sitting here watching the sun and the clock, and I've decided to do just that. I'm going to smile if it kills me, then do what I want when he's not looking. Maybe," he added, grinning, "I can help drive him to that early retirement you guys are always talking about."

"I wish you all the luck in the world," I said, returning the grin, though more relieved that he was still with us than responding to his humor.

"But listen, Eddie," he said. "I'll tell you one thing: I'm not going to take that kind of abuse in public again. And neither is anyone else." And for a frightening moment, his anger returned.

"Sure thing. Whatever you say, Marty," I said, standing quickly. "Just play it safe for a while, will you? See which way the wind blows. I doubt that Jollie's after your hide. He just doesn't like original thinkers, you know what I mean?"

"I think we'd better get going, don't you? The education of our nation's children lies perilously within our hands."

"Yea, and verily," I said. "Onward. I'll meet you there. I think you'd better shave."

"Brutus was right, though," Marty said as he held open the door for me. "We all stand against the spirit of Caesar, but unfortunately, the spirit doesn't bleed."

"Come again?" But the door was shut before I could get an answer. And I didn't remember his remark until after Thanksgiving, when my own classes were destroying Shakespeare's poetry. When the lines Marty had paraphrased came up in the discussion,

I became unaccountably nervous, and I kept seeing Jollie draped in a toga. When I passed the fantasy on to those I could trust not to run immediately to the boss, they laughed, and soon enough, Jolliet became Caesar, and Marty was an instant celebrity for inspiring the analogy.

What a blow it was, then, when we received a party invitation from the old man.

I was sitting in my classroom, commiserating with Val over an impossible malcontent who was disrupting her classes, when our departmont bird watcher and sapling look-alike, Wendy Buchwall, scurried in waving a pink slip of paper. "You're not going to believe this," she said, "but we've been invited to a costume ball."

"You're right," I said. "I don't believe it. Who's passing that insane idea around? It sounds like Guidance is on a new kick."

"No, him," she said, holding the paper in front of my glasses just long enough for me to make out Jolliet's pompous scrawl.

"Him?"

"The Man, Val."

"You're kidding. Cut it out. It isn't funny."

Wendy, obviously still unbelieving herself, handed her the invitation, and we sat for a quiet moment wondering if we'd stumbled into an alternate universe that delighted in perversity.

"It figures," Val said finally. "A Shakespearean ball, yet."

"That's ridiculous," I said when Wendy handed the paper to me. I read it, blinked and hoped it would go away. "Hey, this thing is on the Friday over Christmas vacation. Brother, he sure knows how to ruin a holiday."

Wendy perched on the edge of my desk and shook her head. "There is absolutely no way I am going to drag my husband to such a farce. He'll divorce me. He'll have good reason."

"Dream on," Val said. "Unfortunately, I don't see how you can gracefully get out of it. Unless you're dying."

"Says who?"

"Says tenure, dear. We three unholies are bucking for that lovely piece of security. We're stuck. And," she added as Wendy turned to her, "if I remember correctly, we all advised Marty to play the game. What's he going to think of us if we don't go along? We, honey, are on the same team."

Wendy stuck out her tongue and pouted, kicking her heels against the metal side of my desk until I was more than tempted to dump her onto the floor. But Val, as usual, was right. The three of us had drifted into this valley high school at the same time, each running from a city faculty horrific in its brutality. All of us had at least ten years behind us, and it was a wonder that we were hired at all. Now we were facing the final step—no tenure this time and it was back to housekeeping for Wendy, a library for Val, and God only knew what for me. It was times like this that made me want to strangle the wag who said, "Them's that can't, teach."

I began doodling on the desk blotter. A noose first. When I drew in a stick man, I couldn't decide who it was.

"I don't want to go," Wendy near whispered, sadly now.

"No choice," Val said. "No goddamned choice."

"It's the principle of the thing," I said, suddenly angry. "I don't know why the hell we let that man push us around like this. Christ, we're like children as far as he's concerned."

"Principle," said Val in her maddeningly calm way, "does not put bread on the table."

And silence. I remembered when I had been as idealistic as Marty Schubert, and mourned myself those days. I began to see just why he had reasons for hating me, and I wondered if, in fact, he had. Right then, it suddenly mattered very much. Not only did I care that he understood what I was doing and why I didn't fight the world as he did, I was also a little frightened. For the last two weeks, pranksters of a most unfunny lot had been dumping mutilated fowl on our doorsteps. Mine (two barn owls) were missing their hearts, Wendy's and Val's their entrails. Jolliet, too, had been similarly victimized, and although we had been passing the incidents off on some kid who was too eager to delve into the literal meanings of the occult in Shakespeare's more gruesome moments, I couldn't help thinking of Marty, his rage, and those tears in his eyes.

"My God," I finally shouted, getting out of my chair and tossing the pencil into the wastebasket. "Whose damnable idea was this in the first place?"

"Mine."

I looked up and Marty came in, hands clasped in front of him like a marching priest. Wendy jumped off the desk and punched him twice on the arm, hard. He laughed and ducked playfully away from her further attack. Val threw an eraser at him, and I stalked around until I slumped against the chalkboard and glared at him. "Traitor," I said.

Marty smiled innocently. "I thought you wanted me to go along with him."

"Oh, brother," I said. "That was the general idea, yes, but did you have to go for assistant god? A Shakespearean ball? Jesus, Marty, couldn't you have done better?"

He glanced around at the three of us, shrugged and appropriated my chair. Immediately he sat, his feet were crossed on the desk's top, scattering several papers. "But Willy is his favorite man. All I did was kind of ease him around until he fell into it himself. He, uh, really didn't care for it at first. It took a lot of talking." He smiled again, but this time there was no mirth, and I knew he was lying. Jolliet would have died before going through a year, a goddamned day with Lear, Hamlet and all the rest of the bloody crew. Marty, for his own reasons, knew exactly what he was doing. I didn't know if the women caught on, but I didn't like it and abruptly lost the will to banter any more. The game had turned sour; I wanted to spit.

"I wish you hadn't done it," I said.

Marty shrugged his indifference to my opinion.

Val, meanwhile, was mimicking an ultrasensuous walk up and down an aisle, tossing kisses to the pale green walls. "I'm not ashamed to say that Cleopatra would suit me just fine."

"You'll make an asp of yourself," I said.

"You'll go to hell for that," she said and blew me a kiss, a real one, and I couldn't help but admit to myself that she could easily slay my bachelorhood dragon.

"Too obvious," Wendy said, off on a track of her own. "Why not beat the bastard at his own game and go as the conspirators? Who knows, maybe the Ides of March'll come early this season."

"That's the spirit," Marty said, abandoning my chair and heading for the door, a little too quickly. "I might be Marc Antony."

"But he was a double-crosser," Wendy said.

"Yeah," he answered. "How about that?"

After he'd gone, I picked up a piece of chalk and began scribbling what I could remember of the "Friends, Romans, countrymen" speech on the blackboard. It helped me not to think.

A few minutes later, Val picked up her coat and purse and took Wendy by the arm. "Come on, bird girl," she said. "Let's hit the road. Eddie, if all you've got is your famous TV dinners, drop around. I'll see what the larder has hidden from payday."

I stopped writing and nodded without committing myself. Then I listened to their heels tracing a unison beat down the hall. Outside my window I could hear a snowball fight. From the back of the school came the muffled shouts of an afternoon basketball game, the cadenced pounding of feet responding to a cheer. "I still don't like it," I said to the empty chairs.

The Christmas break arrived none too soon for my rapidly decaying nerves. Though there had been no repetition of the practical jokes that had stained my doorstep, Marty's increasingly foul temper had strained our not-too-deep friendship. More and more he sniped at me for surrendering my ideals, would then immediately laugh as if to salve the wounds he knew he was inflicting. And there was fury in the dust he raised when he left school each night.

Since I was without a family, and Val had headed for an aunt's, I treated myself, on Christmas Day, to a gluttonous delight at a nearby restaurant that deserved a better fate than being buried in the hills. The more I ordered, the better the service was; and when the meal finally ended, I was actually laughing with the waitress. It was a good, rare feeling, and I drove home slowly in order to preserve it. There had been a snowfall two days before, and the lawns and fields had not yet been all trampled by children and snowmobiles. The snow had hardened, filmed with thin ice and contoured smooth like unbroken clouds. I grinned; I whistled; and when the telephone rang just as I was hanging up my overcoat, I even said "hello" instead of the usual "yeah?"

"Marty here, Ed. I just wanted to wish you a merry, and all that. Also, I have a friendly reminder of this Friday's gay festivities."

The measure of my good will weathered even this miserable reminder of that costume affair. "Bless you, Tiny Tim," I said.

"Having a good day?"

"So-so. I'm at my, uh, uncle's place now. Where the party's going to be, you know? Strange old guy, but he's teaching me a few things, and I'll put up with anything for a free meal. Can't complain. You?"

"Just great, just great. But as long as you brought it up, what are you going as?"

"Huh?"

"Oh, come on. The extravaganza, my boy. What ingenious rig have you devised, or is it a secret?"

"Oh, that. Nothing special. Since everyone seems on a Caesar kick—"

"I wonder why," I muttered.

"—I thought I would just grab a sheet and go as the soothsayer."

He laughed, but somehow I failed to see the joke. For all the scheming he had done, I thought the least he'd go as was the Poet himself. A soothsayer just didn't seem to fit the occasion. I told him I was thinking of Macbeth, but he didn't seem to care. As soon as he learned I was still going, he chatted meaninglessly for a while, then rang off, leaving me with an absolutely preposterous image of him wandering the halls of this uncle's house trailing a permanent-press sheet beneath Japanese sandals and whispering "Beware the Ides of January" into everyone's ears. The image, unbidden, was immediately replaced with one equally unwelcome: of a figure in immaculate white posturing on a rounded dais while all the English Department sprawled at his cloven feet and drank hemlock laced with sulfur. The man's face was in clouds, and I couldn't tell if it were Marty or Jolliet. I held the picture as long as I could, working to eliminate its inexplicably obscene horror by trying to think of an appropriate theme for it. But the only song I could come up with was "After the Ball," in dirge time.

For the rest of the day I had the feeling that, while some entertained the ghost of Christmas Future, I was hosting the Scrooge of Hellsmas Past.

Quickly I grabbed a bottle from my private, not-very-select stock and sloshed out three quarters of a glass, most of which I finished before I'd lost my nerve. At the same time, I delved into my puny knowledge of Freud and attempted to fashion an explanation for the vision, if vision it were; but I was interrupted, gratefully, by the telephone. This time it was Wendy, slightly drunk and wishing slurred season's greetings for nearly five minutes before apologizing and hanging up. I hadn't even had the chance to say hello.

I had dreams after that, better forgotten, and finally came the night, the Friday evening when not even the Second Coming would have cheered me up. Feeling as ridiculous as I ever had, I climbed into my car, decked out in the closest approximation of Shakespearean Italian the local theatrical costumer could dredge up. If anyone asked, I would be Romeo, or Petruchio, or perhaps even Iago; at any rate, no one was going to get the same answer twice, and I didn't really care. For the moment all I worried about was being stopped by a local policeman and having to explain, while taking a drunkometer test, why I was dressed in tights, a scarf and a red-plumed hat.

It wasn't until I reached the house and was getting out of the car that I saw the still-red heart of a bird lying on the seat next to me. I gagged, tossed it away and leaned against the car hood, trying hard to breathe. I told myself to turn right around and go on home. But I spotted Val's car and decided I'd better stick around, although I wasn't sure why.

Originally, the house had been a development ranch which successive owners had bastardized by splicing on additions so often that it sprawled idiotically over a full acre, if not more. I'd passed it often and had never known who'd lived there, but I wasn't surprised to learn that it was Marty's uncle's. Somehow it seemed to fit. At least, however, he'd tried to even things off a bit by enclosing two inner courtyards, one behind the other, with a roof of glass, thus providing his guests with green grass and roof-high shrubbery to hide in while the snow fell and turned the sky white. This I discovered not two minutes after I'd rung the doorbell and had been admitted to a living-room-cum-foyer by a woman I didn't recognize and who apparently didn't know that harem girls seldom appeared at the Globe. She was, however, friendly, and immediately guided me to the first garden, where most of my fellow sufferers were rapidly draining the first of seemingly endless punch bowls.

Val, true to her threat, was Cleopatra, so much so that I began at once to make plans for later. Wendy and her husband struggled valiantly, and lost, as Bottom and Titania. The others were dressed as I was or were tripping over homemade togas. The masks we wore seemed less to hide than scream our identities, and what laughter there was seemed false.

I squirmed and was uncomfortable, and welcomed Val's offering of a drink with a smile and a kiss just this side of rape. She grinned. "Down, whoever you are. We've only just begun to play."

"But, Madame Egypt," I protested, sitting gingerly on a plaster, gingerly because the tights I was wearing were that and more. "This is too much. What are we supposed to do, sit around and drink all night? For that I could have gone to a bar."

Val coiled beside me, hugging my arm, and we watched as the newcomers were ushered in, grabbed by Wendy and hustled away with filled glasses before we could identify them. I blinked and shook my head. "I didn't know we had this many in the department."

She laughed, making quite sure I noticed she was not about to let go of my arm. "You should see the back patio. Courtyard. Whatever. I guess Marty told Jollie he could have anyone he wanted. It's amazing. I didn't think he knew that many people."

"Speaking of which, where is mine host? It'd be just like him not to come."

"Oh, he's around. He looks like a drip-dry bed with all his sheets.

But, Eddie, his beard, his face . . . it looks too real." I frowned and was about to get an elaboration when Wendy staggered over and punched me viciously on the arm. For the first time in months I was in no mood for her imitation heavyweight, and I think I would have hit her back if her husband, Dan, hadn't followed her over. I shook his hand without standing as we passed the usual acquaint-ances-who-don't-really-know-each-other's greetings.

"Where is the creep?" he growled, and I could see, even with his ass's head, that he wasn't kidding. I looked to Wendy, who smiled dryly and waved a hand toward the roof. "I told him about Jollie and Marty. And us."

"Bastard," Dan muttered belligerently. "Men like him shouldn't be allowed to work."

"Smart guy," I said to his wife, but she wasn't listening, staring instead at the glass over our head.

The snow, which had started nearly an hour before I'd left, was powder, and a slight wind was skating it across the glass in swirls and nebulae, which made me think of watching herds of antelope stampeding before a pursuing helicopter. I sensed Val watching me, and I grinned and said without looking at her, "Beautiful. Stare at it long enough and you'll forget where you are." There were scratches in the glass, and snow caught and held there, then quickly escaped to be replaced and replaced again. Suddenly Val tugged at my arm. I looked down, with the odd feeling that I was actually looking up, and then saw Marty enter from the glass-walled breezeway that divided the two courtyards. I was going to laugh at the preposterous sight, but something about the ancient way he walked stopped me. He nodded at each guest, but passed them as if they were statuary, stalking rather than winding his way toward us. When he arrived, however, he was smiling, his grayed head bobbing as he looked quickly around.

"Beware—"

"—the Ides of January," I interrupted, and was surprised at the glare he shot at me.

"How'd you know I was going to say that?" he said, his voice matching his made-up age.

I shrugged. "ESP. Besides, it suits you."

The glare shifted reluctantly to a frown, to a bland smile. "Oh, well, nobody was laughing anyway. How do you like the ball?"

"Where's the music and dancing?" Val wanted to know. "How can you have a ball without an orchestra, or even a radio? I'm disappointed in you, Marty boy, really I am."

Marty said nothing. He only resumed his bobbing. "Don't worry. Everything's all right. All these people are for show anyway. They'll be gone soon, and then the real party begins. By the way, have you seen our fearless leader?"

We shook our heads, and he grinned, yellow and brown-black.

"Caesar," he said without elaboration.

"Why not?" Val said.

"That," I said, "is the most disgusting thing I've ever heard. The man can't be serious, he just can't be. And before I forget, old man, I found a bird's heart in my car tonight. I don't suppose you know anything about it."

"So did I," Val said. "Wendy too." She tried smiling, but I saw the way she swallowed convulsively. Fully angry now, I turned back to Marty, but he stopped me with a feeble wave.

"Don't worry about it. Bad joke. Like Jollie's costume."

I wanted to pursue that "bad joke" of his, certain now that he was the one who'd been deviling us, but Val must have known what I was thinking because she placed a gentle finger on my lips and mouthed "Caesar." "Him? What about him? You know, if you tell me he's wearing a plastic laurel wreath, I'll vomit, if you'll pardon the vulgarity."

"No," Marty said. "It's real. He said it took him two hours to get it right. He didn't want to use any string. Authenticity, he said."

I had a comment, several of them, but suddenly there was a crackling, ripping flash of lightning, followed hard by a deafening explosion of thunder. The entire house quieted, and a couple of women shrieked. Only a few times before had I ever witnessed such a phenomenon, and each time, the feeling of watching snow falling while thunder and lightning played out of season was as close to staring dead on into an open grave as I'd like to get. There was an encore as eerie as the first, but this served to shatter the silence and everyone began talking at once, the noise rapidly regaining its former level until, without realizing it, I found myself listening to some canned music. Quite accidentally, I discovered the speakers hidden within the huge, junglelike thickets of forsythia that lined the garden's perimeter and served to screen most of the house from those in the center. Curious it was, and impulsively, I grabbed Val's hand.

"Come on," I said. "There's something I want to see."

"Hey, wait a minute," Marty said. "Don't you want to see Jollie?"

"No, thanks," I said. "That can wait, if you don't mind."

Marty frowned until he appeared to make a decision. "Oh, well, you can see him later, I guess. It won't make any difference. Where are you going?"

I pointed. "The other courtyard."

"Oh. Well, look, try not to wander around the house, okay? Even with a single floor, all those additions make it too easy to get lost." He laughed. "I ought to know. I came through the back door once, and it took me two hours to get to the front. You know, when I told my uncle about this party, I thought he—"

"Marty," I said, not altogether politely, "you have other guests. Val and I'll talk to you later on, after you've done the host bit. I'm sure you wouldn't want to offend anyone."

"Now what was that supposed to mean?" I could see it then, the reason why he looked so old, weighted, weary—the rage was still there, and no longer merely directed at Jolliet. The old saying "If looks could kill" came disturbingly to mind, and I involuntarily stepped back.

"I didn't mean anything," I said. "Forget it. Come on, Val." And once into the corridor, I pulled her close to me, felt her shivering. "Sorry, love, but I have a feeling I'm not exactly in the spirit of things."

"Relax, Eddie," she said as I guided her into the back garden. "I think I'm going to develop a splitting headache in a few minutes. In fact, as soon as Jollie sees us and we smile a little."

"I have this odd feeling I'm going to have to be chivalrous. Coincidence."

We laughed quietly as we stepped onto the grass and looked around. Except for a slightly denser crowd, there seemed to be no difference between the two party areas. Then I noticed the red and purple streamers, and the red balloons dangling from string taped to the glass roof. If the idea was to make the room more festive, it failed miserably. All it did was make a pleasant garden look tawdry.

"Notice something?" I asked.

"What?"

"Except for spaces cleared for doors, you can't see into the house from here. And vice versa, I imagine. I wonder why someone would bother to make a place like this if you couldn't see it unless you were in it?"

Val stepped in front of me then, crossing her arms over her barely covered chest. "Why don't you really relax a little, Ed? Try to enjoy. Worry about something else besides the architecture. Like my dry throat, for instance."

I stared dumbly for a moment. And I wondered. None of this—the bizarre party, the birds' hearts and entrails, the people who now seemed to be leaving—none of it affected her. As I led her to the refreshment table, I began to think I was far too susceptible to atmosphere, especially when it seemed to be of my own creation.

"You're so cheerful," Val said suddenly. "I don't think I can stand it."

"Try," I said, nearly choking on a swallow of cheap whiskey. "And if you want entertainment, turn around and blink rapidly before it goes away." As she did, I added, "Jesus Christ, I never thought I'd live to see the day."

Both of us indulged for a moment in the cinematic cliché of allowing our mouths to drop open. Entering the garden through a door in the back was Jolliet, all six-plus feet of him so elegantly swathed in a toga laced with purple that he actually commanded a slight bow. His longish brown hair was combed straight back and held by a laurel wreath twined with some kind of gold metallic thread. Big in a suit, he was huge in that costume, and no one, least of all myself, laughed. For some reason, we didn't dare.

"My God," Val said weakly. "That's spooky."

"It's downright unnatural," I said sourly. I had expected to find the man a supreme source for derision, and he had double-crossed me. I became furious and poured myself another drink while Val waved and sent him striding regally toward us. The still-thinning crowd parted wordlessly, and when he stood before us, he took Val's hand and bowed over it, his lips barely brushing her skin.

"Caesar," she said, easing her voice up from her throat in a way I'd never heard before.

"My dearest Cleo," he said, ignoring me, but not her cleavage. "Egypt misses you, I've no doubt. The serendipity of your counte-nance entices me. Would you care to join me in a devilish concoc-tion I invented myself?"

Val laughed and gently disengaged her hand while holding up her still-full glass with the other. "I have one, thanks. Romeo, here, makes a good servant."

"Thanks," I said, extending my hand to my boss, who barely touched it.

"Grand celebration, isn't it, Eddie? I really believe the old man would have been delighted to be here."

The "old man" was Shakespeare. The way Jolliet talked about him, I've often thought they were roommates in boarding school.

"Marty's done a fine job," I admitted. "And if you don't mind me asking, where in God's name did you get that costume? You could have been born in it."

"I've often wished I had, Eddie."

"Surely not as Caesar," Val said. "Your life would have been shortened considerably."

Jolliet smiled wickedly. "Not mine."

All I could say was, "Oh." Then, "Did you ever find out who's been playing those jokes?"

Immediately he stiffened. "I'm sorry, Ed, but I'm afraid I cannot call that a joke, especially when I discovered the severed head of an owl in my automobile this evening. No, not a joke. Some misbegotten prankster, perhaps. More likely someone deathly afraid of facing me himself, and therefore he uses less direct, less committed means of expressing his displeasure. You, possibly?"

"Not me," I said, laughing. "That's too original for me."

"Hardly original, Ed. The disemboweled chicken, the owls, are straight out of the so-called occult literature available in any shoddy paperback. The child obviously has problems and has decided to use me as a focus of his aberration."

"That oo," I muttered into my glass, not bothering to note that the "old man" himself was not above employing the so-called occult. The conversation, continuing with Val while I sulked, might have been funny to someone unused to his instant analyses, but having been subjected to them several times myself, I was definitely not amused. And during a pause, I said, "How do you figure it's a kid? One of your students?"

He waved an arm and a yard of cloth, gathering both Val and me into a circle of apparent great confidence. "My students? Absolutely not, Eddie. They know better. I've taught them better. They all have come to realize the value of reason, and this is hardly the act of a reasonable man. No, I rather think it's the result of an overimaginative mind that somehow feels I've wronged it. As much as I dislike those things, however, I must admit I'm intrigued. I can't wait for the next manifestation."

"Oh?" I said. "Very interesting, really. I'll hope you let us know what happens next. I really hadn't looked at it your way before."

Jolliet nodded, smiling too much like a shark to please me. "Of course I will. Glad to see your interest. We should talk about this sometime. I'd like to hear what you think about these occult things. *Rosemary's Baby*, and such."

"Great," I said. "It's a date."

Someone called his name, then, and when he looked up, it was Marty, beckoning from the doorway. "Ah, excuse me, Eddie, Val, Marty has a surprise for me. A contest or something, I imagine. I'll talk to you later."

When he disappeared through the rear door, Val snatched away
my empty glass and slammed it onto the table. "I hope you'll let
us know what happens next," she mimicked. "I really hadn't seen
it that way. Oh, brother, Eddie." And she rolled her eyes skyward.

Doing my best to imitate her slinking walk, I sidled up to her
and grabbed her hand. "Oh, Caesar, baby," I said as huskily as I
could. "Oh, Caesar, darling."

We stared at each other for a long second, and we didn't laugh.

The music grew, then, as did the voices, the laughter and not
a few high-pitched shrieks. People were moving as if in a quiet
panic from garden to garden. I looked for Wendy and Dan and saw
only sequined masks and faces like raccoons. I found myself staring
at mouths, since eyes were forbidden to me, and their grotesque
writhings made me dizzy. I started to curse the whiskey and
looked feebly around for a chair. The room had become perceptibly colder, the snow fell more heavily and seemed now to be
freezing on the glass roof despite the warmth beneath. I shook off
an impression that the house was beginning to move, ignored
another ghostly display of thunder, and watched as the people
began to leave, with none replacing them. Val, unaware of my
gathering nightmare, hugged my arm and whispered something
about Wendy and Dan. I nodded mutely and, when she left,
renewed my friendship with Miniver Cheevy, cursing the fates
and drinking.

Through a slowly descending curtain, then, I lost vision of the
rest of the evening. I wandered. I drank. I shook off a woman in
a harem costume who wanted to see what my codpiece was hiding. I tried to vomit, and couldn't.

I do remember standing at a window and watching the snow
fall.

I do remember standing by a speaker and listening to muted
trombones.

And when next I opened my eyes and could see without falling,
I was in a bed in a hideously dark-blue bedroom. A single light
burned on a wrought-iron night table. I struggled to sit up, then
waited for dizziness to pass. There was a constant pounding at the

back of my head, and my mouth was dry to rasping.

And still the house was silent.

In a foolish moment, I searched the bed for my hat, realized what I was doing and laughed, stopping immediately when my throat burned.

Carefully, I pushed myself off the bed onto my feet and, using the walls for support until I was sure I wouldn't fall, I made my way to a dimly lighted hallway. Ruefully remembering Marty's warning about too much unguided wandering, I left the door open and walked to the nearest corner. I could hear snatches of mournful music, and I tried to locate its direction. When it became obvious I was losing it, I headed back the other way, staring without seeing the paintings on the dark-papered walls. None of them were striking enough to recall individually, except for their color: night. I cannot even now remember seeing one brush-stroked sun or noon-drenched meadow. I'm sure there were no people, no animals, no houses. Just . . . night.

I've since tried to locate that hallway again to verify these vague impressions. But I'm unable to.

Maybe later.

But I doubt it.

And then, quite by accident, I found a corridor I knew led to the gardens. Immediately I began to hurry, uneasily imagining some humiliating scene when Marty and Jolliet discovered I'd missed a fair portion of the party. It was all I needed to end a perfect evening.

But the gardens were empty, the tables, refreshments, folding chairs gone. The balloons were broken, the streamers shredded and hanging loosely. I called out for Val, half expecting my voice to echo. Then I called for Marty. Wendy. Even Dan. But when there was no response, I went into the front room where I'd met the harem girl. It was a small room, heavily paneled in walnut with an ugly moose's head perched over the front window. After a quick look around, I opened the door, shuddered at the shock of the cold and looked out. There was snow yet, and an oddly gathering fog. I could see, just this side of that wall-like mist, a couple of cars, including my own, still in the drive; so at least I wasn't alone. Under the circumstances, that was the greatest comfort I'd known in ages.

But when Marty snuck up behind me and whispered, "Beware the Ides of winter," I immediately lost everything I'd drunk onto the front stoop. Marty became solicitous at once and helped me back into the house.

"Now that was a stupid thing to do," I snapped, yanking my arm from his grip. "What the hell are you trying to do?"

"Shut up," he said, glaring. "We're waiting for you in the back garden."

"Oh, now wait a minute," I said, one hand to the wall to aid my abruptly uncooperative legs. "As soon as I can, I'm leaving, fella. This bullshit has gone on long enough."

Marty only stood there. I shook my head in a vain effort to clear it, then rubbed my face vigorously.

"If Val is still here," I said, "tell her to come out if she still needs a ride."

Marty shook his head. "The back garden. Come on, Eddie, you're holding up the works."

"What the hell are you babbling about?" I demanded, but he had already turned to leave. At the door he switched off the lights and looked back at me. Right then I was tempted to leave, even without my coat, but curiosity more than his heavy-handed manner made me follow him.

Through the first, still-empty garden. And the second.

"All right, all right, Mr. Barrymore, where is everyone?"

"I said the back garden," Marty said without turning around. "The back garden."

I was too frustrated and confused to be apprehensive about the way Marty spoke to me, and I had to hurry to catch up with him as he made a sharp left through the rear exit and strode rapidly along a corridor that felt as if it had been carpeted in velvet. Another turn, and yet another before we stood in front of a glass wall streaked with dust and through which I could see what at first I refused to believe.

Here the house was two stories high, and in the courtyard framed by walls of stone were Val, Wendy and Dan, Jolliet and a man I'd never seen before. They were sitting on the sparse grass, but far from comfortably. As soon as Val spotted me, she ran into my arms before I realized they were open to receive her. Dan was dazed, his plaster ass's head broken on the ground beside him, his wife huddled in the protection of his arm.

And Jollie. I saw then that he wasn't sitting at all. He was propped up against a white stone bench, and there was more than purple on his toga. There was blood, drying like rust, pooling at his twisted legs. In his left hand he clutched the laurel wreath.

Before reason returned and all the scene's implications penetrated my own daze, I said, "I'm ashamed of you, Marty. That's hardly original."

Val, not understanding, gave a cry like a struck bird and backed away to stare at me, horrified. And while she did, I admitted to myself that I wasn't sorry. That he was dead, it grieved me because he was human and deserved better, but because he was Jolliet, I felt nothing but morbid curiosity.

Marty, meanwhile, had come around to face me, grinning. Beneath the beard his teeth seemed yellow-aged, and his eyes only echoed his grin. That look, more than anything else, snapped me awake, and I turned away to find a telephone. Marty snapped something I didn't quite catch, and the old man placed himself in front of the door. He was shorter than I, and easily forty years beyond me, but I checked myself and stared at him. Val, who had slumped wearily to the ground where she'd been standing, said, "That's the uncle, Eddie."

I nodded; he nodded back. And suddenly I began to laugh. Ludicrous: a murdered man, five teachers and an eccentric. And still I laughed. The hero's image I'd had of myself in fantasies that had lifted me from my more than prosaic life shattered like a twisted mirror with all the pieces shredding my eyes. I turned back to Marty, gagging now at the sight of Jollie's blood. He gestured and I sat, heavily. Val crawled slowly over to me, and we huddled, reflections of Wendy and Dan. I think I said "It's going to be all right" a few times, but neither Val nor I were listening or believing. One of us was shivering.

At last Marty seemed to tire of watching us and dragged a folding chair from behind a bush. The old man stayed where he was.

"You're going to die, you know," Marty said. "But not like that," and he nodded toward Jollie's body. "It's not the way you want to, is it? Do you like uncle's place, by the way? He used to be an illusionist; that's why the house seems bigger than it really is. He doesn't talk; so don't ask him any questions. The snow's coming down a bit more than earlier. Bad driving, not that you'll care."

"Okay, pal," I said, tired of his rambling. "Just get to the point and stop this . . . this . . . whatever."

"Why, Eddie, you're frightened."

"No kidding."

At that moment, Dan came out of his stupor, and Wendy began crying. When Marty saw it, he waved a hand at his uncle, who hurried crablike to the Buchwalls and stood over them. Dan scowled, Wendy tried to crawl behind him, but the old man only looked until Dan eased himself to his feet and pulled Wendy up beside him. The former illusionist must have also been a mesmerist because they didn't speak, didn't see us, only followed the old man out of the garden.

"Where are they going?" Val asked, straightening and pulling out of my arms.

"To hell," Marty said flatly.

"And what are you, an angel?" I said.

He laughed. "Oh, my God, no. Is that what you're thinking? That this is the end of the world and I'm Gabriel in drag? Oh, Christ, Eddie, no wonder you've never gotten anywhere."

"Then where are they going?" Val repeated, her matter-of-fact tone the only sane thing in the world at the time.

"Nowhere," Marty said. "Nowhere at all." And he grinned, and that grin was rapidly fraying my nerves, or what was left of them.

"So what do we do now?"

"Wait."

That did it. His damnable calm and refusal to let us in on his

cosmic plans infuriated me to the edge and over. I jumped to my
feet before he could raise a hand to stop me. Head down, I struck
him dead on the chest, my hands scrabbling for his neck. We fell
off the chair and were separated when the ground struck us.
Quickly I got to my feet, but not soon enough. Marty was waiting,
swinging. There was no pain at first, nor did some magical part of
my brain tell me I didn't know how to fight. I just stood there,
trying to hit him while he pounded me to my knees. When sensation came, tears came and I fell to my side, sobbing, aching and
utterly humiliated. There was salt in my mouth and one eye was
closing. Val cradled my head and murmured nothings until my
agony extended beyond the physical. I pressed my face into her
breasts and continued to sob.

"You all played the game, you see," I could hear Marty saying,
his disgust no longer hiding. "Too afraid to be even the slightest
bit idealistic outside your own private ravings. You rationalized
your powerlessness against a single man until you actually believed it. You convinced yourselves that you could do nothing but
teach, and marked that damned school as the ends of your lines.
Tell me something, Eddie: how many new teachers have you
wiped out in the past three years? And how many at the school
before that? And the one before that? How many teachers have
you murdered?"

"Go to hell," Val said. "And leave him alone."

"Oh, I intend to do just that, Miss Stern."

"All right, then, you've made your point, little man. Now how
about letting us go?"

"I'll think about it."

"What's to think about? You've murdered a man, and I doubt
you'll get away with it. You've destroyed Eddie here, and you've
made me harder than I thought I could be. What more do you
want?"

Marty righted his chair and sat, crossing his arms over his chest
while I rolled over and pushed myself up. I knew I was hurt, but
whatever pain there was had dulled to a permanent, background
throbbing easy to ignore. And while he was busy tormenting Val,

I finally realized what had happened, what was going to happen, and I knew I wasn't man enough to fight it, or even explain it to Val. She was right. I was finished.

Marty, the soothsayer, had taken to himself the standard of the dreamers against the realities of the world. He had ranted more than we had, raged and railed until he had literally accumulated for himself a massive vortex of powered righteous indignation. Gully Jimson, Don Quixote and every dream of perfection and transformation twisted around him until he could, finally, strike back. Once. That was all he needed. And he paid, dearly.

"That man," I finally said, not stronger but more sure. "Nickels to dimes he's not your uncle."

Val looked quizzically at me; Marty smiled, genuine respect and grateful humor revived in his eyes.

"You know," he said, and I nodded. "This battle is very tiring, you see. He tried it when he was twenty-six. You'd never believe it, but he's thirty-four now. I met him last summer and thought he was crazy until he explained how it could be done and showed me a newspaper clipping of an unsolved disappearance. When that department meeting was over, I knew I could do it but was undecided until just before you came over to pick up my resignation. I wasn't mad enough until I saw you. He won't live much longer, though. It takes a lot out of you."

"Then why bother?"

"Because sooner or later—"

"What are you two talking about?" Val demanded.

She was frightened now, her shell pierced and peeling. Marty reached for her shoulder to comfort her, but she twisted away, shuddering.

"Sooner or later what?" I pursued. "All us cynics and realists will be gone, and the world will become a better place to live? The dreamers will march, the sunrise will come, and all God's children will be free at last to roam among the flowers?" I trembled, wanting to yell, feeling more like weeping. "When this is over, you'll be as aged as your friend, and just as useless. Don't you think you'll do more good by inculcating your students than destroying your so-called enemies?"

"What enemies?" Val said. "Eddie, this isn't funny at all. Please help me."

I reached out and took her hand, softly, and turned back to Marty. "I'm sorry to say there are more of us than there are of you."

"Bastard," he said.

At that, Val leaped to her feet, her face streaked and shining. She was naked now, and her exposure belied the clothes that covered her. "I want to go home, and damn both of you," she said. "Marty, damn you, let me out of here."

Marty looked at me, then behind me. The old-young man shuffled in, stood silently by the door while I wondered how many he had banished in his pitiful moment of glory.

"Take her out," Marty said.

The old man nodded, and Val, after a wild, almost feral stare at me, hurried after him. I made no move to stop her, called no reassuring words after her. I had been vampirized, and could only wait.

Marty stood, then, and slowly followed them. I turned on the ground. I thought of jumping and killing him, but dismissed it. Marty would die sooner than he thought, and would live to regret it. His friend must have learned how to harness and focus that rage/power from others before him; Marty had obviously learned it from him, and I suppose now that it must take a special kind of fury that only dreamers can muster. But why he didn't learn, why he didn't take the warning of the after effects, I still don't know. I don't even know if that other man had been a teacher, a preacher or a young-and-coming politician. Not that it matters.

And I have to admit he did try to warn us with those Shakespearean omens, to remind us of the Prince's caution not to take lightly that which we do not know.

"The house is yours," Marty said. "Take care of it, while it lasts."

"Hey, mind if I ask you something? How many places like this one are there?"

"As many as there are people like me. And him."

"Do we all get a house?"

"No. Some just walk. Others float. One or two fly. It's all the same, Eddie. It's all the same."

And he left, and I rose to my feet and staggered around until my legs decided they'd work for a while longer. I explored and found food, though I didn't think I'd need it. I decided this must be a thing . . . a something about time and space displacement, a nondimensional locus of a dreamer's rage. There's probably an empty field now where the house was. And as long as Marty lived, I knew I'd be here. And when he died, the hold on the house and me, and all the others, would be gone; and thus would I die.

I did wonder, though, who had the worst of this nightmare. Marty, I often thought, because he could only call upon this power once and is even now trapped in the world of the living to watch his dreams shred like so much yellowing cloth. Of course, I've also collapsed in self-pity, repenting my cynicism and wordliness to all the walls of his house, promising the sky and apple pie. But never for long.

If I am doomed to be a cynic, then he is doomed to be a romantic. What comes after, I don't like to consider. If it's more of the same . . .

And the end cometh. Marty is dying. The lights begin to fail room by room, and there is cold. Outside, where there is nothing but fog, the light turns black. I have a radio that had somehow— thanks, Marty, for that anyway—kept me in touch with the musical world, but the bands fade one by one. I can find only a single station now, and I wonder if Val can hear it, floating, walking, encased in her own fog, and dying. I still twiddle around until I can finally catch it, then hold the radio close to my ear and listen as if it were the laugh of little children. But all I can hear is "After the Ball."

The rest, dear Hamlet, is silence.

ROBERT SILVERBERG

Born with the Dead

"Born with the Dead" won the Nebula Award for the best science-fiction novella of 1974. Winning awards is nothing new to Robert Silverberg, who has won three other Nebulas for "Passengers," the best short story of 1969, and *A Time of Changes* and "Good News from the Vatican," the best novel and short story of 1971. For those who keep score, this ties him with Samuel R. Delany, who also has won four Nebulas (just as Ursula Le Guin's two Nebulas in one year tie her with Silverberg, Delany, and Zelazny in that distinction). A former president of SFWA and a former New Yorker who now lives in Oakland, Bob Silverberg has always been a writer. He graduated from Columbia University in 1956 already a published author and never has done anything else. For a while he was the most prolific author around; then, in an astonishing transformation, he changed himself into a writer of keen perception, startling originality, and sensitive skill. In the story that follows he deals with the quick and the dead in a world where both exist but separated by the gulf of life itself.

❧

────────

❧

1.

And what the dead had no speech for, when living,
They can tell you, being dead: the communication
Of the dead is tongued with fire beyond the language of
  the living.

—T. S. ELIOT, *Little Gidding*

Supposedly his late wife Sybille was on her way to Zanzibar. That
was what they told him, and he believed it. Jorge Klein had
reached that stage in his search when he would believe anything,
if belief would only lead him to Sybille. Anyway, it wasn't so absurd
that she would go to Zanzibar. Sybille had always wanted to go
there. In some unfathomable obsessive way the place had seized
the center of her consciousness long ago. When she was alive it
hadn't been possible for her to go there, but now, loosed from all
bonds, she would be drawn toward Zanzibar like a bird to its nest,
like Ulysses to Ithaca, like a moth to a flame.

The plane, a small Air Zanzibar Havilland FP-803, took off more
than half empty from Dar es Salaam at 0915 on a mild bright

174

morning, gaily circled above the dense masses of mango trees, red-flowering flamboyants, and tall coconut palms along the aquamarine shores of the Indian Ocean, and headed northward on the short hop across the strait to Zanzibar. This day—Tuesday, the 9th of March, 1993—would be an unusual one for Zanzibar: five deads were aboard the plane, the first of their kind ever to visit that fragrant isle. Daud Mahmoud Barwani, the health officer on duty that morning at Zanzibar's Karume Airport, had been warned of this by the emigration officials on the mainland. He had no idea how he was going to handle the situation, and he was apprehensive· these were tense times in Zanzibar. Times are always tense in Zanzibar. Should he refuse them entry? Did deads pose any threat to Zanzibar's ever-precarious political stability? What about subtler menaces? Deads might be carriers of dangerous spiritual maladies. Was there anything in the Revised Administrative Code about refusing visas on grounds of suspected contagions of the spirit? Daud Mahmoud Barwani nibbled moodily at his breakfast—a cold chapatti, a mound of cold curried potato—and waited without eagerness for the arrival of the deads.

Almost two and a half years had passed since Jorge Klein had last seen Sybille: the afternoon of Saturday, October 13, 1990, the day of her funeral. That day she lay in her casket as though merely asleep, her beauty altogether unmarred by her final ordeal: pale skin, dark lustrous hair, delicate nostrils, full lips. Iridescent gold and violet fabric enfolded her serene body; a shimmering electrostatic haze, faintly perfumed with a jasmine fragrance, protected her from decay. For five hours she floated on the dais while the rites of parting were read and the condolences were offered— offered almost furtively, as if her death were a thing too monstrous to acknowledge with a show of strong feeling; then, when only a few people remained, the inner core of their circle of friends, Klein kissed her lightly on the lips and surrendered her to the silent dark-clad men whom the Cold Town had sent. She had asked in her will to be rekindled; they took her away in a black van to work their magic on her corpse. The casket, retreating on their

broad shoulders, seemed to Klein to be disappearing into a throbbing gray vortex that he was helpless to penetrate. Presumably he
would never hear from her again. In those days the deads kept
strictly to themselves, sequestered behind the walls of their self-
imposed ghettos; it was rare ever to see one outside the Cold
Towns, rare even for one of them to make oblique contact with
the world of the living.

So a redefinition of their relationship was forced on him. For
nine years it had been Jorge and Sybille, Sybille and Jorge, I and
thou forming *we*, above all *we*, a transcendental *we*. He had loved
her with almost painful intensity. In life they had gone everywhere together, had done everything together, shared research
tasks and classroom assignments, thought interchangeable
thoughts, expressed tastes that were nearly always identical, so
completely had each permeated the other. She was a part of him,
he of her, and until the moment of her unexpected death he had
assumed it would be like that forever. They were still young, he
38, she 34, decades to look forward to. Then she was gone. And
now they were mere anonymities to one another, she not Sybille
but only a dead, he not Jorge but only a warm. She was somewhere
on the North American continent, walking about, talking, eating,
reading, and yet she was gone, lost to him, and it behooved him
to accept that alteration in his life, and outwardly he did accept
it, but yet, though he knew he could never again have things as
they once had been, he allowed himself the indulgence of a lingering wistful hope of regaining her.

Shortly the plane was in view, dark against the brightness of the
sky, a suspended mote, an irritating fleck in Barwani's eye, growing larger, causing him to blink and sneeze. Barwani was not ready
for it. When Ameri Kombo, the flight controller in the cubicle next
door, phoned him with the routine announcement of the landing,
Barwani replied, "Notify the pilot that no one is to debark until I
have given clearance. I must consult the regulations. There is
possibly a peril to public health." For twenty minutes he let the
plane sit, all hatches sealed, on the quiet runway. Wandering goats

emerged from the shrubbery and inspected it. Barwani consulted no regulations. He finished his modest meal; then he folded his arms and sought to attain the proper state of tranquility. These deads, he told himself, could do no harm. They were people like all other people, except that they had undergone extraordinary medical treatment. He must overcome his superstitious fear of them: he was no peasant, no silly clove-picker, nor was Zanzibar an abode of primitives. He would admit them, he would give them their anti-malaria tablets as though they were ordinary tourists, he would send them on their way. Very well. Now he was ready. He phoned Ameri Kombo. "There is no danger," he said. "The passengers may exit."

There were nine altogether, a sparse load. The four warms emerged first, looking somber and a little congealed, like people who had had to travel with a party of uncaged cobras. Barwani knew them all: the German consul's wife, the merchant Chowdhary's son, and two Chinese engineers, all returning from brief holidays in Dar. He waved them through the gate without formalities. Then came the deads, after an interval of half a minute: probably they had been sitting together at one end of the nearly empty plane and the others had been at the other. There were two women, three men, all of them tall and surprisingly robust-looking. He had expected them to shamble, to shuffle, to limp, to falter, but they moved with aggressive strides, as if they were in better health now than when they had been alive. When they reached the gate Barwani stepped forward to greet them, saying softly, "Health regulations, come this way, kindly." They were breathing, undoubtedly breathing: he tasted an emanation of liquor from the big red-haired man, a mysterious and pleasant sweet flavor, perhaps anise, from the dark-haired woman. It seemed to Barwani that their skins had an odd waxy texture, an unreal glossiness, but possibly that was his imagination; white skins had always looked artificial to him. The only certain difference he could detect about the deads was in their eyes, a way they had of remaining unnervingly fixed in a single intense gaze for many seconds before shifting. Those were the eyes, Barwani thought, of people who had

looked upon the Emptiness without having been swallowed into
it. A turbulence of questions erupted within him: What is it like,
how do you feel, what do you remember, where did you go? He
left them unspoken. Politely he said, "Welcome to the isle of
cloves. We ask you to observe that malaria has been wholly eradicated here through extensive precautionary measures, and to pre-
vent recurrence of unwanted disease we require of you that you
take these tablets before proceeding further." Tourists often ob-
jected to that; these people swallowed their pills without a word
of protest. Again Barwani yearned to reach toward them, to
achieve some sort of contact that might perhaps help him to tran-
scend the leaden weight of being. But an aura, a shield of strangeness, surrounded these five, and, though he was an amiable man
who tended to fall into conversations easily with strangers, he
passed them on in silence to Mponda the immigration man. Mponda's high forehead was shiny with sweat, and he chewed at his
lower lip; evidently he was as disturbed by the deads as Barwani.
He fumbled forms, he stamped a visa in the wrong place, he
stammered while telling the deads that he must keep their passports overnight. "I shall post them by messenger to your hotel in
the morning," Mponda promised them, and sent the visitors onward to the baggage pickup area with undue haste.

Klein had only one friend with whom he dared talk about it, a
colleague of his at UCLA, a sleek little Parsee sociologist from
Bombay named Framji Jijibhoi, who was as deep into the elaborate
new subculture of the deads as a warm could get. "How can I
accept this?" Klein demanded. "I can't accept it at all. She's out
there somewhere, she's alive, she's—"
Jijibhoi cut him off with a quick flick of his fingertips. "No, dear
friend," he said sadly, "not alive, not alive at all, merely rekindled.
You must learn to grasp the distinction." Klein could not learn to
grasp the distinction. Klein could not learn to grasp anything having to do with Sybille's death. He could not bear to think that she
had passed into another existence from which he was totally ex-
cluded. To find her, to speak with her, to participate in her experi-

ence of death and whatever lay beyond death, became his only purpose. He was inextricably bound to her, as though she were still his wife, as though Jorge-and-Sybille still existed in any way.

He waited for letters from her, but none came. After a few months he began trying to trace her, embarrassed by his own compulsiveness and by his increasingly open breaches of the etiquette of this sort of widowerhood. He traveled from one Cold Town to another—Sacramento, Boise, Ann Arbor, Louisville—but none would admit him, none would even answer his questions. Friends passed on rumors to him, that she was living among the deads of Tucson, of Roanoke, of Rochester, of San Diego, but nothing came of these tales, then Jijibhoi, who had tentacles into the world of the rekindled in many places, and who was aiding Klein in his quest even though he disapproved of its goal, brought him an authoritative-sounding report that she was at Zion Cold Town in southeastern Utah. They turned him away there too, but not entirely cruelly, for he did manage to secure plausible evidence that that was where Sybille really was.

In the summer of '92 Jijibhoi told him that Sybille had emerged from Cold Town seclusion. She had been seen, he said, in Newark, Ohio, touring the municipal golf course at Octagon State Memorial in the company of a swaggering red-haired archaeologist named Kent Zacharias, also a dead, formerly a specialist in the mound-building Hopewellian cultures of the Ohio Valley. "It is a new phase," said Jijibhoi, "not unanticipated. The deads are beginning to abandon their early philosophy of total separatism. We have started to observe them as tourists visiting our world—exploring the life-death interface, as they like to term it. It will be very interesting, dear friend." Klein flew at once to Ohio and, without ever actually seeing her, tracked her from Newark to Chillicothe, from Chillicothe to Marietta, from Marietta into West Virginia, where he lost her trail somewhere between Moundsville and Wheeling. Two months later she was said to be in London, then in Cairo, then Addis Ababa. Early in '93 Klein learned, via the scholarly grapevine—an ex-Californian now at Nyerere University in Arusha—that Sybille was on safari in Tanzania and was planning to go, in a few weeks, across to Zanzibar.

Of course. For ten years she had been working on a doctoral thesis on the establishment of the Arab Sultanate in Zanzibar in the early nineteenth century—studies unavoidably interrupted by other academic chores, by love affairs, by marriage, by financial reverses, by illnesses, death, and other responsibilities—and she had never actually been able to visit the island that was so central to her. Now she was free of all entanglements. Why shouldn't she go to Zanzibar at last? Why not? Of course: she was heading for Zanzibar. And so Klein would go to Zanzibar too, to wait for her.

As the five disappeared into taxis, something occurred to Barwani. He asked Mponda for the passports and scrutinized the names. Such strange ones: Kent Zacharias, Nerita Tracy, Sybille Klein, Anthony Gracchus, Laurence Mortimer. He had never grown accustomed to the names of Europeans. Without the photographs he would be unable to tell which were the women, which the men. Zacharias, Tracy, Klein . . . ah. *Klein.* He checked a memo, two weeks old, tacked to his desk. Klein, yes. Barwani telephoned the Shirazi Hotel—a project that consumed several minutes—and asked to speak with the American who had arrived ten days before, that slender man whose lips had been pressed tight in tension, whose eyes had glittered with fatigue, the one who had asked a little service of Barwani, a special favor, and had dashed him a much-needed hundred shillings as payment in advance. There was a lengthy delay, no doubt while porters searched the hotel, looking in the man's room, the bar, the lounge, the garden, and then the American was on the line. "The person about whom you inquired has just arrived, sir," Barwani told him.

2.

The dance begins. Worms underneath fingertips, lips beginning to pulse, heartache and throat-catch. All slightly out of step and out of key, each its own tempo and rhythm. Slowly, connections. Lip to lip, heart to heart, finding self in other,

dreadfully, tentatively, burning . . . notes finding themselves in
chords, chords in sequence, cacophony turning to polyphonous
contrapuntal chorus, a diapason of celebration.

—R. D. LAING, *The Bird of Paradise*

Sybille stands timidly at the edge of the municipal golf course at
Octagon State Memorial in Newark, Ohio, holding her sandals in
her hand and surreptitiously working her toes into the lush, immaculate carpet of dense, close-cropped lime-green grass. It is a
summer afternoon in 1992, very hot; the air, beautifully translu-
cent, has that timeless Midwestern shimmer, and the droplets of
water from the morning sprinkling have not yet burned off the
lawn. Such extraordinary grass! She hadn't often seen grass like
that in California, and certainly not at Zion Cold Town in thirsty
Utah. Kent Zacharias, towering beside her, shakes his head sadly.
"A golf course!" he mutters. "One of the most important prehis-
toric sites in North America and they make a golf course out of it!
Well, I suppose it could have been worse. They might have bull-
dozed the whole thing and turned it into a municipal parking lot.
Look, there, do you see the earthworks?"

She is trembling. This is her first extended journey outside the
Cold Town, her first venture into the world of the warms since her
rekindling, and she is picking up threatening vibrations from all
the life that burgeons about her. The park is surrounded by pleasant little houses, well kept. Children on bicycles rocket through
the streets. In front of her, golfers are merrily slamming away.
Little yellow golf carts clamber with lunatic energy over the rises
and dips of the course. There are platoons of tourists who, like
herself and Zacharias, have come to see the Indian mounds. There
are dogs running free. All this seems menacing to her. Even the
vegetation—the thick grass, the manicured shrubs, the heavy-
leafed trees with low-hanging boughs—disturbs her. Nor is the
nearness of Zacharias reassuring, for he too seems inflamed with
undeadlike vitality; his face is florid, his gestures are broad and
overanimated, as he points out the low flat-topped mounds, the

grassy bumps and ridges making up the giant joined circle and octagon of the ancient monument. Of course, these mounds are the mainspring of his being, even now, five years post mortem. Ohio is his Zanzibar.

"—once covered four square miles. A grand ceremonial center, the Hopewellian equivalent of Chichen Itza, of Luxor, of . . ." He pauses. Awareness of her distress has finally filtered through the intensity of his archaeological zeal. "How are you doing?" he asks gently.

She smiles a brave smile. Moistens her lips. Inclines her head toward the golfers, toward the tourists, toward the row of darling little houses outside the rim of the park. Shudders.

"Too cheery for you, is it?"

"Much," she says.

Cheery. Yes. A cheery little town, a magazine-cover town, a chamber-of-commerce town. Newark lies becalmed on the breast of the sea of time: but for the look of the automobiles, this could be 1980 or 1960 or perhaps 1940. Yes. Motherhood, baseball, apple pie, church every Sunday. Yes. Zacharias nods and makes one of the signs of comfort at her. "Come," he whispers. "Let's go toward the heart of the complex. We'll lose the twentieth century along the way."

With brutal imperial strides he plunges into the golf course. Long-legged Sybille must work hard to keep up with him. In a moment they are within the embankment, they have entered the sacred octagon, they have penetrated the vault of the past, and at once Sybille feels they have achieved a successful crossing of the interface between life and death. How still it is here! She senses the powerful presence of the forces of death, and those dark spirits heal her unease. The encroachments of the world of the living on these precincts of the dead become insignificant: the houses outside the park are no longer in view, the golfers are mere foolish incorporeal shadows, the bustling yellow golf carts become beetles, the wandering tourists are invisible.

She is overwhelmed by the size and symmetry of the ancient site. What spirits sleep here? Zacharias conjures them, waving his hands like a magician. She has heard so much from him already about these people, these Hopewellians—What did they call themselves? How can we ever know?—who heaped up these ramparts of earth twenty centuries ago. Now he brings them to life for her with gestures and low urgent words. He whispers fiercely:

—Do you see them?

And she does see them. Mists descend. The mounds reawaken; the mound-builders appear. Tall, slender, swarthy, nearly naked, clad in shining copper breastplates, in necklaces of flint disks, in bangles of bone and mica and tortoise-shell, in heavy chains of bright lumpy pearls, in rings of stone and terra-cotta, in armlets of bears' teeth and panthers' teeth, in spool-shaped metal ear-ornaments, in furry loincloths. Here are priests in intricately woven robes and awesome masks. Here are chieftains with crowns of copper rods, moving in frosty dignity along the long earthen-walled avenue. The eyes of these people glow with energy. What an enormously vital, enormously profligate culture they sustain here! Yet Sybille is not alienated by their throbbing vigor, for it is the vigor of the dead, the vitality of the vanished.

Look, now. Their painted faces, their unblinking gazes. This is a funeral procession. The Indians have come to these intricate geometrical enclosures to perform their acts of worship, and now, solemnly parading along the perimeters of the circle and the octagon, they pass onward, toward the mortuary zone beyond. Zacharias and Sybille are left alone in the middle of the field. He murmurs to her:

—Come. We'll follow them.

He makes it real for her. Through his cunning craft she has access to this community of the dead. How easily she has drifted backward across time! She learns here that she can affix herself to the sealed past at any point; it's only the present, open-ended and unpredictable, that is troublesome. She and Zacharias float through the misty meadow, no sensation of feet touching ground; leaving the octagon, they travel now down a long grassy causeway to the place of the burial mounds, at the edge of a dark forest of wide-crowned oaks. They enter a vast clearing. In the center the

ground has been plastered with clay, then covered lightly with
sand and fine gravel; on this base the mortuary house, a roofless
four-sided structure with walls consisting of rows of wooden pali-
sades, has been erected. Within this is a low clay platform topped
by a rectangular tomb of log cribbing, in which two bodies can be
seen: a young man, a young woman, side by side, bodies fully
extended, beautiful even in death. They wear copper breastplates,
copper ear ornaments, copper bracelets, necklaces of gleaming
yellowish bears' teeth.

Four priests station themselves at the corners of the mortuary
house. Their faces are covered by grotesque wooden masks
topped by great antlers, and they carry wands two feet long,
effigies of the death-cup mushroom in wood sheathed with copper.
One priest commences a harsh, percussive chant. All four lift their
wands and abruptly bring them down. It is a signal; the depositing
of grave-goods begins. Lines of mourners bowed under heavy
sacks approach the mortuary house. They are unweeping, even
joyful, faces ecstatic, eyes shining, for these people know what
later cultures will forget, that death is no termination but rather
a natural continuation of life. Their departed friends are to be
envied. They are honored with lavish gifts, so that they may live
like royalty in the next world: out of the sacks come nuggets of
copper, meteoric iron, and silver, thousands of pearls, shell beads,
beads of copper and iron, buttons of wood and stone, heaps of
metal ear-spools, chunks and chips of obsidian, animal effigies
carved from slate and bone and tortoise-shell, ceremonial copper
axes and knives, scrolls cut from mica, human jawbones inlaid with
turquoise, dark coarse pottery, needles of bone, sheets of woven
cloth, coiled serpents fashioned from dark stone, a torrent of offer-
ings, heaped up around and even upon the two bodies.

At length the tomb is choked with gifts. Again there is a signal
from the priests. They elevate their wands and the mourners,
drawing back to the borders of the clearing, form a circle and
begin to sing a somber, throbbing funereal hymn. Zacharias, after
a moment, sings with them, wordlessly embellishing the melody
with heavy melismas. His voice is a rich *basso cantante*, so unex-

pectedly beautiful that Sybille is moved almost to confusion by it, and looks at him in awe. Abruptly he breaks off, turns to her, touches her arm, leans down to say:

—You sing too.

Sybille nods hesitantly. She joins the song, falteringly at first, her throat constricted by self-consciousness; then she finds herself becoming part of the rite, somehow, and her tone becomes more confident. Her high clear soprano soars brilliantly above the other voices.

Now another kind of offering is made: boys cover the mortuary house with heaps of kindling—twigs, dead branches, thick boughs, all sorts of combustible debris—until it is quite hidden from sight, and the priests cry a halt. Then, from the forest, comes a woman bearing a blazing firebrand, a girl, actually, entirely naked, her sleek fair-skinned body painted with bizarre horizontal stripes of red and green on breasts and buttocks and thighs, her long glossy black hair flowing like a cape behind her as she runs. Up to the mortuary house she sprints; breathlessly she touches the firebrand to the kindling, here, here, here, performing a wild dance as she goes, and hurls the torch into the center of the pyre. Skyward leap the flames in a ferocious rush. Sybille feels seared by the blast of heat. Swiftly the house and tomb are consumed.

While the embers still glow, the bringing of earth gets under way. Except for the priests, who remain rigid at the cardinal points of the site, and the girl who wielded the torch, who lies like discarded clothing at the edge of the clearing, the whole community takes part. There is an open pit behind a screen of nearby trees; the worshippers, forming lines, go to it and scoop up soil, carrying it to the burned mortuary house in baskets, in buckskin aprons, in big moist clods held in their bare hands. Silently they dump their burdens on the ashes and go back for more.

Sybille glances at Zacharias; he nods; they join the line. She goes down into the pit, gouges a lump of moist black clayey soil from its side, takes it to the growing mound. Back for another, back for another. The mound rises rapidly, two feet above ground level now, three, four, a swelling circular blister, its outlines governed

by the unchanging positions of the four priests, its tapering contours formed by the tamping of scores of bare feet. Yes, Sybille
thinks, this is a valid way of celebrating death, this is a fitting rite.
Sweat runs down her body, her clothes become stained and
muddy, and still she runs to the earth-quarry, runs from there to
the mound, runs to the quarry, runs to the mound, runs, runs,
transfigured, ecstatic.

Then the spell breaks. Something goes wrong, she does not
know what, and the mists clear, the sun dazzles her eyes, the
priests and the mound-builders and the unfinished mound disap-
pear. She and Zacharias are once again in the octagon, golf carts
roaring past them on every side. Three children and their parents
stand just a few feet from her, staring, staring, and a boy about ten
years old points to Sybille and says in a voice that reverberates
through half of Ohio, "Dad, what's wrong with those people? Why
do they look so weird?" Mother gasps and cries, "*Quiet,* Tommy,
don't you have any manners?" Dad, looking furious, gives the boy
a stinging blow across the face with the tips of his fingers, seizes
him by the wrist, tugs him toward the other side of the park, the
whole family following in their wake.

Sybille shivers convulsively. She turns away, clasping her hands
to her betraying eyes. Zacharias embraces her. "It's all right," he
says tenderly. "The boy didn't know any better. It's all right."

"Take me away from here!"

"I want to show you—"

"Some other time. Take me away. To the motel. I don't want to
see anything. I don't want anybody to see me."

He takes her to the motel. For an hour she lies face down on the
bed, racked by dry sobs. Several times she tells Zacharias she is
unready for this tour, she wants to go back to the Cold Town, but
he says nothing, simply strokes the tense muscles of her back, and
after a while the mood passes. She turns to him and their eyes
meet and he touches her and they make love in the fashion of the
deads.

3.

Newness is renewal: *ad hoc enim venit, ut renovemur in illo;* making it new again, as on the first day; *herrlich wie am ersten Tag.* Reformation, or renaissance; rebirth. Life is Phoenix-like, always being born again out of its own death. The true nature of life is resurrection; all life is life after death, a second life, reincarnation. *Totus hic ordo revolubilis testatio est resurrectionis mortuorum.* The universal pattern of recurrence bears witnooo to tho roourreotion of the dead

—NORMAN O. BROWN, *Love's Body*

"The rains shall be commencing shortly, gentleman and lady," the taxi driver said, speeding along the narrow highway to Zanzibar Town. He had been chattering steadily, wholly unafraid of his passengers. He must not know what we are, Sybille decided. "Perhaps in a week or two they begin. These shall be the long rains. The short rains come in the last of November and December."

"Yoo, I know," Sybille said

"Ah, you have been to Zanzibar before?"

"In a sense," she replied. In a sense she had been to Zanzibar many times, and how calmly she was taking it, now that the true Zanzibar was beginning to superimpose itself on the template in her mind, on that dream-Zanzibar she had carried about so long! She took everything calmly now: nothing excited her, nothing aroused her. In her former life the delay at the airport would have driven her into a fury: a ten-minute flight, and then be trapped on the runway twice as long. But she had remained tranquil throughout it all, sitting almost immobile, listening vaguely to what Zacharias was saying and occasionally replying as if sending messages from some other planet. And now Zanzibar, so placidly accented. In the old days she had felt a sort of paradoxical amazement whenever one landmark familiar from childhood geography lessons or the movies or travel posters—the Grand Canyon, the Manhattan skyline, Taos Pueblo—turned out in reality to look exactly as she imagined it would; but now here was Zanzibar, unfolding predictably and unsurprisingly before her, and she observed it with a camera's cool eye, unmoved, unresponsive.

The soft, steamy air was heavy with a burden of perfumes, not only the expected pungent scent of cloves but also creamier fragrances which perhaps were those of hibiscus, frangipani, jacaranda, bougainvillea, penetrating the cab's open window like probing tendrils. The imminence of the long rains was a tangible pressure, a presence, a heaviness in the atmosphere: at any moment a curtain might be drawn aside and the torrents would start. The highway was lined by two shaggy green walls of palms broken by tin-roofed shacks; behind the palms were mysterious dark groves, dense and alien. Along the edge of the road was the usual tropical array of obstacles: chickens, goats, naked children, old women with shrunken, toothless faces, all wandering around untroubled by the taxi's encroachment on their right-of-way. On through the rolling flatlands the cab sped, out onto the peninsula on which Zanzibar Town sits. The temperature seemed to be rising perceptibly minute by minute; a fist of humid heat was clamping tight over the island. "Here is the waterfront, gentleman and lady," the driver said. His voice was an intrusive hoarse purr, patronizing, disturbing. The sand was glaringly white, the water a dazzling glassy blue; a couple of dhows moved sleepily across the mouth of the harbor, their lateen sails bellying slightly as the gentle sea breeze caught them. "On this side, please—" An enormous white wooden building, four stories high, a wedding cake of long verandahs and cast-iron railings, topped by a vast cupola. Sybille, recognizing it, anticipated the driver's spiel, hearing it like a subliminal pre-echo: "Beit al-Ajaib, the House of Wonders, former government house. Here the Sultan was often make great banquets, here the famous of all Africa came homaging. No longer in use. Next door the old Sultan's Palace, now Palace of People. You wish to go in House of Wonders? Is open: we stop, I take you now."

"Another time," Sybille said faintly. "We'll be here awhile."

"You not here just a day like most?"

"No, a week or more. I've come to study the history of your island. I'll surely visit the Beit al-Ajaib. But not today."

"Not today, no. Very well: you call me, I take you anywhere. I am Ibuni." He gave her a gallant toothy grin over his shoulder and swung the cab inland with a ferocious lurch, into the labyrinth of winding streets and narrow alleys that was Stonetown, the ancient Arab quarter.

All was silent here. The massive white stone buildings presented blank faces to the streets. The windows, mere slits, were shuttered. Most doors—the famous paneled doors of Stonetown, richly carved, studded with brass, cunningly inlaid, each door an ornate Islamic masterpiece—were closed and seemed to be locked. The shops looked shabby, and the small display windows were speckled with dust. Most of the signs were so faded Sybille could barely make them out:

PREMCHAND'S EMPORIUM
MONJI'S CURIOS
ABDULLAH'S BROTHERHOOD STORE
MOTILAL'S BAZAAR

The Arabs were long since gone from Zanzibar. So were most of the Indians, though they were said to be creeping back. Occasionally, as it pursued its intricate course through the maze of Stonetown, the taxi passed elongated black limousines, probably of Russian or Chinese make, chauffeur-driven, occupied by dignified self-contained dark-skinned men in white robes. Legislators, so she supposed them to be, en route to meetings of state. There were no other vehicles in sight, and no pedestrians except for a few women, robed entirely in black, hurrying on solitary errands. Stonetown had none of the vitality of the countryside; it was a place of ghosts, she thought, a fitting place for vacationing deads. She glanced at Zacharias, who nodded and smiled, a quick quirky smile that acknowledged her perception and told her that he too had had it. Communication was swift among the deads and the obvious rarely needed voicing.

The route to the hotel seemed extraordinarily involuted, and
the driver halted frequently in front of shops, saying hopefully,
"You want brass chests, copper pots, silver curios, gold chains from
China?" Though Sybille gently declined his suggestions, he continued to point out bazaars and emporiums, offering earnest
recommendations of quality and moderate price, and gradually
she realized, getting her bearings in the town, that they had
passed certain corners more than once. Of course: the driver must
be in the pay of shopkeepers who hired him to lure tourists.
"Please take us to our hotel," Sybille said, and when he persisted
in his huckstering—"Best ivory here, best lace"—she said it more
firmly, but she kept her temper. Jorge would have been pleased
by her transformation, she thought; he had all too often been the
immediate victim of her fiery impatience. She did not know the
specific cause of the change. Some metabolic side effect of the
rekindling process, maybe, or maybe her two years of communion
with Guidefather at the Cold Town, or was it, perhaps, nothing
more than the new knowledge that all of time was hers, that to let
oneself feel hurried now was absurd?

"Your hotel is this," Ibuni said at last.

It was an old Arab mansion—high arches, innumerable balco-
nies, musty air, electric fans turning sluggishly in the dark hall-
ways. Sybille and Zacharias were given a sprawling suite on the
third floor, overlooking a courtyard lush with palms, vermilion
nandi, kapok trees, poinsettia, and agapanthus. Mortimer, Gracchus, and Nerita had long since arrived in the other cab and were
in an identical suite one floor below. "I'll have a bath," Sybille told
Zacharias. "Will you be in the bar?"

"Very likely. Or strolling in the garden."

He went out. Sybille quickly shed her travel-sweaty clothes. The
bathroom was a Byzantine marvel, elaborate swirls of colored tile,
an immense yellow tub standing high on bronze eagle-claw-and-
globe legs. Lukewarm water dribbled in slowly when she turned
the tap. She smiled at her reflection in the tall oval mirror. There
had been a mirror somewhat like it at the rekindling house. On the
morning after her awakening, five or six deads had come into her

room to celebrate with her her successful transition across the interface, and they had had that big mirror with them; delicately, with great ceremoniousness, they had drawn the coverlet down to show herself to her in it, naked, slender, narrow-waisted, high-breasted, the beauty of her body unchanged, marred neither by dying nor by rekindling, indeed enhanced by it, so that she had become more youthful-looking and even radiant in her passage across that terrible gulf.

—You're a very beautiful woman.

That was Pablo. She would learn his name and all the other names later.

I feel much a flood of relief. I was afraid I'd wake up and find myself a shriveled ruin.

—That could not have happened, Pablo said.

—And never will happen, said a young woman. Nerita, she was.

—But deads do age, don't they?

—Oh, yes, we age, just as the warms do. But not *just* as.

—More slowly?

—Very much more slowly. And differently. All our biological processes operate more slowly, except the functions of the brain, which tend to be quicker than they were in life.

—Quicker?

—You'll see.

—It all sounds ideal.

—We are extremely fortunate. Life has been kind to us. Our situation is, yes, ideal. We are the new aristocracy.

—The new aristocracy—

Sybille slipped slowly into the tub, leaning back against the cool porcelain, wriggling a little, letting the tepid water slide up as far as her throat. She closed her eyes and drifted peacefully. All of Zanzibar was waiting for her. *Streets I never thought I should visit.* Let Zanzibar wait. Let Zanzibar wait. *Words I never thought to speak. When I left my body on a distant shore.* Time for everything, everything in its due time.

—*You're a very beautiful woman,* Pablo had told her, not meaning to flatter.

Yes. She had wanted to explain to them, that first morning, that she didn't really care all that much about the appearance of her body, that her real priorities lay elsewhere, were "higher," but there hadn't been any need to tell them that. They understood. They understood everything. Besides, she *did* care about her body. Being beautiful was less important to her than it was to those women for whom physical beauty was their only natural advantage, but her appearance mattered to her; her body pleased her and she knew it was pleasing to others, it gave her access to people, it was a means of making connections, and she had always been grateful for that. In her other existence her delight in her body had been flawed by the awareness of the inevitability of its slow steady decay, the certainty of the loss of that accidental power that beauty gave her, but now she had been granted exemption from that: she would change with time but she would not have to feel, as warms must feel, that she was gradually falling apart. Her rekindled body would not betray her by turning ugly. No.

—We are the new aristocracy—

After her bath she stood a few minutes by the open window, naked to the humid breeze. Sounds came to her: distant bells, the bright chatter of tropical birds, the voices of children singing in a language she could not identify. Zanzibar! Sultans and spices, Livingstone and Stanley, Tippu Tib the slaver, Sir Richard Burton spending a night in this very hotel room, perhaps. There was a dryness in her throat, a throbbing in her chest: a little excitement coming alive in her after all. She felt anticipation, even eagerness. All Zanzibar lay before her. Very well. Get moving, Sybille, put some clothes on, let's have lunch, a look at the town.

She took a light blouse and shorts from her suitcase. Just then Zacharias returned to the room, and she said, not looking up, "Kent, do you think it's all right for me to wear these shorts here? They're—" A glance at his face and her voice trailed off. "What's wrong?"

"I've just been talking to your husband."

"He's *here?*"

"He came up to me in the lobby. Knew my name. 'You're Zacharias,' he said, with a Bogarty little edge to his voice, like a deceived movie husband confronting the Other Man. 'Where is she? I have to see her.' "

"Oh, no, Kent."

"I asked him what he wanted with you. 'I'm her husband,' he said, and I told him, 'Maybe you were her husband once, but things have changed,' and then—"

"I can't imagine Jorge talking tough. He's such a *gentle* man, Kent! How did he look?"

"Schizoid," Zacharias said. "Glassy eyes, muscles bunching in his jaws, signs of terrific pressure all over him. He knows he's not supposed to do things like this, doesn't he?"

"Jorge knows exactly how he's supposed to behave. Oh, Kent, what a stupid mess! Where is he now?"

"Still downstairs. Nerita and Laurence are talking to him. You don't want to see him, do you?"

"Of course not."

"Write him a note to that effect and I'll take it down to him. Tell him to clear off."

Sybille shook her head. "I don't want to hurt him."

"Hurt him? He's followed you halfway around the world like a lovesick boy, he's tried to violate your privacy, he's disrupted an important trip, he's refused to abide by the conventions that govern the relationships of warms and deads, and you—"

"He loves me, Kent."

"He loved you. All right, I concede that. But the person he loved doesn't exist any more. He has to be made to realize that."

Sybille closed her eyes. "I don't want to hurt him. I don't want you to hurt him either."

"I won't hurt him. Are you going to see him?"

"No," she said. She grunted in annoyance and threw her shorts and blouse into a chair. There was a fierce pounding at her temples, a sensation of being challenged, of being threatened, that she had not felt since that awful day at the Newark mounds. She strode to the window and looked out, half expecting to see Jorge arguing with Nerita and Laurence in the courtyard. But there was no one down there except a houseboy who looked up as if her bare breasts were beacons and gave her a broad dazzling smile. Sybille turned her back to him and said dully, "Go back down. Tell him that it's impossible for me to see him. Use that word. Not that I *won't* see him, not that I *don't want to* see him, not that it isn't *right* for me to see him, just that it's impossible. And then phone the airport. I want to go back to Dar on the evening plane."

"But we've only just arrived!"

"No matter. We'll come back some other time. Jorge is very persistent; he won't accept anything but a brutal rebuff, and I can't do that to him. So we'll leave."

Klein had never seen deads at close range before. Cautiously, uneasily, he stole quick intense looks at Kent Zacharias as they sat side by side on rattan chairs among the potted palms in the lobby of the hotel. Jijibhoi had told him that it hardly showed, that you perceived it more subliminally than by any outward manifestation, and that was true; there was a certain look about the eyes, of course, the famous fixity of the deads, and there was something oddly pallid about Zacharias' skin *beneath* the florid complexion, but if Klein had not known what Zacharias was he might not have guessed it. He tried to imagine this man, this red-haired red-faced dead archaeologist, this digger of dirt mounds, in bed with Sybille. Doing with her whatever it was that the deads did in their couplings. Even Jijibhoi wasn't sure. Something with hands, with eyes, with whispers and smiles, not at all genital—so Jijibhoi believed. *This is Sybille's lover I'm talking to. This is Sybille's lover.* How strange that it bothered him so. She had had affairs when she was living; so had he; so had everyone; it was the way of life. But he felt threatened, overwhelmed, defeated, by this walking corpse of a lover.

Klein said, "Impossible?"

"That was the word she used."

"Can't I have ten minutes with her?"

"Impossible."

"Would she let me see her for a few moments, at least? I'd just like to find out how she looks."

"Don't you find it humiliating, doing all this scratching around just for a glimpse of her?"

"Yes."

"And you still want it?"

"Yes."

Zacharias sighed. "There's nothing I can do for you. I'm sorry."

"Perhaps Sybille is tired from having done so much traveling. Do you think she might be in a more receptive mood tomorrow?"

"Maybe," Zacharias said. "Why don't you come back then?"

"You've been very kind."

"De nada."

"Can I buy you a drink?"

"Thanks, no," Zacharias said. "I don't indulge any more. Not since—" He smiled.

Klein could smell whiskey on Zacharias' breath. All right, though. All right. He would go away. A driver waiting outside the hotel grounds poked his head out of his cab window and said hopefully, "Tour of the island, gentleman? See the clove plantations, see the athlete stadium?"

"I've seen them already," Klein said. He shrugged. "Take me to the beach."

He spent the afternoon watching turquoise wavelets lapping pink sand. The next morning he returned to Sybille's hotel, but they were gone, all five of them, gone on last night's flight to Dar, said the apologetic desk clerk. Klein asked if he could make a telephone call, and the clerk showed him an ancient instrument in an alcove near the bar. He phoned Barwani. "What's going on?" he demanded. "You told me they'd be staying at least a week!"

"Oh, sir, things change," Barwani said softly.

4.

What portends? What will the future bring? I do not know, I have no presentiment. When a spider hurls itself down from some fixed point, consistently with its nature, it always sees before it only an empty space wherein it can find no foothold however much it sprawls. And so it is with me: always before

me an empty space; what drives me forward is a consistency
which lies behind me. This life is topsy-turvy and terrible, not
to be endured.

—SOREN KIERKEGAARD, *Either/Or*

Jijibhoi said, "In the entire question of death who is to say what
is right, dear friend? When I was a boy in Bombay it was not
unusual for our Hindu neighbors to practice the rite of suttee—
that is, the burning of the widow on her husband's funeral pyre
—and by what presumption may we call them barbarians? Of
course"—his dark eyes flashed mischievously—"we *did* call them
barbarians, though never when they might hear us. Will you have
more curry?"

Klein repressed a sigh. He was getting full, and the curry was
fiery stuff, of an incandescence far beyond his usual level of tolerance; but Jijibhoi's hospitality, unobtrusively insistent, had a certain hieratic quality about it that made Klein feel like a blas-
phemer whenever he refused anything in his home. He smiled
and nodded, and Jijibhoi, rising, spooned a mound of rice into
Klein's plate, buried it under curried lamb, bedecked it with chut-
neys and sambals. Silently, unbidden, Jijibhoi's wife went to the
kitchen and returned with a cold bottle of Heinekens. She gave
Klein a shy grin as she set it down before him. They worked well
together, these two Parsees, his hosts.

They were an elegant couple—striking, even. Jijibhoi was a tall,
erect man with a forceful aquiline nose, dark Levantine skin,
jet-black hair, a formidable mustache. His hands and feet were
extraordinarily small; his manner was polite and reserved; he
moved with a quickness of action bordering on nervousness. Klein
guessed that he was in his early forties, though he suspected his
estimate could easily be off by ten years in either direction. His
wife—strangely, Klein had never been told her name—was
younger than her husband, nearly as tall, fair of complexion—a
light olive tone—and voluptuous of figure. She dressed invariably
in flowing silken saris; Jijibhoi affected Western business dress,

suits and ties in styles twenty years out of date. Klein had never seen either of them bareheaded: she wore a kerchief of white linen, he a brocaded skullcap that might lead people to mistake him for an Oriental Jew. They were childless and self-sufficient, forming a closed dyad, a perfect unit, two segments of the same entity, conjoined and indivisible, as Klein and Sybille once had been. Their harmonious interplay of thought and gesture made them a trifle disconcerting, even intimidating, to others. As Klein and Sybille once had been.

Klein said, "Among your people—"

"Oh, very different, very different, quite unique. You know of our funeral custom?"

"Exposure of the dead, isn't it?"

Jijibhoi's wife giggled. "A very ancient recycling scheme!"

"The Towers of Silence," Jijibhoi said. He went to the dining room's vast window and stood with his back to Klein, staring out at the dazzling lights of Los Angeles. The Jijibhois' house, all redwood and glass, perched precariously on stilts near the crest of Benedict Canyon, just below Mulholland: the view took in everything from Hollywood to Santa Monica. "There are five of them in Bombay," said Jijibhoi, "on Malabar Hill, a rooky ridge overlooking the Arabian Sea. They are centuries old, each one circular, several hundred feet in circumference, surrounded by a stone wall twenty or thirty feet high. When a Parsee dies—do you know of this?"

"Not as much as I'd like to know."

"When a Parsee dies, he is carried to the Towers on an iron bier by professional corpse-bearers; the mourners follow in procession, two by two, joined hand to hand by holding a white handkerchief between them. A beautiful scene, dear Jorge. There is a doorway in the stone wall through which the corpse-bearers pass, carrying their burden. No one else may enter the Tower. Within is a circular platform paved with large stone slabs and divided into three rows of shallow, open receptacles. The outer row is used for the bodies of males, the next for those of females, the innermost one for children. The dead one is given a resting-place; vultures rise from the lofty palms in the gardens adjoining the Towers; within an hour or two, only bones remain. Later, the bare, sun-dried skeleton is cast into a pit at the center of the Tower. Rich and poor crumble together there into dust."

"And all Parsees are—ah—buried in this way?"

"Oh, no, no, by no means," Jijibhoi said heartily. "All ancient traditions are in disrepair nowadays, do you not know? Our younger people advocate cremation or even conventional interment. Still, many of us continue to see the beauty of our way."

"Beauty?—"

Jijibhoi's wife said in a quiet voice, "To bury the dead in the ground, in a moist tropical land where diseases are highly contagious, seems not sanitary to us. And to burn a body is to waste its substance. But to give the bodies of the dead to the efficient hungry birds—quickly, cleanly, without fuss—is to us a way of celebrating the economy of nature. To have one's bones mingle in the pit with the bones of the entire community is, to us, the ultimate democracy."

"And the vultures spread no contagions themselves, feeding as they do on the bodies of—"

"Never," said Jijibhoi firmly. "Nor do they contract our ills."

"And I gather that you both intend to have your bodies returned to Bombay when you—" Aghast, Klein paused, shook his head, coughed in embarrassment, forced a weak smile. "You see what this radioactive curry of yours has done to my manners? Forgive me. Here I sit, a guest at your dinner table, quizzing you about your funeral plans!"

Jijibhoi chuckled. "Death is not frightening to us, dear friend. It is—one hardly needs say it, does one?—it is a natural event. For a time we are here, and then we go. When our time ends, yes, she and I will give ourselves to the Towers of Silence."

His wife added sharply, "Better there than the Cold Towns! Much better!"

Klein had never observed such vehemence in her before.

Jijibhoi swung back from the window and glared at her. Klein had never seen that before either. It seemed as if the fragile web of elaborate courtesy that he and these two had been spinning all evening was suddenly unraveling, and that even the bonds between Jijibhoi and his wife were undergoing strain. Agitated now, fluttery, Jijibhoi began to collect the empty dishes, and after a long awkward moment said, "She did not mean to give offense."

"Why should I be offended?"

"A person you love chose to go to the Cold Towns. You might think there was implied criticism of her in my wife's expression of distaste for—"

Klein shrugged. "She's entitled to her feelings about rekindling. I wonder, though—"

He halted, uneasy, fearing to probe too deeply.

"Yes?"

"It was irrelevant."

"Please," Jijibhoi said. "We are old friends."

"I was wondering," said Klein slowly, "if it doesn't make things hard for you, spending all your time among deads, studying them, mastering their ways, devoting your whole career to them, when your wife evidently despises the Cold Towns and everything that goes on in them. If the theme of your work repels her you must not be able to share it with her."

"Oh," Jijibhoi said, tension visibly going from him, "if it comes to that, I have even less liking for the entire rekindling phenomenon than she."

"You do?" This was a side of Jijibhoi that Klein had never suspected. "It repels you? Then why did you choose to make such an intensive survey of it?"

Jijibhoi looked genuinely amazed. "What? Are you saying one must have personal allegiance to the subject of one's field of scholarship?" He laughed. "You are of Jewish birth, I think, and yet your doctoral thesis was concerned, was it not, with the early phases of the Third Reich?"

Klein winced. *"Touché!"*

"I find the subculture of the deads irresistible, as a sociologist," Jijibhoi went on. "To have such a radical new aspect of human existence erupt during one's career is an incredible gift. There is no more fertile field for me to investigate. Yet I have no wish, none at all, ever to deliver myself up for rekindling. For me, for my wife, it will be the Towers of Silence, the hot sun, the obliging vultures —and finish, the end, no more, terminus."

"I had no idea you felt this way. I suppose if I'd known more about Parsee theology, I might have realized—"

"You misunderstand. Our objections are not theological. It is that we share a wish, an idiosyncratic whim, not to continue beyond the allotted time. But also I have serious reservations about the impact of rekindling on our society. I feel a profound distress at the presence among us of these deads, I feel a purely private fear of these people and the culture they are creating, I feel even an abhorrence for—" Jijibhoi cut himself short. "Your pardon. That was perhaps too strong a word. You see how complex my attitudes are toward this subject, my mixture of fascination and repulsion? I exist in constant tension between those poles. But why do I tell you all this, which if it does not disturb you must surely bore you? Let us hear about your journey to Zanzibar."

"What can I say? I went, I waited a couple of weeks for her to show up, I wasn't able to get near her at all, and I came home. All the way to Africa and I never even had a glimpse of her."

"What a frustration, dear Jorge!"

"She stayed in her hotel room. They wouldn't let me go upstairs to her."

"They?"

"Her entourage," Klein said. "She was traveling with four other deads, a woman and three men. Sharing her room with the archaeologist, Zacharias. He was the one who shielded her from me, and did it very cleverly, too. He acts as though he owns her. Perhaps he does. What can you tell me, Framji? Do the deads marry? Is Zacharias her new husband?"

"It is very doubtful. The terms 'wife' and 'husband' are not in use among the deads. They form relationships, yes, but pair-bonding seems to be uncommon among them, possibly altogether unknown. Instead they tend to create supportive pseudo-familial groupings of three or four or even more individuals, who—"

"Do you mean that all four of her companions in Zanzibar are her lovers?"

Jijibhoi gestured eloquently. "Who can say? If you mean in a physical sense, I doubt it, but one can never be sure. Zacharias seems to be her special companion, at any rate. Several of the others may be part of her pseudo-family also, or all, or none. I have reason to think that at certain times every dead may claim a familial relationship to all others of his kind. Who can say? We perceive the doings of these people, as they say, through a glass, darkly."

"I don't see Sybille even that well. I don't even know what she looks like now."

"She has lost none of her beauty."

"So you've told me before. But I want to see her myself. You can't really comprehend, Framji, how much I want to see her. The pain I feel, not able—"

"Would you like to see her right now?"

Klein shook in a convulsion of amazement. "What? What do you mean? Is she—"

"Hiding in the next room? No, no, nothing like that. But I do have a small surprise for you. Come into the library." Smiling expansively, Jijibhoi led the way from the dining room to the small study adjoining it, a room densely packed from floor to ceiling with books in an astonishing range of languages—not merely English, French, and German, but also Sanskrit, Hindi, Gujerati, Farsi, the tongues of Jijibhoi's polyglot upbringing among the tiny Parsee colony of Bombay, a community in which no language once cherished was ever discarded. Pushing aside a stack of dog-eared professional journals, he drew forth a glistening picture-cube, activated its inner light with a touch of his thumb, and handed it to Klein.

The sharp, dazzling holographic image showed three figures in a broad grassy plain that seemed to have no limits and was without trees, boulders, or other visual interruptions, an endlessly unrolling green carpet under a blank death-blue sky. Zacharias stood at the left, his face averted from the camera; he was looking down, tinkering with the action of an enormous rifle. At the far right stood a stocky, powerful-looking dark-haired man whose pale, harsh-featured face seemed all beard and nostrils. Klein recognized him: Anthony Gracchus, one of the deads who had accompanied Sybille to Zanzibar. Sybille stood beside him, clad in khaki slacks and a crisp white blouse. Gracchus' arm was extended; evidently he had just pointed out a target to her, and she was intently aiming a gun nearly as big as Zacharias'.

Klein shifted the cube about, studying her face from various angles, and the sight of her made his fingers grow thick and clumsy, his eyelids to quiver. Jijibhoi had spoken truly: she had lost none of her beauty. Yet she was not at all the Sybille he had known. When he had last seen her, lying in her casket, she had seemed to be a flawless marble image of herself, and she had that same surreal statuary appearance now. Her face was an expressionless mask, calm, remote, aloof; her eyes were glossy mysteries; her lips registered a faint, enigmatic, barely perceptible smile. It frightened him to behold her this way, so alien, so unfamiliar. Perhaps it was the intensity of her concentration that gave her that forbidding marmoreal look, for she seemed to be pouring her entire being into the task of taking aim. By tilting the cube more extremely, Klein was able to see what she was aiming at: a strange awkward bird moving through the grass at the lower left, a bird larger than a turkey, round as a sack, with ash-gray plumage, a whitish breast and tail, yellow-white wings, and short, comical yellow legs. Its head was immense and its black bill ended in a great snubbed hook. The creature seemed solemn, rather dignified, and faintly absurd; it showed no awareness that its doom was upon it. How odd that Sybille should be about to kill it, she who had always detested the taking of life: Sybille the huntress now, Sybille the lunar goddess, Sybille-Diana!

Shaken, Klein looked up at Jijibhoi and said, "Where was this taken? On that safari in Tanzania, I suppose."

"Yes. In February. This man is the guide, the white hunter."

"I saw him in Zanzibar. Gracchus, his name is. He was one of the deads traveling with Sybille."

"He operates a hunting preserve not far from Kilimanjaro," Jijibhoi said, "that is set aside exclusively for the use of the deads. One of the more bizarre manifestations of their subculture, actually. They hunt only those animals which—"

Klein said impatiently, "How did you get this picture?"

"It was taken by Nerita Tracy, who is one of your wife's companions."

"I met her in Zanzibar too. But how—"

"A friend of hers is an acquaintance of mine, one of my informants, in fact, a valuable connection in my researches. Some months ago I asked him if he could obtain something like this for me. I did not tell him, of course, that I meant it for you." Jijibhoi looked close. "You seem troubled, dear friend."

Klein nodded. He shut his eyes as though to protect them from the glaring surfaces of Sybille's photograph. Eventually he said in a flat, toneless voice, "I have to get to see her."

"Perhaps it would be better for you if you would abandon—"

"*No.*"

"Is there no way I can convince you that it is dangerous for you to pursue your fantasy of—"

"No," Klein said. "Don't even try. It's necessary for me to reach her. Necessary."

"How will you accomplish this, then?"

Klein said mechanically, "By going to Zion Cold Town."

"You have already done that. They would not admit you."

"This time they will. They don't turn away deads."

The Parsee's eyes widened. "You will surrender your own life? Is this your plan? What are you saying, Jorge?"

Klein, laughing, said, "That isn't what I meant at all."

"I am bewildered."

"I intend to infiltrate. I'll disguise myself as one of them. I'll slip into the Cold Town the way an infidel slips into Mecca." He seized Jijibhoi's wrist. "Can you help me? Coach me in their ways, teach me their jargon?"

"They'll find you out instantly."

"Maybe not. Maybe I'll get to Sybille before they do."

"This is insanity," Jijibhoi said quietly.

"Nevertheless. You have the knowledge. Will you help me?"

Gently Jijibhoi withdrew his arm from Klein's grasp. He crossed the room and busied himself with an untidy bookshelf for some moments, fussily arranging and rearranging. At length he said, "There is little I can do for you myself. My knowledge is broad but not deep, not deep enough. But if you insist on going through with this, Jorge, I can introduce you to someone who may be able to assist you. He is one of my informants, a dead, a man who has rejected the authority of the Guidefathers, a person who is *of* the deads but not *with* them. Possibly he can instruct you in what you would need to know."

"Call him," Klein said.

"I must warn you he is unpredictable, turbulent, perhaps even treacherous. Ordinary human values are without meaning to him in his present state."

"Call him."

"If only I could discourage you from—"

"Call him."

5.

Quarreling brings trouble. These days lions roar a great deal. Joy follows grief. It is not good to beat children much. You had better go away now and go home. It is impossible to work today. You should go to school every day. It is not advisable to follow this path, there is water in the way. Never mind, I shall be able to pass. We had better go back quickly. These lamps use a lot of oil. There are no mosquitoes in Nairobi. There are no lions here. There are people here, looking for eggs. Is there water in the well? No, there is none. If there are only three people, work will be impossible today.

—D. V. PERROTT, *Teach Yourself Swahili*

Gracchus signals furiously to the porters and bellows, *"Shika njia hii hii!"* Three turn, two keep trudging along. *"Ninyi nyote!"* he calls. *"Fanga kama hivi!"* He shakes his head, spits, flicks sweat from his forehead. He adds, speaking in a lower voice and in English, taking care that they will not hear him, "Do as I say, you malevolent black bastards, or you'll be deader than I am before sunset!"

Sybille laughs nervously. "Do you always talk to them like that?"

"I try to be easy on them. But what good does it do, what good does any of it do? Come on, let's keep up with them."

It is less than an hour after dawn but already the sun is very hot, here in the flat dry country between Kilimanjaro and Serengeti. Gracchus is leading the party northward across the high grass, following the spoor of what he thinks is a quagga, but breaking a trail in the high grass is hard work and the porters keep veering away toward a ravine that offers the tempting shade of a thicket of thorn trees, and he constantly has to harass them in order to hold them to the route he wants. Sybille has noticed that Gracchus shouts fiercely to his blacks, as if they were no more than recalcitrant beasts, and speaks of them behind their backs with a rough contempt, but it all seems done for show, all part of his white-hunter role: she has also noticed, at times when she was not supposed to notice, that privately Gracchus is in fact gentle, tender, even loving among the porters, teasing them—she supposes—with affectionate Swahili banter and playful mock-punches. The porters are role-players too: they behave in the traditional manner of their profession, alternately deferential and patronizing to the clients, alternately posing as all-knowing repositories of the lore of the bush and as simple, guileless savages fit only for carrying burdens. But the clients they serve are not quite like the sportsmen of Hemingway's time, since they are deads, and secretly the porters are terrified of the strange beings whom they serve. Sybille has seen them muttering prayers and fondling amulets whenever they accidentally touch one of the deads, and has occasionally detected an unguarded glance conveying unalloyed fear, possibly revulsion. Gracchus is no friend of theirs, however jolly he may get with them: they appear to regard him as some sort of monstrous sorcerer and the clients as fiends made manifest.

Sweating, saying little, the hunters move in single file, first the porters with the guns and supplies, then Gracchus, Zacharias, Sybille, Nerita constantly licking her camera, and Mortimer. Patches of white cloud drift slowly across the immense arch of the sky. The grass is lush and thick, for the short rains were unusually heavy in December. Small animals scurry through it, visible only in quick flashes, squirrels and jackals and guineafowl. Now and then larger creatures can be seen: three haughty ostriches, a pair of snuffling hyenas, a band of Thomson gazelles flowing like a tawny river across the plain. Yesterday Sybille spied two warthogs, some giraffes, and a serval, an elegant big-eared wildcat that slithered along like a miniature cheetah. None of these beasts may be hunted, but only those special ones that the operators of the preserve have introduced for the special needs of their clients; anything considered native African wildlife, which is to say anything that was living here before the deads leased this tract from the Masai, is protected by government decree. The Masai themselves are allowed to do some lion-hunting, since this is their reservation, but there are so few Masai left that they can do little harm. Yesterday, after the warthogs and before the giraffes, Sybille saw her first Masai, five lean, handsome, long-bodied men, naked under skimpy red robes, drifting silently through the bush, pausing frequently to stand thoughtfully on one leg, propped against their spears. At close range they were less handsome—toothless, fly-specked, herniated. They offered to sell their spears and their beaded collars for a few shillings, but the safarigoers had already stocked up on Masai artifacts in Nairobi's curio shops, at astonishingly higher prices.

All through the morning they stalk the quagga, Gracchus pointing out hoofprints here, fresh dung there. It is Zacharias who has asked to shoot a quagga. "How can you tell we're not following a zebra?" he asks peevishly.

Gracchus winks. "Trust me. We'll find zebras up ahead too. But you'll get your quagga. I guarantee it."

Ngiri, the head porter, turns and grins. *"Piga quagga m'uzuri, bwana,"* he says to Zacharias, and winks also, and then—Sybille sees it plainly—his jovial confident smile fades as though he has had the courage to sustain it only for an instant, and a veil of dread covers his dark glossy face.

"What did he say?" Zacharias asks.

"That you'll shoot a fine quagga," Gracchus replies.

Quaggas. The last wild one was killed about 1870, leaving only three in the world, all females, in European zoos. The Boers had hunted them to the edge of extinction in order to feed their tender meat to Hottentot slaves and to make from their striped hides sacks for Boer grain, leather *veldschoen* for Boer feet. The quagga of the London zoo died in 1872, that in Berlin in 1875, the Amsterdam quagga in 1883, and none was seen alive again until the artificial revival of the species through breedback selection and genetic manipulation in 1990, when this hunting preserve was opened to a limited and special clientele.

It is nearly noon, now, and not a shot has been fired all morning. The animals have begun heading for cover; they will not emerge until the shadows lengthen. Time to halt, pitch camp, break out the beer and sandwiches, tell tall tales of harrowing adventures with maddened buffaloes and edgy elephants. But not quite yet. The marchers come over a low hill and see, in the long sloping hollow beyond, a flock of ostriches and several hundred grazing zebras. As the humans appear, the ostriches begin slowly and warily to move off, but the zebras, altogether unafraid, continue to graze. Ngiri points and says, *"Piga quagga, bwana."*

"Just a bunch of zebras," Zacharias says.

Gracchus shakes his head. "No. Listen. You hear the sound?"

At first no one perceives anything unusual. But then, yes, Sybille hears it: a shrill barking neigh, very strange, a sound out of lost time, the cry of some beast she has never known. It is a song of the dead. Nerita hears it too, and Mortimer, and finally Zacharias. Gracchus nods toward the far side of the hollow. There, among the zebras, are half a dozen animals that might almost be zebras, but are not—unfinished zebras, striped only on their heads and fore-parts; the rest of their bodies are yellowish-brown, their legs are white, their manes are dark brown with pale stripes. Their coats sparkle like mica in the sunshine. Now and again they lift their

heads, emit that weird percussive whistling snort, and bend to the
grass again. Quaggas. Strays out of the past, relicts, rekindled
specters. Gracchus signals and the party fans out along the peak
of the hill. Ngiri hands Zacharias his colossal gun. Zacharias kneels,
sights.

"No hurry," Gracchus murmurs. "We have all afternoon."

"Do I seem to be hurrying?" Zacharias asks. The zebras now
block the little group of quaggas from his view, almost as if by
design. He must not shoot a zebra, of course, or there will be
trouble with the rangers. Minutes go by. Then the screen of zebras
abruptly parts and Zacharias squeezes his trigger. There is a vast
explosion; zebras bolt in ten directions, so that the eye is bom-
barded with dizzying stroboscopic waves of black and white; when
the convulsive confusion passes, one of the quaggas is lying on its
side, alone in the field, having made the transition across the
interface. Sybille regards it calmly. Death once dismayed her,
death of any kind, but no longer.

"*Piga m'uzuri!*" the porters cry exultantly.

"*Kufa,*" Gracchus says. "Dead. A neat shot. You have your trophy."

Ngiri is quick with the skinning-knife. That night, camping below Kilimanjaro's broad flank, they dine on roast quagga, deads
and porters alike. The meat is juicy, robust, faintly tangy.

Late the following afternoon, as they pass through cooler
stream-broken country thick with tall, scrubby gray-green vase-
shaped trees, they come upon a monstrosity, a shaggy shambling
thing twelve or fifteen feet high, standing upright on ponderous
hind legs and balancing itself on an incredibly thick, heavy tail. It
leans against a tree, pulling at its top branches with long forelimbs
that are tipped with ferocious claws like a row of sickles; it
munches voraciously on leaves and twigs. Briefly it notices them,
and looks around, studying them with small stupid yellow eyes;
then it returns to its meal.

"A rarity," Gracchus says. "I know hunters who have been all
over this park without ever running into one. Have you ever seen
anything so ugly?"

"What is it?" Sybille asks.

"Megatherium. Giant ground sloth. South American, really, but we weren't fussy about geography when we were stocking this place. We have only four of them, and it costs God knows how many thousands of dollars to shoot one. Nobody's signed up for a ground sloth yet. I doubt anyone will."

Sybille wonders where the beast might be vulnerable to a bullet: surely not in its dim peanut-sized brain. She wonders, too, what sort of sportsman would find pleasure in killing such a thing. For a while they watch as the sluggish monster tears the tree apart. Then they move on.

Gracchus shows them another prodigy at sundown: a pale dome, like some huge melon, nestling in a mound of dense grass beside a stream. "Ostrich egg?" Mortimer guesses.

"Close. Very close. It's a moa egg. World's biggest bird. From New Zealand, extinct since about the eighteenth century."

Nerita crouches and lightly taps the egg. "What an omelet we could make!"

"There's enough there to feed seventy-five of us," Gracchus says. "Two gallons of fluid, easy. But of course we mustn't meddle with it. Natural increase is very important in keeping this park stocked."

"And where's mama moa?" Sybille asks. "Should she have abandoned the egg?"

"Moas aren't very bright," Gracchus answers. "That's one good reason why they became extinct. She must have wandered off to find some dinner. And—"

"Good God," Zacharias blurts.

The moa has returned, emerging suddenly from a thicket. She stands like a feathered mountain above them, limned by the deep blue of twilight: an ostrich, more or less, but a magnified ostrich, an ultimate ostrich, a bird a dozen feet high, with a heavy rounded body and a great thick hose of a neck and taloned legs sturdy as saplings. Surely this is Sinbad's rukh that can fly off with elephants in its grasp! The bird peers at them, sadly contemplating the band of small beings clustered about her egg; she arches her neck as

though readying for an attack, and Zacharias reaches for one of the
rifles, but Gracchus checks his hand, for the moa is merely rearing
back to protest. It utters a deep mournful mooing sound and does
not move. "Just back slowly away," Gracchus tells them. "It won't
attack. But keep away from the feet; one kick can kill you."

"I was going to apply for a license on a moa," Mortimer says.

"Killing them's a bore," Gracchus tells him. "They just stand
there and let you shoot. You're better off with what you signed up
for."

What Mortimer has signed up for is an aurochs, the vanished
wild ox of the European forests, known to Caesar, known to Pliny,
hunted by the hero Siegfried, altogether exterminated by the year
1627. The plains of East Africa are not a comfortable environment
for the aurochs and the herd that has been conjured by the genetic
necromancers keeps to itself in the wooded highlands, several
days' journey from the haunts of quaggas and ground sloths. In this
dark grove the hunters come upon troops of chattering baboons
and solitary big-eared elephants and, in a place of broken sunlight
and shadow, a splendid antelope, a bull bongo with a fine curving
pair of horns. Gracchus leads them onward, deeper in. He seems
tense: there is peril here. The porters slip through the forest like
black wraiths, spreading out in arching crab-claw patterns, com-
municating with one another and with Gracchus by whistling.
Everyone keeps weapons ready in here. Sybille half expects to see
leopards draped on overhanging branches, cobras slithering
through the undergrowth. But she feels no fear.

They approach a clearing.

"Aurochs," Gracchus says.

A dozen of them are cropping the shrubbery: big short-haired
long-horned cattle, muscular and alert. Picking up the scent of the
intruders, they lift their heavy heads, sniff, glare. Gracchus and
Ngiri confer with eyebrows. Nodding, Gracchus mutters to Mortimer, "Too many of them. Wait for them to thin off." Mortimer
smiles. He looks a little nervous. The aurochs has a reputation for
attacking without warning. Four, five, six of the beasts slip away,

and the others withdraw to the edge of the clearing, as if to plan strategy; but one big bull, sour-eyed and grim, stands his ground, glowering. Gracchus rolls on the balls of his feet. His burly body seems, to Sybille, a study in mobility, in preparedness.

"Now," he says.

In the same moment the bull aurochs charges, moving with extraordinary swiftness, head lowered, horns extended like spears. Mortimer fires. The bullet strikes with a loud whonking sound, crashing into the shoulder of the aurochs, a perfect shot, but the animal does not fall, and Mortimer shoots again, less gracefully ripping into the belly, and then Gracchus and Ngiri are firing also, not at Mortimer's aurochs but over the heads of the others, to drive them away, and the risky tactic works, for the other animals go stampeding off into the woods. The one Mortimer has shot continues toward him, staggering now, losing momentum, and falls practically at his feet, rolling over, knifing the forest floor with its hooves.

"*Kufa,*" Ngiri says. "*Piga nyati m'uzuri, bwana.*"

Mortimer grins. "*Piga,*" he says.

Gracchus salutes him. "More exciting than moa," he says.

"And these are mine," says Nerita three hours later, indicating a tree at the outer rim of the forest. Several hundred large pigeons nest in its boughs, so many of them that the tree seems to be sprouting birds rather than leaves. The females are plain—light brown above, gray below—but the males are flamboyant, with rich, glossy blue plumage on their wings and backs, breasts of a wine-red chestnut color, iridescent spots of bronze and green on their necks, and weird, vivid eyes of a bright, fiery orange. Gracchus says, "Right. You've found your passenger pigeons."

"Where's the thrill in shooting pigeons out of a tree?" Mortimer asks.

Nerita gives him a withering look. "Where's the thrill in gunning down a charging bull?" She signals to Ngiri, who fires a shot into the air. The startled pigeons burst from their perches and fly in low circles. In the old days, a century and a half ago in the forests of North America, no one troubled to shoot passenger pigeons on the wing: the pigeons were food, not sport, and it was simpler to blast them as they sat, for that way a single hunter might kill thousands of birds in one day. Thus it took only fifty years to reduce the passenger pigeon population from uncountable sky-blackening billions to zero. Nerita is more sporting. This is a test of her skill, after all. She aims her shotgun, shoots, pumps, shoots, pumps. Stunned birds drop to the ground. She and her gun are a single entity, sharing one purpose. In moments it is all over. The porters retrieve the fallen birds and snap their necks. Nerita has the dozen pigeons her license allows: a pair to mount, the rest for tonight's dinner. The survivors have returned to their tree and stare placidly, unreproachfully, at the hunters. "They breed so damned fast," Gracchus mutters. "If we aren't careful, they'll be getting out of the preserve and taking over all of Africa."

Sybille laughs. "Don't worry. We'll cope. We wiped them out once and we can do it again, if we have to."

Sybille's prey is a dodo. In Dar, when they were applying for their licenses, the others mocked her choice: a fat flightless bird, unable to run or fight, so feeble of wit that it fears nothing. She ignored them. She wants a dodo because to her it is the essence of extinction, the prototype of all that is dead and vanished. That there is no sport in shooting foolish dodos means little to Sybille. Hunting itself is meaningless for her.

Through this vast park she wanders as in a dream. She sees ground sloths, great auks, quaggas, moas, heath hens, Javan rhinos, giant armadillos, and many other rarities. The place is an abode of ghosts. The ingenuities of the genetic craftsmen are limitless; someday, perhaps, the preserve will offer trilobites, tyrannosaurs, mastodons, saber-toothed cats, baluchitheria, even—why not?—packs of australopithecines, tribes of Neanderthals. For the amusement of the deads, whose games tend to be somber. Sybille wonders whether it can really be considered killing, this slaughter of laboratory-spawned novelties. Are these animals real or artificial? Living things, or cleverly animated constructs? Real, she decides.

Living. They eat, they metabolize, they reproduce. They must seem real to themselves, and so they are real, realer, maybe, than dead human beings who walk again in their own cast-off bodies.

"Shotgun," Sybille says to the closest porter.

There is the bird, ugly, ridiculous, waddling laboriously through the tall grass. Sybille accepts a weapon and sights along its barrel. "Wait," Nerita says. "I'd like to get a picture of this." She moves slantwise around the group, taking exaggerated care not to frighten the dodo, but the dodo does not seem to be aware of any of them. Like an emissary from the realm of darkness, carrying good news of death to those creatures not yet extinct, it plods diligently across their path. "Fine," Nerita says "Anthony, point at the dodo, will you, as if you've just noticed it? Kent, I'd like you to look down at your gun, study its bolt or something. Fine. And Sybille, just hold that pose—aiming—yes—"

Nerita takes the picture.

Calmly Sybille pulls the trigger.

"Kazi imekwisha," Gracchus says. "The work is finished."

6.

Although to be driven back upon oneself is an uneasy affair at best, rather like trying to cross a border with borrowed credentials, it seems to be now the one condition necessary to the beginnings of real self-respect. Most of our platitudes notwithstanding, self-deception remains the most difficult deception. The tricks that work on others count for nothing in that very well-lit back alley where one keeps assignations with oneself: no winning smiles will do here, no prettily drawn lists of good intentions.

—JOAN DIDION, *On Self-Respect*

"You better believe what Jeej is trying to tell you," Dolorosa said. "Ten minutes inside the Cold Town, they'll have your number. Five minutes."

Jijibhoi's man was small, rumpled-looking, forty or fifty years old, with untidy long dark hair and wide-set smoldering eyes. His skin was sallow and his face was gaunt. Such other deads as Klein had seen at close range had about them an air of unearthly serenity, but not this one: Dolorosa was tense, fidgety, a knuckle-cracker, a lip-gnawer. Yet somehow there could be no doubt he was a dead, as much a dead as Zacharias, as Gracchus, as Mortimer.

"They'll have my what?" Klein asked.

"Your number. Your number. They'll know you aren't a dead, because it can't be faked. Jesus, don't you even speak English? Jorge, that's a foreign name. I should have known. Where are you from?"

"Argentina, as a matter of fact, but I was brought to California when I was a small boy. In 1955. Look, if they catch me, they catch me. I just want to get in there and spend half an hour talking with my wife."

"Mister, you don't have any wife any more."

"With Sybille," Klein said, exasperated. "To talk with Sybille, my—my former wife."

"All right. I'll get you inside."

"What will it cost?"

"Never mind that," Dolorosa said. "I owe Jeej here a few favors. More than a few. So I'll get you the drug—"

"Drug?"

"The drug the Treasury agents use when they infiltrate the Cold Towns. It narrows the pupils, contracts the capillaries, gives you that good old zombie look. The agents always get caught and thrown out, and so will you, but at least you'll go in there feeling that you've got a convincing disguise. Little oily capsule, one every morning before breakfast."

Klein looked at Jijibhoi. "Why do Treasury agents infiltrate the Cold Towns?"

"For the same reasons they infiltrate anywhere else," Jijibhoi said. "To spy. They are trying to compile dossiers on the financial dealings of the deads, you see, and until proper life-defining legis-lation is approved by Congress there is no precise way of compelling a person who is deemed legally dead to divulge—"

Dolorosa said, "Next, the background. I can get you a card of residence from Albany Cold Town in New York. You died last December, okay, and they rekindled you back east because—let's see—"

"I could have been attending the annual meeting of the American Historical Association in New York," Klein suggested. "That's what I do, you understand, professor of contemporary history at UCLA. Because of the Christmas holiday my body couldn't be shipped back to California, no room on any flight, and so they took me to Albany. How does that sound?"

Dolorosa smiled. "You really enjoy making up lies, Professor, don't you? I can dig that quality in you. Okay, Albany Cold Town, and this is your first trip out of there, your drying-off trip—that's what it's called, drying-off—you come out of the Cold Town like a new butterfly just out of its cocoon, all soft and damp, and you're on your own in a strange place. Now, there's a lot of stuff you'll need to know about how to behave, little mannerisms, social graces, that kind of crap, and I'll work on that with you tomorrow and Wednesday and Friday, three sessions; that ought to be enough. Meanwhile let me give you the basics. There are only three things you really have to remember while you're inside:

"1) Never ask a direct question.

"2) Never lean on anybody's arm. You know what I mean?

"3) Keep in mind that to a dead the whole universe is plastic, nothing's real, nothing matters a hell of a lot, it's all only a joke. Only a joke, friend, only a joke."

Early in April he flew to Salt Lake City, rented a car, and drove out past Moab into the high plateau rimmed by red-rock mountains where the deads had built Zion Cold Town. This was Klein's second visit to the necropolis. The other had been in the late summer of '91, a hot, parched season when the sun filled half the sky and even the gnarled junipers looked dazed from thirst; but now it was a frosty afternoon, with faint pale light streaming out of the wintry western hills and occasional gusts of light snow whirl-

ing through the iron-blue air. Jijibhoi's route instructions pulsed
from the memo screen on his dashboard. Fourteen miles from
town, yes, narrow paved lane turns off highway, yes, discreet little
sign announcing PRIVATE ROAD, NO ADMITTANCE, yes, a second
sign a thousand yards in, ZION COLD TOWN, MEMBERS ONLY, yes,
and then just beyond that the barrier of green light across the
road, the scanner system, the roadblocks sliding like scythes out of
the underground installations, a voice on an invisible loudspeaker
saying, "If you have a permit to enter Zion Cold Town, please
place it under your left-hand windshield wiper."

That other time he had had no permit, and he had gone no
farther than this, though at least he had managed a little colloquy
with the unseen gatekeeper out of which he had squeezed the
information that Sybille was indeed living in that particular Cold
Town. This time he affixed Dolorosa's forged card of residence to
his windshield, and waited tensely, and in thirty seconds the roadblocks slid from sight. He drove on, along a winding road that
followed the natural contours of a dense forest of scrubby conifers,
and came at last to a brick wall that curved away into the trees as
though it encircled the entire town. Probably it did. Klein had an
overpowering sense of the Cold Town as a hermetic city, ponderous and sealed as old Egypt. There was a metal gate in the brick
wall; green electronic eyes surveyed him, signaled their approval,
and the wall rolled open.

He drove slowly toward the center of town, passing through a
zone of what he supposed were utility buildings—storage depots,
a power substation, the municipal waterworks, whatever, a bunch
of grim windowless one-story cinderblock affairs—and then into
the residential district, which was not much lovelier. The streets
were laid out on a rectangular grid; the buildings were squat,
dreary, impersonal, homogeneous. There was practically no automobile traffic, and in a dozen blocks he saw no more than ten
pedestrians, who did not even glance at him. So this was the
environment in which the deads chose to spend their second lives.
But why such deliberate bleakness? "You will never understand
us," Dolorosa had warned. Dolorosa was right. Jijibhoi had told

him that Cold Towns were something less than charming, but Klein had not been prepared for this. There was a glacial quality about the place, as though it were wholly entombed in a block of clear ice: silence, sterility, a mortuary calm. Cold Town, yes, aptly named. Architecturally, the town looked like the worst of all possible cheap-and-sleazy tract developments, but the psychic texture it projected was even more depressing, more like that of one of those ghastly retirement communities, one of the innumerable Leisure Worlds or Sun Manors, those childless joyless retreats where colonies of that other kind of living dead collected to await the last trumpet. Klein shivered.

At last, another few minutes deeper into the town, a sign of activity, if not exactly of life: a shopping center, flat-topped brown stucco buildings around a U-shaped courtyard, a steady flow of shoppers moving about. All right. His first test was about to commence. He parked his car near the mouth of the U and strolled uneasily inward. He felt as if his forehead were a beacon, flashing glowing betrayals at rhythmic intervals:

FRAUD   INTRUDER   INTERLOPER   SPY

Go ahead, he thought, seize me, seize the impostor, get it over with, throw me out, string me up, crucify me. But no one seemed to pick up the signals. He was altogether ignored. Out of courtesy? Or just contempt? He stole what he hoped were covert glances at the shoppers, half expecting to run across Sybille right away. They all looked like sleepwalkers, moving in glazed silence about their errands. No smiles, no chatter: the icy aloofness of these self-contained people heightened the familiar suburban atmosphere of the shopping center into surrealist intensity, Norman Rockwell with an overlay of Dali or De Chirico. The shopping center looked like all other shopping centers: clothing stores, a bank, a record shop, snack bars, a florist, a TV-stereo outlet, a theater, a five-and-dime. One difference, though, became apparent as Klein wandered from shop to shop: the whole place was automated. There were no clerks anywhere, only the ubiquitous data screens, and no doubt a battery of hidden scanners to discourage shoplifters. (Or did the impulse toward petty theft perish with the body's first death?) The customers selected all the merchandise themselves, checked it out via data screens, touched their thumbs to charge plates to debit their accounts. Of course. No one was going to waste his precious rekindled existence standing behind a counter to sell tennis shoes or cotton candy. Nor were the dwellers in the Cold Towns likely to dilute their isolation by hiring a labor force of imported warms. Somebody here had to do a little work, obviously—how did the merchandise get into the stores?—but, in general, Klein realized, what could not be done here by machines would not be done at all.

For ten minutes he prowled the center. Just when he was beginning to think he must be entirely invisible to these people, a short, broad-shouldered man, bald but with oddly youthful features, paused in front of him and said, "I am Pablo. I welcome you to Zion Cold Town." This unexpected puncturing of the silence so startled Klein that he had to fight to retain appropriate deadlike imperturbability. Pablo smiled warmly and touched both his hands to Klein's in friendly greeting, but his eyes were frigid, hostile, remote, a terrifying contradiction. "I've been sent to bring you to the lodging-place. Come: your car."

Other than to give directions, Pablo spoke only three times during the five-minute drive. "Here is the rekindling house," he said. A five-story building, as inviting as a hospital, with walls of dark bronze and windows black as onyx. "This is Guidefather's house," Pablo said a moment later. A modest brick building, like a rectory, at the edge of a small park. And, finally: "This is where you will stay. Enjoy your visit." Abruptly he got out of the car and walked rapidly away.

This was the house of strangers, the hotel for visiting deads, a long low cinderblock structure, functional and unglamorous, one of the least seductive buildings in this city of stark disagreeable buildings. However else it might be with the deads, they clearly had no craving for fancy architecture. A voice out of a data screen in the spartan lobby assigned him to a room: a white-walled box, square, high of ceiling. He had his own toilet, his own data screen, a narrow bed, a chest of drawers, a modest closet, a small window that gave him a view of a neighboring building just as drab as this. Nothing had been said about rental; perhaps he was a guest of the city. Nothing had been said about anything. It seemed that he had been accepted. So much for Jijibhoi's gloomy assurance that he would instantly be found out, so much for Dolorosa's insistence that they would have his number in ten minutes or less. He had been in Zion Cold Town for half an hour. Did they have his number?

"Eating isn't important among us," Dolorosa had said.
"But you do eat?"
"Of course we eat. It just isn't *important.*"
It was important to Klein, though. Not *haute cuisine*, necessarily, but some sort of food, preferably three times a day. He was getting hungry now. Ring for room service? There were no servants in this city. He turned to the data screen. Dolorosa's first rule: *Never ask a direct question.* Surely that didn't apply to the data screen, only to his fellow deads. He didn't have to observe the niceties of etiquette when talking to a computer. Still, the voice behind the screen might not be that of a computer after all, so he tried to employ the oblique, elliptical conversational style that Dolorosa said the deads favored among themselves:
"Dinner?"
"Commissary."
"Where?"
"Central Four," said the screen.
Central Four? All right. He would find the way. He changed into fresh clothing and went down the long vinyl-floored hallway to the lobby. Night had come; streetlamps were glowing; under cloak of darkness the city's ugliness was no longer so obtrusive, and there was even a kind of controlled beauty about the brutal regularity of its streets.
The streets were unmarked, though, and deserted. Klein walked at random for ten minutes, hoping to meet someone head-

ing for the Central Four commissary. But when he did come upon someone, a tall and regal woman well advanced in years, he found himself incapable of approaching her. *(Never ask a direct question. Never lean on anybody's arm.)* He walked alongside her, in silence and at a distance, until she turned suddenly to enter a house. For ten minutes more he wandered alone again. This is ridiculous, he thought: dead or warm, I'm a stranger in town, I should be entitled to a little assistance. Maybe Dolorosa was just trying to complicate things. On the next corner, when Klein caught sight of a man hunched away from the wind, lighting a cigarette, he went boldly over to him.

"Excuse me, but—"

The other looked up. "Klein?" he said. "Yes. Of course. Well, so you've made the crossing too!"

He was one of Sybille's Zanzibar companions, Klein realized. The quick-eyed, sharp-edged one—Mortimer. A member of her pseudo-familial grouping, whatever that might be. Klein stared sullenly at him. This had to be the moment when his imposture would be exposed, for only some six weeks had passed since he had argued with Mortimer in the gardens of Sybille's Zanzibar hotel, not nearly enough time for someone to have died and been rekindled and gone through his drying-off. But a moment passed and Mortimer said nothing. At length Klein said, "I just got here. Pablo showed me to the house of strangers and now I'm looking for the commissary."

"Central Four? I'm going there myself. How lucky for you." No sign of suspicion in Mortimer's face. Perhaps an elusive smile revealed his awareness that Klein could not be what he claimed to be. *Keep in mind that to a dead the whole universe is plastic, it's all only a joke.* "I'm waiting for Nerita," Mortimer said. "We can all eat together."

Klein said heavily, "I was rekindled in Albany Cold Town. I've just emerged."

"How nice," Mortimer said.

Nerita Tracy stepped out of a building just beyond the corner —a slim athletic-looking woman, about forty, with short reddish-brown hair. As she swept toward them Mortimer said, "Here's

Klein, who we met in Zanzibar. Just rekindled, out of Albany."

"Sybille will be amused."

"Is she in town?" Klein blurted.

Mortimer and Nerita exchanged sly glances. Klein felt abashed. *Never ask a direct question.* Damn Dolorosa!

Nerita said, "You'll see her before long. Shall we go to dinner?"

The commissary was less austere than Klein had expected: actually quite an inviting restaurant, elaborately constructed on five or six levels divided by lustrous dark hangings into small, secluded dining areas. It had the warm, rich look of a tropical resort. But the food, which came automat-style out of revolving dispensers, was prefabricated and cheerless—another jarring contradiction. *Only a joke, friend, only a joke.* In any case he was less hungry than he had imagined at the hotel. He sat with Mortimer and Nerita, picking at his meal, while their conversation flowed past him at several times the speed of thought. They spoke in fragments and ellipses, in periphrastics and aposiopeses, in a style abundant in chiasmus, metonymy, meiosis, oxymoron, and zeugma; their dazzling rhetorical techniques left him baffled and uncomfortable, which beyond much doubt was their intention. Now and again they would dart from a thicket of indirection to skewer him with a quick corroborative stab: Isn't that so, they would say, and he would smile and nod, nod and smile, saying, Yes, yes, absolutely. Did they know he was a fake, and were they merely playing with him, or had they, somehow, impossibly, accepted him as one of them? So subtle was their style that he could not tell. A very new member of the society of the rekindled, he told himself, would be nearly as much at sea here as a warm in deadface.

Then Nerita said—no verbal games, this time—"You still miss her terribly, don't you?"

"I do. Some things evidently never perish."

"Everything perishes," Mortimer said. "The dodo, the aurochs, the Holy Roman Empire, the T'ang Dynasty, the walls of Byzantium, the language of Mohenjo-daro."

"But not the Great Pyramid, the Yangtze, the coelacanth, or the

skullcap of Pithecanthropus," Klein countered. "Some things per-
sist and endure. And some can be regenerated. Lost languages
have been deciphered. I believe the dodo and the aurochs are
hunted in a certain African park in this very era."

"Replicas," Mortimer said.

"Convincing replicas. Simulations as good as the original."

"Is that what you want?" Nerita asked.

"I want what's possible to have."

"A convincing replica of lost love?"

"I might be willing to settle for five minutes of conversation
with her."

"You'll have it. Not tonight. See? There she is. But don't bother
her now." Nerita nodded across the gulf in the center of the
restaurant; on the far side, three levels up from where they sat,
Sybille and Kent Zacharias had appeared. They stood for a brief
while at the edge of their dining alcove, staring blandly and emo-
tionlessly into the restaurant's central well. Klein felt a muscle
jerking uncontrollably in his cheek, a damning revelation of undeadlike uncoolness, and pressed his hand over it, so that it
twanged and throbbed against his palm. She was like a goddess up
there, manifesting herself in her sanctum to her worshippers, a
pale shimmering figure, more beautiful even than she had become
to him through the anguished enhancements of memory, and it
seemed impossible to him that that being had ever been his wife,
that he had known her when her eyes were puffy and reddened
from a night of study, that he had looked down at her face as they
made love and had seen her lips pull back in that spasm of ecstasy
that is so close to a grimace of pain, that he had known her
crotchety and unkind in her illness, short-tempered and impatient
in health, a person of flaws and weaknesses, of odors and
blemishes, in short a human being, this goddess, this unreal rekindled creature, this object of his quest, this Sybille. Serenely she
turned, serenely she vanished into her cloaked alcove. "She knows
you're here," Nerita told him. "You'll see her. Perhaps tomorrow."
Then Mortimer said something maddeningly oblique, and Nerita
replied with the same off-center mystification, and Klein once

more was plunged into the river of their easy dancing wordplay, down into it, down and down and down, and as he struggled to keep from drowning, as he fought to comprehend their inter-changes, he never once looked toward the place where Sybille sat, not even once, and congratulated himself on having accomplished that much at least in his masquerade.

That night, lying alone in his room at the house of strangers, he wonders what he will say to Sybille when they finally meet, and what she will say to him. Will he dare bluntly to ask her to describe to him the quality of her new existence? That is all that he wants from her, really, that knowledge, that opening of an aperture into her transfigured self; that is as much as he hopes to get from her, knowing as he does that there is scarcely a chance of regaining her, but will he dare to ask, will he dare even that? Of course his asking such things will reveal to her that he is still a warm, too dense and gross of perception to comprehend the life of a dead; but he is certain she will sense that anyway, instantly. What will he say, what will he say? He plays out an imagined script of their conver-sation in the theater of his mind:

—Tell me what it's like, Sybille, to be the way you are now.

—Like swimming under a sheet of glass.

—I don't follow.

—Everything is quiet where I am, Jorge. There's a peace that passeth all understanding. I used to feel sometimes that I was caught up in a great storm, that I was being buffeted by every breeze, that my life was being consumed by agitations and fren-zies, but now, now, I'm at the eye of the storm, at the place where everything is always calm. I observe rather than let myself be acted upon.

—But isn't there a loss of feeling that way? Don't you feel that you're wrapped in an insulating layer? Like swimming under glass, you say—that conveys being insulated, being cut off, being almost numb.

—I suppose you might think so. The way it is is that one no longer is affected by the unnecessary.

.—It sounds to me like a limited existence.

—Less limited than the grave, Jorge.

—I never understood why you wanted rekindling. You were such a world-devourer, Sybille, you lived with such intensity, such passion. To settle for the kind of existence you have now, to be only half alive—

—Don't be a fool, Jorge. To be half alive is better than to be rotting in the ground. I was so young. There was so much else still to see and do.

—But to see it and do it half alive?

—Those were your words, not mine. I'm not alive at all. I'm neither less nor more than the person you knew. I'm another kind of being altogether. Neither less nor more, only different.

—Are all your perceptions different?

—Very much so. My perspective is broader. Little things stand revealed as little things.

—Give me an example, Sybille.

—I'd rather not. How could I make anything clear to you? Die and be with us, and you'll understand.

—You know I'm not dead?

—Oh, Jorge, how funny you are!

—How nice that I can still amuse you.

—You look so hurt, so tragic. I could almost feel sorry for you. Come: ask me anything.

—Could you leave your companions and live in the world again?

—I've never considered that.

—Could you?

—I suppose I could. But why should I? This is my world now.

—This ghetto.

—Is that how it seems to you?

—You lock yourselves into a closed society of your peers, a tight subculture. Your own jargon, your own wall of etiquette and idiosyncrasy. Designed, I think, mainly to keep the outsiders off balance, to keep them feeling like outsiders. It's a defensive thing. The hippies, the blacks, the gays, the deads—same mechanism same process.

—The Jews, too. Don't forget the Jews.

—All right, Sybille, the Jews. With their little tribal jokes, their special holidays, their own mysterious language, yes, a good case in point.

—So I've joined a new tribe. What's wrong with that?

—Did you need to be part of a tribe?

—What did I have before? The tribe of Californians? The tribe of academics?

—The tribe of Jorge and Sybille Klein.

—Too narrow. Anyway, I've been expelled from that tribe. I noodod to join another one.

—Expelled?

—By death. After that there's no going back.

—You could go back. Any time.

—Oh, no, no, no, Jorge, I can't, I can't, I'm not Sybille Klein any more, I never will be again. How can I explain it to you? There's no way. Death brings on changes. Die and see, Jorge. Die and see.

Nerita said, "She's waiting for you in the lounge."

It was a big, coldly furnished room at the far end of the other wing of the house of strangers. Sybille stood by a window through which pale, chilly morning light was streaming. Mortimer was with her, and also Kent Zacharias. The two men favored Klein with mysterious oblique smiles—courteous or derisive, he could not tell which. "Do you like our town?" Zacharias asked. "Have you been seeing the sights?" Klein chose not to reply. He acknowledged the question with a faint nod and turned to Sybille. Strangely, he felt altogether calm at this moment of attaining a years-old desire: he felt nothing at all in her presence, no panic, no yearning, no dismay, no nostalgia, nothing, nothing. As though he were truly a dead. He knew it was the tranquility of utter terror.

"We'll leave you two alone," Zacharias said. "You must have so much to tell each other." He went out, with Nerita and Mortimer. Klein's eyes met Sybille's and lingered there. She was looking at him coolly, in a kind of impersonal appraisal. That damnable smile

of hers, Klein thought: dying turns them all into Mona Lisas.
She said, "Do you plan to stay here long?"
"Probably not. A few days, maybe a week." He moistened his
lips. "How have you been, Sybille? How has it been going?"
"It's all been about as I expected."
What do you mean by that? Can you give me some details? Are
you at all disappointed? Have there been any surprises? What has
it been like for you, Sybille? Oh, Jesus—
—Never ask a direct question—
He said, "I wish you had let me visit with you in Zanzibar."
"That wasn't possible. Let's not talk about it now." She dis-
missed the episode with a casual wave. After a moment she said,
"Would you like to hear a fascinating story I've uncovered about
the early days of Omani influence in Zanzibar?"
The impersonality of the question startled him. How could she
display such absolute lack of curiosity about his presence in Zion
Cold Town, his claim to be a dead, his reasons for wanting to see
her? How could she plunge so quickly, so coldly, into a discussion
of archaic political events in Zanzibar?
"I suppose so," he said weakly.
"It's a sort of Arabian Nights story, really. It's the story of how
Ahmad the Sly overthrew Abdullah ibn Muhammad Alawi."
The names were strange to him. He had indeed taken some
small part in her historical researches, but it was years since he had
worked with her, and everything had drifted about in his mind,
leaving a jumbled residue of Ahmads and Hasans and Abdullahs.
"I'm sorry," he said. "I don't recall who they were."
Unperturbed, Sybille said, "Certainly you remember that in the
eighteenth and early nineteenth centuries the chief power in the
Indian Ocean was the Arab state of Oman, ruled from Muscat on
the Persian Gulf. Under the Busaidi dynasty, founded in 1744 by
Ahmad ibn Said al-Busaidi, the Omani extended their power to
East Africa. The logical capital for their African empire was the
port of Mombasa, but they were unable to evict a rival dynasty
reigning there, so the Busaidi looked toward nearby Zanzibar—a
cosmopolitan island of mixed Arab, Indian, and African popula-

tion. Zanzibar's strategic placement on the coast and its spacious and well-protected harbor made it an ideal base for the East African slave trade that the Busaidi of Oman intended to dominate."

"It comes back to me now, I think."

"Very well. The founder of the Omani Sultanate of Zanzibar was Ahmad ibn Majid the Sly, who came to the throne of Oman in 1811 —do you remember?—upon the death of his uncle Abd-er-Rahman al-Busaidi."

"The names sound familiar," Klein said doubtfully.

"Seven years later," Sybille continued, "seeking to conquer Zanzibar without the use of force, Ahmad the Sly shaved his beard and mustache and visited the island disguised as a soothsayer, wearing yellow robes and a costly emerald in his turban. At that time most of Zanzibar was governed by a native ruler of mixed Arab and African blood, Abdullah ibn Muhammad Alawi, whose hereditary title was Mwenyi Mkuu. The Mwenyi Mkuu's subjects were mainly Africans, members of a tribe called the Hadimu. Sultan Ahmad, arriving in Zanzibar Town, gave a demonstration of his soothsaying skills on the waterfront and attracted so much attention that he speedily gained an audience at the court of the Mwenyi Mkuu. Ahmad predicted a glowing future for Abdullah, declaring that a powerful prince famed throughout the world would come to Zanzibar, make the Mwenyi Mkuu his high lieutenant, and would confirm him and his descendants as lords of Zanzibar forever.

" 'How do you know these things?' asked the Mwenyi Mkuu.

" 'There is a potion I drink,' Sultan Ahmad replied, 'that enables me to see what is to come. Do you wish to taste of it?'

" 'Most surely I do,' Abdullah said, and Ahmad thereupon gave him a drug that sent him into rapturous transports and showed him visions of paradise. Looking down from his place near the footstool of Allah, the Mwenyi Mkuu saw a rich and happy Zanzibar governed by his children's children's children. For hours he wandered in fantasies of almighty power.

"Ahmad then departed, and let his beard and mustache grow again, and returned to Zanzibar ten weeks later in his full regalia as Sultan of Oman, at the head of an imposing and powerful armada. He went at once to the court of the Mwenyi Mkuu and proposed, just as the soothsayer had prophesied, that Oman and Zanzibar enter into a treaty of alliance under which Oman would assume responsibility for much of Zanzibar's external relations—including the slave trade—while guaranteeing the authority of the Mwenyi Mkuu over domestic affairs. In return for his partial abdication of authority, the Mwenyi Mkuu would receive financial compensation from Oman. Remembering the vision the soothsayer had revealed to him, Abdullah at once signed the treaty, thereby legitimizing what was, in effect, the Omani conquest of Zanzibar. A great feast was held to celebrate the treaty, and, as a mark of honor, the Mwenyi Mkuu offered Sultan Ahmad a rare drug used locally, known as *borgash,* or 'the flower of truth.' Ahmad only pretended to put the pipe to his lips, for he loathed all mind-altering drugs, but Abdullah, as the flower of truth possessed him, looked at Ahmad and recognized the outlines of the soothsayer's face behind the Sultan's new beard. Realizing that he had been deceived, the Mwenyi Mkuu thrust his dagger, the tip of which was poisoned, deep into the Sultan's side and fled the banquet hall, taking up residence on the neighboring island of Pemba. Ahmad ibn Majid survived, but the poison consumed his vital organs and the remaining ten years of his life were spent in constant agony. As for the Mwenyi Mkuu, the Sultan's men hunted him down and put him to death along with ninety members of his family, and native rule in Zanzibar was therewith extinguished."

Sybille paused. "Is that not a gaudy and wonderful story?" she asked at last.

"Fascinating," Klein said. "Where did you find it?"

"Unpublished memoirs of Claude Richburn of the East India Company. Buried deep in the London archives. Strange that no historian ever came upon it before, isn't it? The standard texts simply say that Ahmad used his navy to bully Abdullah into signing the treaty, and then had the Mwenyi Mkuu assassinated at the first convenient moment."

"Very strange," Klein agreed. But he had not come here to listen to romantic tales of visionary potions and royal treacheries. He groped for some way to bring the conversation to a more personal level. Fragments of his imaginary dialogue with Sybille floated through his mind. *Everything is quiet where I am, Jorge. There's a peace that passeth all understanding. Like swimming under a sheet of glass. The way it is is that one no longer is affected by the unnecessary. Little things stand revealed as little things. Die and be with us, and you'll understand.* Yes. Perhaps. But did she really believe any of that? He had put all the words in her mouth; everything he had imagined her to say was his own construct, worthless as a key to the true Sybille. Where would he find the key, though?

She gave him no chance. "I will be going back to Zanzibar soon," she said. "There's much I want to learn about this incident from the people in the back country—old legends about the last days of the Mwenyi Mkuu, perhaps variants on the basic story—"

"May I accompany you?"

"Don't you have your own research to resume, Jorge?" she asked, and did not wait for an answer. She walked briskly toward the door of the lounge and went out, and he was alone.

7.

I mean what they and their hired psychiatrists call "delusional systems." Needless to say, "delusions" are always officially defined. We don't have to worry about questions of real or unreal. They only talk out of expediency. It's the *system* that matters. How the data arrange themselves inside it. Some are consistent, others fall apart.

—THOMAS PYNCHON, *Gravity's Rainbow*

Once more the deads, this time only three of them, coming over on the morning flight from Dar. Three was better than five, Daud

Mahmoud Barwani supposed, but three was still more than a suffi-
ciency. Not that those others, two months back, had caused any
trouble, staying just the one day and flitting off to the mainland
again, but it made him uncomfortable to think of such creatures
on the same small island as himself. With all the world to choose,
why did they keep coming to Zanzibar?

"The plane is here," said the flight controller.

Thirteen passengers. The health officer let the local people
through the gate first—two newspapermen and four legislators
coming back from the Pan-African Conference in Capetown—and
then processed a party of four Japanese tourists, unsmiling owlish
men festooned with cameras. And then the deads: and Barwani
was surprised to discover that they were the same ones as before,
the red-haired man, the brown-haired man without the beard, the
black-haired woman. Did deads have so much money that they
could fly from America to Zanzibar every few months? Barwani
had heard a tale to the effect that each new dead, when he rose
from his coffin, was presented with bars of gold equal to his own
weight, and now he thought he believed it. No good will come of
having such beings loose in the world, he told himself, and certainly none from letting them into Zanzibar. Yet he had no choice.
"Welcome once again to the isle of cloves," he said unctuously, and
smiled a bureaucratic smile, and wondered, not for the first time,
what would become of Daud Mahmoud Barwani once his days on
earth had reached their end.

"—Ahmad the Sly versus Abdullah Something," Klein said.
"That's all she would talk about. The history of Zanzibar." He was
in Jijibhoi's study. The night was warm and a late-season rain was
falling, blurring the million sparkling lights of the Los Angeles
Basin. "It would have been, you know, gauche to ask her any
direct questions. Gauche. I haven't felt so gauche since I was
fourteen. I was helpless among them, a foreigner, a child."

"Do you think they saw through your disguise?" Jijibhoi asked.

"I can't tell. They seemed to be toying with me, to be having
sport with me, but that may just have been their general style with

any newcomer. Nobody challenged me. Nobody hinted I might be
an impostor. Nobody seemed to care very much about me or what I
was doing there or how I had happened to become a dead. Sybille
and I stood face to face, and I wanted to reach out to her, I wanted
her to reach out to me, and there was no contact, none, none at all, it
was as though we had just met at some academic cocktail party and
the only thing on her mind was the new nugget of obscure history
she had just unearthed, and so she told me all about how Sultan
Ahmad outfoxed Abdullah and Abdullah stabbed the Sultan." Klein
caught sight of a set of familiar books on Jijibhoi's crowded shelves
—Oliver and Mathew, *History of East Africa,* books that had
traveled everywhere with Sybille in the years of their marriage.
He pulled forth Volume I, saying, "She claimed that the standard
histories give a sketchy and inaccurate description of the incident
and that she's only now discovered the true story. For all I know,
she was just playing a game with me, telling me a piece of established history as though it were something nobody knew till last
week. Let me see—Ahmad, Ahmad, Ahmad—"
He examined the index. Five Ahmads were listed, but there was
no entry for a Sultan Ahmad ibn Majid the Sly. Indeed an Ahmad
ibn Majid was cited, but he was mentioned only in a footnote and
appeared to be an Arab chronicler. Klein found three Abdullahs,
none of them a man of Zanzibar. "Something's wrong," he murmured.
"It does not matter, dear Jorge," Jijibhoi said mildly.
"It does. Wait a minute." He prowled the listings. Under *Zanzibar, Rulers,* he found no Ahmads, no Abdullahs; he did discover
a Majid ibn Said, but when he checked the reference he found that
he had reigned somewhere in the second half of the nineteenth
century. Desperately Klein flipped pages, skimming, turning
back, searching. Eventually he looked up and said, "It's all wrong!"
"The Oxford History of East Africa?"
"The details of Sybille's story. Look, she said this Ahmad the Sly
gained the throne of Oman in 1811 and seized Zanzibar seven
years later. But the book says that a certain Seyyid Said al-Busaidi
became Sultan of Oman in 1806 and ruled for *fifty years.* He was

the one, not this nonexistent Ahmad the Sly, who grabbed Zanzibar, but he did it in 1828, and the ruler he compelled to sign a treaty with him, the Mwenyi Mkuu, was named Hasan ibn Ahmad Alawi, and—" Klein shook his head. "It's an altogether different cast of characters. No stabbings, no assassinations, the dates are entirely different, the whole thing—"

Jijibhoi smiled sadly. "The deads are often mischievous."

"But why would she invent a complete fantasy and palm it off as a sensational new discovery? Sybille was the most scrupulous scholar I ever knew! She would never—"

"That was the Sybille you knew, dear friend. I keep urging you to realize that this is another person, a new person, within her body."

"A person who would lie about history?"

"A person who would tease," Jijibhoi said.

"Yes," Klein muttered. "Who would tease." *Keep in mind that to a dead the whole universe is plastic, nothing's real, nothing matters a hell of a lot.* "Who would tease a stupid, boring, annoyingly persistent ex-husband who has shown up in her Cold Town, wearing a transparent disguise and pretending to be a dead. Who would invent not only an anecdote but even its principals, as a joke, a game, a *jeu d'esprit.* Oh, God. Oh, God, how cruel she is, how foolish I was! It was her way of telling me she knew I was a phony dead. *Quid pro quo,* fraud for fraud!"

"What will you do?"

"I don't know," Klein said.

What he did, against Jijibhoi's strong advice and his own better judgment, was to get more pills from Dolorosa and return to Zion Cold Town. There would be a fitful joy, like that of probing the socket of a missing tooth, in confronting Sybille with the evidence of her fictional Ahmad, her imaginary Abdullah. Let there be no more games between us, he would say. Tell me what I need to know, Sybille, and then let me go away; but tell me only truth. All the way to Utah he rehearsed his speech, polishing and embellishing. There was no need for it, though, since this time the gate of

Zion Cold Town would not open for him. The scanners scanned his forged Albany card and the loudspeaker said, "Your credentials are invalid."

Which could have ended it. He might have returned to Los Angeles and picked up the pieces of his life. All this semester he had been on sabbatical leave, but the summer term was coming and there was work to do. He did return to Los Angeles, but only long enough to pack a somewhat larger suitcase, find his passport, and drive to the airport. On a sweet May evening a BOAC jet took him over the Pole to London, where, barely pausing for coffee and buns at an airport shop, he boarded another plane that carried him southeast toward Africa. More asleep than awake, he watched the dreamy landmarks drifting past: the Mediterranean, coming and going with surprising rapidity, and the tawny carpet of the Libyan Desert, and the mighty Nile, reduced to a brown thread's thickness when viewed from a height of ten miles. Suddenly Kilimanjaro, mist-wrapped, snow-bound, loomed like a giant double-headed blister to his right, far below, and he thought he could make out to his left the distant glare of the sun on the Indian Ocean. Then the big needle-nosed plane began its abrupt swooping descent, and he found himself, soon after, stepping out into the warm humid air and dazzling sunlight of Dar es Salaam.

Too soon, too soon. He felt unready to go on to Zanzibar. A day or two of rest, perhaps: he picked a Dar hotel at random, the Agip, liking the strange sound of its name, and hired a taxi. The hotel was sleek and clean, a streamlined affair in the glossy 1960's style, much cheaper than the Kilimanjaro where he had stayed briefly on the other trip, and located in a pleasant leafy quarter of the city, near the ocean. He strolled about for a short while, discovered that he was altogether exhausted, returned to his room for a nap that stretched on for nearly five hours, and, awakening groggy, showered and dressed for dinner. The hotel's dining room was full of beefy red-faced fair-haired men, jacketless and wearing open-throated white shirts, all of whom reminded him disturbingly of Kent Zacharias; but these were warms, Britishers from their accents, engineers, he suspected, from their conversation. They were building a dam and a power plant somewhere up the coast, it seemed, or perhaps a power plant without a dam; it was hard to follow what they said. They drank a good deal of gin and spoke in hearty booming shouts. There were also a good many Japanese businessmen, of course, looking trim and restrained in dark blue suits and narrow ties, and at the table next to Klein's were five tanned curly-haired men talking in rapid Hebrew—Israelis, surely. The only Africans in sight were waiters and bartenders. Klein ordered Mombasa oysters, steak, and a carafe of red wine, and found the food unexpectedly good, but left most of it on his plate. It was late evening in Tanzania, but for him it was ten o'clock in the morning, and his body was confused. He tumbled into bed, meditated vaguely on the probable presence of Sybille just a few air-minutes away in Zanzibar, and dropped into a sound sleep from which he awakened, what seemed like many hours later, to discover that it was still well before dawn.

He dawdled away the morning sightseeing in the old native quarter, hot and dusty, with unpaved streets and rows of tin shacks, and at midday returned to his hotel for a shower and lunch. Much the same national distribution in the restaurant—British, Japanese, Israeli—though the faces seemed different. He was on his second beer when Anthony Gracchus came in. The white hunter, broad-shouldered, pale, densely bearded, clad in khaki shorts, khaki shirt, seemed almost to have stepped out of the picture-cube Jijibhoi had once shown him. Instinctively Klein shrank back, turning toward the window, but too late: Gracchus had seen him. All chatter came to a halt in the restaurant as the dead man strode to Klein's table, pulled out a chair unasked, and seated himself; then, as though a motion-picture projector had been halted and started again, the British engineers resumed their shouting, sounding somewhat strained now. "Small world," Gracchus said. "Crowded one, anyway. On your way to Zanzibar, are you, Klein?"

"In a day or so. Did you know I was here?"

"Of course not." Gracchus' harsh eyes twinkled slyly. "Sheer coincidence is what this is. She's there already."

"She is?"

"She and Zacharias and Mortimer. I hear you wiggled your way into Zion."

"Briefly," Klein said. "I saw Sybille. Briefly."

"Unsatisfactorily. So once again you've followed her here. Give it up, man. Give it up."

"I can't."

"*Can't!*" Gracchus scowled. "A neurotic's word, *can't.* What you mean is *won't.* A mature man can do anything he wants to that isn't a physical impossibility. Forget her. You're only annoying her, this way, interfering with her work, interfering with her—" Gracchus smiled. "With her life. She's been dead almost three years, hasn't she? Forget her. The world's full of other women. You're still young, you have money, you aren't ugly, you have professional standing—"

"Is this what you were sent here to tell me?"

"I wasn't sent here to tell you anything, friend. I'm only trying to save you from yourself. Don't go to Zanzibar. Go home and start your life again."

"When I saw her at Zion," Klein said, "she treated me with contempt. She amused herself at my expense. I want to ask her why she did that."

"Because you're a warm and she's a dead. To her you're a clown. To all of us you're a clown. It's nothing personal, Klein. There's simply a gulf in attitudes, a gulf too wide for you to cross. You went to Zion drugged up like a Treasury man, didn't you? Pale face, bulgy eyes? You didn't fool anyone. You certainly didn't fool *her.* The game she played with you was her way of telling you that. Don't you know that?"

"I know it, yes."

"What more do you want, then? More humiliation?"

Klein shook his head wearily and stared at the tablecloth. After a moment he looked up, and his eyes met those of Gracchus, and he was astounded to realize that he trusted the hunter, that for the first time in his dealings with the deads he felt he was being met with sincerity. He said in a low voice, "We were very close, Sybille and I, and then she died, and now I'm nothing to her. I haven't been able to come to terms with that. I need her, still. I want to share my life with her, even now."

"But you can't."

"I know that. And still I can't help doing what I've been doing."

"There's only one thing you *can* share with her," Gracchus said. "That's your death. She won't descend to your level: you have to climb to hers."

"Don't be absurd."

"Who's absurd, me or you? Listen to me, Klein. I think you're a fool, I think you're a weakling, but I don't dislike you, I don't hold you to blame for your own foolishness. And so I'll help you, if you'll allow me." He reached into his breast pocket and withdrew a tiny metal tube with a safety catch at one end. "Do you know what this is?" Gracchus asked. "It's a self-defense dart, the kind all the women in New York carry. A good many deads carry them, too, because we never know when the reaction will start, when the mobs will turn against us. Only we don't use anesthetic drugs in ours. Listen, we can walk into any tavern in the native quarter and have a decent brawl going in five minutes, and in the confusion I'll put one of these darts into you, and we'll have you in Dar General Hospital fifteen minutes after that, crammed into a deep-freeze unit, and for a few thousand dollars we can ship you un-thawed to California, and this time Friday night you'll be undergoing rekindling in, say, San Diego Cold Town. And when you come out of it you and Sybille will be on the same side of the gulf, do you see? If you're destined to get back together with her, ever, that's the only way. That way you have a chance. This way you have none."

"It's unthinkable," Klein said.

"Unacceptable, maybe. But not unthinkable. Nothing's unthinkable once somebody's thought it. You think it some more. Will you promise me that? Think about it before you get aboard that plane for Zanzibar. I'll be staying here tonight and tomorrow, and then

I'm going out to Arusha to meet some deads coming in for the hunting, and any time before then I'll do it for you if you say the word. Think about it. Will you think about it? Promise me that you'll think about it."

"I'll think about it," Klein said.

"Good. Good. Thank you. Now let's have lunch and change the subject. Do you like eating here?"

"One thing puzzles me. Why does this place have a clientele that's exclusively non-African? Does it dare to discriminate against blacks in a black republic?"

Gracchus laughed. "It's the blacks who discriminate, friend. This is considered a second-class hotel. All the blacks are at the Kilimanjaro or the Nyerere. Still, it's not such a bad place. I recommend the fish dishes, if you haven't tried them, and there's a decent white wine from Israel that—"

8.

O Lord, methought what pain it was to drown!
What dreadful noise of waters in mine ears!
What sights of ugly death within mine eyes!
Methought I saw a thousand fearful wrecks;
A thousand men that fishes gnawed upon;
Wedges of gold, great anchors, heaps of pearl,
Inestimable stones, unvalued jewels,
All scatt'red in the bottom of the sea.
Some lay in dead men's skulls, and in the holes
Where eyes did once inhabit there were crept,
As 'twere in scorn of eyes, reflecting gems
That wooed the slimy bottom of the deep
And mocked the dead bones that lay scatt'red by.
                              —SHAKESPEARE, *Richard III*

"—Israeli wine," Mick Dongan was saying. "Well, I'll try anything once, especially if there's some neat little irony attached to it. I mean, there we were in Egypt, in *Egypt*, at this fabulous dinner party in the hills at Luxor, and our host is a Saudi prince, no less, in full tribal costume right down to the sunglasses, and when they bring out the roast lamb he grins devilishly and says, Of course we could always drink Mouton-Rothschild, but I do happen to have a small stock of select Israeli wines in my cellar, and because I think you are, like myself, a connoisseur of small incongruities I've asked my steward to open a bottle or two of—Klein, do you see that girl who just came in?" It is January, 1981, early afternoon, a fine drizzle in the air. Klein is lunching with six colleagues from the history department at the Hanging Gardens atop the Westwood Plaza. The hotel is a huge ziggurat on stilts; the Hanging Gardens is a rooftop restaurant, ninety stories up, in freaky neo-Babylonian decor, all winged bulls and snorting dragons of blue and yellow tile, waiters with long curly beards and scimitars at their hips— gaudy nightclub by dark, campy faculty hangout by day. Klein looks to his left. Yes, a handsome woman, mid-twenties, coolly beautiful, serious-looking, taking a seat by herself, putting a stack of books and cassettes down on the table before her. Klein does not pick up strange girls: a matter of moral policy, and also a matter of innate shyness. Dongan teases him. "Go on over, will you? She's your type, I swear. Her eyes are the right color for you, aren't they?"

Klein has been complaining, lately, that there are too many blue-eyed girls in Southern California. Blue eyes are disturbing to him, somehow, even menacing. His own eyes are brown. So are hers: dark, warm, sparkling. He thinks he has seen her occasionally in the library. Perhaps they have even exchanged brief glances. "Go on," Dongan says. "Go *on*, Jorge. Go." Klein glares at him. He will not go. How can he intrude on this woman's privacy? To force himself on her—it would almost be like rape. Dongan smiles complacently; his bland grin is a merciless prod. Klein refuses to be stampeded. But then, as he hesitates, the girl smiles too, a quick shy smile, gone so soon he is not altogether sure it happened at all, but he is sure enough, and he finds himself rising, crossing the alabaster floor, hovering awkwardly over her, searching for some inspired words with which to make contact, and no words come, but still they make contact the old-fashioned way, eye to eye, and he is stunned by the intensity of what passes between them in that first implausible moment.

"Are you waiting for someone?" he mutters, stunned.

"No." The smile again, far less tentative. "Would you like to join me?"

She is a graduate student, he discovers quickly. Just got her master's, beginning now on her doctorate—the nineteenth-century East African slave trade, particular emphasis on Zanzibar. "How romantic," he says. "Zanzibar! Have you been there?"

"Never. I hope to go some day. Have you?"

"Not ever. But it always interested me, ever since I was a small boy collecting stamps. It was the last country in my album."

"Not in mine," she says. "Zululand was."

She knows him by name, it turns out. She had even been thinking of enrolling in his course on Nazism and Its Offspring. "Are you South American?" she asks.

"Born there. Raised here. My grandparents escaped to Buenos Aires in '37."

"Why Argentina? I thought that was a hotbed of Nazis."

"Was. Also full of German-speaking refugees, though. All their friends went there. But it was too unstable. My parents got out in '55, just before one of the big revolutions, and came to California. What about you?"

"British family. I was born in Seattle. My father's in the consular service. He—"

A waiter looms. They order sandwiches offhandedly. Lunch seems very unimportant now. The contact still holds. He sees Conrad's *Nostromo* in her stack of books; she is halfway through it, and he has just finished it, and the coincidence amuses them. Conrad is one of her favorites, she says. One of his, too. What about Faulkner? Yes, and Mann, and Virginia Woolf, and they share even a fondness for Hermann Broch, and a dislike for Hesse. How odd. Operas? *Freischütz, Holländer, Fidelio*, yes. "We have very Teutonic tastes," she observes. "We have very similar tastes," he adds. He finds himself holding her hand. "Amazingly similar," she says.

Mick Dongan leers at him from the far side of the room; Klein gives him a terrible scowl. Dongan winks. "Let's get out of here," Klein says, just as she starts to say the same thing.

They talk half the night and make love until dawn. "You ought to know," he tells her solemnly over breakfast, "that I decided long ago never to get married and certainly never to have a child."

"So did I," she says. "When I was fifteen."

They were married four months later. Mick Dongan was his best man.

Gracchus said, as they left the restaurant, "You will think things over, won't you?"

"I will," Klein said. "I promised you that."

He went to his room, packed his suitcase, checked out, and took a cab to the airport, arriving in plenty of time for the afternoon flight to Zanzibar. The same melancholy little man was on duty as health officer when he landed, Barwani. "Sir, you have come back," Barwani said. "I thought you might. The other people have been here several days already."

"The other people?"

"When you were here last, sir, you kindly offered me a retainer in order that you might be informed when a certain person reached this island." Barwani's eyes gleamed. "That person, with two of her former companions, is here now."

Klein carefully placed a twenty-shilling note on the health officer's desk.

"At which hotel?"

Barwani's lips quirked. Evidently twenty shillings fell short of expectations. But Klein did not take out another banknote, and after a moment Barwani said, "As before. The Zanzibar house. And you, sir?"

"As before," Klein said. "I'll be staying at the Shirazi."

Sybille was in the garden of the hotel, going over that day's research notes, when the telephone call came from Barwani. "Don't let my papers blow away," she said to Zacharias, and went inside. When she returned, looking bothered, Zacharias said, "Is there trouble?"

She sighed. "Jorge. He's on his way to his hotel now."

"What a bore," Mortimer murmured. "I thought Gracchus might have brought him to his senses."

"Evidently not," Sybille said. "What are we going to do?"

"What would you like to do?" Zacharias asked.

She shook her head. "We can't allow this to go on, can we?"

The evening air was humid and fragrant. The long rains had come and gone, and the island was in the grip of the new season's lunatic fertility: outside the window of Klein's hotel room some vast twining vine was putting forth monstrous trumpet-shaped yellow flowers, and all about the hotel grounds everything was in blossom, everything was in a frenzy of moist young leaves. Klein's sensibility reverberated to that feeling of universal vigorous thrusting newness; he paced the room, full of energy, trying to devise some feasible stratagem. Go immediately to see Sybille? Force his way in, if necessary, with shouts and alarums, and demand to know why she had told him that fantastic tale of imaginary sultans? No. No. He would do no more confronting, no more lamenting; now that he was here, now that he was close by her, he would seek her out calmly, he would talk quietly, he would invoke memories of their old love, he would speak of Rilke and Woolf and Broch, of afternoons in Puerto Vallarta and nights in Santa Fe, of music heard and caresses shared, he would rekindle not their marriage, for that was impossible, but merely the remembrance of the bond that once had existed, he would win from her some acknowledgment of what had been, and then he would soberly and quietly exorcise that bond, he and she together, they would work to free him by speaking softly of the change that had come over their lives, until, after three hours or four or five, he had brought himself with her help to an acceptance of the unacceptable. That was all. He would demand nothing, he would beg for nothing, except only that she assist him for one evening in ridding his soul of this useless destructive obsession. Even a

dead, even a capricious, wayward, volatile, whimsical, wanton
dead, would surely see the desirability of that, and would freely
give him her cooperation. Surely. And then home, and then new
beginnings, too long postponed.

He made ready to go out.

There was a soft knock at the door. "Sir? Sir? You have visitors
downstairs."

"Who?" Klein asked, though he knew the answer.

"A lady and two gentlemen," the bellhop replied. "The taxi has
brought them from the Zanzibar House. They wait for you in the
bar."

"Tell them I'll be down in a moment."

He went to the iced pitcher on the dresser, drank a glass of cold
water mechanically, unthinkingly, poured himself a second,
drained that too. This visit was unexpected; and why had she
brought her entourage along? He had to struggle to regain that
centeredness, that sense of purpose understood, which he thought
he had attained before the knock. Eventually he left the room.

They were dressed crisply and impeccably this damp night,
Zacharias in a tawny frock coat and pale green trousers, Mortimer
in a belted white caftan trimmed with intricate brocade, Sybille
in a simple lavender tunic. Their pale faces were unmarred by
perspiration; they seemed perfectly composed, models of poise.
No one sat near them in the bar. As Klein entered, they stood to
greet him, but their smiles appeared sinister, having nothing of
friendliness in them. Klein clung tight to his intended calmness.
He said quietly, "It was kind of you to come. May I buy drinks for
you?"

"We have ours already," Zacharias pointed out. "Let us be your
hosts. What will you have?"

"Pimm's Number Six," Klein said. He tried to match their frosty
smiles. "I admire your tunic, Sybille. You all look so debonair
tonight that I feel shamed."

"You never were famous for your clothes," she said.

Zacharias returned from the counter with Klein's drink. He took
it and toasted them gravely.

After a short while Klein said, "Do you think I could talk privately with you, Sybille?"

"There's nothing we have to say to one another that can't be said in front of Kent and Laurence."

"Nevertheless."

"I prefer not to, Jorge."

"As you wish." Klein peered straight into her eyes and saw nothing there, nothing, and flinched. All that he had meant to say fled his mind. Only churning fragments danced there: Rilke, Broch, Puerto Vallarta. He gulped at his drink.

Zacharias said, "We have a problem to discuss, Klein."

"Go on."

"The problem is you. You're causing great distress to Sybille. This is the second time, now, that you've followed her to Zanzibar, to the literal end of the earth, Klein, and you've made several attempts besides to enter a closed sanctuary in Utah under false pretenses, and this is interfering with Sybille's freedom, Klein, it's an impossible, intolerable interference."

"The deads are dead," Mortimer said. "We understand the depths of your feelings for your late wife, but this compulsive pursuit of her must be brought to an end."

"It will be," Klein said, staring at a point on the stucco wall midway between Zacharias and Sybille. "I want only an hour or two of private conversation with my—with Sybille, and then I promise you that there will be no further—"

"Just as you promised Anthony Gracchus," Mortimer said, "not to go to Zanzibar."

"I wanted—"

"We have our rights," said Zacharias. "We've gone through hell, literally through hell, to get where we are. You've infringed on our right to be left alone. You bother us. You bore us. You annoy us. We hate to be annoyed." He looked toward Sybille. She nodded. Zacharias' hand vanished into the breast pocket of his coat. Mortimer seized Klein's wrist with astonishing suddenness and jerked his arm forward. A minute metal tube glistened in Zacharias' huge fist. Klein had seen such a tube in the hand of Anthony Gracchus only the day before.

"No," Klein gasped. "I don't believe—*no!*"

Zacharias plunged the cold tip of the tube quickly into Klein's forearm.

"The freezer unit is coming," Mortimer said. "It'll be here in five minutes or less."

"What if it's late?" Sybille asked anxiously. "What if something irreversible happens to his brain before it gets here?"

"He's not even entirely dead yet," Zacharias reminded her. "There's time. There's ample time. I spoke to the doctor myself, a very intelligent Chinese, flawless command of English. He was most sympathetic. They'll have him frozen within a couple of minutes of death. We'll book cargo passage aboard the morning plane for Dar. He'll be in the United States within twenty-four hours, I guarantee that. San Diego will be notified. Everything will be all right, Sybille!"

Jorge Klein lay slumped across the table. The bar had emptied the moment he had cried out and lurched forward: the half-dozen customers had fled, not caring to mar their holidays by sharing an evening with the presence of death, and the waiters and bartenders, big-eyed, terrified, lurked in the hallway. A heart attack, Zacharias had announced, some kind of sudden attack, maybe a stroke, where's the telephone? No one had seen the tiny tube do its work.

Sybille trembled. "If anything goes wrong—"

"I hear the sirens now," Zacharias said.

From his desk at the airport Daud Mahmoud Barwani watched the bulky refrigerated coffin being loaded by grunting porters aboard the morning plane for Dar. And then, and then, and then? They would ship the dead man to the far side of the world, to America, and breathe new life into him, and he would go once more among men. Barwani shook his head. These people! The man who was alive is now dead, and these dead ones, who knows what they are? Who knows? Best that the dead remain dead, as was intended in the time of first things. Who could have foreseen a day when the dead returned from the grave? Not I. And who can foresee what we will all become, a hundred years from now? Not I. Not I. A hundred years from now I will sleep, Barwani thought. I will sleep, and it will not matter to me at all what sort of creatures walk the earth.

9.

We die with the dying:
See, they depart, and we go with them.
We are born with the dead:
See, they return, and bring us with them.
—T. S. ELIOT, *Little Gidding*

On the day of his awakening he saw no one except the attendants at the rekindling house, who bathed him and fed him and helped him to walk slowly around his room. They said nothing to him, nor he to them; words seemed irrelevant. He felt strange in his skin, too snugly contained, as though all his life he had worn ill-fitting clothes and now had for the first time encountered a competent tailor. The images that his eyes brought him were sharp, unnaturally clear, and faintly haloed by prismatic colors, an effect that imperceptibly vanished as the day passed. On the second day he was visited by the San Diego Guidefather, not at all the formidable patriarch he had imagined, but rather a cool, efficient executive, about fifty years old, who greeted him cordially and told him briefly of the disciplines and routines he must master before he could leave the Cold Town. "What month is this?" Klein asked, and Guidefather told him it was June, the seventeenth of June, 1993. He had slept four weeks.

Now it is the morning of the third day after his awakening, and he has guests: Sybille, Nerita, Zacharias, Mortimer, Gracchus. They file into his room and stand in an arc at the foot of his bed, radiant in the glow of light that pierces the narrow windows. Like demigods, like angels, glittering with a dazzling inward brilliance, and now he is of their company. Formally they embrace him, first Gracchus, then Nerita, then Mortimer. Zacharias advances next to his bedside, Zacharias who sent him into death, and he smiles at Klein and Klein returns the smile, and they embrace. Then it is Sybille's turn: she slips her hand between his, he draws her close, her lips brush his cheek, his touch hers, his arm encircles her shoulders.

"Hello," she whispers.

"Hello," he says.

They ask him how he feels, how quickly his strength is returning, whether he has been out of bed yet, how soon he will commence his drying-off. The style of their conversation is the oblique, elliptical style favored by the deads, but not nearly so clipped and cryptic as the way of speech they normally would use among themselves; they are favoring him, leading him inch by inch into their customs. Within five minutes he thinks he is getting the knack.

He says, using their verbal shorthand, "I must have been a great burden to you."

"You were, you were," Zacharias agrees. "But all that is done with now."

"We forgive you," Mortimer says.

"We welcome you among us," declares Sybille.

They talk about their plans for the months ahead. Sybille is nearly finished with her work on Zanzibar; she will retreat to Zion Cold Town for the summer months to write her thesis. Mortimer and Nerita are off to Mexico to tour the ancient temples and pyramids; Zacharias is going to Ohio, to his beloved mounds. In the autumn they will reassemble at Zion and plan the winter's amusement: a tour of Egypt, perhaps, or Peru, the heights of Machu Picchu. Ruins, archaeological sites, delight them; in the places where death has been busiest, their joy is most intense. They are flushed, excited, verbose—virtually chattering, now. Away we will go, to Zimbabwe, to Palenque, to Angkor, to Knossos, to Uxmal, to Nineveh, to Mohenjo-daro. And as they go on and on, talking with hands and eyes and smiles and even words, even words, torrents of words, they blur and become unreal to him, they are mere dancing puppets jerking about a badly painted stage, they are droning insects, wasps or bees or mosquitos, with all their talk of travels and festivals, of Boghazköy and Babylon, of Megiddo and Massada, and he ceases to hear them, he tunes them out, he lies there smiling, eyes glazed, mind adrift. It perplexes him that he has so little interest in them. But then he realizes that it is a mark of his liberation. He is freed of old chains now. Will he join their set? Why should he? Perhaps he will travel with them, perhaps not, as the whim takes him. More likely not. Almost certainly not. He does not need their company. He has his own interests. He will follow Sybille about no longer. He does not need, he does not want, he will not seek. Why should he become one of them, rootless, an amoral wanderer, a ghost made flesh? Why should he embrace the values and customs of these people who had given him to death as dispassionately as they might swat an insect, only because he had bored them, because he had annoyed them? He does not hate them for what they did to him, he feels no resentment that he can identify, he merely chooses to detach himself from them. Let them float on from ruin to ruin, let them pursue death from continent to continent; he will go his own way. Now that he has crossed the interface he finds that Sybille no longer matters to him.

—*Oh, sir, things change*—

"We'll go now," Sybille says softly.

He nods. He makes no other reply.

"We'll see you after your drying-off," Zacharias tells him, and touches him lightly with his knuckles, a farewell gesture used only by the deads.

"See you," Mortimer says.

"See you," says Gracchus.

"Soon," Nerita says.

Never, Klein says, saying it without words, but so they will understand. Never. Never. Never. I will never see any of you. I will never see you, Sybille. The syllables echo through his brain, and the word *never, never, never* rolls over him like the breaking

surf, cleansing him, purifying him, healing him. He is free. He is
alone.

"Goodbye," Sybille calls from the hallway.

"Goodbye," he says.

It was years before he saw her again. But they spent the last days
of '99 together, shooting dodos under the shadow of mighty Kilimanjaro.

The Nebula Winners 1965-1974

The method of choosing the winners of the Nebula Awards is of the utmost simplicity. During the course of the year the active members of Science Fiction Writers of America nominate stories and novels as they appear in print. There is no limit to this list that grows to an unwieldy length as the year draws to an end. There is then a final nominating ballot and this time there is a limit in order that the final ballot be short enough for everyone to read everything on it. At every stage only the active members of the organization are permitted to vote. The final ballot and the winning stories are selected by writers, judging other writers. The stories in this volume, number ten of the series, were published in 1974. There also is a Dramatic Presentation Award and, new this year, a Grand Master Award.

1965

Best Novel: DUNE *by Frank Herbert*
Best Novella: "The Saliva Tree" *by Brian W. Aldiss*
         "He Who Shapes" *by Roger Zelazny* (tie)
Best Novelette: "The Doors of His Face, the Lamps of His Mouth" *by*
         Roger Zelazny
Best Short Story: " 'Repent, Harlequin!' Said the Ticktockman" *by Harlan Ellison*

1966

Best Novel: FLOWERS FOR ALGERNON *by Daniel Keyes*
 BABEL-17 *by Samuel R. Delany* (tie)
Best Novella: "The Last Castle" *by Jack Vance*
Best Novelette: "Call Him Lord" *by Gordon R. Dickson*
Best Short Story: "The Secret Place" *by Richard McKenna*

1967

Best Novel: THE EINSTEIN INTERSECTION *by Samuel R. Delany*
Best Novella: "Behold the Man" *by Michael Moorcock*
Best Novelette: "Gonna Roll the Bones" *by Fritz Leiber*
Best Short Story: "Aye, and Gomorrah" *by Samuel R. Delany*

1968

Best Novel: RITE OF PASSAGE *by Alexei Panshin*
Best Novella: "Dragonrider" *by Anne McCaffrey*
Best Novelette: "Mother to the World" *by Richard Wilson*
Best Short Story: "The Planners" *by Kate Wilhelm*

1969

Best Novel: THE LEFT HAND OF DARKNESS *by Ursula K. Le Guin*
Best Novella: "A Boy and His Dog" *by Harlan Ellison*
Best Novelette: "Time Considered as a Helix of Semi-Precious Stones"
 by Samuel R. Delany
Best Short Story: "Passengers" *by Robert Silverberg*

1970

Best Novel: RINGWORLD *by Larry Niven*
Best Novella: "Ill Met in Lankhmar" *by Fritz Leiber*
Best Novelette: "Slow Sculpture" *by Theodore Sturgeon*
Best Short Story: No award

1971

Best Novel: A TIME OF CHANGES, *by Robert Silverberg*
Best Novella: "The Missing Man" *by Katherine MacLean*
Best Novelette: "The Queen of Air and Darkness" *by Poul Anderson*
Best Short Story: "Good News from the Vatican" *by Robert Silverberg*

1972

Best Novel: THE GODS THEMSELVES *by Isaac Asimov*
Best Novella: "A Meeting with Medusa" *by Arthur C. Clarke*
Best Novelette: "Goat Song" *by Poul Anderson*
Best Short Story: "When It Changed" *by Joanna Russ*

1973

Best Novel: RENDEZVOUS WITH RAMA *by Arthur C. Clarke*
Best Novella: "The Death of Doctor Island" *by Gene Wolfe*
Best Novelette: "Of Mist, and Grass, and Sand" *by Vonda N. McIntyre*
Best Short Story: "Love Is the Plan the Plan Is Death" *by James
                           Tiptree, Jr.*

1974

Best Novel: THE DISPOSSESSED *by Ursula K. Le Guin*
Best Novella: "Born with the Dead" *by Robert Silverberg*
Best Novelette: "If the Stars Are Gods" *by Gordon Eklund and Gregory
                           Benford*

Best Short Story: "The Day Before the Revolution" *by Ursula K. Le Guin*

Grand Master: *Robert A. Heinlein*

THE HUGO WINNERS

The Science Fiction Achievement Awards, a title rarely used, became known as "Hugo" Awards shortly after the first such awards were presented, in 1953. The "Hugo" is after Hugo Gernsback, author, editor and publisher and one of the "fathers" of modern science fiction. The Hugo Awards have been made annually since 1955, and their winners are determined by popular vote. Because each year's awards have been under the administration of a different group, the committee in charge of the year's World Science Fiction Convention, rules and categories has fluctuated from year to year, sometimes drastically.

From their inception, the Hugo Awards have been made for amateur as well as for professional achievement. Thus there are usually awards for Best Fanzine (the initiate's term for amateur magazine), Best Fan Writer and Best Fan Artist as well as the awards for professional writing, for Best Professional Editor, and for Best Professional Artist. Only the more standardized awards for professional writing are listed here.* In recent years voting on both the nominating and final ballot has been limited to those who have purchased memberships in the World Science Fiction Convention. The Hugo Trophy is a miniature rocket ship poised for takeoff, though details of design and materials have varied from year to year. In the following list, the year given is the year of publication for the winning entries, and this is followed by the name, place and year of the World Science Fiction Convention at which the awards were made.

*The reader is referred to *A History of the Hugo, Nebula and International Fantasy Awards*, published by Howard DeVore, 4705 Weddel Street, Dearborn, Michigan, for the history of the awards and a detailed listing of Hugo winners and nominees in all categories. The book also contains a complete listing of Nebula Award nominees.

1965 ("Tricon," Cleveland, 1966)

Best Novel: . . . AND CALL ME CONRAD *by Roger Zelazny*
DUNE *by Frank Herbert* (tie)
Best Short Fiction: "'Repent, Harlequin!' Said the Ticktockman" *by Harlan Ellison*

1966 ("NYCon III," New York City, 1967)

Best Novel. THE MOON IS A HARSH MISTRESS *by Robert A. Heinlein*
Best Novelette: "The Last Castle" *by Jack Vance*
Best Short Story: "Neutron Star" *by Larry Niven*

1967 ("Baycon," Oakland, California, 1968)

Best Novel: LORD OF LIGHT *by Roger Zelazny*
Best Novella: "Riders of the Purple Wage" *by Philip José Farmer*
"Weyr Search" *by Anne McCaffrey* (tie)
Best Novelette: "Gonna Roll the Bones" *by Fritz Leiber*
Best Short Story: "I Have No Mouth, and I Must Scream" *by Harlan Ellison*

1968 ("St. Louiscon," St. Louis, 1969)

Best Novel: STAND ON ZANZIBAR *by John Brunner*
Best Novella: "Nightwings" *by Robert Silverberg*
Best Novelette: "The Sharing of Flesh" *by Poul Anderson*
Best Short Story: "The Beast That Shouted Love at the Heart of the World" *by Harlan Ellison*

1969 ("Heicon," Heidelberg, Germany, 1970)

Best Novel: THE LEFT HAND OF DARKNESS *by Ursula K. Le Guin*
Best Novella: "Ship of Shadows" *by Fritz Leiber*
Best Short Story: "Time Considered as a Helix of Semi-Precious Stones" *by Samuel R. Delany*

1970 ("Noreascon," Boston, 1971)

Best Novel: RINGWORLD *by Larry Niven*
Best Novella: "Ill Met in Lankhmar" *by Fritz Leiber*
Best Short Story: "Slow Sculpture" *by Theodore Sturgeon*

1971 ("L.A. Con," Los Angeles, 1972)

Best Novel: TO YOUR SCATTERED BODIES GO *by Philip José Farmer*
Best Novella: "The Queen of Air and Darkness" *by Poul Anderson*
Best Short Story: "Inconstant Moon" *by Larry Niven*

1972 ("Torcon," Toronto, 1973)

Best Novel: THE GODS THEMSELVES *by Isaac Asimov*
Best Novella: "The Word for World Is Forest" *by Ursula K. Le Guin*
Best Novelette: "Goat Song" *by Poul Anderson*
Best Short Story: "Eurema's Dam" *by R. A. Lafferty*
              "The Meeting" *by Frederik Pohl and Cyril M. Korn-
              bluth* (tie)

1973 ("Discon," Washington, D.C., 1974)

Best Novel: RENDEZVOUS WITH RAMA *by Arthur C. Clarke*
Best Novella: "The Girl Who Was Plugged In" *by James Tiptree, Jr.*
Best Novelette: "The Deathbird" *by Harlan Ellison*
Best Short Story: "The Ones Who Walk Away from Omelas" *by Ursula
              K. Le Guin*

1974 ("Aussiecon," Melbourne, Australia, 1975)

Best Novel: THE DISPOSSESSED *by Ursula K. Le Guin*
Best Novella: "A Song for Lya" *by George R. R. Martin*
Best Novelette: "Adrift Just Off the Islets of Langerhans" *by Harlan
              Ellison*
Best Short Story: "The Hole Man" *by Larry Niven*